W9-BDH-358

DRAMA
QUEENS
in the house

DRAMA QUEENS
in the house

julie
williams

roaring brook press
new york

Copyright © 2014 by Julie Williams

Published by Roaring Brook Press

Roaring Brook Press is a division of Holtzbrinck Publishing Holdings Limited Partnership

175 Fifth Avenue, New York, New York 10010

macteenbooks.com

Library of Congress Cataloging-in-Publication Data

Williams, Julie, 1948 September 2–
    Drama queens in the house / Julie Williams.—First edition.
        pages cm
        Summary: "A La Cage aux Folles–inspired YA novel about a girl genius who must thwart
her unconventional theater family's demise in which her mother, her father, and her father's
new boyfriend, all live under the same roof"—Provided by publisher.
        ISBN 978-1-59643-735-7 (hardback)
        [1. Family life—Fiction.   2. Gifted children—Fiction.   3. Theater—Fiction.   4. Gays—
Fiction.   5. Racially mixed people—Fiction.   6. African Americans—Fiction.]   I. Title.
        PZ7.W66654Dr 2014
        [Fic]—dc23   2013028529

Roaring Brook Press books may be purchased for business or promotional use.

For information on bulk purchases please contact Macmillan Corporate and Premium Sales

Department at (800) 221-7945 x5442 or by e-mail at specialmarkets@macmillan.com.

First edition 2014

Printed in the United States of America

10 9 8 7 6 5 4 3 2 1

To my daughter, Jennifer, and our jumble of a chosen family

the luckiest girl in the world

The theater is lit up like an opening-night gala celebrating the first show of a new season. It's graduation night, the second Thursday in June, and this gala is all about me.

JESSIE JASPER LEWIS . . . my name on the marquee in lights.

Well, the marquee actually reads THE JUMBLE PLAYERS. But a dozen Japanese maples dotting the patio are sparkling with lights. All the windows in the old mansion part of the theater are twinkling, too.

And there IS a huge banner strung across the stage door that reads WAY TO GO, JESSIE!

My dad hops out of the front passenger seat and runs around to open the limo door for me.

My best friend Bits leans over me, letting out a huge sigh. "Oooooh! I never see it like this. I'm always inside by now."

"I know! It's gorgeous, isn't it?"

"Like Broadway!" From Bits that's the highest praise. "And tonight it's all for you!"

She gives me a shove.

I tumble out onto the driveway. For such a tiny person—not even five feet tall—Bits sure is strong.

She slides out after me. "Let's go see what David's got to eat . . ." She's also skinny as a rail and always hungry. I'm always hungry, too. But when you're five foot eight at fifteen that's a given.

Mom has gracefully alighted from the massive Hummer limo. I envy that grace. She and Bits are the same height and so much alike you'd think Bits was her kid, not her niece. (My aunt Loretta looks like a linebacker.) Like Bits and unlike me, Mom has full control of all her limbs.

She grabs my dad's hand, and they lead the way toward the stage door.

Let me just say, that though we live a dramatic life, we are not accustomed to this extravagant mode of transportation. Okay, the truth is I've never ridden in any kind of a limo before. And Hummers are—well, kind of disgusting. Plus, we live only two houses down from the theater (572 steps to be exact), and my main transportation going anywhere else has always been the city bus system. If it weren't for our tech director's other life running a limo service, we'd be in the theater van.

I grab Grandmama's arm and help her out of the limo. I think it's safe to say she's never had such a fancy ride either. Although you never know. She's wearing her red suit and her favorite red church hat and looking pretty sharp for a lady who just turned eighty.

Suddenly the stage door is thrown open and the entire JUM-BLE acting and tech company, administrators, students, and all their families explode out and down the stairs shouting, "Way to go, Jessie!"

When I open my eyes again, I see they are all wearing theatrical costumes of one sort or another. And those who just got here from the school ceremony are madly pulling on capes and hats and sashes and masks and swords and things.

Ooooh, I see. It's more than costumes. We've got a little theatrical production going on here.

Lydia and Edward (co-founders with my parents of the theater and my friend David's parents) hold up a sign that reads JESSIE JUMBLE—YOUNGEST VALEDICTORIAN OF UMLS!

Everybody reads it out loud. Sort of in unison.

My cousin Bartle has grabbed a sign that reads YOUNGEST UMLS GRADUATE EVER!

More people read aloud, or I should say, shout aloud.

"She's the first black graduate, too," Grandmama mutters.

"Biracial," Mom counters. It's an old argument, one neither of them will ever win.

My dad pulls her toward the steps where a bunch of theater school kids are waving signs announcing my university choices, prompting huge cheers from the crowd.

"Ahhhh, gee," I say, doing an awkward curtsy and nearly spraining an ankle.

Today, I'm the star. "Thanks, everyone . . . I could get used to this."

But, of course, they're not done.

Brad, our costumer and dear friend, cues the entire group, and they pull out smaller signs that say SHE CHOSE THE JUMBLE!

That makes me laugh.

And then they launch into a song-and-dance routine. Yup. Right there on the steps of the stage door, down onto the patio, and out into the parking lot.

The theater name is an acronym for the founders' names—*J* for Jasper Lewis (my last name), *U* for Una, my mom, and *M* for Mark, my dad. And then the Benedicts—Lydia and Edward. J-U-M-B-L-E. Oh, and it also stands for our six cats (Judge, Uncle, Maggie, Brick, Lettuce, and Elbows). But that's another story.

Now a news team has pulled into the driveway and they are filming us.

Good grief.

They're here—as always—because of my parents. Actors, directors, teachers—they are very well known not just here in the Twin Cities, but all over the Midwest. The JUMBLE Players even won a regional Tony a few years ago for a show my parents starred in. They're used to having their pictures in the paper and on the Internet and TV.

Not me.

Looking at me, you'd never guess I grew up in this crazy theater community.

"Jessie! You're wearing a dress!" Susie, one of the theater school students, blurts this out in front of everyone.

"I know," Bits says. "I had to drag her to the mall to buy one. She didn't even own one."

"Oh, my god! And are those heels?" Susie's already high-pitched voice rises in a squeal.

Yes, and they are uncomfortable in the extreme. I slip out of them and in one swift move, I've kicked them into a corner by the stairs.

"Oh, there's the news crew that was at graduation," Bits says. "You should have heard Jessie's speech!" She sounds as proud as if she was my mother not my cousin.

"Of course you were valedictorian!" Susie says. "You are like the smartest person I have ever known."

"It was sweet," Bits says. "She said that she loved the theater and I quote, 'As much as I love my crazy black father and itsy-bitsy white mother!' The audience roared. Especially when she made Una and Mark stand up and take a bow. They loved it, of course."

"I made you stand up and take a bow, too," I remind her.

"And she loved it, didn't she?" Susie chirps. She and Bits are friends but they are also constant competitors for roles.

"How come you're not going to college?" Susie's mother, Trish, has joined us. "I heard you got several scholarship offers."

"I'm not ready for college yet. At least, not going away to school. And the University of Minnesota would be . . . I don't know . . . like continuing at the Lab School."

"I can see that," Trish says. "So, what are you going to do?"

"I'm not sure," I say, although I do have a plan. "I want to really focus here and see if I can find my strengths in the theater."

This is true, but it sounds kind of gaggy. It's also the scary part. I mean, what if I have no place in the theater?

Susie and her mom go back inside.

My mom and dad are over talking to the reporter, who is eyeing me—probably to get a picture—so I duck behind one of the maple trees (a small, decorative tree that doesn't hide me, it just makes me look like an idiot).

David comes out with a big mug of café au lait for me. It's topped with whipped cream and fresh-shaved chocolate. My favorite.

"Congratulations, kid!" He gives me a hug. "I'm next."

"If you're lucky!"

"I wish I were graduating with you today," Bits says, more than a touch of wistfulness in her voice. She would have loved all this hoopla directed at her. But her mother, Loretta (my aunt and a religious fanatic of the worst kind) pulled her out of the university Lab School a year ago. In order to prepare for the end of the world. Can you believe that? Bits had to finish high school online.

"We'll celebrate when you turn eighteen," I promise.

It's amazing really. Loretta (who I stopped calling Aunt Loretta a long time ago) tried to pull her out of the theater school, too, but Mom and Bits's dad, Lee, intervened. Lee's had a lot more control over what happens to Bits since the divorce, I've noticed. And that's a good thing! It's too bad Bits can't live with him. He's a drummer and on the road too much with the band. That would be Auntie Ellie's band (Auntie Ellie, who is not my real aunt, but my mom's best friend from forever and who I keep calling Auntie

6

because she seems way more like family to me than nutcase Loretta does. I'm just saying.)

Maybe after Bits turns eighteen she can move in with us. You know, for those three days before the world ends.

I sure hope Loretta's insanity is not hereditary.

"Where's my café au lait?" Bits asks David, who rushes off to get her a cup. It cracks me up the way she rules that boy.

My mom signals me, so I set the cup down and drag Bits with me to talk to the reporters. My motto: if you have to talk to them, at the very least, CONFUSE them. Not all that hard to do, considering I'm nearly as tall as my dad, though not as dark, of course. Then Mom and Bits are a foot shorter and look like twins. Then there's Bartle, who is the same color as my dad (his uncle) but six feet three inches tall. Here he comes and, did I mention? He's in drag.

"And here we have the graduate herself, Jessie Jasper Lewis. Any regrets that you've chosen to stay here at the theatre school instead of accepting one of the scholarships you were offered?" the reporter asks, jamming the microphone in my face.

"No regrets," I answer, a surge of happiness washing over me. The camera guy comes in for a close-up. It hits me all of a sudden— I'm through with high school! I don't have to go on to college just yet. "How could I have regrets?"

I can feel the grin spreading over my face. "I'm the luckiest girl in the world to have parents who love me, love each other, and love the theater—not necessarily in that order—as much as I do."

"That's a wrap," the reporter says. "Nice line."

I turn to hug my parents, but they've already started back to the stage door. Mom and Bits have their heads together as usual. My dad is talking to Brad, who's appeared out of nowhere.

The party is my graduation present from Edward, Lydia, and David. Of course my parents contributed. And Auntie Ellie's band is playing. Normally we'd have a more personal party at our house, but the theater is bigger and it's got a catering kitchen. I can't believe how many people showed up. The only students missing are the ones that are also graduating today. That's only a handful. Most of the theater school kids are younger, like me.

The food is incredible. We stuff our faces.

And then we stuff our faces some more.

David keeps bringing me things to try. "Your favorite," he says, handing me his special deviled eggs.

Bartle grabs one in each hand, shoveling them in his enormous mouth in two quick bites. "What do you put in these . . . ?"

"Do not try to speak until you've swallowed those," I say, reaching for the last egg on the plate. "You are so gross. Why do you do that?"

Bartle says something else, but it's impossible to know what. He swallows. Tries again.

"No, you are not going to blame your lack of manners on your mother kicking you out!" I whack him on the arm with the plate. "That was three years ago!"

David has returned with another platter, larger this time, featuring his fabulous paté and slices of baguette. He grabs the empty plate from me before I can hit Bartle again.

Bartle swallows, and manages to say while David is still within hearing, "This is incredible. Are you sure that boy isn't gay?"

"Yes," I say. "He's NOT gay."

"He's NOT," Bits adds, slathering another piece of baguette with paté.

"I'm not," David throws this back over his shoulder. "If I were, I would walk like THIS." He mimics Bartle's walk all the way back to the stage door.

Bartle laughs, twirls the feather boa that's hanging around his neck, throwing it over his shoulder like an imitation of Vanessa Redgrave playing Isadora Duncan. (I love that movie!) His mother (my dad's only sister and my other aunt—Mary) was so stupid to kick him out when he told her he was gay. What is wrong with adults sometimes?

"Where's Tim?" I ask, realizing I haven't seen him anywhere. Tim Chang and Bartle are inseparable. They're best friends. At first I thought they were, you know, together. But they're not.

"Had to work. He's coming over afterward. He and the other girrrrrls."

David comes back out with a platter of rib tips.

"Would you go back in and get us some of that fresh limeade?" I shamelessly beg, while licking BBQ sauce off my fingers.

David stands there. I know that look. He's searching for a comeback. Stubbornly searching.

Bits smiles up at him. "Please?"

And off he runs.

"Shameless," I say.

Bartle, assuming I'm talking about him, says, "I am NOT!"

Bartle goes off with the empty platter and the rest of our trash. Bits turns to me and says, "What did you mean when you told Susie's mom you wanted to 'find your strength in the theater'? I mean, what are you going to do?"

"Do?"

"Yeah," she says, flipping her head around so her curls bounce like they've got springs in them. How does her hair do that?

"You know, that's different from what you've been doing?" She goes back to gnawing on the last rib tip.

And just like that all my happiness and excitement (and relief) at being done with school drops away.

One minute I'm flying high. The next I'm totally crashed.

Because, honestly, even though I have a plan for what classes to take and all that, I don't really know the answer to her question.

And I see a year, two years, of nothing but the usual coming at me. Classes in the theater school that I've taken over and over and over with—I hate to admit it but it is oh, too true—little success. Running lines with my parents and Bits. Struggling like the enormous klutz I am with yet another movement class.

I meant it when I said I don't want to go away to college. Not yet.

But, oh, I don't want this year at the theater to be the same as last year or the year before or the year before that.

"Something exciting, please . . ." The words say themselves.

"Huh?" Bits is looking for a place to dump the rib bone now that our human garbage can is gone.

"What?"

"You said . . ." She pauses, waving the rib bone. "You said something . . . exciting?"

"I did?"

"Uh-huh."

"I said that out loud?" I laugh.

She nods.

Geez, what a dumb conversation. "I did say that." I can't help but laugh. "It's true—I do! I want something EXCITING to happen! Something completely different."

"Jessie," Bits says, her voice lowering. "You hate change."

She's right, of course. I am notorious for hating change.

"Aren't you bored with everything being exactly the same?" I push it.

"No," she says. "No. I love it here. I hated high school, but I love the theater school."

"Yeah, yeah. But don't you get tired of it?" What is wrong with me?

"The only thing different I want from this year," she says, "is I want to get at least one really good part. Not school shows. On the main stage. So I have that to take with me to New York."

"Well, I'm not going to New York," I say, taking the rib bone from her and walking over to the trash can. Geez. "And I don't want any parts, good or not. And I do want to be right here, at the theater."

"So . . . ?"

"So I want something different to happen . . ."

A little voice in my head is saying SHUT UP! but for some reason I insist on ignoring it. "Something exciting . . ."

something exciting, please . . .

A UPS truck drives up and instead of double-parking at the curb, pulls into the parking lot. It's our regular UPS guy, who's schlepping a small but evidently heavy package.

"Aren't you delivering kind of late tonight, Al?" I ask.

"Yeah, I was on my way into the lot, but saw this one and decided to drop it off. Congratulations!"

"Thanks! Take it in to Mom and she'll give you a piece of cake . . ."

He doesn't come back out so I figure Mom must have remembered his passion for chocolate. I saw that huge torte that David made in there. Unreal.

We head back in for dessert and to see if the band's ready to start playing. Nope, they're all stuffing themselves with that amazing cake.

"You'd better get some," David says. "It's going fast."

Mom's waving a huge card at me. It has this creepy artwork on the front. One of those super-realistic paintings you see in some religious books and magazines. You know, one of those Biblical scenes where lions are lying down with lambs and all kinds of people are wandering around in gardens, and it ought to be beautiful but it's just weirdly perfect.

"Your aunt," she says as I grab the card out of her hand. "Your aunt is nuts!"

"In order to become my aunt," I say. "She had to first be YOUR sister."

The card is one of those oversized cards you can buy at Hallmark stores. Only this one is clearly NOT of the mass-produced variety. There's a quote from Revelations (yes, book of the Bible, Revelations) hand printed on the inside. And Loretta has written a rather longish note addressed, I see, to both me and Mom.

"Oh, yeah," Bits says, "I saw her working on that the other day . . ."

Nowhere in the card does it say, "Happy Graduation!" or "Congratulations, Graduate!"

As far as I can tell, Loretta doesn't celebrate anything.

I check the envelope. Nope. There's no money in there either. Figures.

Auntie Ellie grabs the card from me and reads it out loud.

> *Dear Una and Jessie,*
>
> *Thank you for the invitation to attend Jessie's graduation ceremony and party. While I appreciate the thought, you know I can't support such a WORLDLY activity,*

especially not in the year—this year, 2012—when the
WORLD IS PREDICTED TO END at the Battle of
Armageddon.

Una, you have fallen far away from the FAITH in the
years you've been with Mark and in the theater. But you
still have a chance to REPENT YOUR SINS and to save
yourself and your child. Jessie deserves to live forever in a
RIGHTEOUS NEW WORLD.

Big laughter from the gathered crowd. Like my mom has sins
to repent. Right.

So, in lieu of a graduation gift (which, of course, I don't
celebrate) I am sending you each a Living Prophecy Transla-
tion of the Bible and several books that I know our smart girl
will gobble up in minutes. Please, Una, leave Mark and that
terrible theater and join me in the quest for righteousness.

I look around to see how my dad's reacting to Loretta's plea,
but he's nowhere in sight. Neither is Grandmama.

It may be your ONLY CHANCE of survival.
                              Your loving sister, Loretta

Mom has picked up the two Bibles and looks like she's going
to throw them into the fireplace (which would not be a good idea
because it's lit). It's an unusually cool day for mid-June.

No two ways about it. Loretta's a lunatic.

Auntie Ellie and Mom take the Bibles and other books out to the kitchen. Mom's still grumbling over Loretta's innate ability to ruin a good time.

David waves his arms to get everyone's attention.

"Quick cure for religious hysteria," he says. Who could resist that? We all gather around.

"What we need is a game of JUMBLE Hide and Seek."

Hide and Seek is one of our traditions that goes back years. The story is that my mom started it here at the theater to entertain David (and me) one time when she was the one watching us and David kept going into the kitchen and climbing up the cupboards in the butler's pantry.

Lydia has embraced a child-rearing philosophy in which she has never (to my knowledge) said no to David. Not once in nearly eighteen years. Think about that. It's really amazing that he's as nice as he is.

The game changed as we got older, and now everyone plays— all the actors and directors, the tech crew, not just the students. The rules (like the original game) are simple. The entire theater including the old carriage house (where the set shop and costume shop are) is allowed. The only space that's off limits is the office upstairs in the mansion—the main theater building. Oh, and you can't hide in the bathrooms because of the male/female thing although honestly when does anyone pay attention to that in this place? Really.

I suddenly see where David's going with this.

Tradition is that Mom is always the first one who's IT. Always.

Perfect way to get her attention off my crazy aunt and back to me. Oh, I mean, to the celebration.

Where's my dad anyway? And Grandmama? My dad must have driven her home.

Here comes my mom and she's laughing, and David's blindfolded her and she's counting (up to fifty) and we are all running in different directions. At first we're all shrieking and then everyone goes silent in order to fool her. If I live to be a hundred I will always love the sound of everyone running and laughing on the first ten count and then the sneaky quiet that follows.

I slip around the side of the studio theater wing and wait until everyone's out of sight and then I run for the carriage house. There's a little closet under the stairs right before you go up to the costume shop that is the perfect hiding place. It's full of bolts of fabric, and I have never once gotten found there. I'm surprised I still fit, but I do.

The trouble is, the minute I settle behind several bolts of brown corduroy, I realize I have to pee. I seriously have to pee.

No problem. There's a bathroom in the costume shop. I think I heard someone go into the set shop, but no one went up the stairs. So I sneak out of the closet and take the stairs two at a time, thanking heaven for my long legs, which allow me to do that and still go quietly. Mom had to have yelled, "Ready or not, here I come!" by now, but I didn't hear her stuck in the closet.

I slip into the costume shop and tiptoe (just in case) across the room and into the dye room where the bathroom is.

And there's my dad.

Wrapped around Brad.

And they are kissing.

Really, really kissing.

They pull apart and swing around. Did I gasp or something? I don't know.

"Jessie!" my dad says, like I've done something wrong. "What are you doing here?"

"What are . . ." I stop. I can SEE what they're doing. "Brad?"

Brad thinks I'm asking him something and starts to answer. "Jessie, I . . . we . . ."

"Hide and seek," I say, quickly, so I don't have to hear some kind of bogus explanation.

"Huh?" my dad says, he and Brad looking at each other. There is a lot of information in that easy look, and I don't want to see that, either.

"Pee—" I blurt out. "I've . . . got to . . ."

And I run into the bathroom and slam the door shut.

I can hear them talking but can't hear what they're saying. I'm puking and I'm peeing and I'm thinking maybe I'll just stay here. Like until tomorrow.

My dad and Brad were KISSING.

And that was not like a first kiss or experiment or something. That was like . . . "we've done this a lot and really know what we're doing" kind of kiss.

Does my mother know about this?

No. She couldn't. Could she?

I mean, I don't even know. This. Whatever this is.

What is this?

18

My dad and Brad kissing.

There's a tap on the door.

"Jessie?" It's my dad. "Are you okay?"

I don't answer. Answering that question would mean I'd have to know what I'm feeling.

What am I feeling?

Well, for one thing that my wonderful celebration went down the toilet with all that great food I just upchucked.

I look at myself in the mirror while I'm washing my face. Yup, still here.

"Jessie?"

I flush the toilet a second time, run the water in the tap some more and, when I can't postpone it with either action or esoteric thoughts, open the door.

My dad and Brad are still there, standing a little too close to each other, looking like . . . looking like a . . . and suddenly everything shifts and it all makes sense. I don't mean I could explain it. It's that on some level I get it.

And then I get this flashing set of images of things that have been happening for . . . I don't know . . . months. Somewhere inside of me I know that when I am alone in my room (hopefully soon) this will all make sense. You know, sense with words attached.

"Does Mom know?"

My dad and Brad give each other a quick glance and then look away.

"So, no?"

They shake their heads.

"You have to tell her," I say.

My dad flinches, and Brad looks terrified.

I can feel something rising up in me. Some loud girl. Some bossy girl (that's not really me most of the time). But in THIS moment of . . . whatever this is . . . I have this picture of me going out of here and having to face Mom. And I know I can't hide this. And I'm sure not going to be the one to tell her I caught my dad kissing one of her best friends. Who's a GUY.

They're still not saying anything.

"No, I mean it," I say, my voice rising. "You HAVE to tell Mom!"

"Tell me what?"

None of us heard her coming. Probably because I was shouting.

Now she looks from me to my dad to Brad.

"Oh . . ." she says.

And I know she's figured it out. I don't know how exactly, but probably the same way it all suddenly makes sense to me.

"Oh . . ." she says again, her voice so light it can hardly be heard. And then again. "Oh . . ."

I don't know what happens in the dye room after that. Because I run out of there. My dad and Brad . . . And I run home.

But the house is huge and dark and empty and I can't go up to my room because then I'd be trapped there if my parents came home.

So I run down the back stairs and out the back door and across to David's house. Well, it's a condo really. But of course no one is home because they are all at the theater, probably still in their hiding places waiting for Mom to come find them.

My dad and Brad . . .

I'm barefoot because I slipped out of my new shoes the minute we got to the theater. So I'm running over grass and gravel and sticks and who knows what. My dad and Brad . . . And eventually I'm back in the theater and I head straight for where Bits always hides.

Tears are rolling down my face now, and I can't stop them. My dad and Brad . . .

"What's going on?" Bits whispers, when I grab her and yank her out from behind the desk in the library.

"I can't tell you right now," I say, snuffling and gulping down tears and snot. "But I'm it. So play like you just caught me."

I swipe at my face with the sleeve of my dress and run out into the lobby yelling, "I'm it!"

Bits doesn't ask any questions. She runs out behind me shouting like it's an acting class improv, "Jessie's IT!"

And when everyone reconvenes around us, I say, "Carriage house is off limits!" And then I cover my eyes with my hands and start to count to fifty. LOUD. Tears are dribbling out of my closed eyes and through my fingers and running off my chin, but I keep wiping them away.

"Ready or not, here I come!" I shout, and run for the main theater. I don't know why but it feels like it's my job to cover for my parents, to keep this party going, to keep everything the same as it was before I walked in on them.

My dad and Brad.

That look on my mom's face.

Like this is something I can control.

Lydia and Edward, Auntie Ellie, and the guys from the band have pulled out of the game and are sitting at the tables outside the kitchen door having coffee and cake.

Auntie Ellie takes one look at my face and grabs my arm. "Jessie, what's going on?"

I pull away, but she grabs me again. "Honey, what's going on? Where's Una?"

Now I'm pulling her, away from Edward and Lydia and Lee. "Dye shop. You better go . . ."

"Oh, shit," she says.

And then I'm pretty sure she either knows or she's got a good idea what's going down. I wonder who else knows. And I wonder why I didn't.

You know, I'm the genius, aren't I?

Yet I'm the one who's totally unprepared for this. My dad and Brad . . .

Did I really ask out loud back there for something exciting and different to happen? Shit.

When Auntie Ellie comes back from the costume shop, she says something to Lydia. The party breaks up pretty fast after that. All it takes are a few whispered conversations and people stealing looks at me (I can't imagine what I must look like— probably a cross between Godzilla and the Mask of Tragedy). I refuse to go into the bathroom to check.

It ends with Bits and David and me sitting on the back steps of the theater. I'm afraid to go home, which is where my parents have gone.

I don't know where Brad went, but I do know he wasn't with them.

Bartle joins us. He won't look me in the eye.

"You knew, didn't you?" I ask him, unwilling to let him off the hook.

"I didn't," Bits says. And not for the first time. I believe her. She has an uncanny knack for seeing what she wants to see. I think it's what's gotten her through the past few years with the divorce and her crazy mother.

Or am I describing MYSELF?

I stare at Bartle until he's forced to look at me.

He nods.

"How?"

"I saw them downtown at the bars."

"Do they know you know?"

He shrugs. "I don't think so," he says, fingering the tattered feather boa. "We didn't talk about it."

"Why didn't you tell me?"

"Jessie . . ."

"You should have told me. Or Mom."

"Una already knows . . ."

"About Brad? No she didn't . . . she was really surprised . . ."

"No," Bartle says, suddenly looking panicky. "I mean . . . she knows . . ."

"She knows Mark is gay," David says. "Everyone knows Mark is gay . . ."

I stand up.

I sit back down.

Look at Bits.

"I didn't," she says. "Honest, Jessie, I really didn't." Her eyes have welled up with tears.

I stand back up.

Nothing makes any sense.

"I'm going home," I say.

"I don't think you should do that yet," David says, and Bartle agrees with him.

But I'm already walking.

Bits runs to catch up with me but I push her away. I see the hurt look in her eyes and I don't even care.

"Jessie!" Bartle yells after me, but I'm already way past 500 of the 572 steps it takes to get from the theater home.

# of COURSE my dad is gay

The front door is unlocked. In the entryway everything is dark and quiet like no one's here. Not even the cats. For a second I think, maybe that really didn't happen.

And then I think, maybe they're already making up . . .

But I know that's not it.

This is way bigger than . . . those kinds of fights . . . they haven't had those kinds of fights for a long time.

I turn on a light and tiptoe over to the base of the stairs and lean in, listening. Nothing. I know they're up there, but it's really quiet.

I so wish I could yell, "Mom! Dad! I'm home!" and have time go flying back to before this happened.

But my head is filling up with images that I do NOT want to see.

I sit down on the step at the first landing and lean against the rail.

My dad falling asleep every night on the sofa and still being there when I get up in the morning.

The way he slips out of my mom's arms whenever she goes to hug him.

The look on her face when that happens.

How he goes down to the theater bar without her after a show opening, and how he goes after rehearsals and on regular production nights. It hasn't always been like that. We used to always be together after shows. When did that change, and why didn't I notice it?

Well, for one thing, someone's always here.

First Bartle moved in three years ago when Aunt Mary kicked him out. He could have gone to stay with Grandmama, but he came here instead. My mom said it was so there wouldn't be such a rift between Grandmama and Aunt Mary. But it wasn't just that, of course. We all knew he would be more comfortable here. Bartle is . . . like . . . quintessentially gay . . . he is stereotypically, swishily gay. And that is so NOT cool in the black community.

In the theater? Hey, he fits right in.

Auntie Ellie moved in shortly after that. She's on the road a lot, but when she's here, so are Lee and the other band guys. Bits is here a lot. Lydia and sometimes Edward. David.

Then there's Tim Chang and Bartle's other crazy friends.

And Brad.

If my dad's here, he's on the sofa watching TV with Maggie and Brick (the two of our cats that follow my dad around like they're dogs). I usually watch TV with him until he makes me go up to bed.

Mom doesn't. She fixes herself a drink, kisses us both on the tops of our heads, and goes upstairs, or if Auntie Ellie's here, she and Mom will sit in the kitchen talking until late and I'm in bed by the time she comes up. But she's always alone.

Maybe I didn't notice this so much because at the theater everything's been the same.

My parents are the most incredible team. Not like Edward and Lydia who each have THEIR OWN THING and who treat each other at work like they're not even married. My mom and dad finish each other's sentences. And when they're leading acting exercises they seem to know what the other one is thinking so it's like you're working with one person that's been split in two.

And, oh, my god, when they act together—everyone says it's magical. I know what they mean when they say that. I feel it, too.

My dad is gay.

Of course he is.

Now they're yelling. I can't make out what they're saying. Only a few words here and there. As dramatic as they both are, they've never fought much. Not out loud anyway.

It makes my stomach twist and turn into a knot so tight I can hardly breathe.

Auntie Ellie finds me there on the stair landing, curled up, clutching my stomach. All six cats are sitting there with me, which is sweet, but doesn't help calm me down. (Especially since Elbows, the Siamese, is yowling.) Auntie Ellie drags me out to the kitchen where she makes me a cup of tea and then forces me to drink it. It's hot and sweet and it actually helps unkink my stomach.

She tries to get me to go over to David's house, but I refuse.

The cats and I end up on the sofa with the TV turned up loud enough I can hardly hear the shouting. Or the silence that follows. Or my mom's loud sobs.

Auntie Ellie comes and sits with me, but we don't talk. I can't.

We watch show after show on the Home and Garden channel where people are hunting for houses all over the world.

I fall asleep there and don't wake up until I hear my dad coming down the stairs. He's trying to be quiet, I can tell, but he's lugging a big suitcase and his computer bag and he can't help bumping into things.

I stop him at the door. "Where are you going?"

"Jessie, what are you doing down here? I thought you were asleep."

"What time is it?" Like I care.

"I don't know," he says. "Late."

"Don't go," I say. "You can sleep on the couch. I'll go upstairs."

"No," he says, setting down his bags and pulling me into his arms. "No, I've got to go. But I'll see you tomorrow, I promise. We'll talk then, okay?"

"Daddy, please . . ." I'm begging, and I can't remember the last time I called him Daddy. "Please don't go . . ."

"Honey, I have to. But I'll see you tomorrow."

I don't ask him where he's going. I'm pretty sure I know. And what difference does it make once he's gone?

He kisses me on the forehead. And then he slips out the door, his bag bumping against it.

The quiet after that is huge.

I don't know what to do, so I watch him as he walks down the street away from the theater, away from us. He's going in the direction of Brad's apartment. But he could just as well be walking to the bus stop. Maybe he's going to Grandmama's. I find my phone and check the time. It's 5:30 a.m. Yes, the buses are running again.

The house feels enormous and so empty. Even the cats have disappeared. I wonder if Bartle ever came home.

I climb the stairs and stand outside Mom's room. It's been Mom's room, not their room, for quite a while, and I'm only now realizing that. What else do I know that I don't know? Or maybe the question is what else don't I know that I actually do know?

My head hurts from not crying.

The door's open and, though it's dark in there, enough light is starting to come up outside that after I've stood there a while I can see her, standing over in the bay window with the curtain pulled back. My dad's long gone, but she's still standing there, watching. Like if she watches hard enough time will reverse and he'll come walking back up the steps and be here with us where he belongs.

Where he belongs, whether or not he's gay.

"Mom?"

It takes her a very long time to turn around. Her face is in shadows, but I can see from the way she's standing how much pain she's in.

I take a step toward her. "Mom?"

"Not now, Jessie," she says, her voice cracking. And then she's doubled over, sobbing. "Not now . . . go away . . ."

And I pull back like she's hit me (not something she's ever done but that's how it feels) and she shuts the door.

And I'm standing there in the hallway outside her room and my dad's gone and I feel like I'm ten, not fifteen.

I sure don't feel like someone who graduated from high school . . . Was that really only yesterday? I stand there for a long time.

And then I go get Auntie Ellie and send her up to comfort Mom.

When Auntie Ellie doesn't come back, I know Mom's let her in. So I go into Auntie Ellie's room off the kitchen and curl up in her bed and cry myself to sleep. At noon the smell of coffee wakes me up, and I start to get up because I want some, but then I remember what happened . . .

And I hear my dad's voice out there.

"Mark, she's still asleep." It's Auntie Ellie talking.

I pull myself up and sit on the edge of the bed. I'm wearing a big old T-shirt, not the dress I was wearing yesterday. I don't remember changing.

"I told Jessie I'd talk with her today," my dad says.

"It can wait." Auntie Ellie's voice is curt.

I strain to hear.

Mom would have interrupted them if she'd been there. And I don't hear Bartle, either. I'll bet he never even came home, the wuss.

"No, Ell, it can't. I promised," my dad says, and my eyes fill up with tears.

"I'm up," I say from the doorway. "Sorry I hogged your room last night . . ."

"Oh, baby," Auntie Ellie says, giving me a quick hug. She disappears into her room, and I go stand by the counter where my dad is pouring me a cup of coffee. Handing me the milk and sugar. His hands are shaking. So are mine when I take the cup.

"I don't care if you're gay," I blurt out, coffee spilling all over the table as I set the cup down. "I just don't want you to leave us for Brad . . ."

And then my dad has his arms around me and we are standing there in the kitchen sobbing.

we walk

"You want to go for a walk?" my dad asks.

"Uh-huh," I say and fly upstairs in a mad scramble to throw on jeans and rebraid my hair—quickly, quickly—for the first time in my life I'm afraid if I don't hurry I'll lose him. My dad will bolt, and I'll never see him again. I know this isn't true. He's in the show tonight. I can track the guy down. But that's what it feels like.

Still in a rush, I come tumbling down the back stairs, bumping against the wall where the steps turn before you enter the kitchen. The Victorian architects were sadists and, to prove it, I am perennially black and blue.

We walk.

Away from the theater, down to Grand Avenue. But that's a little too busy. It's Friday and a gorgeous early summer day so everyone's out up and down the street, walking dogs, sitting at sidewalk cafés. In Minnesota you can eat outdoors for only about four months out of the year max, so the minute the temperature exceeds 60 degrees, every establishment throws open its doors and sets up tables and chairs wherever there's a few feet of extra space.

We cross the street and head into the residential area south of Grand. Big old houses, most of them restored and beautiful. Lots of huge old trees. It's a little chilly in the sudden shade and I shiver.

My dad lets out a breath in a long sigh.

We walk. We're close to the same height—I'm only about an inch shorter than he is—so it's easy to match strides, not like when my mom and I walk anywhere together and I'm either slowing myself down to match her short legs or she's running to catch up.

He stops and looks down at the poured cement sidewalk, so old it's cracked and heaving from tree roots and our crazy-cold winters.

"I don't know how to do this," he says.

This scares me again. My dad never admits to not knowing how to do anything. He's got a pretty flamboyant confidence.

Of course, I don't know how to do this, either, but why would I? We walk some more.

"You could ask me questions," he says finally. We're nearly to Snelling Avenue; we've been walking so long. Snelling is busy, too, but in a different way from Grand. It's all traffic noises—trucks and police cars and fire engines and buses.

We turn around and start walking back the way we came.

"How long have you and Brad . . . have you been with . . . have you and Brad been . . . ?"

"Not very long," he says. "A couple months. Right before the show opened."

"*PRIVATE LIVES?*"

"Yes."

I'm thinking—wow, that timing couldn't be worse. For Mom, I mean. She has this THING about that particular Noël Coward play. It's like her big romantic icon or something. She and my dad did it in college back when they were interested in each other but not going out yet. She always refers to it as "their play."

"Why?"

"Why what?" he asks.

Oops. I forgot he wasn't in my head with me.

"Why then?"

"Why then what?"

In the interest of clarity, I stop walking. "Were you interested in him before and, if not, why then?"

"Oh."

We walk.

"You know, I always thought of Brad as Una's friend. I mean, she was the one into costuming. She hired him and trained him. And she supervises him. And any time he came over it was because she invited him or he needed to see her for some reason."

I don't say anything. I'm really curious all of a sudden about what brought them together and I'm kind of laughing inside—you know, around all the screaming, hurting places—because

34

I'm pretty sure this wasn't the direction my dad meant for this talk to go.

"Your mom's always on me about not being interested in the technical aspects of theater," he says with a snort.

"So it's HER fault?" I can't help myself.

"No! Oh, god . . . no. It's just ironic . . ."

I hate irony.

"I was trying to appease her and I decided the costume shop was the best—well, you know, easiest—place to start since I've been surrounded by all her costuming stuff for nearly twenty years. As you know, I am not fond of power tools . . ."

"Including vacuum cleaners and sewing machines . . ."

"Very true. Long story short . . . something was different about those conversations with Brad. One thing led to another . . . and, ta-da, here we are."

Ta-da, indeed. "Are you in love with him?"

We stop walking again. There's a long pause.

"Yes."

I can feel tears welling up behind my eyes. They're hot and urgent. But there's a lot more I need to know, and crying can wait until later. I blink them back.

"Dad, have you always been gay?"

This answer comes quickly. "Yes."

"Then why did you marry Mom?"

"I loved her . . . I still love her . . . but back then I loved her so much. Our, I don't know, our . . . connection . . . knocked me off my feet. It came as a complete surprise that I could have that.

With anyone, but especially with a woman. I wanted to make a life together. And you were on the way. It seemed so possible . . ."

"Did Mom know? Back then, I mean?"

"No. No, she didn't. I was very much in the closet."

"Why? I mean, yeah, that was a long time ago, but it's not like it was the 1960s or 1970s. I thought everyone came out of the closet in the 1970s."

"Good lord!" He laughs. "What have you been reading?"

"Everything I could find on the subject pretty much since Bartle came to live with us."

"Of course you have."

"Maybe it was Grandmama and Aunt Mary and her church and the whole black community thing about homosexuality," I say, searching his face to see if I've hit on something.

"Welllllll . . ." My dad draws the word out in that funny teasing way he always does when he thinks I'm cashing in on my smarts. Only now all of a sudden I realize how . . . you know . . . GAY he sounds.

Funny, I couldn't see that before.

"Does Grandmama know?"

"I imagine she does, but we've never talked about it."

"I rest my case."

"Yes, darling," he says. "You are more than likely right about that."

"How did Mom find out?"

"You mean that I'm gay?"

"Uh-huh."

"I don't remember exactly . . ."

I'll bet my mom does, I'm thinking. I keep my mouth shut. Log that in as one of the questions I'll ask her if she ever stops crying long enough for me to have a conversation with her.

"No, that's not true. Of course I remember. But there are some things I don't feel right about telling you."

I still don't say anything. One thing I know is how to wait my dad out.

"Okay. There was a guy in one of our shows. Quite a while ago—nine or ten years. I couldn't hide my interest in him, I guess. Una put that together with other things . . ."

I'm about to ask what, but he says, "No, I really can't talk with you about this in any detail. Not now. I'm sorry. I can't."

We walk.

"Okay," he says. "The short version—she confronted me, and I spilled my guts, and we came to an agreement."

"And that's why you stayed in the closet?"

"Yes. Because of Grandmama. And because of Loretta. You know she's even more rabid about homosexuality than she is about me being black. And because as long as we were married, that was the agreement . . ."

"Love . . ." I say.

"Yes, love," he swallows hard. "Love . . . and . . . marriage . . . and you."

"Okay."

"Okay?"

"Uh-huh."

We're back at Grand waiting to cross the street.

"Anything else you want to know?"

37

"Where are you staying?"

"At Brad's."

"Are you ever coming back?"

"Jess . . ."

I have to swallow hard against the tears that rise up. My throat aches.

"Is it all right if I talk to Grandmama about this?" I'm pretty sure Grandmama must know about my dad. She's a very cool lady, but she's just like the rest of the black community. Knowing's one thing, talking about it is another.

He hesitates for a second, but then he says, "Yes. You can talk with anyone you want to about this."

That surprises me more than anything. It seems to make it so . . . irrevocable. And I have a ton of other questions but not one ounce of energy to ask them or to hear my dad's answers.

"You have a show tonight."

"I do," my dad smiles at me and gives my arm a whack. It reminds me of Grandmama. That's what she does instead of hugging. "Did you think I was going to forget?"

"I guess, I don't know." I whack back at him, and he steps off the sidewalk in an attempt to avoid it.

"Are you coming?"

"Uh-huh."

"Well, then, I'll see you afterward."

We're at the house, and I can see he's not coming in.

He reaches over and gives me a quick hug and bolts as if he can't wait to get out of there.

At the door, I turn back, figuring he'll be gone, but having to check anyway.

He's stopped and turned, and is watching me. He watches until I get in the house.

And when I look out the window, this time he's gone.

UN-private lives

Mom stays in her room the entire day. She lets Auntie Ellie come and go, but when I try to get in to talk to her she says, "Not now. I'm sorry, Jess. Not now."

I stand outside her room for a long time listening to her sob. I want to go in and comfort her.

Shit, let's get real here. I want to go in there and shake her until she pulls herself together, remembers she has a daughter, and comforts ME.

Only I'm not the one who's crying. My tears all dried up after talking with my dad and all I have is this heaviness in my chest. Like in the autumn when the leaf mold makes us all gasp for air until we have the first big freeze. Like that.

Auntie Ellie finally pulls me away from Mom's door and downstairs to the kitchen.

"You can run up the back stairs if anyone comes home," she says, knowing without me telling her that I don't want to see anyone else.

Mom always says Auntie Ellie's the sister Loretta could never be. They both escaped from that small town up north, determined to never go back. Auntie Ellie knows Mom probably better than anyone.

"There's a show tonight," I say, like Auntie Ellie doesn't know it's Friday night.

She nods.

"Hey, don't you have a gig?"

"Canceled it," she says.

"Whoa . . ."

She shrugs. "Figured you guys might need me."

"But, I can . . ."

"Of course you can. But you shouldn't have to."

"But . . ."

"Geez, Jessie." Auntie Ellie squeezes my shoulder. "You're the kid here. You shouldn't have to take care of the grown-ups."

Well, that's a nice sentiment, I'm thinking.

My dad has risen to the occasion a little better than Mom, which is kind of unusual. At the moment, taking care of her seems like the only viable method of establishing contact.

Auntie Ellie and I sit at the kitchen table and play gin rummy. I should have known she wasn't going anywhere. She's wearing her favorite pair of jeans that are washed so thin they have holes in the butt. And her Western shirt is the same way. Even Auntie Ellie, who looks really good no matter what she has on, can't get away with this outfit.

My stomach is queasy but eating the party leftovers David brought over when I was walking with my dad helps. We drink about three pots of coffee. And for once Auntie Ellie doesn't get on my case about it.

Bartle doesn't come home.

Neither does my dad. Not that I expected him to.

And Grandmama doesn't call or come over, either. I'm wondering if maybe my dad talked to her. We always either see her or hear from her on Fridays.

At 6:15 p.m. when Mom should be heading to the theater for first call, Lydia shows up with the makeup kit and Mom's costume. This isn't her usual job. Other than teaching and occasionally acting, Lydia's the main administrator of the theater. But she's also one of Mom's oldest friends and probably the only person over there that dared to show up at our house today.

She and Auntie Ellie go into Mom's room. Then, with Mom in tow, they take over the upstairs hall bathroom—it's the largest one plus it's got a vanity.

I get a glimpse of my mother through the open doorway when one of them steps aside for a minute. Her face is beet red and swollen up like she's been stung by about a thousand bees.

"We really have to think about putting an understudy program into place," Lydia is saying as she ices down my mother's eyes with frozen cucumber slices in preparation for applying makeup.

Every time my mother opens her eyes tears start running down her cheeks and they have to calm her down and start all over again.

The curtain goes up at 8:00 p.m. This is going to be a long, long night.

At 7:00 p.m. Lydia finally has my mom's face dry and is troweling on stage makeup. I'm not kidding. It looks like she's applying it with a big spatula or something.

At 7:15 p.m. Kate, the hair stylist from the theater, shows up. When she enters the bathroom, she takes one look at Mom, gasps, and Auntie Ellie shoves her back out into the hallway. Kate pulls herself together and goes back inside.

At 7:35 p.m. Mom comes out of the bathroom looking almost human. I duck out of sight behind my open doorway. I'm afraid if she sees me she will start crying again.

Without even looking in a mirror, I pull off my dingy T-shirt, pull on a nicer, clean one, slip into sandals, and race to the theater. I'm there before I remember my hair's a mess, but then it's too late.

It's the second-to-the-last night of our production of Noël Coward's *Private Lives*. The show got incredible reviews when it opened two months ago, so of course, the house is packed with people trying to get in to see it before it closes. Usually by 7:55 p.m. Edward is in the back of the house doing his directorial pacing routine. Tonight he's nowhere in sight.

My guess is he's backstage giving Mom a pep talk.

I'm there about a minute when David slips in next to me. Bits joins us a few minutes later. And then, as the lights start to dim and the doors close, Bartle is there, too. We don't say anything; we tuck up against the wall in the back, as far away from the last audience row as we can get, which isn't very far.

I don't know about them, but I feel like I'm about to watch an accident happen. One of those accidents you feel like you shouldn't watch but you can't take your eyes away.

43

The curtain goes up revealing the terrace of a hotel in France. I've run lines with all four of the actors so I've memorized the entire script. My dad is playing the male lead, Elyot. My mother is playing the female lead, Amanda. In the story, they are a couple who were married to each other and have been divorced for five years. They meet unexpectedly at a hotel in France where they are each on their honeymoon with a new partner. How ridiculously ironic, given the circumstances.

Have I mentioned how much I hate irony?

The first scene is my dad as Elyot with his new wife, Sybil, and it goes smoothly. He's a little stiff, but that's not all that unusual. He can't stand the actress who's playing Sybil so sometimes he doesn't overcome that completely. The next scene is Mom as Amanda with her new husband, Victor. Amanda has the title speech in this scene, the one that reveals the theme of the play.

I bite my lip to keep from mouthing the words with her. But they're still ricocheting around in my pinball machine head. Amanda's going on about how when you dig down into people's private lives, hardly anyone is what you'd call normal.

I hadn't really thought about it when I was running lines with her, but Noël Coward knew what he was talking about. Basically that if all the cosmic connections, you know, CONNECT, anything can happen.

No shit, Sherlock.

I'm holding my breath because I know in about a minute and a half, Victor will leave the stage and Elyot will come out and he and Amanda will "discover each other" and realize they are deeply, madly, irrevocably in love, not with their new spouses, but with each other.

They pull it off.

They are amazing, they really are.

Each time my mom comes back onstage after she's been off for a while I can see that Lydia has slapped on another layer of makeup. Mom's eyes are nearly swollen shut. But when she opens her mouth, we are transported into another world, another time period, into the person of this brittle, sophisticated Amanda, who loves her first husband with all her heart.

The play is a comedy. The laughs keep coming. The audience is enthralled.

When they enter together to take their curtain calls, they grab each other's hands the way they always do. Take their bows to each other and to the audience. Then my dad stands back and lets my mom take a single bow.

They receive a long and vigorous standing ovation.

I feel like my heart is going to leap out of my chest and be trampled under the audience's departing feet.

Bits and Bartle and David are all talking at once, evidently at me. My head is in such a fog, I can't make out what they're saying. Something about food. Bits coming over to spend the night. Bartle saying something stupid about how everything will turn out all right.

I step back, away from them all.

"No!" I say, more loudly than I mean to.

And I slip out the back way and run home.

This is the night when I shut my bedroom door and lock it.

It's an old house, and everything creaks. Lying there, not crying, I hear the stairs creak when Bits follows me home. She taps on my door and calls my name. It's mean, I know, but I ignore her.

Then I hear the stairs creak as she goes back down them. I don't know whether she leaves or not. I can hear the front door opening and closing, opening and closing. It's Grand Central Station down there tonight, apparently.

People are in the kitchen talking. I don't think my dad is here. I don't hear his voice. There's no shouting. Every once in a while someone laughs. I hear the clink of glasses. The refrigerator door.

I hear my mom come up the back stairs and go to her room. I think about trying again to talk to her, but I can't move. It doesn't seem likely she'll have the focus or the energy for me tonight, either. Maybe after the show closes. Tomorrow night or the next day.

I hear the cats out in the hallway. Probably looking for an open bedroom door. Not mine. Not tonight.

Sometime later, I hear Bartle come up and go to his room. I don't know why I'm so mad at Bartle. But I hate it that he knew about my dad and didn't tell me. At the same time, I know if he HAD told me, I'd have been even madder about that.

Nothing about what I'm feeling is reasonable.

What I want is to close my eyes, drift off to sleep, and wake up two days ago, with everyone happy and excited about my graduation honors.

I want to declare to the universe that it is perfectly all right if nothing exciting ever happens to me. Or to any of us.

Ever again.

all the world's a stage

After the insanity of *Private Lives* and lying awake listening to everyone go up and down the stairs until the wee hours, I finally fall asleep. When I wake up around nine, the house is still quiet. That's pretty typical for a Saturday morning because there's always a play on Friday nights, or rehearsal. Or someone's auditioning somewhere, or out partying. In Auntie Ellie's case, she's usually out of town with the band.

This Saturday morning feels like it should be different. Everything else is.

I sneak downstairs to put on a pot of coffee.

My head feels like it's going to explode. Or maybe that's all six of the cats yowling for food. I dump some in their bowls. I should check their litter boxes, but I can't quite bring myself to go down to the basement before coffee. Ick.

The doorbell chimes. I can see through the peephole that it's some kind of religious duo, probably Jehovah's Witnesses, as they seem to dominate the Saturday-morning-knock-on-your-door scene. From the porch where they are waiting (J.W.s, like Mormons, always travel in pairs, or sometimes in threesomes if they've got a mini Witness with them), I know they can hear "Boogie Woogie Bugle Boy of Company B" blasting through all three stories of our Victorian house. (Sung by Bette Midler ages ago, this extremely GAY doorbell music was a gift to Mom and Dad from the tech crew at the theater the year Mom bought the house. Well, that's one of those rather huge clues I somehow managed to miss, isn't it?)

I go back to the kitchen and pour a cup of coffee.

The song continues its blare through the living and dining rooms and rousts me back out of the kitchen. Geez.

Anyway, no one has had the heart to change the song or lower the volume, although all of us at one point or another have been sorely tempted to take a hammer and permanently disable the system. I would do it right now if there weren't someone at the door.

Cup in hand, I answer it. No, these aren't the J.W.s. If they were, they would be more neatly dressed and carrying book bags with the *Watchtower* and *Awake* peeking out. I could be wrong, but I think these are Loretta's Church of the Living Prophesy—CLP—folks, looking like a cross between New Age gurus and J.W./Mormons. A dangerous combination, I might add.

None of those groups ever identify themselves first thing. It's always something like, "We are out in the service of God today, spreading this good news of the kingdom."

I say, "No thank you," and close the door. Stand inside the door, listening to the doorbell go off one more time—this is what clues

49

me that these self-appointed ministers were SENT (undoubtedly by my lunatic aunt). I suppose we should be grateful that she's not coming herself.

I ignore the doorbell.

Even before 2012, as far back as I can remember, once or twice a year the CLP folks would show up. Mom always denies that Loretta sends them. It's too terrible a thought. But I'm sure she does. I mean, come on, she pulled Bits out of high school in preparation for Armageddon. That's when I stopped calling her AUNT Loretta. I don't think anyone's even noticed. But it makes me feel better.

The thing I've noticed (even before Loretta sent her graduation "present") is that because it's 2012 the CLP messengers—that's what they call themselves—have been coming even more often.

Today, given what's going on at our house and given the state Mom's in, I'm just thankful I was the only one up and that no one else is a light sleeper.

After the CLP scare, I hide out in my room most of the day, sneaking down to the kitchen to refill my coffee. Yes, I know I am too young to drink this much coffee, but I add lots of milk. Lots of it.

Mom stays in her room, too, and I don't know where Bartle is, unless he's still asleep. Around noon Auntie Ellie comes up and taps on my door until I open it a crack. She's got her shiny, retro Western shirt on over her good jeans. And my favorite turquoise-and-orange cowboy boots. It works with her long legs and long brown hair. I don't know why, but it does.

"I've got to go, Jess. We are taking off for Madison. We'll be back in the morning."

"Yeah, okay."

"I can't cancel another night." The way she's looking at me, I think she may be reconsidering it.

"No, no you can't," I say. "Really, it's okay . . ."

"Call Lydia if you need . . . I mean, if Una . . ." She doesn't finish whatever she was going to say. I don't want to know what that was.

"Sure."

She reaches in and cups my chin with her hand. I know if I weren't standing there clutching the door three-quarters shut she would hug me. Normally I would like that. I like it that we are a huggy family. Today I can't stand the thought of anyone touching me.

"Okay then," she says. "I'll see you in the morning."

For a second I consider running after her and begging her to take me with her. I could sit in the back of the van with all the instruments. I could schlepp them into the bar and help set up. Only then what would I do? They don't allow fifteen-year-olds in bars. Not even in Wisconsin, the underage, beer-bar capital of the world.

By 5:00 p.m. I'm overloaded with information from doing online research on my laptop. (Yes, I am a research geek and, yes, it is one of my major coping mechanisms, so sue me.) And I'm so hungry I risk going down to the kitchen.

No one's there, so I make myself a sandwich, eat it, have some orange juice, and an apple. Loretta must have taken Bits somewhere. Usually she comes over on Saturdays.

I'm starting to get worried about my mom. I mean, tonight's closing night of the show. What if she's unconscious up there or something? My stomach goes all queasy and I'm about to head for the bathroom when I hear the front door opening and closing.

It's Lydia, and she's holding Mom's makeup kit and this time she's got Kate, the hair stylist, with her from the start. And Brad, carrying Mom's first act costume.

Oh, dear. I don't think that's a very good idea.

I'm about to run up the stairs to warn Mom, but Lydia cuts me off.

"Better let me go," she says, handing me the makeup kit.

At least they aren't ALL descending on her bedroom. I go back out to the kitchen, leaving Brad and Kate standing in the living room.

Hey, I am not a hostess. I am a teenager with many years practice being a diva's only child.

The front door bangs open and bangs shut.

It's Bartle. So he WAS out somewhere.

"Brad!" he shouts. "What are you doing here?"

Subtle.

I peek around the corner of the door leading from the kitchen to the dining room. Brad is holding up Mom's first act costume and waving it like a surrender flag.

Save that for Mom, I'm thinking. You're going to need more than a costume to get you past that one.

Now Brad and Bartle look like long-lost buddies, whispering together in there. I jump back from the door as Kate wanders out to the kitchen. She's an ex-JUMBLE theater student who's doing some intern work with us while she completes her degree at the U. We know each other pretty well because she used to babysit for me before Bartle moved in.

She reaches into the fridge for a diet soda.

"You okay?" she asks, popping the top and taking a long swig.

I shrug my shoulders. Words are eluding me.

I DON'T KNOW HOW I AM. Is what I'm thinking. In caps. I WISH I KNEW. And then: WHERE'S MY MOM? WHAT IS MY DAD THINKING? WHY IS BRAD HERE? NO MORE COFFEE OR I WILL FLY THROUGH THE ROOF! WILL WE HAVE TO CANCEL THE SHOW TO-NIGHT? IT'S CLOSING NIGHT. FULL HOUSE. WE CAN'T AFFORD TO CANCEL.

I start calculating tonight's box office. If we don't cancel. If we do cancel. Ahhhh, math can be soothing, even when the results are mostly in red.

Bartle sweeps into the kitchen. Grabs a bottle of water from the fridge. Avoids meeting my eyes.

What is with him anyway?

He and Kate start talking like they haven't seen each other for ages and have so much catching up to do. She was at my party two nights ago. What is with him?

I'm considering getting the hell out of the kitchen when the whole rest of the entourage sails in.

Mom and Lydia come flying down the back stairs so I can't escape that way. Especially since the cats are following them. Brad marches in from the living room, with a look of simultaneous terror and determination plastered all over his face. Of course he's still clutching Mom's costume. It doesn't help his case that Dad's cats, Maggie and Brick, are twining themselves around his ankles. Good grief!

Now would be a good time to run for it, but not only are they blocking the exits and turning this into *No Exit* from Sartre, it's that whole watching an accident scenario all over again.

Let's see. How to describe it.

Okay, I've got it.

Mom's in character already. Yes, that's it. She's not Una; she's Amanda. Her eyes aren't nearly as puffy as they were last night. In fact, her face has almost gone back to normal. But now that the puff is gone, you can actually see her eyes. And it's not pretty.

Words to describe her eyes: hard, brittle, maybe even a little mean. For the first time, I notice a physical resemblance to Loretta. Scary.

I back into the open doorway of Auntie Ellie's room. Like I'm easy to hide.

Actually, I am easy to hide. I am so not the focus of this scene. Let's say that given the immensity of Mom's performance, I have been rendered part of the scenery.

What is it my dad always says? Oh, yeah, it's his favorite Shakespearean quote: "All the world's a stage."

Yup. That's it. From the play, *As You Like It*.

Like it? Nope. Not that much. Especially when the play is shaping up to be a melodrama and the stage is our kitchen.

"Brad, darrrlllling," Mom says, her voice dripping with sarcasm. "I was wondering when you were going to show up."

Brad starts sputtering and turns bright pink. He's waving her costume again like that proverbial surrender flag. I almost feel sorry for the guy.

Almost.

Lydia gets her into makeup. Kate does her hair. Brad does her costume. (Yeah, she lets Brad do her costume. I am impressed. Although I don't think it's an accident when she pokes him in the eye twice in the process.)

Bartle makes sure she has a few sips of a protein smoothie and a bottle of water. And then they all escort her over to the theater in the nick of time for first call.

By this time I'm so mad I can hardly see straight. It's not like I expect to be the center of anyone's attention, not even my mother's. But I sure don't want to be invisible.

She hasn't said ONE WORD to me about what happened Thursday night. I'm trying to give her the space she needs to get through the rest of the run. But come on.

I want to cry. You know that weird spurting crying that happens when you're really angry and have no outlet? But this time, I'm too mad to do even that.

I hate my mother.

I hate my father.

I hate Brad.

I hate this whole stupid theater.

I hate this old Victorian house that my mother loves.

I hate St. Paul, Minnesota.

I hate my friends.

I hate *Private Lives* and Noël Coward! (Which is such a

bald-faced lie—I love Noël Coward—it snaps me out of my litany of hates.)

Suddenly, panic sets in. I mean, you do know what's on the flip side of the hate coin, right?

That would be love.

I race upstairs, quickly rebraid my hair, which is sticking up all around my head like a curly, matted mop, pull on some un-wrinkled jeans and a tank top and run to the theater.

Just in time. The house closes. The curtain goes up.

David slips in beside me and gives me a quick hug before I can pull away.

Then Bits is there, too, her hand in mine, holding on so tight, there's no use fighting her.

It's always like this. You grow up in a theater and you are drawn to it . . . you can't stay away. Especially not when something crazier than usual is going down.

So we clutch each other and huddle there watching the best performance we've ever seen from my deranged parents.

There's a closing party afterward, a benefit for the theater that's been scheduled for months. Lydia told me she and Edward gave Mom the option of canceling it, but Mom said no. Then they suggested—carefully, I might add—she not attend, but by the end of the show she's so hyped up on acting adrenaline, she changes her mind and decides to go.

Edward tries to tell my dad it would be better if HE left, but there are people here from the other theaters in town, and some of the original reviewers are here, people he wants to schmooze with, plus he hates it when Edward tries to tell him anything, so he digs in his heels and stays, too.

It's not a huge party because all of the tech people are in the middle of striking the set and props and costumes. We don't usually have these kinds of events at closing, but it's always good to have a fund-raiser right before the theater goes dark for the rest of June.

Normally I would help with the costume strike, but I'm not going anywhere near Brad if I can help it. And anyway, Bartle's helping him. For some reason, ever since we found out about my dad and Brad, Bartle's become Brad's best friend. Go figure.

Bits, David, and I mostly hang out in the kitchen, playing cards and taking turns going to the door to check on what's happening. There's a DJ tonight, since Auntie Ellie and the band are in Wisconsin. Pretty soon everyone's sloshed on champagne and the dancing starts.

When my mom drinks it's usually scotch. On the rocks. But tonight she's drinking champagne like it's water. And she and champagne . . . let's say they have history. Plus, I haven't seen her take a bite of food. And I doubt if she's slept since Thursday.

When she's so drunk she can hardly stand up, she heads for my dad and pulls him out on the dance floor.

I've been watching through the open doorway, but now I get up right in the middle of our game and go stand against the wall outside the door.

"They're doing that routine they always do . . ." Bits's voice is priceless. Filled with something that's a cross between awe and horror.

"You mean the one that's like ballroom dancers," David abandons the cards and joins us. "Only more . . . uh . . ."

"Musical comedy-ish?" I finish for him.

"Yeah, that one," Bits whispers.

See, everywhere my parents go, someone always asks them to dance. One of their favorite memories is of dancing on the tables at the Holiday Inn one time when Auntie Ellie and her band were playing there.

Yup. On the tables.

I've pretty much always taken it for granted. I'm not stupid, so I don't think this is what everyone else's parents do. I mean, there's not much about my family that's like anyone else's (at least not any I've ever met). No, I mean that they've been doing these kinds of things since before I was born, so it seems . . . normal . . . to me.

Tonight it seems . . .

"Surreal," David says, making me wonder if I've been talking out loud.

"It's so sad," Bits adds, and even though that's exactly what I'm thinking, I want to scream at her to SHUT UP.

And anyway, *desperate* is the word I'm thinking—at least in the case of my mother.

My dad?

"What's the word when you give into something that's coming at you like a freight train?"

"Huh?" Bits is still all wrapped up in the sad story.

"You know, because what else can you do but give in?"

They're both looking at me as though I've lost my mind. Maybe I have. I almost feel sorry for my dad. Almost.

Anyway. They do the whole damned routine—just like they've been doing it my entire life.

I glance over at Brad, who has popped in (evidently the costume strike is done). His shoulders kind of sag as he watches them. What's he feeling, I wonder? I'll bet he's asking what he got himself into. If there's any way this can ever turn out okay.

I almost feel sorry for him, too. Except that my definition of "turn out okay" is, like, on the other end of the continuum from his.

"Here comes the kiss thing," Bits says, nearly breathless.

That would be where my dad always pulls my mother up close to him and she arches her back and throws her leg up and they kiss. Very stagey, very theatrical, but very cute. And always a part of the dance.

Not tonight. Tonight he reverses the move and spins her out. She's a little wobbly and ends up flying into Edward's arms.

Edward takes Mom into the kitchen. I'm not about to leave her alone with Edward—who has what we will call a *reputation*—especially not when she's had too much to drink and is, shall we say, emotionally overwrought.

Bits and David evidently have the same idea. We all converge on the kitchen. Edward doesn't even know what hit him. We are good.

David, Bits, and I drag Mom home. I'm fervently wishing Auntie Ellie were here. She's the only person (other than my dad)

59

who knows how to handle Mom when she's had too much to drink.

It's not like she drinks all the time, but when she does, especially champagne, she has a habit of getting sloshed. And, of course, these are extraordinary times.

Bartle's nowhere in sight, either. He and Tim must have gone downtown after the strike.

"Should I get my mom?" David asks.

I shake my head. Lydia, in these circumstances? Nuh-uh. Lydia's rational intelligence isn't a good fit with Mom all drunk and sobbing. Auntie Ellie? Now, she is the perfect fit. Unfortunately she's still in Wisconsin.

"Stay here, though."

He sits down on the landing while Bits and I drag Mom up the stairs and into her room.

She's been sobbing all the way home and is asleep by the time we dump her, fully clothed, on her bed.

I'm quivering with exhaustion and sadness and other feelings I can't even find words for. I'm so mad at my mom I don't know what to do. What am I doing, having to put her to bed because she's so drunk she can't stand up? I mean, was it wrong of me to think maybe she'd be able to talk with me tonight?

When Bits goes down to tell David he can go home, I lock myself in my room again. I know it's mean. This isn't Bits's fault. I know I should be grateful to her and to David, too. And I am.

But I can't help this. I have to be alone.

I hear Bits go down the stairs. Dang, those stairs creak. I know she doesn't want to go home—she never wants to go home and who can blame her—so she'll probably sleep on the couch or in Auntie Ellie's room. That way she'll be here when her dad drops Auntie Ellie off.

In the morning, I think. I'll apologize in the morning.

And then I am blissfully, soundly asleep.

when the theater goes dark

The theater goes dark twice during each year. That's from Christmas until the end of January. And then during the summer, two weeks in June and three weeks in August. I suppose you could consider that three periods of going dark, but for some reason we always talk about it as two.

Most often these days you hear the term *theater goes dark* when a theater loses its funding and closes for good. Sometimes people say it about the house lights going down, you know, signaling the start of the show. But what I'm talking about are the periods when the theater shuts down between scheduled runs, mostly to let everyone rest and relax. Or, in the case of my parents and Edward and Lydia, to gear up for the next round.

After *Private Lives* closes, after Mom's drunken dance with my dad, after Bits and David and I dump her into bed and I lock myself in my room, after I manage to call my dad the next day to wish him a Happy Father's Day, let's just say everything goes dark.

My dad sounds surprised that I called. Almost like he's shocked to still be recognized as a father. Is this what it's going to be like from now on? I'm thinking. Erasing everything backward until we get to before family?

A lump the size of Lake Harriet forms in my throat.

I am so desperate I go across the hall and stand outside my mom's closed door.

I want to open it the way I usually would and I want her to see me and say, "Honey . . ." like she always does. And we'll sit down on the bed and she'll talk with me about what's going on.

She'll tell me what she's feeling. She's an actress, so she always knows what she's feeling. That must be nice.

Her door's closed. And for the first time EVER I don't feel like I can just open it. Maybe I could knock. I should be able to knock, shouldn't I?

But I'm scared to.

I mean, what if she didn't open it?

Now the lump in my throat is the size of Lake Superior. It takes a gargantuan effort to swallow it down.

Auntie Ellie and the band have a six-week summer gig coming up in Baraboo, Wisconsin, so I'm about to lose the one person running interference.

Right before they're scheduled to leave, she makes me let her into my room.

"Jess, if you want me to, I will cancel this gig."

"You can't do that!"

"Yes, I can, and I will if you need me."

I honestly don't know what I would have done without Auntie Ellie since graduation night. Mom must feel that way, too. I mean, as far as I know, Auntie Ellie's the only one she's let in.

"No, it's okay." I want so badly to say, "YES, yes, please, please stay." But instead I find the words, "You guys all need the money. I know this gig pays well."

"It does," she says. "It keeps us going all the way into the fall. But I can send the band and get one of my friends to sub in for me."

"You're the draw," I say.

She smiles. She knows I'm right about her being the star. Her deep, smoky singing voice is the best thing about that band.

"Will you be okay?"

"Yeah, sure."

She gives me a big hug, and because I don't want her to think for a second that I'm upset or mad or whatever because I'm not, I don't pull away. Who am I kidding? I need that hug.

"Mom . . . I don't know . . . what if Mom . . ."

"Honey, Una will pull herself together. I know she will."

Tears well up until my eyes feel burning hot.

"Jess, I'm so sorry Una's not paying any attention to you . . ."

The tears spill over, and I swipe at my face. I'd like to throttle my mom, but it hurts me to have someone else saying what she's doing is wrong.

"Auntie Ellie, thanks so much." I swallow the tears down. "For everything. We'll be okay . . ."

"I'll call you," she says, giving me another quick hug. "At least you're not spending a month in Baraboo!"

In spite of how lousy I feel I can't help but laugh remembering our one disastrous trip to Baraboo. She laughs, too, and leaves looking a little less worried about me.

The house feels cavernous. I stay on my computer doing on-line research. Maybe I will go to college after all. The campus in Chapel Hill, North Carolina, looks really appealing all of a sudden.

Every day Bits comes and pounds on my door and then when I won't open it, she stands there and talks to me through the door. It's crazy that I won't open the door to Bits. I just can't. I stand there and listen to her tell me about what's going on with her mom and how she wishes Summer Street Theater would start.

And I don't let her in.

I would feel bad about this if I had any room in my being for feeling anything other than what I'm trying so hard NOT to feel.

I'm not mad at her anymore. I'm kind of embarrassed, I guess. And sad.

And I don't want to talk about it.

David, Edward, and Lydia have gone to Florida to visit Lydia's parents.

"Florida in late June—ugh," David said when he called me the night before they left. "Thank god they live near the beach!"

Lydia, in an enormous act of sacrifice, actually asked if I want to go along. I thought about it but I couldn't do it. I mean, I love them, but not to live with. Not even on vacation. And Lydia's parents drive me crazy.

Mom, apparently, also said no. I don't know why. It seems to me she would want me out of her hair, I mean, given how she's acting.

Bartle's suddenly getting paid by Brad to clean and organize the costume shop and costume storage. He's still got his busboy job, so whenever he's not working at the café he's over at the shop throwing his mojo around. My guess is he's pretending he's one of those decorator/organizers on HGTV.

I entertain a brief fantasy about Bartle and Brad falling madly in love and running off to San Francisco. This gets me through an afternoon.

I don't know what my dad's doing, but I do know he's not putting in an appearance here. At least he calls me every other day or so. Sometimes I answer.

Sunday night I sneak out of the house after I've heard my mom come up from eating dinner. I'm assuming she ate dinner. I heard the microwave ding.

I'm so stir crazy I have to get out of the house. So I make myself a peanut butter sandwich and walk over to the theater. This is the only place I can think to go, especially at night.

I head upstairs to the main theater. There's something about that proscenium stage that feels most like home.

My mom tells a story about when I was really little—I don't know, two or three I guess—and had never really gone to church much. At that point, Mom kept me away from Grandmama's black Baptist Church, a kind of knee-jerk reaction to her own crazy religious upbringing, I suppose. Anyway, the story goes that she and my dad took me with them to a wedding of friends of theirs down in Chicago.

When we got into the big, elaborate church and got ourselves seated, Mom says I looked all around the huge space and then turned to my parents and said, in a loud, theatrical stage whisper that could be heard in every corner of the church, "What is this place anyway? A theater?"

Brought down the house.

We're a superstitious bunch here in the theater. Whenever the theater goes dark, whether it's for the night or for two weeks or a month, the last stagehand out leaves a lighted lamp on the stage.

Some people say it's to keep the ghosts away.

Some people say it's to light the stage so the ghosts can play.

My dad says maybe it's both. What's irrefutable is that any great theater is haunted.

I can say for sure as I sit here eating my peanut butter sandwich, this one is.

or i'll blow your house down

Bits is pounding on my bedroom door. She's pounding so hard the water is sloshing in the toilet in my bathroom. I'm not kidding. For someone so tiny she sure is strong.

I'd say it was someone bigger—Bartle perhaps—pounding but it's unmistakably Bits who is yelling as she pounds.

"Jessie! Let me in or I'm going to call the fire department . . ."

Pound, pound, pound!

"And six huge fire trucks with their sirens blaring will pull up and, using a fire ax, they will knock down this damned door!"

Pound, pound, pound!

Bits, who never swears, said *damned*.

Where's my mom? She must have gone over to the theater.

"Open this door or I'm going to go get a screwdriver and take the hinges off!"

"The hinges are on the inside, you moron!" My voice is rusty from over a week of hardly ever using it. And I just called my cousin a MORON.

She stops pounding.

I've done it now.

"Bits?" I still can't bring myself to open the door. "Bits are you there?"

No answer.

I unlock the door and open it a crack. I don't see her.

I open it a little more.

There she is, sitting next to the door with her back against the wall.

"You are unbelievable!" she says without looking at me. She's fiddling around with her phone.

Good lord! Was she actually going to call the fire department?

"I mean it," she says, putting her phone back in her pocket. "I don't know why I keep trying to get you out of there."

I step out into the hallway. It's blindingly bright. Apparently I've turned into Mole Woman.

"Maybe because you've never done anything like this before . . ." Suddenly she starts to cry. And the next thing I know she's wailing.

"I'm sorry!" I say, throwing myself down onto the rug next to her. "Stop crying! I'm so sorry!"

She gulps and hiccups, but can't seem to stop sobbing.

"I . . . I can't . . ."

"I'm the moron . . ."

We say this together and then stop and look at each other.

"You're a mess," she says, reaching up to push my hair out of my eyes.

I nod. Not much to say to that. I am. I am definitely a mess.

"Where's Mom?"

"She went to the theater. She's starting to gear up for the start of Summer Street next week."

"Street Theatre starts NEXT week?" How long have I been holed up here? You talked to her?"

"Yeah, a little while ago."

My stomach does one of those jumpy things and I feel kind of dizzy all of a sudden. That's what happens when you go so long without much food and the only light in the room is from your laptop.

I put my head down between my knees.

"I made some coffee," she says, smiling for the first time.

"You did?" That brings my head back up.

"Uh-huh."

She leaps up, but my legs are kind of wobbly, so my attempt to follow her fails.

"Well, what are we waiting for?" I say, trying again. This time she reaches down and pulls me the rest of the way to my feet.

"I've been feeding the cats."

Thank goodness.

"I haven't cleaned out their litter, though. I hate your basement."

Join the club, I'm thinking. I can't imagine that Bartle did it, either.

"Well, I can't smell it," I say, once we hit the kitchen.

"You can't smell this coffee?" Bits asks, pouring us cups.

"The cat litter," I say, smiling. The coffee smells wonderful.

"I was so scared," Bits says.

"Yeah, I know . . ." I say, getting the milk out of the fridge. "I was, too."

Bits waits until I've had a couple sips of coffee and then she reaches into the big tote bag she schlepps everywhere and pulls out a handful of cards. She plops them down on the table between us.

"I've committed a felony," she says.

"Mail fraud, I presume?" I say, reaching for the top postcard.

It only takes me a second to see what she's been collecting. Postcards to Mom from Loretta. Each one entreating her to SAVE HERSELF (and me) BEFORE IT'S TOO LATE.

The woman lives six blocks away. I wonder if she knows this is the twenty-first century?

"What did I do to deserve a cousin like you?" I ask after I've read them all.

"Are you going to give them to Una?" Bits asks, her voice a little shaky.

"Are you kidding? Now?" The thought makes me shudder.

"What are you going to do with them?"

"Well, I want to rip them up and throw them away," I say, spreading them all out on the table with the pictures face up, like a tarot reading. The postcards are typical Minnesota tourist cards like you can buy everywhere. What's kind of weird is that they are all nature shots from the country. Birch trees, loons, lake shots, an overhead shot of a small town spreading out from the lakeshore.

Deer standing at the edge of a pine forest. I mean, we all live in the city, you know—even Loretta.

I flip them over, one after another, to reveal Loretta's beautiful handwriting and her words . . . her indescribably stupid words.

"Did you tell your mom about what's going on with my dad and Brad?"

"God, no!" Bits looks horrified.

"Okay, good . . . Don't tell her."

"I won't! She'd be . . . I don't know . . . I won't tell her . . ."

"I'm going to hide these postcards in my room and bring them out if and when I need them. And your part in this will never be mentioned . . ."

Bits beams at me and refills my coffee cup. "It's not only Una Mom's after. She has started calling me when she knows I'm busy and leaving me end-of-the-world voice mail."

"No! She doesn't!"

"Yeah. Thank goodness she refused to get me text messaging when my dad got me this phone. Can you imagine?"

"One good thing about this awful week is Mom's probably forgotten all about Loretta's package and letter . . ."

"You say you forgot me?" The back door opens and in comes Grandmama, lugging a huge shopping bag and surrounded by the most delicious smells.

"Grandmama!" In one second I feel about two thousand times better than I did the second before. Grandmama has that effect on people. I leap up to grab the bag from her. She whacks me on the arm and yes, I feel as hugged as if she'd actually hugged me.

Bits runs over and gives Grandmama a big kiss on the cheek.

Grandmama grins. I don't know what it is about Bits, but she can get away with it. Not only with Grandmama, either. Maybe it's because she's so small. And cute.

"Una come out of her bedroom yet?" Grandmama asks, stirring three teaspoons of sugar into her coffee. I hand her the milk.

"How'd you . . . ?" I stop myself. Of course someone's been calling her and keeping her up on what's going down. Bartle? My dad? Probably both.

She smiles and takes a long sip.

"Una's at the theater," Bits says, leaning over my arm to peer into Grandmama's shopping bag.

"Go on, you," Grandmama says, shoving the bag with her foot in our direction. "Dig in there. I didn't cook and bake all morning to have that sit there and get cold."

It would be a lie if I said that I didn't feel a lot better after eating two pieces of Grandmama's fried chicken and three cinnamon rolls.

"I've got to go," Bits says. "I told Una I'd meet her in an hour and I'm late."

"Okay," I say, wondering what she's meeting mom about. Well, Summer Street Theater, I imagine. But why today?

Bits is standing there, shifting nervously from one foot to the other.

"It's okay," I say again. "Really. Are you coming back later?"

"Yeah, unless my mom insists I come home."

"Go!" I say. "You know Mom hates it when anyone's late . . ."

It's only when she's gone I realize, uh-oh, now I'm alone with

Grandmama and I don't have any idea how to talk about what's happening.

I needn't have worried about that.

Grandmama digs down into the bottom of her cloth shopping bag and pulls out her set of dominoes.

"Some things it don't do much good to talk about," she says, opening up the case and dumping the tiles out onto the table.

"You know?"

She nods. "About your dad and that chubby costumer?"

"Brad—his name is Brad . . ."

She nods again, deftly turning tiles over with her long fingers. I have Grandmama's hands, only mine aren't as worn from work as hers are.

I turn tiles, too.

"You knew about Dad before?"

"Mmm-hmm," she says, nodding again.

We keep turning tiles.

"You're . . . um . . . okay with him being gay?"

She looks up from the tiles, fixes me with that stare of hers, the one that scares a lot of people until they get to know her. Then they'd do just about anything to call up that look from her, the way it lets you know she knows who you are and how it makes you feel alive.

"Something goes that deep, who am I to question?" Grandmama goes back to turning the tiles.

"Aunt Mary . . ."

"Is a fool," Grandmama snaps. "She's a bigger fool than her mama was!"

"I wish I'd known my dad's mother."

"You got to talk today, don't you?" Grandmama says, turning the last tile. "I suppose that's what comes of shutting yourself up in your room for so long."

So she knows about that, too.

"Pour me some more coffee, then," she says. "The game can wait a minute or two."

I pour her another cup, put in the milk and push the sugar bowl over to her side of the table.

"You know she left him with me when he was just a baby, run off."

"So, my dad didn't really ever know her then?"

Grandmama shakes her head. I can see this pains her. "Huh-uh, he didn't. Mary, she might remember her. Not that she'd admit it."

"What did she die of?"

"Some kind of infection, staph I think it was . . ." Grandmama eyes the tiles. "We goin' to play here?"

"You start," I say, because Grandmama always starts.

"I love that boy," Grandmama says without looking up from the tiles.

"My dad?"

She nods, still concentrating on the game.

"Mary, she was hard-headed and stubborn like her mama, right from the start. Only . . ." Grandmama searches for words, shaking her head again. "Only she went so far into righteous she's stupid with it."

I play my tile. "Like Loretta . . ."

"Not as bad as Loretta," Grandmama says, shaking her head. "Bad enough, though. Now Mark . . . your daddy . . . I knew the day Lou drop him off he was goin' to be something special. And he is."

She looks at me again, that see-through-you look.

I nod. She's right. He is.

"Honey, he'll always be your daddy . . ."

She's right. He will.

"Your turn," she says, calling me back to the game.

Good grief, see what she did while I wasn't looking.

"Grandmama!" Bartle shouts, sweeping into the kitchen looking like the proverbial bag lady.

"What are you wearing?" I have to ask. I'm used to Bartle being in drag. But this is strange even for him.

"Cleaning the costume storage," he says. "Stuff Brad was getting rid of . . ." His mouth is full of chicken. I mean, literally, there's a drumstick hanging out of his huge mouth. Gross.

"So you decided it was your responsibility to wear it home? All of it? All at the same time?"

"Welcome back, Jess," he says, polishing off the drumstick and reaching for his second cinnamon roll. Good thing Grandmama made a triple batch.

For her, food is the cure-all for whatever ails us.

She may be right.

"You see why I don't worry too much about Mark," she says to me, nodding her head toward Bartle. "This one takes up all my worry space."

"No, I don't," Bartle laughs.

"Close your mouth and chew!" I can't help myself. Trying to teach Bartle manners gives my life purpose.

Grandmama pulls herself to her feet. "I need to be getting home."

I glance at the clock over the stove. "Aren't you going to stay for dinner?"

"Yeah," Bartle says. "Una will be home in a few minutes."

That seems to get Grandmama moving even faster. She ducks out the back door right as Mom comes breezing through the front. I wonder what that's about.

Mom comes straight to the kitchen and she's alone, so Loretta must have claimed Bits for the evening. I'm kind of sorry she's not here. I mean, I've been feeling bad about my mom ignoring me, but now that I see her, I'd just as soon be left alone.

getting her groove back

"Tomorrow I need you to pull out all the improv and theater game supplies and make sure everything's there and in good shape," Mom says, pouring herself the last cup of coffee.

Well, hello to you, too. Gee, it's good to see that you've finally come out of your room. How are you? I've been so concerned . . .

Mom's eyeing the twelve-cup coffeemaker like she could convince it to make itself another pot of coffee.

"Jessie?" Mom asks, a question mark hanging at the end of my name.

"Yeah?" I look over my shoulder at her, the pot full of water threatening to dump all over the counter.

"Tomorrow . . ." she says.

I turn back around and pour the water into the coffeemaker. Turn it on. Stand there watching it begin its brew cycle, something I would rather do than talk to my mother at this point.

Bartle is sitting at the table eating yet another cinnamon roll and removing (while in a seated position) one article of clothing after another.

"The improv supplies . . ." Mom says.

"What?" I say, mesmerized by Bartle's strip act. "I thought you were talking to Bartle."

At least I hoped she was.

"I'm helping Brad with the costumes," Bartle says.

Mom stiffens when she hears Brad's name. Makes me wonder how she's behaving when they're together.

A picture of this summer's theater program for younger kids suddenly flashes through my head. The big circus tent in the middle of the JUMBLE parking lot. Screaming hordes of six- to twelve-year-old kids descending on the theater. Day after day of theater games and improvs. All of us working together nearly twenty-four hours a day.

It's crazy, wild, chaotic, exhausting. And one of my favorite things on the face of the earth.

"I need your help starting tomorrow," Mom says, this time actually making eye contact.

I stare right back at her and keep staring until she drops her eyes first.

I am pretty sure that's never happened before.

"I'll help you get everything set up," I hear myself saying. "But I'm not working Summer Street this year."

Bartle chokes on whatever he's currently chewing.

Mom's head snaps up and she looks at me, I mean really looks at me like she's seeing me, for the first time in two weeks.

"What do you mean? Of course you're working Summer Street . . ."

"No," I say.

We're staring at each other. Wow. Two staring contests in one day. We're making history here.

Bartle has quit choking. He's staring, too.

"But we need you. You've been doing this for years and know it like the back of your hand . . ."

This is the moment when I can say, "You're right. I don't know what I was thinking. Of course I'll do Summer Street."

Because, you know, I LOVE IT. And at least then, in this one thing, everything will be the same as always.

"Mom, come on," I say. "Half the teenagers at the theater would kill to be a Summer Street intern. Not only that, their parents will pay you so they can do it. You don't need me."

My mouth has a mind of its own.

Mom looks at me as if she's weighing the idea. Carefully weighing it.

Since Mom and I were both shut up in our separate bedrooms for the last ten days, I really have no idea how she went from sobbing shut-in who has no time or energy for her only daughter to having her "Okay, kids, it's time to get ready for the summer" hat on. But I can see she does.

I'm wondering why somewhere between incapacitated and this she couldn't have come across the hall to my bedroom to check on how I was doing.

My mouth, however, chooses not to say that out loud, either. Not with Bartle sitting there gaping at us.

"Susie, for one," my mouth says. Yeah, my mouth and my head have definitely lost connection with one another. And let's not even get started on what my heart is doing. "That's who I would get. She's been in Summer Street since she was six. And she's almost as good as Bits at acting. Better at dancing, really."

Bartle raises one eyebrow at this. "I'm going to tell Bits you said that . . ."

I ignore him.

"That's true," Mom says, looking interested now.

"And, Mom, Susie's parents are loaded. No tuition problems there. Maybe you guys should create a new intern position and charge an arm and a leg . . ."

What they've been doing is taking away the summer tuition for a handful of kids who've exceeded the age limit but want to continue being part of the program. They help out and get to take the classes for free. Like Bits, except with her it's because she's family.

Mom's nodding. I can tell she's interested in this idea. The theater always needs money. And the truth is, it's a good idea. I don't know why I'm positing it at the moment, but it's a very good idea.

"Well, what are you going to do if you don't help with Summer Street?"

DANGED IF I KNOW is the real answer to my mom's question. What I actually say is "I just graduated from high school. How about I take a vacation?"

Wrong answer. We don't do vacations in this family.

Mom wrinkles up her brow, looking as though she's straining to remember what interests me. I don't help her out. Summer Street, I'm wailing inside. I love Summer Street! I love the kids and the games and the wild success of the productions.

"You could take a class at the U," she says.

"I don't want to take a class at the U," I snap. Was she even listening to my valedictorian speech?

Now I'm studiously avoiding her eyes until my head and mouth have had a chance to get completely in sync. "I thought maybe I would help out here by . . . cleaning and organizing the—swallow, gulp, take a deep breath—basement."

"The BASEMENT?" Bartle mouths, looking from Mom to me, and back again.

I sneak a glance Mom's way. Okay, it's a dumb idea. But that basement has needed some serious attention for nearly as long as we've been in the house, which is about seven years now.

Short version: It's gross! And at the moment I can't think of anything else I could do. Pathetic.

"I'll need to talk with . . . your dad . . . and make sure he's okay with it . . ."

"The house is yours," I blurt out without stopping to think.

Bartle, who has just grabbed another cinnamon roll, gasps.

"Well, it is," I say to him. "You know Mom bought this house with her inheritance."

"It's a community property state," Mom says, with a sigh. "I may have used my money for the house, but it belongs to both of us."

She's right, of course. If I'd been thinking clearly I'd have remembered that.

"Anyway," she says, putting her coffee cup in the dishwasher and starting for the back stairs, "I meant I needed to talk to Mark about you not participating in Summer Street, not whether or not you should . . . clean the basement."

After she's gone upstairs, I sit down across from Bartle.

"You're crazy!" he says, looking up from the clothing items he's gone back to folding and stacking in a neat (for Bartle) pile on the table.

"I'm crazy?" I reach over and pick up the tiny fur stole he had been wearing around his neck. I've seen these before. The head is still on the fur piece and it's the mouth that has the catch in it that hooks the two ends together. An animal activist nightmare. "This is a period piece. Doesn't Brad need this for the costume shop?"

"No, he says he'd rather fake it. Anything to avoid being doused in red paint."

He's got a point.

"Aren't you the one who said you were going to devote the next two years of your life to finding your place in the theater?" Bartle has hit the nail on the head and is looking smug about it.

"Get those ratty costumes out of here," I say, ignoring him. "I'm going to fix dinner for everyone."

He stacks them up on the bottom step where our oldest cat, Judge, is sitting peering around the door frame. Judge promptly climbs onto the pile of clothes, does that circling thing cats do, and then settles in.

"Ahhh," I say, with a grin. "New cat bed. Good going, Judge."

"Finding your place in the theater . . ." Bartle says. "I'm not letting you off the hook. Come on, diva, cough it up . . ."

"Oh, I thought you were talking to the cat."

Bartle laughs and waves the floral scarf he's just pulled from the pile of clothes.

"I meant what I said about the theater. I'm just . . . not going to start until the fall . . ."

"You love Summer Street," Bartle says, wrapping the scarf around his head.

Now there's a look.

"Yes." I might as well admit it. "Yes, I do."

Bartle goes to the fridge and starts unloading Grandmama's containers of food. I can't believe we're making supper. We've been eating nonstop for hours.

"If Una and Mark can work together," Bartle says, staring me down. "And if Brad is willing to hang in there . . . why can't you?"

"It's not about that," I say, dumping food into pans and adjusting the burners. I don't convince even myself.

I mean, is it going to be weird (probably) or hard (yes) to see my dad and Brad together? Until I caught them kissing, I'd always liked Brad a lot. At the moment, I wish he'd hop a plane for the East Coast or go back to Kansas where he grew up.

Mom is the real unknown quantity in this scenario. Today she's acting like she's got her groove back (thank you, Terry McMillan . . . I enjoyed your books better than the movies made of them). But how long is that going to last? And is she ever going to see what this is doing to me?

I don't say any of this to Bartle. I mean, he's looking at me like he understands. But does he? Honestly, he seems not to mind any of this at all.

take it to the streets

"When you are biracial you embody an innate understanding of compromise . . ." This is the now *in*famous quote of my—for the most part—sane mother. This notion is nearly as peculiar (and offensive) as my lunatic aunt warning Mom when she was pregnant with me that I would come out striped like a zebra.

Though I don't buy either notion (not for an instant) let me say this: I do hold the Family Record for "Most Likely to Compromise." And my favorite cats are the striped ones.

I'm just saying.

For the next week and a half, I compromise and help my parents get ready for Summer Street Theater. The work is no big deal. I could do it in my sleep.

And it's not like I'm in a huge hurry to clean the basement.

In addition to the circus tent, we have gazebos set up all over the big yard. One for each age group. My dad will work with the oldest kids (eleven- to twelve-year-olds). There are seven in the group this year. My mom has the eight- to ten-year-olds and Susie will be helping her. That's the largest group—twelve kids. And for the first time, Bits is handling the youngest group by herself. It's small—only five kids. For an only child, she's GREAT with the six- and seven-year-olds. Maybe because she's like a little kid herself.

Lee has managed—all the way from Baraboo, Wisconsin—to get Loretta to let Bits move in with us for the duration of the summer program. She's so excited about this she can't stop dancing around like a twelve-year-old. Her pure, unadulterated glee is catching.

"FIVE WEEKS!" she shrieks. "five weeks I don't have to go to CLP meetings!"

"Hallelujah!" Bartle shouts, sounding as though he's at a tent revival.

Bits giggles. "five weeks I don't have to sit at dinner waiting ten minutes for my mom to stop praying so we can eat before the food gets cold!"

"Hallelujah!" I shout, caught up in their enthusiasm.

"And it's always cold!" Bits shouts back.

Bartle throws in an, "Amen!"

Bits hauls all her stuff over a couple days later and then it's already the Fourth of July. My dad's singing at Lake Harriet in Minneapolis, so we all pile into the JUMBLE van and go over there for a picnic. He's fantastic as always. Mom and Brad spend all evening acting like they're a couple. This is so weird Bits and I decide to sit on the other side of the band shell from them. When we get home, we celebrate with sparklers. Dad and Brad go downtown to the bars and Mom celebrates with a double shot of scotch.

The Benedicts come back at the end of the first week of July a few days before Summer Street starts. David's got a gorgeous suntan. It makes him look, I don't know, kind of hot.

"Since you're not doing Summer Street," Lydia says, handing me a piece of paper, "I thought you might be interested in this."

ASPIRING PLAYWRIGHTS:
Creative Journaling Intensive. Two weekends:
Saturday and Sunday—July 14–15 and Sunday, July 22, 2012.
JUMBLE Players Library.
What to do before, during, and after you write the play.
Come prepared to write.

"It's at the theater?"

Lydia nods. "We're going to start having groups from the community rent space here. It's a way of doing outreach that benefits us and them."

"Who's teaching it?"

"A guy I know at the university."

"Is it something I could take? I mean, is it open to everyone?"

"I don't see why not," Lydia says. "I think you'd like James. He's a really nice guy, and I hear he's a good teacher."

"Are you an aspiring playwright?" David asks as soon as Lydia's gone on to the office.

"I don't know," I say, folding the paper in half and then

folding it over again so it will fit in the pocket of my denim work shirt.

"Well, you should do it," Bits says. "I mean, you're a really good writer."

"How do you know I'm a good writer?"

"School papers . . . All A's and A pluses . . . your senior thesis . . ."

"I got A's on everything . . ."

"Yeah, rub it in," Bits says, but with a grin.

"It's only three sessions," David interrupts. "Give it a try."

"I'll think about it."

Bits and David are beaming and going all parental on me.

I've managed all week to get home in time to grab the mail, sort through it, and weed out Loretta's cards. Except for missing one day, she has not let up with her barrage of SAVE YOUR-SELF postcards. I know I should let it go and let Mom deal with it. Loretta's her sister. But at the moment, this seems an easier solution.

I'd throw the cards out, but I keep thinking they will come in handy some day. Blackmail?

Yeah, like that's going to work.

If I'm honest with myself, I really want to do Summer Street. But something's holding me back. I want to do it only if it can be like it's always been. But Mom's all wrapped up in training Susie and Bits, and my dad's all wrapped up in Brad. And neither of them is insisting I do it.

Let me be clear—I didn't say no so that they'd insist I do it. But I can't help wishing one of them would.

So I'm squirreling away Loretta's crazy-ass postcards, waiting for an opportunity to use them against my mother.

I'd like to talk with my mom about it. I would talk with her about all of this if she . . . well, you know . . . if this were a month ago.

double-whammy day

It is Saturday morning, and once again I am the first one up because, well, because it's Saturday and in this house everyone stays
up late on Friday nights. Last night we had Edward and Lydia
and David over for dinner. They were exhausted from their vacation and hadn't gone grocery shopping yet. Even David couldn't
get it together to shop and cook.

Mom didn't invite my dad and Brad, for which I was grateful,
I guess, though it was weird not having them here.

Bartle and Tim Chang were here. Bits, of course, since she's
living with us right now.

It was kind of a fun night. The first gathering Mom's had since
my dad moved out. She drank a little too much. And it seemed
as though Edward was flirting with her. Maybe that was my
imagination.

Anyway, I'm up at my usual time and in the kitchen making
coffee in the hopes that the smell will wake Bits up because I

really don't feel like being alone when I hear the doorbell do its boogie-woogie thing. I'm mid-measurement with the coffee, so I finish what I'm doing and by the time I get to the entry hall, Mom's at the open door.

I'm assuming she forgot that she's wearing her pajamas and that she hasn't brushed her hair yet because she hasn't had her coffee yet and she pretty much doesn't do ANYTHING until she's had her coffee.

Maybe she didn't hear the doorbell and opened the door to get the newspaper. It's anyone's guess.

Is it the Jehovah's Witnesses? Nope, no eerily neat clothing and regulation book bags. Is it the Mormons? Nope, no white shirts and ties. One look at the long gauzy dress circa 1978 that the woman is wearing and it's clear that it's those pesky Church of the Living Prophesy folks again. You'd think with their incessant postcard and voice-mail campaigns they could leave off with the door-to-door stuff.

I'm standing right behind Mom trying to catch her attention so that I can encourage a rapid refusal and the closing of the door. This is not working any better today than it ever does.

In fact, Mom freezes when she sees who it is.

Talk, talk, talk . . . less than six months left until the end of the world . . . talk, talk, talk . . . enlightenment vs impending destruction . . . talk, talk, talk . . . not only Biblical but Mayan and Hopi and Nostradamus and . . . talk, talk, talk . . . Armageddon . . .

Yup, Mom is frozen stiff in the middle of the doorway (a

benefit because they can't very well shove her aside to come in, and she's so paralyzed at least she doesn't invite them in).

For some reason two of our cats—Maggie and Brick—are fascinated by visiting religious fanatics. We have no idea why. They make do with the Witnesses, they snarl at the Mormons, and they like the CLPs best. Anyway, they come tearing down the stairs, rush to the door, and do that winding thing around and around and around this couple's ankles.

The woman starts sneezing. Snuffling, she says, "The earth will undergo a magnetic field shift, reversing the polarity of the planet . . ."

To give Mom credit, she doesn't get sucked into a discussion. But she does allow the man to unload the entire contents of his leather messenger bag into her arms, while the woman asks if she'd like to schedule a New-Age Bible study.

Whoa! At this point, I pull Mom back into the house and close the door.

We walk through the house to the back door, out to the fence, and dump all the goodies into the garbage can. They called it literature but you know, I can't. I just cannot.

Mom follows me back to the kitchen.

The doorbell SINGS a second time. See, what did I say? They were sent. They were.

We ignore it.

Mom lets me pour her a cup of coffee, and I let her tell me AGAIN the story of having been raised by New Age CLP lunatics.

"My mother and Loretta were always dragging me to meetings.

And the rules kept changing all the time. My sophomore year all of a sudden I couldn't date worldly boys anymore."

"What do you mean, *worldly*? No, wait a minute—what do you mean ANYMORE? When did you start dating?"

She must catch my tone, because she stops for a second before she answers. "Kind of early. When I was a freshman. Thirteen."

I lower my forehead to the table and bang it a few times. Most of the time it doesn't bother me that I'm what Grandmama calls a "late bloomer" but come on.

"Way early," she says. "No one should be dating that early."

When I don't raise my head she goes right on with her CLP story.

"So then my junior year I had to go with them warning people about all the 2012 prophesies."

"I can't believe you actually did that!" I always say the same thing at this point in the story because I truly can't believe it. Even knowing it in advance, hearing her say it makes my head pop up off the table. I cannot picture my mother as a practicing CLP.

No, no I can't.

But I sure can picture her rebelling and going to the University of Minnesota (by this time the CLPs were warning their youth against attending a university or getting too focused on a worldly career). What other kind of career can you have?

And I can picture Mom rebelling even further and marrying my father. Because even in 1995 it was a fairly big act of rebellion for a small town Northern Minnesota white girl to marry a black guy from South Minneapolis.

The only rebelling Loretta ever did as far as I can figure out is when she went wild for one summer and got pregnant and ended up marrying a guy who's a drummer in a band. That would be Lee. I wasn't even born yet, but Mom says Loretta was almost human until Bits turned three. (I have to trust Mom on this one.) Anyway, Mom says when their mother died, Loretta went all crazy back to the CLPs.

Thank goodness Mom never even thought about going back.

Now she says, "What if they're right and the world really IS going to end this year?"

"Mom! You don't believe that, do you?"

"What?" Mom's face is doing that thing again. A kind of haze slides over it. She looks all blurry to me, like one of those old movies where they put that fuzzy filter over the female lead so she looks prettier. Only this haze just makes Mom look . . . more distant.

"You don't believe the world is going to end?"

Mom's eyes fill all up with tears. "It already did, didn't it?"

And with a sob, she runs up the back stairs to her room.

Yeah, I guess it did.

an empty house

When everyone goes off to the theater on the first morning of Summer Street I am seriously questioning my sanity at choosing to NOT participate. Bartle is totally involved in the program this year. David is helping out way more than he usually does. And I won't even get to see Bits teaching for the first time.

Bits and I have always been an odd combination of competitive cousins and best friends. Which is not the same thing as competitive best friends. At the Lab School, I left her in the dust with my high IQ and perfect grades. She's long since surpassed me in everything theater-based.

I'm proud of her. And I also like to keep tabs on her, if you know what I mean.

Except for the cats and me, the house is EMPTY. Even Auntie Ellie is still away and she won't be back until the beginning of August.

And the thing is, the start-up of the summer program is a lot of fun. The kids are the most comical combination of scared and excited. Some of them have done it before and they think they are soooooo cool. And then, after the opening ceremony and rules and all that, they spend the whole day playing games, some of them in their own groups, and some as one big group. By the end of the day they are exhausted, but they're also hooked.

I almost sneak down there so I can see Bits with the kids. And, okay, see how my parents are working together. But then I stop myself.

What I need is some time to get used to all this. Dad and Brad acting like newlyweds. Mom going all Jekyll and Hyde on me. Not a good literary comparison, but I can't come up with a better one at the moment.

I wander out to the backyard, which is not much more than a small brick patio with a little bit of grass, two small flower beds, and the vegetable garden Mom shares with Lydia and Edward. It's beautiful out here, a sunny summer morning, cooler than last week after the weekend storm. I can hear the kids from Summer Street chanting some rhyme, and that makes me want to run down to the theater.

Safely back in the kitchen, I take a deep breath and walk down the stairs to the basement. Gross, gross, gross.

I decide to go for a walk first.

This time I head the opposite direction from where my dad and I went. It doesn't help. I can't stop thinking about my parents, my dad's transformation. My mom's odd behavior. It's hard not to be mad at her. She seems like a stranger right now. She still hasn't said one word to me about my dad moving out. Or about him being gay. What parent wouldn't feel like it was necessary to address these issues with their only child?

I mean, really. It's almost like she's the kid and I'm the parent.

Even my walking feels aimless, so I stop in Caribou Coffee and pick up a latte. Drinking it slows me down, and I window shop for a while until I get to the corner where there's a little thrift store. I'm throwing my cup away when I turn around and nearly knock into an old guy who's lugging something into the store. I am such a klutz!

"Jessie!" he says, as he regains his balance. "Jessie, is that really you?"

It's our old friend, Bruce. He and his partner, Arthur, used to have season subscriptions to the theater, but the last few years Arthur's been too frail to attend many shows, so they stopped coming. Before that, I used to feed their cats whenever they went on trips.

It still seems kind of strange calling him by his first name; he's so old. He's older than Grandmama, in his mid-eighties at least. And he's got to be ten years younger than Arthur. I started out calling him Mr. Olson and Arthur, Mr. Rasmussen. But then they had a commitment ceremony and we were all invited, and Bruce took Arthur's last name. It surprised me. I had no idea people did that in same-sex ceremonies. But I read up on it and it's more common than you'd think. So after that it seemed stupid to call them both Mr. Rasmussen. Anyway, they are soooo fine with me calling them Arthur and Bruce.

"How are you?" I ask, helping him sit down on the bench that's outside the store. "How's Arthur?"

He tears up, and I get scared that Arthur died and no one told us. I mean, it could happen. He's really old.

I can see Bruce swallowing hard and gathering himself. He's such a sweet guy. My heart's racing.

"Honey, Arthur is really sick."

"Oh, no, I'm so sorry . . ."

"We're about to head down to Rochester where he's going to be getting some treatments at the Mayo Clinic. He's too frail to go back and forth, so we're staying down there. He'll be in and out of the hospital."

"When are you going?"

"Day after tomorrow . . ." He sighs, looking down at the parcel he's holding. "I've been bringing some things over here to sell on commission. I'd better get moving."

I take the parcel from him and help him up off the bench.

"I still need to find someone to come in and feed the cats, spend a little time with them. I've been asking around, but no one's been able to do it. Probably because we're going to be gone for at least a month."

"I'll do it," I say. "I will. I'm happy to do it."

"Aren't you too busy with Summer Street?" Bruce asks, but looks hopeful. "I know how hard you work every summer!"

"No," I say. "No, I'm not doing Summer Street this year."

I follow him over to his house to get a key and while I'm getting reacquainted with the cats I tell him about Dad and Brad. I expect him to be shocked or surprised, but he isn't.

"So Mark finally came out," he says. "I wondered how long it would take him."

"You knew, too!" I blurt out as both Ariel and Morgan try to climb into my lap at the same time.

"Honey, there are some things you can't hide from another gay man. Even if he's old like me."

I nod. Ariel is up around my neck, and Morgan's butting my chin with the top of his head.

"How's Una holding up?" Bruce asks. "I'll try to give her a call while we're down in Rochester."

"She's . . . she's . . . I don't know how she's doing," I finally say. "Okay, I guess."

Bruce nods. "Arthur will want to see you."

"I want to see him, too," I say.

When I put the cats down, I see how stiff they walk. They're getting old, too, but they're doing a lot better than Arthur.

Arthur cries when he sees me. The cats cry when I leave.

Bruce cries as he gives me instructions and pays me in advance.

Walking home, all I can think about is Arthur and Bruce. I want them to have years and years left together.

And I realize nothing we're going through seems as dire and desperate.

I never make it back down to the basement. I figure getting a cat-sitting job lined up is enough for one day. In the late afternoon, I go upstairs and take a long, hot shower. I even get my head wet (you'd have to see my hair to appreciate the magnitude of the decision). And I'm struggling to get some of the ten thousand snarls out when David calls.

"Pizza night," he says.

Tradition. The first night of Summer Street is always pizza night.

"Thank god," I say back, my big-toothed comb stuck in what appears to be a rat's nest on the left side of my head. I tug. It only gets more stuck.

Where's my dad with a jar of grease when I need him?

"I'm going to try grilling pizzas," he adds.

"You are? That's cool."

"Yeah, so it's going to be over here. The kids are all gone—you can come over now if you want to."

"I'll be there as soon as I get this comb out of my hair."

My parents feel bad that they haven't kept in touch with Arthur and Bruce and are glad that I'm going to help them out. I am, too. I go over for a little while every day to let the cats out in the backyard and feed them and give them some attention. They're used to tons of attention.

I love the cats, but the place gives me the willies. I'd forgotten how full of junk that house is. Bruce always says, "Oh, that Arthur! He is such a packrat!"

Packrat? Nah. He's a hoarder. By any standards.

Since I can't do anything about their house, I go home more than usually motivated to tackle the basement. It's daunting, but I am nothing if not organized. So by the end of a couple days of cleaning, OUR cats have a very comfortable and, I might add, immaculate toilet area. And the basement half bath (i.e., toilet and sink in a closet) is so neat, not to mention sanitary, it squeaks.

The rest of the basement? Horrible.

By the end of the second week I've made huge progress. I seriously do not want our house to EVER be like Bruce and Arthur's. That house could be featured on that TV show, *Hoarding: Buried Alive*. Okay, I admit it. I've become obsessed with cleaning the basement.

And of course it's not just cleaning; I'm opening every single box and going through it. Why? Because there's no one home to stop me or interrupt me or tell me countless stories about their contents.

I spend days transferring all the family memorabilia from cardboard boxes to plastic.

There are boxes and boxes of loose photos that need to be organized. I waste an entire afternoon caught up in all the memories and don't manage to organize any of them. So many fun times, mostly at the theater. There are a whole bunch of photos of me in dance class when I was really little. I don't remember that at all.

Bits runs over for a few minutes on her lunch break, usually to bring me one of David's incredible sandwiches. She can't believe I would choose to clean a basement when I could be working at Summer Street.

It does not escape me that this cleaning and organizing project is a rather transparent attempt to regain some control over . . . well, over . . . US.

Not that it works.

he's not my adorable professor

My intention: leave the house early and get to the theater library so I can pick the seat I want before anyone else gets there. In a typical Lab School classroom I sit in the front row so I don't have to watch everyone else looking at me.

What actually happens: Bartle asks where I'm going and when I tell him, he decides he wants to take the workshop, too. But he's not dressed yet. So he runs upstairs to make himself gorgeous and asks me to ask Mom if he can borrow the money to take the workshop, which basically means will she pay for it.

Mom's in the shower, but fortunately, I have graduation money stashed in my closet, so I grab enough to pay for Bartle, too. Then I realize Bartle doesn't have a notebook or a pen, so I run back to my room to get him one. So, we arrive after everyone else, including the teacher.

Bartle pauses in the door frame, does one of those overly

dramatic sweeping looks at the room and says, "Jessie Jumble! You did not tell me your professor was so adorable!"

MY professor? This is the first session. I've never met the man. Good grief.

It gets worse immediately. The chairs are set up in a circle so there is no front row or back row or rows in between. No. We are all sitting there staring at each other.

I rush to a seat that will get me away from Bartle so I don't have to listen to his running commentary the entire workshop. Of course, there's no place I can sit where I can't SEE him. After I sit I notice I'm between a young woman who is in Emo get-up and a nun wearing a full habit who looks like she's fifty if she's a day. I am surrounded by black (and in a very different way than usual).

Bartle has honed in on a guy I should know. He is a college student who gets small roles sometimes in our shows. He's very handsome in a classical kind of way. Bartle chooses the chair next to him, drops into it, moves the chair closer to the guy, and then dramatically crosses his legs.

After I stop hyperventilating, I am able to really look at the teacher. Dr. James Enomoto—he has written on the portable blackboard in a tight, cramped hand. He has wild, curly black hair that's a bit too long so it almost looks like this very odd, short Afro I had years ago before my mom let me grow my hair out again after the Elmer's glue incident.

"My name is easier to pronounce than it might seem," the professor says. "Japanese names are sounded out the way they look. *En-o-mo-to.* But this is an informal workshop, so please call me James."

I steal a glance at the nun beside me and see she is writing his full name in her notebook.

"It's important, of course, that we get to know one another," he says. "We could do that by simply introducing ourselves. But writing is the focus of this workshop, so instead, we will begin with a writing exercise."

That's cool.

"Okay, write down three things you absolutely DO NOT want us to know about you."

What? That's not cool.

"Don't worry. You won't have to read them out loud or turn them in."

Okay. I can do this.

I DO NOT WANT YOU TO KNOW:

1. That having my dad move out feels like the end of the world.
2. My mom is acting so weird she scares me. And I miss my dad so much . . . so much . . . . it feels like it's killing me.
3. I don't know who I am anymore.

I've finished writing. That's all I can do. I feel a little fluttering in my chest.

Everyone else is still scratching away. I take another peek around. I can't believe there's a nun sitting next to me. An old nun. And she's wearing one of those old fashioned head things—what's it called? A wimple? I didn't think they even wore those anymore—like in the *Sound Of Music*, which my father has forced me to watch exactly fifty-two times. (I am fifteen. That's at least three times a year since I was born. Does that qualify as abuse?)

The woman on the other side of the Emo chick has the most amazing red hair. I've never seen her before. Then the actor guy. Troy! That's his name. And then Bartle. Then the teacher, James Enomoto. Who is kind of cute, though not as adorable as Bartle would have you believe.

Now the professor says, "Okay, write down three things you are willing to share with the group, starting with your name."

1. Jessie Jasper Lewis
2. My parents are Mark Lewis and Una Jasper Lewis of The JUMBLE Players, but everyone calls us the Jumbles.
3. I don't know if I'll be any good at this but I love words and I'm willing to try.

When the professor collects our papers, he says, "Okay, great. Why don't we start with you, Sister Mary Margaret?"

On the way home:

BARTLE: Ooooooh, that man is so adorable! Isn't he adorable?
JESSIE: (*makes a grunting noise*)
BARTLE: He's gay, isn't he? I mean, he's so adorable he's got to be gay!

JESSIE: I don't think he's gay.

BARTLE: Oh, yeah, he's gay. He's got to be gay.

At dinner (*we're at the theater because David is grilling pizzas again*):

BARTLE: You should see the writing teacher! He is so adorable!

BRAD: (*with an arch look at my father*) He iiiiiiissssss?

UNA: (*with an arch look at my father*) He iiiiiiissssss?

MARK: Is he gay?

At breakfast:

BARTLE: Why does the workshop only meet three times?

JESSIE: (*treating it like a riddle or a knock-knock joke, though she knows what's coming*) I don't know, why DOES the workshop meet only three times?

BARTLE: That man is so adorable!

UNA: (*to Jessie*) Do you think he's adorable?

JESSIE: No!

UNA: Then he's probably gay.

At lunch:

BARTLE: I cannot wait until the workshop. That man . . .

JESSIE: His name is James Enomoto . . .

BARTLE: That man . . . James . . . is so adorable . . .

TIM CHANG: Is he gay?

BARTLE/JESSIE: (in unison) YES!!! / NO!!!

TIM CHANG: Can I still sign up for the workshop?

BARTLE/JESSIE: (in unison) NO!!! / YES!!

It goes downhill from there. Geez. Who are these people?

Sunday is the second workshop. Tim Chang has joined Bartle and me, clutching his $20.00 per class workshop fee in his grubby little manicured paws. All the way over to the theater he and Bartle are slavering over the teacher who Bartle has dubbed "Your professor" as if I'd somehow conjured the man from thin air.

The professor—James—is setting up the chairs in the requisite circle. Bartle and Tim Chang rush to help him. For every chair that Bartle puts down, the professor bumps into it, sets it askew, and Tim Chang corrects it. An unholy urge to laugh is bubbling up inside me.

I've been secretly holding out the hope that it's too late for Tim to join the class, but the professor says it's not a class, it's a workshop, so anyone can join at any time. That's why he has the per class fee. Shoot.

The group gathers and, except for Bartle and Tim scrambling to sit on either side of the professor, and me pretending I don't know them, we all sit in the same seats we sat in last time. Which means I'm between Emo Girl, whose name is Bev, and Sister Mary Margaret.

Sitting directly across from me is another new person, a girl. She has beautiful brown hair in one thick braid hanging down past her waist. And the biggest eyes I've ever seen. But she's not really pretty, so much as . . . I don't know . . . striking, I guess.

"Emily is joining us today," Professor Enomoto says, and she smiles. "Emily, do you want to tell us something about yourself?"

"I'm a photographer, and I'm not very good with words," she says, pulling a digital camera out of the pocket of her army-surplus vest and an iPhone out of her other pocket. "I thought a class might help me get better . . . with . . ." She holds up her phone and clicks a picture. "Better with words . . ."

Everyone laughs.

She smiles again, and I smile back. You know in books when they say someone has a contagious smile. She does.

"And also, please welcome Tim," the Professor says, gesturing to Tim, who is sitting right next to him. "Tim, do you want to say something about yourself?"

Tim shakes his head and waves at us.

All right then.

"This is a workshop," Professor Enomoto says. "We're going to do writing exercises. I'll write with you. And we will leave enough time to read what we've written."

Did I gasp out loud? I hope not.

He goes right on, so probably not. "No one will ever have to read if they don't want to."

Whew.

"But, of course, I'm hoping that everyone will read at some point."

Hmm.

"I'll give you prompts, and we'll write for specific periods of time."

"When are we going to start writing plays?" the redhead, whose name is Anne, asks, blurting it out as she raises her hand.

"We're not actually writing plays in this workshop," the professor says. "We're working with writing practice that prepares you to write a play, helps you while you're writing a play, and gets you through the transition to your next play. So, we're going to free write the way you would in a private journal, and then on the last day we will look at how this material can be crafted into scenes."

Everyone's nodding, well, except for Anne. She's sorting through her pile of papers. I'd be willing to bet she's looking for the original flyer so she can argue with him. I also have to mention that Sister Mary Margaret (given that head gear) looks like a duck when she nods. Uncharitable, but true.

"Let's try it and see how it goes," the professor says. "We'll start with five minutes. I'll time and let you know when to wrap up what you're writing. There's only one rule. Start writing as soon as I give you the prompt and don't lift your pen from the page. Keep your hand moving, don't think too much, just write."

"Was that one rule?" Troy asks. Mr. Literal.

"Broken into parts," the professor answers with a quick smile. "The rule is: keep writing."

Anne finally stops pawing through her folder and raises her pen over her open notebook page.

Bartle does a mini drum roll on his leg and says, *"Annnnnnnd* the prompt is . . ."

The professor smiles again, showing off two—yeah, adorable—dimples on each side of his mouth, and says, "Without using your actual name, complete this sentence and then keep writing: My real name is . . ."

We are all frozen, staring at him.

"That's it," he says. "Go!"

And we bend our heads over our notebooks and start to write. It feels like thirty seconds have gone by when the professor calls out, "Time to wrap up . . . finish your sentence . . . stop writing . . ."

"All right," he says. "Great. Now let's try reading it out loud. If you don't want to read, say, 'I pass' . . . okay? No excuses or qualifications either about reading or about not reading. OR about what you've written."

We all nod, although the looks on everyone's faces are priceless. None of us are used to this kind of class structure. I'd venture to say we are all used to explaining and explaining and explaining EVERYTHING.

"Okay," he says, "here are the guidelines for listening and responding to each other. This is raw writing, as I said before."

Again, we all nod. Steal glances at each other. Blush a little.

"So it's not time yet for any kind of criticism. This is about giving and receiving. Yes? It's about voicing and hearing. The only appropriate response is to acknowledge that."

"How?" Good grief. I'm the one who asked that. And I didn't even raise my hand.

"Well," he says, his smile even bigger. "I like applause, don't you?"

There's a huge burst of laughter. We're in a theater after all.

"And it's also okay to *ooooooh* and *ahhhhhhh*. Try it now."

We all let out some big *oooooooohs* and *ahhhhhhhs*. Followed by a round of applause.

"All right," he says. "Who'd like to start?"

Of course Bartle raises his hand.

The professor glances at his notebook, "All right, Mark . . ."

I'm waiting for Bartle to correct him, but he doesn't. What he does is smile. A huge, luminous smile, and starts to read.

My real name is...Kicked Out Too Soon...Shameful Son...Should Have Been A Girl...My real name is...Goes in Search of Himself and Finds a King-dom. My real name is Dressmaker not The Dressmaker's Dummy...the Queen of Patchwork...Goes in Search of Her-self and finds a Whole Rainbow World.

We all applaud at the end. Someone—I don't see who—says, "Ahhhhhh!"

I steal a glance at my cousin. I want to say, "Who are you?"

We don't talk that much at our house about our . . . I don't know . . . identities, I guess. Everybody's too busy working on the roles they're playing. So it surprises me that's what came out in Bartle's first free write. And other people's, too. I want to hear more.

Around the circle we go. Sister Mary Margaret is the first to say, "I pass . . ."

I can see a fleeting moment of disappointment on the professor's face, but he rallies immediately and smiles and says, "That's fine. Another time . . ."

And then it's my turn.

I want to read mine out loud so badly I can taste it. But I can't do it. Instead I open my mouth and out comes, "I pass . . ."

And then I'm blinking back tears and hiding my face in my notebook and Bev's reading what she wrote.

I'm holding my breath as she reads. The words are so different from what you see on the outside.

We all applaud and sigh.

Emily says, "I pass."

For some reason that makes me feel less bad about not reading. And the thing is, I wrote something. I wrote something yesterday and I wrote something today.

We do timed writings for the rest of the workshop. He has us draw pieces of paper out of a hat (very theatrical, Professor! and he manages to do it without dumping the contents of the hat over anyone), and then share the prompt that's on it with the person next to us. And then we write, write, write.

There's no time for us to read these exercises out loud.

I kind of wish there were time.

I've never done this kind of writing before. Only stuff for school.

Now I'm writing about what's happening in our family. The things I wonder about Mom and what's going to happen with Dad and Brad. And I write about me. Why don't I fit in? You know, anywhere? But especially in the theater?

I'm glad Lydia gave me the flyer for this workshop.

I love it when people read. I want to hear what they wrote.

But it's going by so fast.

And I want to be brave enough to read what I wrote out loud.

you're not going to like this

Honestly, why do people preface what they're going to say with a statement like that? I mean, don't you want to run screaming out of the room?

It's Monday, almost dinnertime, and Bartle walks in and says, "You're not going to like this."

I throw the spatula at him. It's greasy and it hits his T-shirt, which happens to be his favorite T-shirt, and he grabs one of my three braids and yanks me nearly off my feet.

Mom waltzes in, takes one look at us acting like five-year-olds, and walks right out the other door.

I retrieve the spatula, wash it off, and go back to browning ground beef for the baked spaghetti I'm making for dinner. Grandmama's recipe, so everyone will be happy.

Bartle sits there, dabbing at the grease stain on his shirt, and looking smug. Knowing something no one else knows does that to a person.

But I can hold out longer than he can. Always.

"Brad's lease is up on his studio apartment," Bartle finally says.

See what I mean?

"You know Brad's been looking for a house. He wants one of those smaller Victorians that you see over on the other side of Grand."

Like I care.

"He wanted to keep renting the studio apartment so he can keep saving money for the house, but the new owner is doing some renovations and won't rent month to month."

Also not news. Why is Bartle telling me this? I DON'T CARE.

I sneak a look at his face. Yeah, still smug. Like there's something in it for me.

"So, the place is way too little anyway, you know, since Mark moved in . . . so there's no way they're going to sign another year lease . . ."

If it's about my dad, of course I'm interested. But I'm draining the ground beef and pretending otherwise.

"So they have to find someplace else to live."

Now I'm being stubborn. With a vengeance.

"Only they can't find a one-bedroom anywhere near the theater," Bartle's staring at me. He hates it when I get all stubborn. Pushes me.

"So they're going to have to move . . . out of this neighborhood for sure."

Do all losses happen like this? In increments, like cutting up a stalk of rhubarb, one chunk at a time?

I don't want my father to move out of the neighborhood. Having him move away from the theater suddenly seems as scary as it felt having him move out of the house. What will he want to do next? Move out of the city? Out of the state? Out of the country?

"There are lots of apartments around here," I say, pulled into the discussion in spite of myself.

"You weren't listening, Bright Girl," Bartle says, smirking at me. "They need cheap rent and no lease so that Brad can buy the first one of those houses that comes available."

"Well, that's kind of crazy, isn't it? I mean, he can't know when one of those is going to open up. This is a high-demand neighborhood. It could be years."

"Exactly," Bartle says, looking even more smug.

What is with him? Does he WANT them to move far away?

"Oh, I see what you mean. They really can't afford to move out of the neighborhood because they don't have a car, and the busses don't run late at night. But if they rent an expensive place here, then Brad won't be able to afford to buy a house . . ."

"I suppose you could think of that as revenge," Bartle says. "I mean, if you're looking to get revenge."

I am studiously avoiding saying the words that are ricocheting around in my cavernous insides. If my dad moves away from the neighborhood, the only time I'll ever see him is when he's working at the theater. And what if he leaves the theater? What if they move so far away they both get other jobs? What if this is the first step of a hundred horrible steps, all of them taking him farther and farther away from . . . ME?

"Hand me the ketchup," I say, holding out my hand.

"You're no fun to talk to anymore," Bartle says, getting up and walking out of the kitchen.

A few days later I've left the basement behind—hopefully for good—and am upstairs reassessing the damage I've done by dragging crates of photos up here for safekeeping.

I'm standing there, trying to figure out if I should tackle cleaning the attic, too, when it hits me.

My dad and Brad can move in up here.

Yeah, I know it's kind of crazy, but . . . well . . . we're kind of crazy. I mean, they're all working together at the theater. From what I can tell and what I hear from Bits and David and Bartle, it's a little tense now and then but nobody seems to be spontaneously combusting.

I walk around the big room for about the fiftieth time. There's a brick chimney that runs up through the room three-quarters of the way toward the back of the house. If you put screens next to that, or hung curtains from the ceiling, that could easily be a bedroom back there. There's even a closet built in under the eaves. And we could get some big wardrobes out at Ikea. Maybe even to use as walls—yes, to flank a door opening. And then hang curtains everywhere else.

The rest of the space is huge. I mean, we'd have to clear out a bunch of the furniture and boxes. But it's way bigger than that dinky studio Brad has been renting. That place is tiny.

This isn't just huge by comparison, it's got . . . What's that expression they use on HGTV all the time? . . . It's got *great bones.*

The more I think about it, the more I like the idea.

Oh, don't get me wrong, I'm not crazy about having Brad living here. But to have my dad back in the house. Even if it's only for a little while, until one of those houses opens up. And who knows what might happen? Maybe he and Brad will break up and then he's, you know, already here, so why not stay?

Okay, the likelihood of that happening is about one in ten thousand. But a girl can dream, can't she?

I'd be willing to bet my mom wants him back in the house with us. But what does my dad want? That's harder to know.

And what's Brad willing to endure in order to get that house he loves so much? He's wanted one of those houses since he took the job at the theater. He talks about it all the time.

This has real possibilities, and I'm starting to get excited.

The place needs to be painted.

I need to pitch this idea to one of them. The question is which one?

worse than mail fraud,
but not a felony

Okay, I've officially lost my mind. This is way worse than hiding Loretta's postcards from my mom. Do I make a rational decision about whether or not it makes the most sense to talk with my dad or to talk with my mom about the attic? No. Do I consult with people I trust whom I know are closemouthed enough and loyal enough to me they won't tell anyone but each other (i.e., Bits and David)? No.

I pitch the idea to all three of them. One at a time. Mom. Dad. Brad.

And then make each of them promise not to tell the other.

And here's the deal. They all promise.

If this seems overly dramatic and complicated, you would be right. If I had any sense I'd go blurt it out at pizza night and let them all duke it out until it's settled. One way or another.

I choose the moment carefully, tell Mom what Bartle told

me. And it turns out, she hasn't heard yet. She flips out, but after a few cups of coffee and my plan, she's got her perk back, and she's just promised not to reveal to Dad or Brad where this fabulous idea came from. And she doesn't even seem to think that's odd.

I'm a horrible person for playing on my mother's heartbreak and desperation.

And apparently I'm not done yet.

A couple days go by but no one says anything, so I'm pretty sure Mom hasn't talked to either Dad or Brad. I wonder what she's waiting for. I know she likes the idea. Maybe she's afraid he'll say no. Or laugh at her or something. No, he wouldn't do that.

But he might say no. There's a pretty good chance he'll say no.

I'm over at the theater looking for David and my dad's in the green room on his laptop. He's waiting for Brad to get done in the costume shop. I already know it's going to be a late night because Bartle said if they didn't get the costumes done for the first gazebo production tonight, they would be in big trouble.

Turns out my dad's looking at apartment rentals online. How's that for a segue?

My dad's a little harder sell than Mom was. Of course he is. He's just gotten his freedom from the intersection of Straightdom and Marriage. Why would he want to move back in? Well, me for one thing. But, you know, it's more complicated than that.

"Think how much money you could sock away. Mom probably wouldn't even charge you rent. Or if she did, it would be way less than what Brad's paying right now."

"I don't know how Brad would feel about living . . . you know . . . with Una," my dad's voice cracks on Mom's name.

I don't even try to deal with this one. "Yeah . . . maybe that's too much to ask."

I wait, let him think about it for a few minutes. The next apartment that pops up on his screen is a studio over by the river. It's even more expensive.

"Well, it wouldn't hurt to talk with him," my dad says with a sigh.

More days go by. Still no one says anything. I've gotten into the habit of stopping over at the theater at lunchtime. I figure as long as I'm eating David's sandwiches, I might as well eat them with everyone else. Plus, I'm trolling for tension.

Medium-to-high today. Nothing out of the ordinary.

Brad, meanwhile, is getting desperate about the apartment search. He's got nearly enough money socked away for a down payment on a house. He loves this neighborhood. He doesn't want to move to either Northeast or South Minneapolis. He refuses to move to one of the suburbs. When Woodbury is mentioned by one of the parents he nearly bites her head off.

He's telling me all this one afternoon while he's doing a fitting on one of the kids. It's the first time I've hung out in the costume shop since graduation day. It's not like I went over there in order to tell him. I didn't. But I was kind of scoping out the situation, wondering if my dad had said anything.

When the fitting's over and the kid runs out, Brad turns to me and says, "I don't know what we're going to do! My lease is up August first!"

"That's not even two weeks from now!" It actually shocks me to realize this.

And then of course I have to tell him my idea about the attic.

"Do you really think Una would be okay with us moving in up there?" he asks me.

"I think . . . I think if I were you I would talk with my dad and see what he says. Probably it would work best if it was my dad who talked to Mom."

Duh.

Long story short, Brad comes home with me so he can look at the attic again. It's safe to do this because both Mom and Dad are with their students and Bartle is running errands for Brad. The attic blows him away. I mean, it's a tad on the rustic side, but it's way bigger than what he's used to.

So now, everything is set up to move forward according to plan.

Only what happens then is what moves this from FRAUDU-LENT to FUNNY.

We are all at the theater for another grilled pizza night (hands down our favorite grill of the summer). Bartle arrives late and out of breath—he's stopped at the house to get me, not realizing I am already here.

"I ran up to the attic to find Jess," he says. "And it hit me—you two should move in up there when your lease runs out!"

Dad and Brad exchange quick, nervous looks.

I gasp and then try to cover it with a cough.

And Mom? Mom chirps right in, "What a great idea! I'm surprised I didn't think of that . . ."

Yeah. Me, too.

I offer to paint the attic. I'm considering it penance for my perfidy. It's a joke! I mean, a scheme isn't truly perfidy is it, when the outcome has nothing to do with all the scheming?

No matter how you look at it, though, painting an attic in the heat and humidity of the last week of July is punishing.

Not to mention that I'm sacrificing what's left of my summer "vacation" to help out my parents. All three of them.

Of course Mom took me up on the offer.

all the men and women
merely players

Friday is hot and muggy, but I spend the entire morning lugging boxes of props from our attic back to the theater, where I store them in the already overcrowded and dingy basement. If he needs me to, I can help Chris, the props guy, go through them in the fall. Add that to my dwindling list of fall theater school options.

Right after lunch it starts to rain. I'm back up in the attic cleaning when Bartle's weather radio blares.

Ever since the tornadoes wiped out a huge chunk of Northeast Minneapolis last summer, Bartle's been hypervigilant about the weather. The roof on his mother's house blew right off.

My dad said, "A judgment on her." (It's his sister so he can say these things.)

Bartle didn't bite. He's been kind of mopey about his mother this year.

Anyway, that was proof positive that tornadoes hit urban areas. Bartle went out and bought a weather radio.

I race down the stairs to his room and shut off that awful noise. SEVERE THUNDERSTORM WATCH. Yup, Ramsey County.

Half an hour later it blares again. I run back down. SEVERE THUNDERSTORM WARNING, it says. For a warning they name the cities in the path of the storm. Yup, St. Paul.

Grill night at the theater is sounding pretty good after all. Well, not the grill part since it's raining, but being over there not alone in this big old house. The sky is getting darker and darker. It's only 5:00 p.m. but it looks like night. Now the rain has stopped and so has the wind. There's a brooding feel that makes me run the last few steps. Of course, the rain has chased them all indoors.

David's set up in the kitchen and is getting ready to bake the pizzas in the double ovens.

Bartle's got Brad's iPhone and is glued to the weather reports on Brad's favorite weather app.

"This is why we should all have iPhones," he says, between reports.

I agree with him that we should all have iPhones, but I don't think this is the reason. I say nothing.

Mom and Bits are huddled in a corner talking shop.

"That circle exercise worked beautifully with your kids," I hear Mom saying.

Bits blushes and looks up long enough to wave at me.

"I've never used it with the youngest group," Mom continues. "What made you decide to try that?"

I duck into the kitchen, not waiting to hear Bits's answer. Yes,

I'm curious. But she will tell me about it later, I'm sure. And I won't have to hear my mother going on and on about how talented she is.

"I hope the power lasts until the pizzas are done," David says, motioning for me to hand him the second one. "I'm staggering them. I found that works better for some reason."

"I hope we don't get blown off the face of St. Paul," I say, handing him the pizza.

He looks at me as though he has no idea what I'm talking about. That's what happens when he's cooking. Nothing else registers, not even an impending tornado.

I stand in the doorway, listening to the babble. Bartle's weather updates. Mom and Bits deconstructing the teaching week.

"Mark, you have to commit," Brad says. My head snaps around. Commit to what?

"If you're going to have a costume worthy of *Tartuffe*, you're going to have to make a decision now!"

Oh, costume commitment. Well then.

DAD: It's not my job to decide on costumes.

BRAD: Since when?

DAD: I'm not directing.

BARTLE: (*butting in as usual*) But you're playing Tartuffe.

BRAD: (*sighs, holds up two drawings*) The blue velvet . . . or the floral upholstery fabric . . ."

DAD: You choose . . .

MOM: (*head snapping up*) You're letting BRAD choose your costume?

DAD: (*pronunciation extremely crisp*) Yes. Yes, I am.

BRAD: (*voice smooth as silk*) Una, which one do you like better for this role?

DAVID: (*shouts from the kitchen*) Two gigantic pizzas. One veggie, one meat. Who wants what?

DAD & BRAD (*in unison*) Meat. (*They giggle.*)

MOM: The floral upholstery.

And since we're all talking about pizza by now we crack up laughing at her.

"Monitor the weather," Bartle says, handing me the iPhone.

I lean around the door frame and watch him as he gathers up the plates and silverware. I'd help, but he's clearly got it under control. And I wouldn't want to mess up his whole server act.

"What are you eating?" David asks.

"Meat," I say, although I'm actually hungry for veggie. If Mom had said meat, I'd be saying veggie. I'm as bad as Bits who is eating veggie just because that's what Mom's having. We're both pathetic.

"The weather," Bartle says, sweeping past me, just as a huge crash of thunder shakes the entire building.

"Ohhhhh, god," he whimpers. "A judgment . . ."

"You DID NOT say that!"

Another crash follows faster than seems normal. And then a gigantic flash of lightning followed by yet another thundery boom.

When I turn around I see that my dad and mom are in a big discussion about costumes, with Brad struggling to keep up. Bits shrugs her shoulders at me and runs into the kitchen to help David.

I am not jealous of Bits. I refuse to be. She's my favorite cousin (yes, even more favorite than Bartle). She loves my mom and my mom loves her. Thank God she's got my mom, since her mother is the biggest nut case on the face of the earth. It's not only selfish to be jealous of her, it's just plain childish, like my five-year-old name for it. I am not jellies. I am not jellies. I am not jellies.

"Weather . . ." Bartle says on another pass. I head over to the stairs and take a seat where I can watch everyone but they have to look hard into the shadows to see me. It goes without saying this is my favorite place to be.

Bits and Bartle are doing a wildly funny server routine, carrying everything up on their shoulders and sashaying around each other.

Am I hearing sirens? I check the weather. Yup, now we've got a TORNADO WARNING. I wonder if we should be in the basement?

I think about all the boxes I've lugged over. All seven of us down there with the spiders and mice. (We really need to loan one of our cats to the theater for a few weeks.)

"Pizza's ready!" David yells, and then the power goes out.

I can hear him pulling the pans out of the big double oven. It's only 6:00 p.m. but now it's dark as midnight.

"What the hell?!" My dad shouts.

"Did the electricity go out?" Bartle squeals.

"Well, yeah!" I bonk him on the arm with his phone. "That's what this sudden darkness means. Duh."

I feel my way to the cupboard and pull out the battery-operated lanterns we use out on the patio at night.

Silence falls as we all sit around eating our pizza, enveloped in the sounds of the storm. Big bursts of wind send rain splattering against the outside walls and windows. More huge crashes of thunder and flashes of lightning.

Is it an old wives' tale that a tornado won't hit in the middle of a heavy thunder storm? I don't care if it's a myth, as long as believing it holds back the gale.

I'm sitting back on the stairs where for some reason I feel safer, eating my third piece of pizza, when Lydia comes wandering down from the office.

"I didn't know you were here," David says, running to grab the pizza pan from the counter in the kitchen.

"Working on the calendar for next season," she says. "So boring, I fell asleep. Is there any vegetarian left?"

"Male or female?" Bartle asks in his best server manner and everyone except Lydia cracks up.

"That is so sexist," she says. Then, "Where's Edward?"

Mom asks "Where's Edward?" at the exact same time. Hmm.

Turns out he's been in the library trying to find this ONE LINE from *A Streetcar Named Desire*. Wow, that's some focus. The theater could have fallen down around him, but he was going to find that one pivotal line. He grabs a piece of pizza and sits down too close to Mom, pizza in one hand and the script in the other.

Lydia sits down on the other side of him, pulling her chair in as close to his as his is to Mom's.

This is a chaos of overlapping dialogue, hidden meanings, innuendo.

Theater, then. A giggle is forming in the back of my throat and I run upstairs to get some paper out of the office. And a pen. Thank goodness for my photographic memory. I've got to get this down.

The storm has run its course and settled into a steady rain.

The pizza and beer have run out. Bits and David have finished cleaning up.

"Let's go back to the house for coffee and ice cream," Mom says, with an arch glance at Edward when Lydia's not looking.

Evidently my dad catches the look because his eyebrows go up and he whispers to me as he walks past, "'All the world's a stage.'"

"'And all the men and women merely players,'" I answer. It may seem strange to anyone not a part of the JUMBLE, but I've known that line since I was three.

Everyone heads over to our house, but I stay in the stairwell, writing. As soon as I finish, I'll follow them home.

overlapping dialogue

Emily's late. I'm at Caribou Coffee waiting for her so we can pull together our scene for tomorrow. Last session when I saw the professor hold out a hat with slips of paper with our names on them, all I could think was: please don't let me pick that obnoxious white lady, Anne. And I don't want Bartle. And I don't want to work with Tim Chang. Emo Bev? No, no, no. She's kind of scary. And I don't want the Nun! I'd really rather do this alone.

With my eyes closed, I reach in to pull out a name, and when I unfold the paper and read EMILY, it suddenly hits me she's the only one I don't mind working with.

"You're the only one I wanted to work with," she whispers as she pulls her chair over by mine.

Bingo! Smile.

The assignment: each of us (separately) is supposed to record some overheard dialogue.

"Eavesdropping is an essential skill and habit for all creative people—but especially for writers and actors and directors," the professor says.

Wicked.

It sounds like a fun exercise. I eavesdrop all the time. I mean, doesn't everyone? The trouble is, I'm by myself almost all the time these days. Unless you count the cats. Fortunately for me, the storm and grill night intervened at the exact last second. My cast of characters: the usual. Though I do change the names to protect the innocent. Ha!

I managed to get most of it down. My only concern is that Bartle will use the same conversation. (He, by the way, drew Emo Bev for his partner.)

We're to get together before our next session and jam the two pieces of dialogue together (my words) to make a short script. It only has to be two to three pages long, five max. We can describe the characters to fit the people we overheard or create completely new characters. But we have to use the dialogue we recorded (and we've got about a 15 percent allowance for editing and tweaking).

Anyway, I've printed out two copies and brought some tape and a small pair of scissors in case we decide to cut and paste for real. And I've got my laptop.

"I'm sorry I'm late," Emily says, pulling up a chair and plunking her own laptop down on the table. "School is nuts right now."

"School?"

"Summer school," she says. "St. Kate's."

"You aren't a freshman then?" St. Catherine's is down the street from us a couple miles. Far as I know they don't offer summer school courses to incoming freshmen.

"Sophomore." Emily flicks her long braid back over her shoulder. "Supposed to be studying business, but I've switched to an art major."

I take a sip of my latte. "You want anything?"

"Yeah, I'll get it," she starts over to the counter, then doubles back. "You good?"

"I'm good."

"Are you in school?" she asks when she returns with her plain black coffee.

"No, I just graduated . . . from high school." I'm thinking—oh, crap—she missed the intros in the workshop, didn't she? She doesn't know I'm fifteen or any of the rest of it for that matter. I still haven't read out loud in the class.

"So, you're not in college?"

"Not yet. I'm taking a year or two off to see how I fit in the theater . . ."

There's this blank look on her face. Like: What theater? Wow, she really did miss all the intros.

"The JUMBLE Players," I say, searching for a very short version. "My parents run it."

"No shit! Wow, that's amazing . . . I mean, that place is amazing. I'd never been there until I came for the workshop but I walked around the other day and looked at everything and met some staff members. Nice!"

"You don't know who my parents are?"

She shakes her head. "No, I'm not from around here. I'm from Connecticut."

Refreshing. Someone who's never heard of my parents. Or me.

"We'd better get to work," I say, pulling out my pages. "I can e-mail these to you if you want."

"Yeah," she says. "Me, too."

We sit reading for a few minutes.

"Is this for real?" she asks, looking up after about her fifth snorting laugh.

I nod. Yeah. I mean, why wouldn't it be?

"Who are all these people?" she asks.

"My family," I say, feeling my face flush from the neck up. "The Jumbles on grill night."

"The Jumbles? Oh, like the theater? But isn't your name something else . . . Jasper something."

"Yeah, Jasper Lewis," I say, grinning. "We call ourselves the Jumbles for reasons you will discover if you hang out at the theater very long. But here's one hint: in addition to being an acronym for the founders' names, it's an acronym for our six cats."

"Named?"

"Judge. Uncle. Maggie. Brick. Lettuce. Elbows."

This time she snorts so loud, she covers her mouth with her hand and falls into a hiccuping giggle.

"So, who's the tall skinny black guy in drag?"

"That's Bartle . . ."

"Our workshop Bartle?" she asks.

I nod.

"So, this other black guy is . . ."

"My dad. Bartle's his nephew . . ."

"And your dad's not with your mom then?"

"No, he's with Brad." This is the first time I've announced this to a stranger and it makes my throat close up and my stomach do a strange flip-flop to say it out loud like that. "Brad's the JUM-BLE costumer."

"Chad in the script?"

"Uh-huh."

"Cool."

I think I'm going to like this girl.

"My dialogue sucks," she says. "It's boring! I kept listening and listening and nothing hit me. Finally I gave in and went to dinner in the school cafeteria. I heard these two girls talking about guys. Lame. But I wrote it down. Then later, I overheard two guys in an elevator and they were saying practically the same thing about girls, only in guy speak. You know. Can we use it?"

"Of course. It's no more boring than mine."

"You're kidding, right?"

I shake my head. And then we both burst out laughing. She's right of course. My crazy family may drive me nuts most of the time, but they're really never boring.

"Look, from what I can figure all we need to do is to jam the two dialogues together, kind of in a mishmash, and then edit it to make some sense. Right?"

"Yeah," she says. "That's exactly it. It's a crazy assignment, but that's pretty much what he said."

"Then, let's jam!"

We stay there for two more hours, drinking coffee and putting our scripts together. I don't usually like group assignments, but I like working with Emily.

Even just figuring out how to give her lines to my characters is so much fun. We give them to David and Bits, who I've already renamed Tony and Maria, a tongue-in-cheek reference to a very well known musical.

"Are you really only fifteen?" Emily asks as we're finishing up.

"Yeah," I say, "I'll be sixteen in August."

"Amazing," she says. "Truly amazing."

And I think about that all the way home, wondering what she means.

to play or not to play . . .

"There are two ways we can go about this today, and I'm going to let you pick."

Emily and I exchange glances and roll our eyes. At the same instant I catch Sister Mary Margaret rolling her eyes, and you have no idea until you've seen it done how funny that looks on a nun wearing an old-fashioned wimple. Only an act of God (or Emily kicking me) keeps me from howling with laughter. As it is, my sudden cough hopefully covers Emily's snort. Sister M&M seems blissfully unaware of our sophomoric struggle to keep from making fun of her.

The professor has, I am certain, picked up on it. In true teacher fashion, suddenly he is directing his explanation right at us.

"This is the only time during our workshop that everyone has to read," he says, reiterating what we already know. Since half of us haven't read out loud in the previous two sessions, there's palpable anxiety dancing in the room.

"Your two choices are to read your own scripts out loud, or to exchange scripts with one other duo and read each other's scripts out loud."

Much muttering going on. I look over at Emily to see how she's reacting and she's doing the same to me. We both shrug our shoulders. And then burst out laughing.

Bartle leans over and stage whispers, "You're in mine, so I don't think you're going to want to read it out loud!"

I snap back, "Well, you're in mine, so maybe you're the most qualified actor for the role!"

"Maybe we wrote the same scene," he says, not even bothering to whisper.

"Even if you did," the professor cuts in, "it won't be the same. I guarantee it."

Nobody wants to read their own script. And nobody wants to relinquish what they wrote to someone else. No one says this, but that's what the hemming and hawing is all about.

"I came prepared for this contingency," the professor says, reaching into his backpack and pulling out a baseball cap. He quickly jots down words on two index cards and folds them up, dropping them into the cap.

"Mark," he says, with his twinkling-eyed smile showing off those adorable (and yes, they really are adorable) dimples. "Why don't you draw?"

Bartle's long arm reaches out, and he makes a big production of picking.

"THEM!" he reads out loud. "What does the other one say?"

"US," the professor says with another wicked grin.

We count off groups and he makes sure that Bartle and I aren't reading each other's scripts. And then the fun begins. He gives us about fifteen minutes to read quietly together to familiarize ourselves with the text. And then he pulls out the tall stools from the corner of the room. He knocks one of the stools over, of course, shaking his head as he picks it back up again.

He really is remarkably awkward.

"One last draw from the cap," he says, handing this one to Anne, who looks like she's ready to burst with some kind of irritation. She's one of those students who always (ALWAYS) thinks she knows a better way to do what we're doing.

We're drawing for reading order, of course. We end up getting right in the middle.

Emily and I have the script Sister M&M and Tim Chang wrote and it's like the scripts my mom uses in her acting classes. It's very brief and you can interpret it all these different ways. Emily and I decide to read it like we're just meeting. I'm not a good actor and she's not an actor at all, but this is Beginning Acting stuff. Easy.

All the scripts are like that, even the one Bartle worked on with Emo Bev. Although theirs is a funny mash-up of her angry rant and his girl talk. Sister M&M and Tim are reading that one. Tim's as good as Bartle at the girl talk and hearing the nun be angry is too funny for words.

I'm kind of glad the script we wrote is being read last, since we didn't do the blank script thing. Ours is more like a fully fleshed-out scene from a wacky comedy.

Anne and Troy are reading it. Now I'm nervous all of a sudden.

The thing I've noticed about writing is that you almost always reveal more than you mean to reveal about whatever it is you're writing.

Which also means revealing more about yourself.

Anne and Troy, it turns out, are both good actors.

Everyone's laughing and there's this one little moment when it gets real quiet in the scene between Tony and Maria (well you know, David and Bits) and it works exactly the way I pictured it. The audience gets quiet, too. I love it when that happens.

When it's over and everyone's talking and laughing and congratulating everyone else, I see the professor looking at me. High IQ Girl knows that look. He likes what we did. It surprised him.

"Thank you all for a great workshop," the professor says, wrapping up our last session.

It's been good. I wish now it was going on for more sessions. And I like working with Emily.

"I'm thinking of offering a more typical six- or eight-week session here later in the fall. Would any of you be interested in continuing?" There are lots of nods and murmurs of assent. Anne's the only one who's packing up her bag and looking grim.

If she thinks this is unorthodox, she ought to take an acting class at the JUMBLE Players!

"Are you going to take his next workshop?" I ask Emily as we are walking out.

"If it works with my classes, yeah, probably," she says. Then her phone rings and with a little wave she moves off to the side to take the call, so I walk home with Bartle and Tim, who are raving about the professor and our scenes.

I glance back once and she's still talking.

She looks up, and I wave at her.

She smiles and nods.

And then we're home.

This is one of those times I wish we didn't live 572 steps from the theater.

to paint or not to paint . . .

If I don't paint the attic immediately, something bad will happen. I know it's not true, but that's how I feel. Dad and Brad will find a better apartment and snap it up. One of those homes will open up and Brad will buy it. Mom will change her mind. (Oh, yeah, like that's going to happen. I'm not sure why she wants Dad and Brad in the house, but I know she does. Almost as much as I do.)

Every morning I wake up with this sense of urgency. And each morning an hour earlier. Today: 4:00 a.m. Ugh.

Even coffee doesn't make it go away.

Of course, timing couldn't be worse.

I'm still going over to the house to feed the cats. Bruce comes up from Rochester about once a week to stay overnight with them. The cats are like their babies. He says Arthur is responding to the treatment but he's really weak.

I tell him not to worry. I can take care of the cats for as long as they need me to.

It's also the very busiest part of Summer Street. Everyone's working around the clock trying to get the big finale production up. Even Brad—who really wants me to get painting—is too busy to help.

Not only that, but now it's only six days until his lease is up. So when he's not in the costume shop tugging at his thinning hair and raving, he's at his place madly packing to move.

"I had no idea I had this much stuff," he keeps saying.

Bartle's given up his job at the omelet place and is handling a lot of the Summer Street costuming, so he's no use. Bits is busy teaching. Plus she's so bad at any of the tech work I'm not sure I want to put a paintbrush in her hand and turn her loose in the attic.

When I check with my dad about paint buying, his response is, "Talk to Brad. He's the one who's going to choose the colors . . ."

Thank goodness Mom's not within hearing. She seems to be handling things pretty well except for those moments between Dad and Brad when they're acting most like a couple. Those either make her bristle all up like a porcupine or dissolve in a puddle of tears.

Finally, I'm able to corner Brad and drag him to the ACE Hardware on Grand Avenue.

At the last second, Bartle decides to come along. Bartle has a habit of doing that. Making up his mind at the last possible moment. Like taking the writing workshop for instance. Annoying.

I am not sure why, but Bartle's picked today to be in full drag in an old wedding dress he must have confiscated from the shop.

It might be because we got the VOTE NO ON THE MARRIAGE AMENDMENT! sign for our front lawn. I didn't even know about the marriage amendment, but the last time Bruce was home I helped him put out their sign so I asked him about it. And since then, I've been bugging my parents about getting one for us. But they are so apathetic when it comes to politics, even when the cause is something that matters to them, they don't take action. Finally I talked Bartle into going with me to get it. He's a registered voter.

Anyway, it would be like him to costume himself to declare his solidarity. Thanks to me (well, and Bruce) we're the first on our block to put out the bright orange sign. None of us want the marriage amendment to pass. Same sex marriage is already banned—who needs it to be unconstitutional?

Fortunately, the ACE people are used to us. It's the hardware store closest to the theater and we're in here a lot.

Brad and I are looking at colors while Bartle sweeps up and down the aisles, pushing a shopping cart as he gathers paint rollers, drop cloths, and stir sticks. I'd planned to borrow most of that from the theater, but anything to keep him over there and not here. He will question and argue with every decision.

"Grays," Brad says, pulling paint chips.

"You're kidding!"

"You don't like gray?" He looks up from the handful of colors with a worried frown creasing his forehead.

"No, I love gray . . . I only meant it wasn't what I was expecting . . ."

"Light gray, medium, and one wall very dark, almost charcoal."

Nice. I smile. He looks relieved.

"And then . . . THIS shade of brown." He holds the chip up to my face. "Yes, exactly."

"What?" Is he talking about the color of my face? "Where?"

"Stripes on the bedroom accent wall . . ."

"Well, thank goodness you're not putting it in the bathroom . . ."

"The bathroom's already painted, isn't it?" His forehead crinkles back up into those worry lines. It seems to me he's had a lot more worry lines since he and my dad got outed.

"Joke," I say, holding the paint card up to my face. "Bathroom. Brown. Me."

"Café au lait," he says, not rising to the bait. "Perfect."

And here I was expecting him to choose lime green and purple. Apparently even I am not immune to stereotyping.

Bartle sails by riding the back of the shopping cart, his wedding dress flying out behind him. Well, geez. There goes my excuse.

When we're lugging all those paint cans and brushes and drop cloths home, I'm glad Bartle decided to come along.

I don't tell him that, of course,

"Did you really have to wear high heels?"

"You don't expect me to get married in FLATS, do you?" he squeals.

No. Oh, heavens no. What was I thinking?

Although I've painted my bedroom twice, I'm kind of nervous

146

about painting a space of this magnitude, not to mention the angles of the ceiling. And what was Brad saying about stripes?

Brad says he'll do the wall of stripes even if he has to do it in the middle of the night.

And, joy of joys, our set director sends two of his guys over to prep the space. That means I don't have to wipe down all the walls and tape all the edges. I help with the drop cloths, though.

After all the extra furniture has been taken out and the walls prepped, suddenly the place looks enormous. And there's nothing left to do but to begin.

I start painting early in the morning while it's still cool. Enormous mess. I make an enormous mess.

After a few hours of this, plus another where I drink an entire pot of coffee while trying to get paint out of my hair, I watch a YouTube video about paint strokes and using a roller and it goes a little better after that.

The dual primer and paint is supposed to cover in one coat, but the dry wall is way too absorbent. It takes me forever to finish the first coat and when it's dry, it's still streaky.

I'm sitting on the top step, aching in every muscle of my body, still pulling paint out of my hair and about to burst into tears of frustration when David shows up with a sandwich and a can of pop. Dr Pepper. My fav.

I've just taken a bite of chicken, pesto, and arugula on asiago bread when he says, "You've got paint in your hair."

I take another bite.

"How come the walls are all streaky like that?"

Suddenly his delicious sandwich tastes like sawdust. I swallow around the lump in my throat. Tears start to dribble out of my eyes and snake down next to my nose. I take another bite of sandwich, a slug of Dr Pepper. Don't answer.

When he sees the tears he gets up and grabs the paint roller. "Why don't I help you with the second coat?"

That coat goes on a lot faster, especially with two of us painting. Even stopping for an iced coffee and a brownie break around three, we are done with the main room before he has to leave to fix supper. And he very kindly doesn't tell about the streaky mess I made with the first coat of paint.

The next morning Brad brings another gallon of paint, this one for an accent wall in the kitchenette part of the living room. A gorgeous rusty orange.

"You'd think we were going to live here a long time," he says. "The way I'm fussing over colors."

Maybe you will be here a long time, I'm thinking. Maybe you'll stay for the next two years until I'm on my feet and know what I'm doing with my life.

Maybe by then Mom and I will stop doing this weird dance around each other and get back to communicating. I don't know why I can't just go talk to her like I always used to. She's like a house with all the doors and windows closed and the blinds drawn. I just can't.

There's still the bedroom area behind the fireplace chimney to do. And Brad insists on doing the stripes himself. It's a great idea and it makes perfect sense for him to be the one to do it, but he's so busy with Summer Street he doesn't have time.

Then we have four days of weather so hot there's no way I

can keep working up there. Even with four fans going, it's too hot to paint.

I sit in the living room in front of an AC vent and read eight books in a row. Two a day. Straight through.

The walk down to feed the cats is excruciating.

It's so hot, I can't imagine how they could be rehearsing in those circus tents. I know two of the days they had to go inside the theater—something we try not to do during the summer program. It's hard for the kids to make that shift.

But we're good.

The Summer Street production goes up and is a huge success as always. Our little local street rag features a review saying that the Grand Avenue Street Fair wouldn't be the same without it.

Bits coaxes a wildly funny scene out of her tiny tots. This makes all the parents melt. And all the JUMBLE folks talk about what a talented teacher Bits is going to be. I wish now I'd taken the time to observe her at work. She's not a funny person—at least not on purpose. It surprises me that she's able to do that, and with the youngest group.

Acting teacher. That's another thing to add to my list of things I don't think I want to be.

So, tell me again, Ms. Jumble . . . what exactly IS it about the theater that you so love?

Beats me.

The closing afternoon performance and celebratory BBQ are nearly over and we still haven't painted the bedroom or the stripes.

Not only that, but tomorrow is moving day.

I'm all for giving up, but we've got the paint and Brad's got the urge. The man is driven. When he announces that's what he's going to go do, nearly everyone at the BBQ follows him to our house, lugging what's left of the food and beverages.

If I had any sense I'd grab David and Bits and Bartle and run for the hills.

But I've put a lot of myself into this project. I mean, not being there for the final painting of the attic would be like walking out on Act Three.

I'm not the one walking out on anyone.

it's a slumber party

My dad puts music on, we eat some more, we drink a pot of coffee, and then Brad says, "It's time!" And everyone heads upstairs. Chris, the only tech guy who followed us home, takes charge of the Incredible Striped Wall Project. Before he can paint, Brad tapes out the stripes, and, of course Bartle's helping. Lydia has taken to calling Dad and Brad and Bartle the Modified Mod Squad. I had to look it up. It's a TV show from the 1970s. Only in the show, the characters were three crime fighters—a white guy, a black guy, and a white woman.

"Those were the days," Lydia says.

"When you were a toddler!" I can't help myself. It has to be said.

"I know. Bummer." Lydia just said *bummer* like it's current slang. She is so retro it's hilarious.

"We can get *Mod Squad* episodes on Netflix, I think," David says, baiting his mother with a wicked smile.

"Let's get them!" Bits leaps up, chortling. "I want to see what all the fuss is about!"

The three of them settle in on the couch to watch the entire first season of the legendary show. Well, that takes care of them for the night.

Mom wanders through on her way back from the bathroom, stops to see what they're watching, lets out a hoot (of derision—I'm sure it's a hoot of derision) and heads to the kitchen for a snack. Mom never snacks this late at night. My guess is she doesn't want to go back upstairs.

I follow her out to the kitchen.

"Are you all right?" I ask when I find her standing with her head in the refrigerator. It's not that hot tonight. And she's been standing there for a couple minutes.

"Huh?" she says, turning to look at me.

"You okay?" I ask again.

"Why wouldn't I be?" she says, finally closing the refrigerator door and reaching up into the cabinet where she keeps her stash of scotch and brandy.

I sit down at the kitchen table.

"Well, Dad and Brad are moving in upstairs in the morning. The entire theater company is here helping them finish painting their bedroom. Summer Street is over. Life's kinda . . . weird . . . isn't it?"

She examines me the way she'd examine a new script. I can almost feel her highlighting her lines. All over my face. I don't think she likes the part.

She turns and gets ice out of the fridge. Pours scotch over the ice. Takes a long sip. Turns and looks at me again.

Honestly, she's looking at me like she's never seen me before. I'm expecting her to say, "Who are you? What are you doing here?"

And I'm about ready to scream at her, "WHO THE HELL ARE YOU? Did you steal my doting mother and lock her up in a dungeon somewhere?" No, I've spent way too much time in the basement, not to mention the attic of this house. Ain't no doting mother hidden anywhere.

Tears rise up behind my eyes, but I blink them back.

She slowly walks over to the table and sits down opposite me.

"Are *you* all right?" she asks, her voice almost recognizable as my pre-graduation night mom.

I dissolve into tears.

She rises and, through all the water pouring down my face, I see she's coming over to me.

And then Bartle bursts through the door and says, "Where are the bandages? Mark sliced his hand open!"

And Mom puts her drink down and runs past him up the back stairs to the second floor linen closet where we keep all that stuff. Which Bartle knows. I suppose he forgot. Either that or he couldn't stop himself from sharing the drama.

"Sorry," he says when he sees what a mess I am.

"You should be," I manage to say before my throat closes up again.

I go out and sit on the back steps instead. Figure if they have to haul my dad to the hospital someone will find me and tell me. Or not.

I can hear laughter floating down from the open attic windows. Sounds like it was no big deal.

For a second there, I had my mom's full attention.

I wonder what would have happened if Bartle hadn't ruined the moment.

When my tears are all dried up and I think I can talk again, I go back in. Lydia is yowling in the living room, "These shows are TERRIBLE! They're terrible!"

David's laughing, "I told you so, Mom!"

"Nothing's ever the way you remember it," Lydia says, her voice sounding sad.

"Thank goodness," Bits says, and then looks surprised when everyone laughs.

I must have dozed off on the couch with Bits. When I come to, there's the wonderful smell of coffee brewing. And David's in the kitchen making breakfast.

"What time is it?" The house is very quiet, and I can hear birds singing full throttle in the backyard. Early. It's really early.

"Only about six," David says, handing me a cup of coffee. "Shhhh, don't wake her . . ."

I peek back into the living room. Bits is still snoring on the couch.

"Where's your mom?"

"She went home. My dad's still upstairs, I think."

"Are they all asleep up there?" Scary thought. I think I've just attended my first slumber party. More proof that I'm a late bloomer.

"Who knows?" he says with a grin. "The smell of food will either wake them up, or you and I will eat it all."

"Ahhhhh, the love of my life!"

"Me?"

"Breakfast . . ."

He fakes a big sigh of disappointment.

He's been doing that lately. Almost like he's flirting with me. Kind of weird given he's like my brother.

Hoards of stomping feet descending both staircases. Brad, my dad, Bartle, and Tim Chang come down the kitchen stairs. Mom and Edward come down the front. Uh-oh. I wonder if David noticed that. Bits wakes up with a small shriek. I do wonder what goes on at her house. She has nightmares all the time.

"Did you finish painting?" I ask, looking right at Mom and Edward.

Brad answers. "Come see . . ."

I'm too curious to ignore him.

We discover Chris asleep draped over the table in the upstairs kitchenette. He wakes up as we go stomping through the room, groans once, and falls back asleep again.

"Oh, my god, it's gorgeous!" And I mean that. I had no idea—even though I am addicted to HGTV shows—what Brad was aiming for with the stripes. They're beautiful.

"I intended to do horizontal," he says, beaming, "but when I stood in the space last night, it seemed like vertical would be perfect."

"You're right!"

The stripes are different widths, all different shades of gray and silver (shiny, metallic silver) and then an occasional stripe of that pretty creamy brown color he showed me.

"Look at the bedding I got," he says, jumping up and down like a little kid.

"Let's put it on," I say. The sheets are striped, kind of like the wall, but the coverlet is this oddly masculine floral pattern in all the same colors, but with the tiniest touch of red here and there. "I want to see what it looks like."

"Fabulous!" Brad says, then blushes bright pink. "Thanks, Jess . . ."

I nod. I can't help but be excited with him. But I cringe to think of what Mom will say when she sees it. The whole room is way prettier than her bedroom.

I foresee another painting project in my future.

"Breakfast's on the table!" David's shouting from the kitchen.

Everyone's already eating when we get down there.

"Round two," he says, pulling a breakfast casserole out of the oven.

"I don't understand where you learned to do this," I say, holding my plate out for a huge helping.

"Fruit?" Brad says, holding out the bowl of cut melons and berries.

"No thank you, I'm straight," David says before I can answer.

"Yes, thank you," I say, dishing up a spoonful. "It keeps me regular."

"Straight?" David asks, grinning.

"Not necessarily . . ." I answer, leaving him with his mouth open. That'll fix him for a while.

Bits is on the couch in the living room, just finishing her breakfast.

"David's got a new casserole—if you hurry you can beat Bartle to his second helping."

No one could possibly have gotten more than two or three hours of sleep. If we had any sense we'd send everyone home and go take a long nap, but now Brad's fretting about making the move from his apartment into the attic. It has to be done by the end of the day, and then his old place has to be cleaned or he won't get his security deposit back.

Chris has to leave right after breakfast. And Tim Chang has a doctor's appointment at nine, so he says he'll go do that and then come back to help.

"You've got a fitting today, too," Bartle reminds him. "I've got to see that dress on you or I'll never be able to get it done in time."

Tim's been cast in a musical review at a really reputable and way-out-there community theater. It's his first big role and he has to provide his own costume. In drag, of course. Bartle's altering a gown from the JUMBLE costume storage. I can't wait to see it on Tim.

My dad, Brad, Bartle, and Edward head over to the studio apartment to begin loading up Brad's stuff. Thank goodness for the JUMBLE van. I don't know what we'd do without it.

David has to run home for a little while, but he promises to come back later to fix us all a late lunch or an early supper, depending. He's amazing. He's not even eighteen yet. It's stuff like this that makes me wonder about reincarnation. I mean, how does anyone get that talented and focused and he's not even out of high school yet?

I'm smart. But I'm not focused. I'm not that talented, either.

One of these days, Lydia and Edward are going to have to give in and realize this is David's true calling.

After all the guys have left, Mom and Bits and I load up the dishwasher and wash up the pots and pans. Like most fabulous chefs David tends to leave a big mess.

Mom and Bits are back talking about the fall season. Who's likely to get what part. What roles Bits should try out for—two of the fall shows allow student auditions but there aren't any really good female roles. How Mom's feeling about playing the lead in *A Streetcar Named Desire* (not my favorite Tennessee Williams play by the way).

I can't help but feel left out.

And if I say anything, they will start in on me about what I'm going to do at the theater in the fall and since I've crossed off nearly everything I had on my original list, I duck out of the room when they're in a heated discussion about the necessity— Mom for, Bits against—of doing a musical comedy sometime in the future, and run upstairs to check my e-mail.

There's an e-mail from Emily. Just when I thought she'd forgotten all about me.

Home in Connecticut. Parents want me to transfer to a school here. Big fight. I prevailed and will be back to St. Kate's in September. See you then?

Yeah, see you then. I decide to wait until later to answer. It's too crazy here right now. I want time to think about what to say.

And I'm grungy as all get out from the day before. Once everyone comes back there will be no let-up until we've got Brad and Dad moved in and his old place cleaned up and David's got lunch or supper on the table, depending on the timing. So I take a quick shower and right after I'm finished, they bring the first load over.

The rest of the morning is as crazy as I expect it to be. But the good news is that even as tired as we all are, everyone's getting along pretty well. Bartle, for some inexplicable reason, keeps talking fake French. The group is divided into two camps over this: ignore him or throw things at him.

Mom's mostly staying out of the way, which surprises me. I can't tell if it's because she's fighting back tears (it doesn't look like it) or that she simply refuses to do Brad's work, especially when it comes to his relationship with my dad.

We haul boxes upstairs and downstairs and over to the costume shop.

Bits and I unpack Brad's kitchen things and put them away. We line drawers. We clean and fix up the bathroom. We shine mirrors.

In the early afternoon, Dad and Brad run back to the studio apartment to clean.

By mid-afternoon they're back home and Tim Chang has arrived for his fitting.

David and Bits are in the kitchen fixing food.

"Call Lydia, will you, and see if they're still coming over to eat." Mom has evidently regrouped, at least for the moment.

She yells this as she heads up the stairs for about the tenth time with another little tidbit she's sharing with Brad. This time it's a framed photo of my dad when he was little.

Who are these people?

let the jumble rumble

"Le Mouse! Le Mouse!" Bartle screeches as he gallops across the living room. No, he's scampering. It should be illegal for a six feet three gangly gay guy to scamper. But he does it. Up the staircase, Mom's long, pink chiffon negligee floating out behind him. He disappears for a moment behind the curving balustrade and re-appears on the landing, revealing pink chiffon with its hastily stitched-on, hot pink feather boa falling to mid-calf.

"Take that thing off!" Mom yells up the stairs.

"It is le prep-ar-a-tion for le design extra-or-din-aire," Bartle yells back.

See, there he goes again. Le???

"You're going to rip out the armholes and I have to wear it tonight!"

"Tonight?" What does she mean she has to wear it tonight?

"Edward and I are rehearsing that big scene of Blanche's . . ."

A Streetcar Named Desire—the JUMBLE's kick-off show of the 2012–2013 season. Mom's playing Blanche Dubois. She's something of a method actor so the rehearsal costume piece is important to her. But rehearsals haven't started yet. Wait, what are she and Edward up to?

"Staging," she snaps in response, I'm assuming, to the look on my face. "I'm helping him with staging."

Right.

"That's one of the hardest scenes in any Tennessee Williams play," Mom says, sounding a bit huffy.

"It is," my dad says, coming up behind my mom and making her jump.

Where did he come from? Isn't he supposed to be . . . you know . . . UPSTAIRS?

My parents love Tennessee Williams, but I personally think he was a sad, sick old Southerner. I say this now in order to get my mom's mind off my dad.

"Jessie! He's one of the only playwrights that wrote decent roles for women . . ."

"That's because he wished he was one," I snap back.

Her mouth falls open practically to her knees and then she howls. With laughter.

She laughs so hard she has to sit down. My dad's laughing even harder. Bartle is trying to remember who Tennessee Williams is.

"Le mouse!" He shrieks again, leaning down over the banister and pointing. "Jessie, my petite fräulein—le petite mouse!"

I spin around in time to see the tiny gray-brown mouse rush into Bartle's overturned boot.

"Boot!" I say, pointing, and then I can't help adding, "*Fräulein* is German." This is an important distinction since Bartle is obviously trying to sound French.

Bartle dashes down the stairs and grabs hold of the rim of the boot.

I run after him to the front door. He throws the door open and leaps out onto the small veranda. Hauling his arm back, he hurls the boot toward the street. I hear the underarm seam of the negligee rip.

Even my loud gasp doesn't prevent Mom from hearing it, too. "Bartle!"

We watch as the boot sails in a graceful arc right over the Ford pickup that has just pulled up to the curb.

When the boot hits the street, it bounces once and flops over on its side. The mouse runs out and without stopping to get its bearings, runs under the truck, up the curb, up all five steps, through Mom's legs and right back into our living room.

Mom and I stand in the doorway yelling, "Mouse! Mouse!"

Not one of our six—count them—SIX cats bothers to put in an appearance.

Bits hates mice, but last time I checked she and David were so engrossed out in the kitchen preparing dinner, I doubt if she's even heard the commotion.

Brad, however, comes rushing down the stairs with his mouth full of straight pins and a tape measure around his neck. Good grief, he moved in minutes ago, and he's already altering something?

Bartle, meanwhile, is straddling the cement balustrade, his legs up in the air to protect himself from the scurrying mouse, the pink robe flapping in the breeze. Thank God he is wearing it over his clothes this time.

We're always wacky but I've got say, everybody's a little wackier than usual after Summer Street closing, the paint session that turned into a slumber party, and the move . . .

At that moment, my dad reappears down the front stairs with only a towel wrapped around his waist, fresh from what must have been the fastest shower in the history of the world. It's one of my mom's favorite hot pink towels. Mom gets that look on her face she gets when she wants to grab my dad and rip all his clothes off. He does look really good, but I'm pretty sure in this case that isn't the reason.

"Those are MY towels now!"

Geez, I hate it when my mom screeches.

"You relinquished them, remember?"

My dad shrugs, and the towel shifts enough so he has to grab it. He is so NOT wearing it over clothes. Brad giggles. Mom shoots him a look that could kill.

At that moment the doors of the pickup open. Ford. Pickup. Sickly, disgusting green.

"Holy shit! It's Loretta!" I transfer my attention from our messed-up household and the disappearing mouse to my aunt, who is unfolding herself from the driver's seat.

"Loretta!" my mother pushes Bartle toward the door and, for a moment anyway, out of sight. "What a . . . surprise!"

"Didn't you get my voice mail this morning?" Loretta's lips pinch together in that older sister I know better than you look that, in a nanosecond, reduces my mother to a babbling idiot.

"It's . . . uh . . . we've been kind of . . . busy . . . this morning . . ."

Now there's an understatement.

Tim Chang's querulous voice drifts out of the dining room. "Bartle! Will you please hurry? This butt-pad and girdle combo is strangling me! Come unhook me so I can pee!"

Words fail me.

They fail Mom, too.

They even fail my dad, who is clutching his towel and looking downright terrified.

Loretta has that effect on people. Especially when she's wearing a dress.

Bartle's disappeared, and Brad is frozen at the base of the stairs staring at Dad looking ravishing in that hot pink towel.

"Dad," I say, but he is now busy shaking water out of his hair and doesn't seem to hear me.

What can I do but rise to the occasion?

"Bits!" I holler at the top of my lungs, "Your mother's here!"

Bits wanders out from the kitchen looking less than interested.

"Hi, Mom," she says, her eyes now fixated on Tim. "Come see the pretty dress Bartle is making for Tim Chang."

Wow. Talk about rising to the occasion.

Meanwhile, Mom has rushed over to Tim and is frantically trying to get him down off the coffee table where he's posing in an aquamarine, floor-length stunner of a gown covered with bugle beads. He is so going to knock them dead in that musical revue.

I suppose Mom hopes to hustle Tim back up the stairs into the sewing room without Loretta seeing him, but after Bits's announcement, there isn't a whole lot she can do.

Do I need to mention that he is also wearing a red wig with champagne highlights?

Earth to Mom, I'm thinking. Each time Loretta comes to the house we've added another layer of complexity to this household. I am fairly certain she doesn't know about Dad and Brad. Because Bits would NEVER tell her. Loretta probably still thinks my dad and mom are happily married. My guess is that even after more than seventeen years she's still trying to digest the fact that he's black.

Mom mouths the words *TAKE TIM UPSTAIRS!* to Bartle, who has reappeared in regular guy clothes. Loretta does know Bartle's gay. I mean, come on, you would have to be 100 years old, blind, deaf, and senile in order to not know Bartle's gay.

Mom drags Dad, still in his towel, and Brad, with pins still stuck in his mouth—I'm surprised he hasn't swallowed them—out to the kitchen where we can all hear her loud murmur as she gives them point-by-point instructions of all the things they can not do or say. You know, just in case they've forgotten what a nut case Loretta is.

At that auspicious moment, Auntie Ellie arrives, home from Wisconsin a whole week early, and she has the entire band with her. The lock's evidently still broken on the back of Lee's ancient—and I do mean ancient—VW van, so they drag their instruments in with them, Auntie Ellie shaking her tambourines.

Oh, good grief, that is so over the top it makes me wish (not for the first time) that I could take a pencil or an eraser and edit my life.

"Hey, guys!" Auntie Ellie's beautiful, smoky voice rises above the jangle. "Hi, baby!" she says to me, which in spite of the chaos makes me smile.

"Oh . . . Hi, Loretta."

"Daddy!" Bits shouts with obvious relief as Lee and the other guys from the band follow Auntie Ellie into the room. She climbs up Lee like she is a monkey and still twelve. She doesn't get to see her dad much when he's on the road with the band.

Loretta's lips prune up until she looks exactly like pictures I've seen of my great-great-grandmother (of course on my maternal side).

Mom comes back out from the kitchen. We can hear Brad and Dad sneaking up the back stairway to the attic. Wow, those steps creak.

"Ellie," Mom's one word is eloquent as a warning bell, but as usual Auntie Ellie ignores her or isn't paying attention.

Am I the only person in this household that picks up on verbal and nonverbal cues? I wonder if David sneaked out the back door.

"Sorry to add to the madness of the day," Auntie Ellie says, "Did Brad and Mark get moved in okay?"

Oh, shit.

Mom's eyes roll back in her head and she opens her mouth as if to speak but no sound comes out.

Now Auntie Ellie wanders toward the coffee table. "Hi, Tim. Nice dress."

Loretta's eyes keep moving from Ellie to Tim, Tim to Ellie.

"Mom," Bits says. "What are you doing here?"

"I have a big meeting downtown," Loretta says, "Minneapolis." Then adds, "Church of the Living Prophesy." As if we didn't know what she was talking about.

Lee snorts, and Auntie Ellie gives him a little kick in the shins.

"It's an important time," Loretta says, reaching down for her tote bag where she keeps all the CLP literature. "We are at the end of six thousand years of human history." Her voice is so crisp it is nearly cracking.

Six thousand—by whose calculations, I'm thinking. Six thousand?

"The end of this wicked system of things is at hand," she snaps, waving a pamphlet like a flag.

Our household. A metaphor for the entire wicked system.

"The predicted year is 2012 . . ." she says, trying to hand the pamphlet to Mom, who appears to be frozen in place, eyes bulging.

"Think about it," Loretta says, nearly throwing the pamphlet at me, "It's August. It's not very long until December 21 . . ."

"And then . . . ?" I ask, picking up the pamphlet, though of course I know the answer.

"The end of the world," she answers.

Mom hasn't moved or spoken.

"What did Ellie mean," Loretta asks Mom. "Did Brad and MARK get moved in?"

sinful times seven

"Helping . . ." Mom says, shifting her gaze to what my dad calls her onstage focus, and what Edward mostly yells at her about when she does it.

The clichéd description "deer in headlights" also applies. (I might add that at the moment Bits is looking more like my mom than ever.)

Mom's not a very good improviser even though she teaches improv. She's said over and over that she's an actress that needs a script. I'd love to provide her with one right about now, but who knows what direction she wants to go with this.

"Helping . . ." she says again, her eyes finally focusing just to the left of Loretta's face. From my angle that makes her look cross-eyed. "Brad's lease ran out . . . and . . . he's renting the attic until he can find a house."

"And Mark?" Loretta asks, staring at her in an attempt, I'm sure, to force Mom to look at her.

"Well, Mark's helping him move today," Mom says, now turning her gaze to the fireplace mantel. "Of course. And . . . we were all so busy Mark ended up doing the bulk of it."

"So . . ." Auntie Ellie says, that tone in her voice that really means "Okay, I may have put my foot in it, but I'm on board now." Of course, she knows Loretta from forever. She'd spent more time at their house than at her own when they were growing up. This makes me seriously wonder what was going on at her house.

"Sooooooo . . ." she says again. "How'd that go? Is Brad all moved in?"

If Aunt Ellie didn't have such a smoky, late-night, too much to drink kind of voice, she'd sound absolutely perky.

"Yep," Mom says, suddenly swinging her head around to look right at Auntie Ellie. She matches Ellie's perky and kicks it up a notch. "They brought the last load over a few minutes ago! And then Mark hopped in the shower."

"Yep," Auntie Ellie says, her tone so much like Mom's it nearly sends me into a spasm of giggles. Bits looks at me with eyes so wide they almost set me off, too, then she spins around and heads to the kitchen.

I follow her.

"Coffee?" I yell back over my shoulder. We're Minnesotans. Coffee is a solution for most everything. No matter what time of day or night or . . . you know . . . weirdness.

"Shit!" Bits says (and she never swears).

"I know, right?" The situation is rendering me inarticulate. Watching my mother lie about something this important is unnerving. I mean, I understand why she'd want to. Loretta can be kind of scary. But come on. Mom's digging a hole and she'll never be able to climb out.

I hear the screen door *whap* and there's Grandmama, standing at the back door with a bag full of goodies. "Grandmama! What are you doing here?"

Has Grandmama ever entered our house through the front door? I don't think so. I run to give her a hug and as usual she bats at me like I've lost my mind.

"Baby, you get any taller, you going to have to play basketball or something," she says, handing me one of her cinnamon rolls.

I personally believe that Grandmama has a sixth sense for chaos and bakes for it.

There's no time for a snotty comeback to the basketball comment. Mom, Auntie Ellie, and Loretta all descend on the kitchen at the same time.

"There's that cute little white girl," Grandmama says, pointing at Mom like she's never seen her before. She does that to rile her up. It works every time. Mom puffs up like an adder. She rolls her eyes in Loretta's direction. "Oh . . . Hi, Loretta . . ."

"When did you get here?" Mom sounds truly puzzled, as if this baking and arriving at our house without notice is a new thing. She's tried and tried to get Grandmama to call ahead. Actually, everyone tries to get her to call ahead. Aunt Mary even bought her a cell phone but she's as bad as Mom about leaving it uncharged.

"Why would I want to be talking on the phone when I'm on the bus? Or walking here with my arms full?"

"If you called someone would come get you . . ." Mom always says.

She should know by now it's no use. Grandmama loves that bus ride. She talks to people all the way over and all the way back. And she endures the walk to our house so she can come in the back door and surprise us.

She's never admitted this, but I know.

Grandmama hands Mom a cinnamon roll and suddenly Mom's all smiles. Such is the power of Grandmama's baked goods. David and I decided a while back if we could get her cinnamon roll recipe down, we could change the world. Imagine the U.N. all peaceful with frosting around their mouths.

Even Loretta lights up a bit when Grandmama hands her a cinnamon roll, too.

Everyone's chomping on rolls, the coffee finishes brewing, I've poured cups for everyone and pushed the milk and sugar into the middle of the table. I've taken a six-pack of beer out to the guys from the band. If I were them I'd leave. But they're not leaving, so they get beer.

Bits has gone back out to sit with her dad. Since the divorce it's always better if Lee and Loretta aren't in the same room. Of course, that was the case before the divorce, too.

Loretta says she can't stay long because she has to register at the conference before the evening meal. I breathe a sigh of relief. Mom's ploy is working. Grandmama's giving nothing away (as usual). We may get away with this after all . . .

And of course that's when Bartle comes crashing down the back stairs, shouting, "Where's the plunger? Mark and Brad's toilet is plugged up. I think Chris must have dumped paint or something down there."

Even Grandmama's fabulous cinnamon rolls can't save us from the chaos that ensues.

"Una?" Loretta's voice sends a shudder down my spine. I'm glad Bits is in the living room. If Loretta were my mother, I'd want to be an orphan.

Mom's frozen again, this time with her eyes so wide open she looks more like Bits than ever. Which is worse, I wonder? Caught lying to her own sister or caught with her husband living in the attic with another man?

"Grandmama!" Bartle says, diving for a cinnamon roll, "When did you get here?"

She doesn't even bat at him or say a word. Clearly he has no idea what he's just done.

"I'll get the plunger," I say.

I nearly fall down the basement stairs I'm in such a hurry.

Above me I hear Loretta say again, "Una?!"

I grab the plunger, race up the stairs through the kitchen where everyone is still stuck in place as if they were on the stage in one of those ridiculously outdated freeze things directors used to use. *Stay frozen*, I'm thinking. *Stay frozen . . . stay frozen . . . stay frozen . . .*

Bartle reaches for the plunger, but I race right past him and up the stairs. He follows me.

Once we're at the top, I tell him what's happening in the kitchen and he goes to get my dad and Brad. Not that I think they should go down and join the fracas but, you know, in case Loretta decides it's her duty to march up to the attic.

"Oh shit," my dad says.

"What?" Brad asks. He really doesn't have the context for this one. Loretta avoids the theater like it's plague-ridden.

"Church of the Living Prophesy," my dad says. "Sinful . . . us . . ."

"Sinful . . ." I say, trying to help. "Sinful . . . times . . . seven . . ."

"Crap!" my dad says.

We all appear to have lost language.

"Una's going to be INSANE!" Bartle adds.

That Brad understands.

their exits and their entrances

We all go tumbling back down the stairs without having made any kind of plan.

"I knew it!" Loretta is saying. "I knew something like this was going on!"

"It's not what . . ."

"If it isn't bad enough you all living the way you do . . ."

"Loretta . . ."

"But NOW, not only do you have two men living in . . . living in . . ."

"The attic?" I prompt from the doorway. Bartle's burst back into the room, but Dad and Brad are cowering behind me on the stairs.

"In mortal sin!" Loretta glares at me as she finishes her sentence. "Plus, I knew when you took that boy in something like this would happen!"

"Bartle?" She's got to be kidding. She thinks it's Bartle's fault my dad's gay?

"If you had any sense, Una, you'd have taken my warning and left this . . . this . . ."

"That's crazy!" I can't help myself.

"Jessie!" Mom comes to life in time to chastise . . . guess who . . . ME. She turns to Loretta. "I can't leave, Loretta. We're about to start a new season. I'm the main acting teacher. I've got major roles in three of the four shows."

Why is she wasting her breath with this kind of argument? As if Loretta's suggestion actually had weight or substance or . . . you know . . . made sense.

"Which will mean exactly nothing when December 21 comes around and Armageddon comes," Loretta retorts. She pulls out another copy of the pamphlet she threw at me earlier, starts reading aloud.

BLAH DE BLAH DE BLAH BLAH BLAH . . .

No, I mean seriously, that's all I hear.

Mayan prophesies . . . BLAH BLAH BLAH . . . *Last days of this wicked system of things* . . . BLAH BLAH BLAH . . . *repent and be saved* . . . BLAH BLAH . . . BLAH!

I look around for support. Grandmama is nowhere to be seen. Bits is gone, too. I hope she grabbed David and ran next door to warn his parents not to come for dinner. If they have any brains they'll stay there.

Auntie Ellie is still here. I'll bet she's kicking herself big time for letting that slip.

"Loretta," she interrupts the reading diatribe. "Loretta, please . . ."

Loretta looks startled, but stops reading. She tries to NEVER speak to Auntie Ellie if she can help it. And I happen to know the feeling is mutual.

"How long has this . . . this TRAVESTY been going on?"

"Frankly"—my dad steps around me and down the last stair into the kitchen—"It's none of your business."

Mom gasps, but she doesn't disagree.

"It's Una's generosity of spirit . . ."

My mom suddenly looks a foot taller.

". . . that allows her to welcome Brad and me back into the house right now."

Mom's not exactly nodding, but she looks as if she could.

". . . And the love we all feel for each other . . ."

Go, Dad!

"I won't stand here and let you denigrate that with your revolting religious intolerance . . ."

Now, there's an actor who doesn't need a script!

Brad steps around me and into the kitchen to stand next to my dad. His face is so red he looks like he might be having a stroke. But there he stands.

The look on Bartle's face nearly breaks my heart. I was only twelve when Aunt Mary kicked him out, but I'll never forget the scene when my parents confronted her. This is a little too close for comfort.

I go stand by him. He grabs my hand, and I squeeze his hard.

"This time, Una, you've gone too far," Loretta says. "I forgave you for marrying that . . . that . . ."

"Nigger?" Mark says.

"Mark!" my mom says, with a gasp.

"Actor!" Loretta says. Racist as I know she is, I honestly believe that being an actor is worse in her book.

But, come on, my mom's an actor, too.

Poor Bits.

My mom looks at Dad and Brad, and then back to Loretta. Her voice is pleading. "Loretta, please . . ."

"I have tried and tried, Una, to bring you back to the Faith."

Yes, she has. She really has. Whatever that means—The Faith.

"And you have over and over again turned your back on The Truth."

My mom's sobbing. No matter how crazy Loretta gets, she's mom's only sibling. They grew up together. I think she always hopes that Loretta will get over this. Like that's ever going to happen.

"Mom didn't turn away from you, Aunt Loretta," I interrupt. I've got to stand up for my mom. And for my dad, too. And for Bartle. "She . . . she turned toward a different way of seeing things."

But Loretta isn't having any of it.

"Jessie," she snaps. "Stay out of it. Children—even overly bright children—should be seen and not heard!"

"Loretta!" Lee says from the arched doorway to the living room. "In this house, Jessie has a voice."

"She does!" Bartle says, speaking for the first time. "We all do!"

Mom is just standing there.

"Obviously my wisdom and guidance aren't welcome in your house," Loretta says, reaching for her purse.

"Now, Loretta, you sit down and have another cup of coffee." Grandmama has reappeared from who knows where. "Let's have a cup of coffee and talk about something else until we're all calmed down . . ."

But Loretta's having none of it. She completely ignores Grandmama. Which is not easy to do. Trust me.

"Una, since you were baptized into the church, I am going to have to report this to the congregation."

"I made this pecan pie this morning on a whim," Grandmama says, holding up the most gorgeous pie. "I know how you love my pecan pie . . ."

Loretta's still having none of it.

"More than likely you will be *dis*fellowshipped . . . for the magnitude of your sins . . ."

"Now, Loretta," Grandmama says, her voice hardening. "You know God is bigger than that . . ."

Loretta looks at Grandmama for a one-two-three beat. It's hard to ignore Grandmama, especially where religion is concerned. Grandmama's on the main line to God, if you know what I mean.

I hold my breath, thinking maybe Grandmama's done it. Nope.

"If you come to your senses, the church . . . and God . . . are forgiving. You are always welcome to return." Suddenly she spins around and reaches for Bits. "And you, you are coming with me!"

Lee grabs Bits and pushes her behind him. "No," he says, his voice more firm than I've ever heard.

"Loretta . . ." Mom takes a step toward her sister and then, for the first time since that truck door opened, she acts like the mother I know (or once knew).

"Loretta," she says, pulling herself up to her full height. Her voice is suddenly loud and very firm. "I've had it with this shit."

Loretta gasps and stutters. Okay, Mom could have been more articulate, but you have to admit it's CLEAR.

"I mean it," Mom says. "There's nothing forgiving about the CLPs . . . and I am sick to death of hearing about the end of the world."

Loretta, for once, is speechless.

"If you can't respect this family, my family, then I want you to get the hell out of my house!" Mom finishes loud and with an appropriate gesture. And then she moves to stand between Bartle and me and Dad and Brad.

Okay, definitely not as eloquent as what my dad said, but much more effective.

Lee, meanwhile, has taken Bits into the front room.

Loretta spins and marches out through the living room, with all of us following her. It's unfortunate that the other guys from the band have all fallen asleep after only one beer and are lying around the room looking particularly degenerate.

Lee's holding on to Bits so there's no chance Loretta will grab her.

"Your blood!" Loretta shouts, her voice shaking. "Your blood is no longer on my hands!"

The front door slams behind her.

It suddenly hits me that she never once mentioned all those postcards Bits and I grabbed out of the mailbox and that are still hidden in my closet.

Maybe God is on my side after all.

"Jessie," Grandmama says, "Go get the ice cream. We're all going to need a double scoop on our pie."

celebration of sixteen

No, that's not me being obtuse or poetic or anything. We are cele-brating not only my sixteenth birthday (*Sweet sixteen never been kissed* . . . as everyone keeps saying all day in a really irritating retro kind of way that makes me want to scream). We are also celebrating sixteen years of dual birthday parties—mine and David's. He turned eighteen yesterday, August 22 (last day of Leo), and I turn sixteen today, August 23 (first day of Virgo). We've been celebrating birthdays together ever since my first.

There were some years in there when that was not fun. Like, say those years when David was six and seven and hated girls for instance. And then there were his first teenage years and "Jessie's a BABY! Why does she have to come to MY party???" What he really hated was that at eleven and twelve I was a foot taller than him.

But as sensitive and progressive and basically loving as our parents are, nothing could stop them from throwing one party for the two of us, alternating years—one year on David's actual day, next year on mine. We thought this was normal for a long time until we discovered that parents who had regular nine-to-five kinds of jobs actually waited and had the party on the weekend. What a concept.

My secret? I love the parties. It never mattered what awkward stage I was in or how annoying (or annoyed) David happened to be that year. There was something special about our parties.

This year? I'm not so sure. If they keep on with that *sweet sixteen, never been kissed* crap I may change my mind.

David and I decided to make it the Last Official Pizza Grill Night of 2012. You never know when fall is going to descend on Minnesota. Last week it felt like October. Today it's hot and sticky and we keep having squalls of rain. The three weeks since Dad and Brad moved into the attic have flown by. And it seems like the confrontation with Loretta cemented everyone's loyalties to each other, so even parental conflict has been virtually invisible.

The biggest thing that happened was a couple weeks ago when Brad bought us all iPhones as a housewarming gift. And then Lee got them for him and Bits and Auntie Ellie. Of course, Mom's phone is still uncharged on her bedside table most of the time.

Anyway, Lydia's annoyed that David's cooking for his own party.

"It's my favorite thing to do," he says, adding capers to my salmon and red onion pizza. Yum!

She sighs.

"Jessie, are you taking my directing class this year?"

Well, there you go. Up against the wall and the party's hardly started.

My dad hands me a can of pop. He's drinking a beer. So is David. DAVID IS DRINKING A BEER!

"Can't I have a beer, too? It's my birthday . . ." (I don't really want a beer, but it's a matter of principle.)

"When you turn eighteen you can have a beer . . ." He and David both take swigs of their beer, adding insult to injury. "Are you taking Lydia's directing class this year?"

Suddenly Mom pops up from behind the kitchen island. What was she doing down there? And what must it be like to be so small you can hide pretty much anywhere?

I wish.

"Yeah, Jess . . . are you taking Directing?"

"Yeah, I thought I might." I don't tell anyone I spent every hot day of the summer reading directing texts from the theater library.

Big smiles all over the room.

Lydia's smile is the biggest, which surprises me. "I'm so glad!"

"Well, that's one down," my dad says. "What's . . ."

". . . the other class going to be?" Mom asks, finishing his sentence for him the way she usually does.

"Now?" I whine. "Do we have to talk about this now . . . ?"

"Jess, will you run over to the house and get me that jar of anchovies we bought yesterday?" says David, saving the day.

When I run in the front door, Bits is coming down the stairs with a script in her hand.

"Why aren't you at the party?"

"I'm coming," she says, eyes still on the script. "I'm coming right now."

"What are you doing? It's our BIRTHDAY PARTY! Come on!"

She follows me out to the kitchen. I can't find the jar of anchovies anywhere. I know we unpacked those groceries from Trader Joe's right here. Where are they?

The cats are lined up in the back stairwell.

"Judge . . . you DIDN'T!"

"Since when can a CAT open a jar of anchovies?" Bits asks, finally looking up from the script.

"Ha! Gotcha!"

"I've got to learn this monologue for my audition," she says, waving the script.

"Which isn't until next week . . . No, it's the week after when school starts. PUT THE SCRIPT DOWN."

Standoff.

"I'll help you with your monologue later."

"You will???"

"Uh, yeah. Like I always do."

She rolls the script up and sticks it in the pocket of the sleeveless hoodie she's wearing.

I yank it out and leave it on the kitchen table.

When we get back to the theater, Edward's joined the group. Lee and Ellie arrive a few minutes later.

"Where's Bartle?"

"He'll be here in a second," Brad says, grabbing the beer my dad's holding out to him. "He's finishing up a vat of dyeing we're doing for *Tartuffe*."

"Wow, Brad," Mom says with a little snicker. "Fall season hasn't even started up again yet. We're supposed to be on break."

"It's only a little dyeing," he says. "Thought I'd get a jump on it. That's going to be a hard show to do at the same time we're doing *Streetcar*."

David's got half a dozen pizzas lined up on the island, each topped with someone's favorite combination. Lydia's tossing a big salad that no one wants, but she's making it anyway.

We've stuffed ourselves on the first round of pizzas, David assuring Lydia we will adopt a Continental approach to the salad she slaved over (i.e., eat it at the end of the meal), when Bartle finally arrives.

"Sweet sixteen and never been kissed," he taunts, grabbing the last piece of the salmon pizza and stuffing it into his big mouth.

"For crying out loud—stop with that already!" I say, smacking him so hard he nearly chokes on the pizza.

"Well you haven't been kissed." He swallows the food he's (as usual) talking around. "Have you?"

"What's the big deal? I just turned sixteen. Today."

Lee takes a big swig of beer. "Una, how old were you for your first kiss?"

Mom actually blushes. Would you look at that? I know the answer, but it still makes me cringe.

"Thirteen," she glances at me. "But that was too young. Way too young."

"Oh, give it up," Auntie Ellie says. "Jackie kissed both of us that day. I was thirteen, too."

"Gotcha!" Lee says, grinning at Auntie Ellie. "Real first kiss?"

"Thirteen," Mom says, still grinning.

"Fourteen," Ellie says at the same time, then she and Mom both burst out laughing. I have no idea why.

"Don't even ask the boys," Mom says.

"It's true," Bits says. "They don't count when it comes to first kisses."

"And what do you know about first kisses, daughter dear?" Lee asks.

"Not much," she says, snuggling up to him.

"And you're almost eighteen," I say, feeling vindicated.

"Stilllllllll," my dad drawls, "*Sweet sixteen and never been kissed . . .*"

Then he and Bartle high-five, which looks so ridiculously GAY on them. We all crack up laughing. Even Mom.

"Where did that phrase come from anyway? It's so stupid."

"Let up on Jessie," David says, "it's time for us to blow out the candles."

"Thank you," I say.

Lydia insisted on getting a cake for us at David's favorite bakery over in South Minneapolis. It was either that or he was going to bake his own.

Edward brings in the cake, literally covered with candles. A quick count reveals they added our ages: thirty-four. How funny.

We lean in over the cake, do our usual eyeball count—one,

two, three—and blow. After all, we have sixteen years of practice at this.

Out the candles go.

And then, David leans in and plants a kiss, right on my lips!

A cheer goes up all around the room.

He hangs on for about a second too long in my opinion. I can feel myself turning red and push him away.

"Sweet sixteen . . ." he says, with a huge grin. "BEEN KISSED!"

Another cheer. I look around the room. What a whacko group! The only person not laughing and shouting is Bits, still curled up next to Lee. Why is she looking so grumpy all of a sudden?

HAS she ever been kissed, I wonder? And if she hasn't, does she mind that now I have? I mean, not seriously. It's only David. It was a joke in front of our parents. But still. It was a pretty nice kiss.

"*Sweet seventeen and never been kissed*," Bartle chortles, pulling Bits up off the love seat.

"I have, too, been kissed!"

"I don't think acting class kisses count . . ." Bartle retorts, and everyone laughs.

"Neither do the ones from your red-neck cousins," Lee says, referring to the ones on his side of the family, and the laughter gets louder. We've met those cousins. Once.

Bits looks like she's going to cry.

David swoops in with a piece of cake and leaning way over, gives her a kiss, too. Right in front of her dad.

"There," Lee says, "Problem solved."

And Bits runs out of the room.

189

I'd go after her, but it's my birthday and Mom's brought out the presents. When Bits doesn't come back after about ten minutes, Auntie Ellie goes to find her. You can always count on Auntie Ellie that way.

No iPad in the pile of gifts, but some great gift cards to buy apps for my new phone. Gift cards for clothes, too. Mom's finally learned not to shop for me or with me. And I need clothes—I'm still growing. All of my jeans are too short.

It's a nice party. Not all that different from any of our summer grill nights. Maybe that's what I like about it the most.

at the altar of the JUMBLE (players)

The text from Loretta comes in just as Bits and I are sitting down in the proscenium theater for the opening assembly.

Jessie, I've been texting Una for days. She isn't answering. Please tell her I won't give up. Armageddon will be here before we know it. Dec 21 isn't that far away. Loretta

Hmm, I thought she said, "our blood was no longer on her hands."

Summer Street opening days are always wild and crazy and fun, but they pale by comparison to the opening of the fall semester at the theater school. I don't think anybody at our house sleeps much the night before. I don't know why, either, because it's pretty much the same every year. Maybe it's that there are always new students to meet. Maybe it's because both my parents love teaching almost as much as they love performing.

Of course I am a little anxious about the directing class. It's going to be mega hard. (Yeah, even for me.) Lydia will pitch it like it's a university course. She's incapable of doing anything else.

And, I have to admit that I am a little on edge because my parents appear to have forgotten that we didn't select a second course for me. It does not escape me that there's a certain irony in me setting a goal to find my place in the theater and then to be unable to select more than one class that I want to take.

Until I outed Dad and Brad, I had a solid plan for this school year. I was going to take Brad's Monday Costuming class. Directing with Lydia, of course. And my dad's Intermediate Acting class. I've taken it before, but I figured he'd let me be like a TA or something. And then I figured I'd take Edward's Set Design class in the spring, Lydia's Directing (Part 2), and maybe I'd get my courage up to take one of the movement classes.

The plan doesn't work for me anymore. I don't want to take the class from Brad. My dad's class is over-full and with a waiting list so he really couldn't let me in. Especially since I've already taken it. And I refuse to take a class with my mom, especially one where she's slavering over Bits's acting ability. Does that make me petty and small? So, sue me.

Regardless, I'm still wildly excited that the JUMBLE school year is starting. Here's how it works—you have to be in high school (at least ninth grade) to enroll. That's because it's been accredited so that certain classes count toward high school graduation, but only if you're in private school, unfortunately. We're still trying to get accepted by the public school system, but so far no go.

Students go to regular school in the morning and to the theater school in the afternoon. This is heaven on earth for anyone who wants to be an actor or a singer or a dancer or a choreographer. I really wish I fell into at least one or more of those categories.

There are about twenty new students (I added up the increase in tuition income and it is significant). They're mostly at the basic level. Some of them are kids who participated in Summer Street. Then there are thirty-six returning students including Bits and me.

I was worried that things would be really different this year, given what's going on with my parents. But here's the weird part. They are doing their usual spiel about how they came together to found the theater. It's as though nothing's changed. They talk. Lydia and Edward talk. The four of them do this comedy routine. It's funny. It's poignant. It's THEATER.

How can they do that when everything is so upside down and inside out?

Now Mom's introducing a new stage movement teacher.

"Ms. Ardella Patterson is from Minnesota originally," Mom says, smiling up at her.

The new teacher is at least as tall as I am and thin as a rail and there's something familiar about her. She's got bright red hair—orange actually—and it's pulled back in a very dancer-y bun.

"We all," Mom gestures at Dad and the Benedicts, "know her from the University. But she's been in New York City for the past ten years dancing and doing choreography, mostly Off-Broadway shows."

Bits gasps at the New York reference. Even Off-Broadway still has BROADWAY in it.

I poke her.

"What?" she says, still breathless.

What a dope.

"Ms. Patterson will be teaching Ballet, Jazz, Modern, and Advanced Stage Movement . . ."

"OMG, I cannot wait!" Bits whispers.

Of course she can't. She's a fabulous dancer. She's excelled in every dance and movement class we've offered.

Now Mom's talking about the projects she'll be doing with her Advanced Acting students. What I like to think of as Una's Elite.

"You're taking that, too, aren't you?" Bits whispers.

"No, I'm not . . ." Is she out of her mind? Me in Una's Elite? I don't think so.

Bits has this funny look on her face. Oh, I know that look.

"I'm NOT . . ."

She wrinkles up her nose and mouth.

"Ohhhhh, they didn't, did they?"

She nods. "I saw the registration sheet when I was helping Lydia with some filing yesterday."

"My name's on it . . ." It's not even a question. This is why they haven't been bugging me. They made the decision without talking to me and they put me on the damned list.

Whatever else Mom says about the coming semester goes right over my reeling head.

And the minute the assembly is over, Bits corners the new movement teacher to talk with her about—what else?—New York City. Bits lives, breathes, eats, talks, dances, walks that place. Like Bartle lives, breathes, eats, talks, and sashays San Francisco. And David has been talking lately about Paris, France.

What is it with everyone, wanting to go somewhere else?

But, more important, how am I going to get out of taking Advanced Acting with my insane mother??? Ditching class is the only thing that comes to mind and it's kind of hard to ditch when your mom is teaching the class.

What good is having an über-brain if these are the kind of problems I'm forced to solve?

Maybe I should have signed up for at least one class at the U. It did occur to me when I turned down the full scholarship offer. But at the time, nothing jumped out at me.

Nope, not now, either.

Bits and I are barely in the house after assembly before she pulls me up the stairs to our room to work on her audition monologue. Okay, I did promise.

But really, when am I not helping someone learn their lines? Maybe I could be an acting coach. I wonder if you can do that without knowing how to act.

"Aren't you going to cue me?"

"It's a monologue," I say, hearing the snip in my voice. I dial back. "Start at the top."

She stumbles through the first few lines with me having to prompt her every other word. As usual, she is having trouble concentrating. Once Bits gets her lines down she is a great actress, but she has a hard time learning them. Her concentration kind of flips and flops around.

"I am so excited about the new movement teacher!" She's wrapping herself up in the bed's canopy curtain and is slowly unrolling herself. Her movement is completely out of sync with the jazzed energy in her voice.

I refuse to engage. This is her excuse to not try with the line she's just butchered.

"She's going to teach us movement techniques right out of New York!"

I crawl up on the bed (it's extra high because it was built for our production of *The Princess And The Pea*) and sit cross-legged at the head. Prop myself up with pillows. Don't reply.

"How can you NOT be excited?" she demands, holding on to the bed post and stretching one leg out behind her. What's the name of that ballet move? See. Even after years of ballet classes— hideous, horrible ballet classes—I'm blanking over a really basic move. "You should drop the advanced acting class and take the movement class . . ."

I read her cue line to her. She ignores it.

"Do you know how much I would love it if my parents actually wanted me to become an actor?"

Of course I know this. A silent *big duh* because there is nothing to say other than I am so sorry I was born to the King and Queen of Theater and you got a loony-tunes mother who is nervously waiting for the end of the world and a father who, though a fun guy and an excellent drummer, has not quite figured out how to be a parent.

Lee's been better lately, though. But her mom . . . Loretta makes mine look like she could be featured in *Parent* magazine.

"You've got so much support from them," she trills. "And you love the theater. You should go for it!"

Now she's wrapping the curtains around her shoulders like a shawl.

I wave the script but she refrains from noticing it.

"What are you complaining about?" She's seriously getting on my nerves. "Between Lee and my parents and Brad and Bartle you have even more support than I do . . ."

"Huh?" She lets the end of the curtain slip a bit.

I wave the script again. I didn't mean to say that last part and I'm hoping in her usual thick way she didn't quite get it. This is not a discussion I'm ready to have.

"Look," she says, pulling the curtain back up around her shoulders. "I get why you don't want to take the advanced acting class right now with your mom. But come on, there's a new dancing teacher . . . I mean, your dancing's not that . . ."

"My dancing sucks. I am quite possibly the world's clumsiest human being. I'm even clumsier than most of the boys. I am clumsier than all of the boys except Robert. Come on, you know that's true . . ."

"Jess, dancing's not your strong suit, but you don't suck," Bits says, winding one of her golden curls around her finger. "You don't suck at anything."

I wave the script a third time, giving her the cue.

"Soooo," she says, ignoring me. "Skip the dancing and go for the acting and singing. You should take a voice class."

It's clear we're going to have this discussion before Bits is willing to learn her lines, so I put the script down.

Okay, I throw it at her. "There's no voice class offered in the fall."

"Well, take one somewhere else then," she says, catching the script, then jumping up and wrapping the curtain around her torso like a toga. She looks like a demented Statue of Liberty holding the script instead of a torch.

I wonder if she's ever been tested for ADD.

"I like to sing. But I'm not that good. I'm just better at it than at all the other theater things I suck at."

She plunks down on the bed and throws the script back at me.

"I'm right."

She sits there with her eyes closed for about three minutes, not answering, ignoring me. I'm used to this, so I spend her down time rereading the monologue. It's Queen Margaret. Such an incredible role. My mom always suggests parts for Bits that she would never get to play for real. I'm sure Mom gave her this one to use as her audition piece.

Suddenly Bits opens her eyes, does a backward roll off the bed (she used to be in gymnastics when she was a kid), stands in the middle of the braided rug, and delivers the entire monologue without one mistake.

If I live to be 100 and Bits is 102, I will never understand how she does it.

I am in tears she is so good.

A few minutes later we're downstairs rewarding her with a cup of freshly brewed hot chocolate with whipped cream.

"Well, you've got to be excited about the directing class," she says, her mouth and the end of her nose covered with the white fluffy stuff. "You've already read most of the directing books."

"Yeah, that's true." I don't mention that in addition to the theater library books, I've ordered five new ones online. "But can I stand to work with Lydia like that for an entire year?"

"Oh, come on," Bits says, "How bad can it be?"

"Remember Theater History?"

"Ohhhhh, yeah . . ."

I can't stand it. I have to wipe the whipped cream off the end of her nose in order to continue with this conversation.

She, meanwhile has grabbed a banana, an apple, and an orange from the fruit bowl on the counter. She balances the apple and orange in her right hand, extends her arm out to the side in a sweeping gesture, the banana in her left hand. Then she successfully juggles all three, depositing first the apple, then the orange back in the bowl. She peels the banana and eats it.

It's hard to believe she's two years older than me.

"Oh," she says, sounding genuinely surprised as she pulls her phone out of her pocket. "Oh. Hi, Mom."

I can hear Loretta yelling on the other end of the line. She's always been a crank but these days she needs medication. I'm glad Bits is staying with us.

"I didn't hear it ring," Bits says, her voice calm and evenly modulated. "I have to keep it on vibrate at the theater."

Never mind that the phone's been in her pocket for HOURS, yup, vibrating away.

She smiles and makes a face at me. I don't know how she does it.

My recent jealousy of my mom's attentions to Bits suddenly seems horrible and unfair. In fact, all my complaints about my own mother seem tiny and insignificant.

Of course that won't last.

the directing class
that wasn't

It's interesting to me that the directing class is Lydia's THING, given that she never directs. I mean, I know she's studying all this for her PhD in Theatre at the U, but still, wouldn't you think she'd want to actually do some directing?

I'm sitting in the classroom next to the library waiting for Lydia to arrive. I'm the only one here.

Thinking about the reading I did all summer, I can see why Lydia's so gung-ho about doing research on the 1970s. Things haven't changed that much in the theater. I mean, there still aren't that many women directing in town. Especially at the big theaters like the Guthrie. There's one all-women company, called Theatre Unbound. And the Children's Theatre Company for the first time ever has an all-woman team of directors and tech people. Even the set designer is a woman. That's really unusual.

Lydia walks in, looks around the empty room, and sighs as she sits down in the desk next to mine. "I'm afraid we're going to have to cancel the directing class."

"No one else signed up?" I'm surprised to discover I'm disappointed.

She nods.

"I think I may have to change my approach to the class," she says finally. "I couldn't even bribe people to take it."

"You didn't?!"

"No," she says with a wry little smile. "But I thought about it."

"I'm sorry it didn't make . . ."

"Jessie, if you're interested in the material, I'd be more than happy to work with you this semester on an independent study basis."

"You would?"

"Absolutely." Lydia reaches down and grabs a handful of papers she'd tossed on the floor. "Here's the reading list. You could start at the top and then . . ."

"Uh . . . I . . ."

"Yes?"

"I already read the books on your list."

"You . . . you read . . ." Lydia looks so surprised she's stuttering. "When did you . . . ?"

"I saw the list in the office this summer and I just started going through the books here in the library."

"And you read them all?"

"Uh-huh."

"Well," she says, sitting back in her chair. "What did you think?"

"Except for the Clurman book, I enjoyed all of them, especially the ones by Peter Brook. I love his books."

"Why don't you like the Clurman?" Lydia asks.

"Male-oriented. Limiting, so limiting. Really white bread," I say, and she nods at each point. "Why's it on the list?"

"His work represents a dominant point of view," she says with a smile. "We need to understand it and then be able to critique it from other perspectives—feminist, cultural studies—that kind of thing."

"Okay. Yeah, I get that."

"And you could also deconstruct it from less well-represented groups. You know, different racial or ethnic groups for instance."

"Like me," I blurt. How wicked is that?

"Yes," she says, her smile even bigger. "Exactly like you. Well, since you've read all the books on the list, let me think about how to approach this."

"Were you waiting until the second semester to read books from this century?"

"From this . . . ? Oh, I . . . well . . ." she says, stuttering again. "Well, yes. Okay, good idea. I'll pull that list for you and we can start there."

"Wicked!" I say, without thinking.

Lydia laughs. "Wicked indeed!"

una's elite (not!)

Okay, so I go all passive-aggressive and don't say anything to Mom about what Bits told me. I want to see how long it will take her to bring the subject up and tell me that she's registered me for her Advanced Acting class.

Only she doesn't.

Meanwhile, Bits is learning yet another audition monologue (yes, suggested by my mother). And every time we sit down to a meal they are talk-talk-talking about what Mom's planning to do in the class.

Wouldn't you think she'd mention it then?

Nope. She doesn't.

Now I'm not only furious about being forced to take the class, I'm just plain furious.

When I mention it to Bits she looks at me like I'm the one who's insane and says, "Well, just ask her . . ."

Hard to argue with that.

Only I can't seem to do it.

So, the first day of class, Bits goes over early with Mom to help her set up the space. She says Mom's planning on jumping right in with some acting exercises.

Oh, goody.

Five minutes before class is scheduled to start, I walk out our front door. Count my steps to the theater . . . 572. On the mark. Good news, I guess. At least it means I haven't grown a foot overnight.

Walk into the green room.

Turn around and walk out before anyone sees me.

Sneak down the hall to the library. Peruse the bookshelves for about ten minutes until I'm sure class has started and Mom's closed the studio theater door. She's a stickler for being on time and the door is locked once class starts. Not only that, but all cell phones are turned off and in a basket by the door. Mom's really old-fashioned where this is concerned.

It seems risky to walk past the studio theater on my way out of the building but I can't help myself. I am too curious to see if she's looking for me. Or if she's holding the class waiting for me (yeah, right).

Nope.

The door is closed. I'm assuming it's locked.

I walk out of the theater and head for Caribou Coffee on Grand Avenue.

My phone doesn't ring.

I don't have any text messages (thank goodness Loretta has stopped texting me).

David's back at school, of course. I actually miss him. We spent a lot of time together this summer. I've only seen him . . . maybe two times since our birthday party and that ridiculous kiss.

It feels strange not to be in high school anymore. I thought I'd feel more done somehow. And for sure, I thought I'd feel more of a sense of purpose at the theater. This summer kind of screwed up all my plans.

I don't have anything to do at Caribou other than drink a latte and play *Angry Birds*. So that's what I do.

I DITCHED MY MOM'S CLASS!

I am so going to catch hell.

i'm not your . . . anything

After the first acting class, Mom waits an entire day and then at dinner in front of everyone she says, "Don't forget acting class tomorrow, Jessie."

"I'm not taking acting class," I say, stuffing a forkful of mashed potatoes in my mouth.

"Yes, you are," she says.

"No," I say. "I'm not."

"That worked for Summer Street," Mom says, getting up to get a glass of water.

I glance around at the others. Everyone's bent over their plates like they're having a sudden intense relationship with their food. Even my dad.

"But it's not working now." Mom sits back down.

I think about pitching a fit (not my style) but decide instead to finish my mashed potatoes. And have another helping of meat loaf. A glass of orange juice. And a piece of bread.

I am channeling Bartle. Ha!

No, I'm not. I'm avoiding talking with my mother about this at the dinner table. I mean, she and I have had next to no conversations about, you know, anything since my graduation night back in June. I'm not having this conversation at the dinner table in front of everyone.

Back in our room, Bits says, "Come on, Jess, just show up at class tomorrow."

Rather than argue, I say, "Okay, I will . . ."

I mean it when I say it. What else can I do? But then, the next day I dawdle so long in the bathroom Bits runs to the theater without me so she won't be late. I can't stay home; I'm too antsy. Let me say that in all my years of schooling, you know all those years where I got nothing but As and A+s, until this week I've never ditched a class.

I didn't even ditch on Senior Ditch Day. Don't ask. It's embarrassing.

Today I walk out our door and breathe in the crisp, sunny early autumn air. And instead of heading for the theater, I walk in the opposite direction.

It's always fun to walk down Grand Avenue because there are so many cool shops and cafes and so much going on. I am walking west, in the direction of Snelling Avenue.

I'm less likely to run into any of the theater folks this way. Plus, it's more interesting.

And, at Snelling there's a Jamba Juice and a great bookstore as a reward for making it all that way. And I can always hop a bus back if I don't want to walk.

I'd never admit to a soul that another consideration is it's also the direction of St. Kate's. And their classes start this week. So everyone from far-away places, you know—like Connecticut—should be back by now. I never answered Emily's e-mail. I'm not sure why.

It's a long way to walk and I'm about to give in and turn back, only then I remember that a few blocks past Snelling is the best art supply store in the Cities. And even though I don't have an artistic bone in my body, I love looking at all the paper and paint and cool sketchbooks and pens and pencils and pastels. So I keep walking.

I happen to know because Emily told me that her favorite coffee hangout is the little café three doors down from Wet Paint (the art store). Closer to the St. Thomas campus than St. Kate's and she says that's why. She has to get away from that place so she can think.

I look in the windows as I go past, and it's practically empty. Wandering around Wet Paint takes up another half hour or so. I buy a notebook and some gel pens. I don't know what for, but I like them.

On the way back past the café I go in, check out the booths, order a latte to go.

And then I walk and sip, taking my time down Grand back to Snelling. Finish my coffee and go into the bookstore. Browsing there takes another half hour.

And then I slowly wander back down Grand toward home. Class is probably letting out about now. So the trick is avoiding my mom until dinnertime when there will be the usual crowd around diverting her attention from me.

Ironic, huh? I spent the whole summer craving her attention and now I'm ducking it.

I hate irony.

I run into David coming out of Kowalski's—our favorite grocery store. Of course he's loaded down with more than he can carry so I rush to help him.

"What are you doing all the way down here?" he asks.

"Ditching acting class," I say, not even bothering to search for a cover-up. I'm too busy covering up my little foray past the grounds at St. Kate's. Embarrassing. And David doesn't even know Emily exists.

"Oh, yeah," he says. "I heard Una'd enrolled you in her acting class without telling you. What is with that?"

I shrug. What is with anything Mom's doing these days? I mean, really.

"What are you going to do?" he asks. I notice that he's not rushing to convince me I should go ahead and take the class. I'm grateful for this.

"I'm doing an independent study with your mom," I say with a shrug. "Tons of work there."

He shifts the grocery bags and looks like he's going to say something.

But he doesn't.

"I don't want to take any of the classes I originally wanted to take." I can hear the petulance in my voice, and it makes me cringe.

"Why not?"

It's a reasonable question. I don't have a reasonable answer, though.

I shake my head.

"Well, you've got to do something. You're going to go stark-raving mad from boredom if you don't."

"Why aren't you in school?" It suddenly hits me it's a Wednesday afternoon.

"Lab Wednesday," he says. "Research day for our senior thesis projects."

"Every Wednesday?" I ask, dumb-founded. He's going to a ridiculously trendy private prep school.

"Yeah. How cool is that?"

"And you are doing research on . . ." I ask, gesturing with my head at our grocery bags, all four of them. How in the world was he planning to get these home if he hadn't run into me?

He grins. "I'm cooking dinner."

"For us, too?"

"Yup, at the theater for the whole gang in time for some big meeting they're having tonight."

Ahhhh, life is good.

"Want to help?"

"Sure," I say, shifting the bags so I can get a better grip. "Just don't tell my mom where you ran into me."

"Deal."

Back at the theater, we unload the groceries and put them away in the fridge and the big pantry. I'm in the middle of filling canisters of rice and sugar, when I feel David move close up behind me.

"What are you . . ." I say, turning to find him RIGHT there.

He kisses me. I kiss back. Kissing is . . . well, it's way nicer than I ever imagined it would be. I'm not exactly attracted to David. But he's a good kisser.

A really good kisser. I wonder where he got all the practice?

"Practice . . ." I say, when we come up for air.

"What?" he says, laughing. "I should practice more?"

"No," I smile. "I'm wondering where you got so much practice . . ."

He blushes a deep, deep pink. Runs his hand through his hair. I decide not to push it.

"And," I continue, "I'm saying that's what we're doing."

"Practicing?" he asks, leaning in and kissing me again.

"I'm not your girlfriend . . ."

"I know that."

"We're just practicing . . ."

what it comes down to

Tonight everyone except Bits is off somewhere doing something else. Bartle went to the gay bars with some of his girrrrrlfriends.

"They'll grow out of this in a few years," Brad says as we watch them waltz out the door.

"Oh, really?!" I say, hiding the smile that's twitching at my lips. "You mean they're NOT going to keep wearing dresses and makeup when they give in to the necessity of earning a living and turn into accountants and stock brokers and school teachers?"

"Off to the costume shop," he says, ignoring me and jamming the last dish into the dishwasher.

Bartle is not old enough to go to the bars, but evidently they only card people they don't want to let in. That's an interesting— not to mention illegal—practice.

Auntie Ellie and Lee are out of town with the band again. La-Crosse, Wisconsin, of all places. They'll be back tomorrow morning. She never misses one of Mom's openings if she can help it.

When Bits asks me to help her with lines for the scene she's working on for her acting class, I look at her like she's lost her mind and walk out of the house.

Yeah, I know. I'm taking out my anger at my mom on Bits. Not fair, but I'm an only child and I'm not used to sharing my room for such a long period of time. And sometimes Little Miss Perfect Theater Person gets on my nerves.

Mom and I are still in a stalemate over the acting class. I keep ditching, and she hasn't mentioned it again since the dinner exchange.

There's nowhere to go and it's mid-September so it's starting to get dark earlier, making walking around the neighborhood not such a great option. I'm kind of hoping David will be hanging out somewhere. Why don't I call him? I should call him. Normally I would call him, but ever since those kisses I feel kind of funny about doing that. That sucks.

I end up at Mom's final dress rehearsal for *A Streetcar Named Desire*. It was a toss-up between that and my dad's rehearsal for *Tartuffe* in the studio theater. But they've barely begun rehearsals, so Mom's seems more interesting.

It's kind of a risk since it may end up in a conversation about the acting class.

And that would be a major drag when there are so many other things I'd love to talk with her about.

I mean, why can't I just run up to her the way I used to and throw my arms around her and say, "I love you, Mom!" And then she would say it back and hug me, and everything would be like it used to be.

But it's not.

Why not?

I don't understand why she's acting like this. She pays attention to Bits. She's all caught up in her life and problems and talents.

It's like she doesn't even see me.

I hate this.

This was the last thing I expected to have happen when I ran in and found Dad and Brad kissing.

And it seems like it's getting worse every day.

I've been avoiding Mom so much, the last time I was at *Streetcar* rehearsal was when they were still doing scene-based improvs. Edward has them do that early on in rehearsal but not until after he's blocked the show. Then he makes changes in his staging based on what the actors come up with. That's about the only way he's flexible, if you ask me.

He gives them staging directions like he's God or something. And he blocks everything in advance. On these big diagram boards with dry-erase markers.

Mom likes working with Edward better than with any of the other directors we use. She says having him that rigid at the beginning gives her the structure she needs later to be her most creative. This doesn't fit with her personality, so it's never made sense to me.

And I don't think I'd want to work like that as a director.

I mean, if I'm ever good enough to be a director.

The run-through is starting when I slip into the back of the theater. They must have been going over some last-minute technical cues or something.

My mom's acting always makes me feel strange. I get this ache inside when I see her do a character that's really different from how she is in our daily life. Like there's this dimension of her that's forever unavailable.

The other thing is, she can pull off roles you'd never expect her to, given how tiny she is. I guess that's why she's so passionate about giving Bits those opportunities.

When I was little, it scared me the way Mom could transform when she acted. Especially wild costumes, wigs, or crazy makeup. The worst, though—was when she had an accent. That would send me into shrieking terror.

Then it became magical, and I wanted to do it, too.

I wonder why my parents are both so talented and I'm not.

Maybe that's the ache.

There are some reviewers here tonight so all the actors are kind of hopped up trying to impress them. Except Mom. She's going to be really good in this role.

I wait for Mom after rehearsal. The truth is, I want to talk with her so bad I'm willing to risk it being about me ditching her class. But my dad's rehearsal gets out the same time as Mom's and we run into him and Brad in the parking lot. She links arms with Brad and asks him how the costumes are coming along. My dad and I talk about the Richard Wilbur translation of *Tartuffe*, which I love and he's not so sure about.

At our front door, Dad and Brad say goodbye and keep going.

They're on their way to catch a bus to downtown Minneapolis to go to Unicorn—the theater bar. The minute they're out of sight, Mom sags and says how tired she is.

But when we walk in the door, Bits is waiting to pounce on Mom with questions about her scene. Mom perks right up, goes to pour herself a glass of scotch, and sits down at the kitchen table to help Bits work through the scene.

When I was younger, I don't know, twelve or thirteen, I actually thought for a while that maybe Bits was really my mother's first kid. She's two years older than I am. Maybe Mom got pregnant, you know, right before she went to the university, and ended up giving her baby to Loretta. You read about stuff like that all the time.

Finally I asked her about it and she laughed so hard I had to believe her. She was so proud of me for being that imaginative.

And then later I saw Bits's birth certificate—you know—the official one she needed for something at school. And Loretta and Lee were on it as parents. Plus, by that date, I realized my mom was already with my dad.

I sit and watch Mom and Bits work together on the scene. Bits is such a good actress. Every suggestion my mom makes, she gets right away and does it like she doesn't even have to stop and think about it.

I refuse to be jealous of Bits and mad at my mom.

This theater thing is my problem. I just need to figure out what I want to do and do it.

mom's opening night

A Streetcar Named Desire turns out to be one of the best shows we've ever done. Ever. Even better than *Private Lives*. There, I said it. I have to admit I've gained a certain amount of appreciation for Tennessee Williams in this one. Any man who could write the character of Blanche Dubois had to have something going for him. But I still think he was sad and sick. And definitely a Southerner.

My dad, Brad, Bartle, and Bits are all at the opening together. Also Lee and Auntie Ellie (they made it home in time), and of course David and Lydia. Lydia very nicely drove me over to get Grandmama. She is dressed to kill. (Like for church, without the hat.)

Of course Edward is here. He directed the show. But he doesn't sit with us when he's the director. He paces in the back. As my dad always says, "Darling, that is soooooo pretentious!"

This is the first show of the fall season, so there is a big reception afterward with catered food and music. This is not a wild and crazy theater party like we usually have. It's primarily for the benefit of donors and the board of directors.

David and I helped set it up this afternoon. We prepped the kitchen for the caterers while Bits and Lydia got the lobby ready.

The critics for the local papers all came to final dress rehearsal last night so they could have reviews in today's paper, but they are back again tonight—more than likely because we serve incredible food and drink at our openings.

Brad pushes my dad to dance with my mom like they always do. That's really nice of him.

My dad comes over to me afterward, and I nearly faint, thinking he's going to ask me to dance. But he doesn't. Thank goodness! I think he's finally given up and I am grateful in the extreme about that. There were so many years when he forced the issue. I'm sure he thought that year would be the year I would gain control of my legs and feet and hands and arms and head and . . . but no. Too embarrassing for words.

This time he's just coming to talk.

About Tennessee Williams, of course. The man died a long time ago, but not at our house.

"Well, darrrrling," he drawls. "Gauging by your enthusiasm, I'm assuming you've changed your mind about our boy Tennessee."

Something about opening nights makes my dad talk like he's a cross between a Shakespearean actor—which he is, of course—and Auntie Mame, the character in the well-known musical of the same name.

He cracks me up.

"And what makes you think I've changed my mind?" I smile, withholding my real opinion long enough to play him a little.

"Oh, I think you know the answer. But I want to hear you admit it."

He reaches for a water cracker and smears a huge dollop of Russian caviar on it, sour cream, red onions. Then instead of popping it in his mouth the way I'm assuming he will, he hands it to me.

David and I have already eaten our share of the caviar out in the kitchen helping the caterers, but I'm hungry again.

He's singing along with the music as he fixes himself the same thing.

"I'm not Tennessee Williams's slave," I say, double meaning and historical allusion intended. "Not the way you and Mom are."

He starts to protest. Use the *slave* word and he will always protest.

"But," I continue, "I am beginning to understand why he won the Pulitzer for this play. Anyone who can create a role like Blanche for Mom to do what she did tonight . . . well, okay . . . I give him credit for that."

"Una was incredible," my dad says, his eyes filling up with tears.

"Yeah," I say, blinking hard. "Yeah, she was."

We're still hashing over whether *Streetcar* is a better show than *Cat On A Hot Tin Roof* (I think it is; he doesn't; they both won the Pulitzer), when Bits pulls me out on the floor to dance with her and David and Bartle. It's a fast song, so I manage that without knocking anyone into the caviar. And it turns out we serve a greater purpose—keeping our retro disco divas, Bartle and Tim, who has raced to the theater after his own rehearsal, from shocking the oldest (very, very white, very, very heterosexual) members of the board of directors.

I am happy to report that as God-fearing and church-abiding as Grandmama is, nothing shocks her. Oh, would you look at that. She's over in the corner dancing with Edward! Get down, Grandmama!

David grabs my hand and pulls me up close to him. "Want to dance?"

"Are you out of your mind?" I pull away so fast I almost fall over. "This is a slow dance. Go dance with Bits."

He glares at me a second and then goes to find her. They make a cute couple on the dance floor. He's so tall and she's so short.

"You're a better actor than Mark," I hear Grandmama say as I walk past her talking to Mom. "You always have been."

My mother suddenly looks like she's six feet tall.

There's a lot of champagne flowing through the room. Even David has a glass or two, I notice, and his parents don't say anything. He gives me a sip, but I don't really like champagne any better than I like beer.

Mom starts to get a little maudlin so Auntie Ellie and I haul her home before she has a chance to embarrass herself in front of the reviewers, the donors, and the B of D. Too much of the bubbly and not enough food is my guess. After we dump her into bed, we all stay up and talk for a long time.

David is a sweetie and drives Grandmama home so she doesn't have to take the bus. Then he comes over and we end up making a midnight breakfast for everyone.

Bits and Lee are curled up in the big overstuffed chair, catching up on their week. Even Dad and Brad forego the after party at the Unicorn and settle in.

David follows me into the pantry and tries to kiss me, but I smack him with the baguette I'm holding, and we crack up laughing and the moment passes.

He needs to get a grip. I need to get a grip. We need to get a grip.

Overall, it's a nice opening night. Too bad Mom's missing most of it.

punishment or bonding
with mom

Another text from Loretta comes in on Saturday morning (8:04 a.m.—geez):

```
Tell Una I read the reviews and am proud of her
even if acting is sinful. But tell her there are
only 81 days left so she needs to WAKE UP now.
Love, L
```

I contemplate the pros and cons of sharing this with Mom and opt (once more) for secrecy. This is becoming habitual. But then, of course it is. I learned from the best.

Over the weekend there are many whispered meetings between Mom and Lydia, which I'm very curious about. Something tells me they were talking about me.

The whispering gets on my nerves, so I shut myself in the

bedroom and start in on the new list of directing books. I've also been rereading *The Empty Space* (that's the Peter Brooks one) because the first reading about took the top of my head off. And I went ahead and ordered every book he's written using some of my Amazon gift cards.

By Monday morning I've made it through three more books, two of them written by (gasp!) women.

"I've got an interview tonight." Bartle slides two pieces of bread out of the bag and pops them in the toaster. Then he adds two more.

"You making ME toast?" Mom's voice shrivels with sarcasm. Bartle's a bottomless pit.

He rolls his eyes at me and grabs the peanut butter AND margarine.

"What for?" I ask. "And why?"

Bartle's working in the costume shop. Of course it's only half-time.

"I'm hungry?"

"No, you dope—the interview. What's it for?"

"Costuming the next show at . . ." he slathers margarine on all four pieces of toast, dragging out the moment as far as he can. "Mixed Blood!"

"That is SICK!" I shout, grabbing one of his pieces of toast. Mixed Blood is one of my favorite theaters in town—after ours of course.

"That is not sick," Mom says. "It's great."

"That's what sick means, Mom."

"Oh."

"Yeahhhhh," Bartle fairly sings. "It is SICK. It is RAW. It is . . ."

"Da bomb," Mom says, trying to keep up.

We both howl.

"Anyway," she says, trying to talk over our raucous laughter. "Oh . . . I don't know if I told you, but Jessie and I are going to Lydia's salon tonight."

"I'm going?" Not only did she not tell Bartle, she (of course) didn't tell me.

"Jessie's going?" Bartle asks, with a smirk at me. He's adding peanut butter to the toast. Crumbs fly everywhere.

Lettuce and Elbows come to assist with the cleanup. Since there are no green veggie things to eat, Lettuce supervises with a superior tilt to his ancient head.

Mesmerized, we watch as Bartle layers his creation with slabs of bologna and puts the whole mess together in a triple-stacked sandwich.

I try never to admit this to Bartle, but he's actually a good-enough looking guy, except for his HUGE mouth. It's a kind of gay male, Steven Tyler mouth with a touch of Mick Jagger thrown in. I'm sure there's some black performer I can include in the description, but right this minute I can't think of one with a mouth that big.

He can even talk when he's taken a huge bite and is chewing it. It's gross, but he can do it. Like right now.

"Remember when Lydia held those psychotherapy sessions and talked you into going?" Bartle's talking and spitting.

"Oh, my god!" Mom shrieks. "I'd forgotten about those!"

"Remember how Mark and I dressed up in drag and came to the third session and rescued you?"

Mom howls even harder. "That probably should have alerted me, huh?"

"Nahhhh," Bartle says, taking another big bite. "That was . . . fun!"

"Hello," I say, waving. No one pays any attention. "Mom! I do NOT want to go to Lydia's salon."

"It will be good for you," Mom says, finally settling on her usual breakfast of cottage cheese and lettuce (most of which she's now feeding to the Cat of the Same Name).

"In what possible way can this be good for me???" The thought of sitting around with a bunch of middle-aged women discussing . . . discussing what? Not the books they've read. Mom would be in trouble then. Except for plays, she doesn't read.

"Am I being punished for something?" I ask, my mouth opening and spewing forth those words before I stop to think.

"Nooooo . . ." she says, her word saying one thing, her voice another.

What you probably should know about punishment in this household is this. They don't. They don't yell. They don't hit. They don't even ground me. They stitch us together (figuratively) and drag me places with them (literally). Or that was what they did before.

"Is there any coffee?"

We all jump at once. Auntie Ellie's head is barely visible sticking out of the door to her room.

"Good lord!" Mom shouts. "I didn't know you were still here."

"What time is it?"

Mom tells her.

"Shit. I didn't hear the alarm. Forget the coffee. Close your eyes so I can make a run for the shower."

We do. She does.

"I'm making her a bathrobe for Christmas," Mom mutters, who apparently didn't close her eyes.

"I don't know why you'd want to," Bartle says.

I can almost hear his demented brain drumming up some soul mate/lesbian joke guaranteed to make Mom howl.

She doesn't bite this time, though.

Auntie Ellie isn't a lesbian. Neither is Mom. Not that I'd mind if she was. They're soul mates, though—a story I've heard oh, so many times.

Mom and Bartle both turn to me. Have they asked me a question and I didn't hear it?

No such luck.

"Think of it as a substitute for the acting class you keep ditching," Mom says, and I can tell by the tone of her voice there's no point in arguing.

No point at all.

to salon or not to salon

"I want to welcome Una Lewis to the group." Lydia is clearly in her element here, which is kind of nice to see. "Una is a wonderful actress. She's been with the JUMBLE Players since the beginning. In fact, if you haven't seen *Streetcar*, you really don't want to miss it. She developed our excellent costume shop, unusual in a theater of this size. And we've been neighbors and friends . . . for years."

The women all smile at Mom and say hello, and she smiles back and says hello.

"This is Una's daughter, Jessie." Lydia gestures toward me. "She's going to be sitting in on our meetings for a while."

A while? Now I'm really curious about those whispered meetings between her and Mom. I've settled in (as directed by my mother) to the book corner that Lydia loves to call the LIBRARY. It's actually the dining room in this condo, but since it's so small and the kitchen's so big Lydia has transformed it into a place with floor-to-ceiling shelves to store their thousands of books. Still, I envy Lydia this library. She and Edward and David are all readers. In my family, I'm kind of on my own there.

Not only am I wondering why Mom's dragging me here, but why in the world is she here? But then I remember that Lydia's unofficial middle name is STEAM ROLLER.

And, where Lydia is concerned, Mom's middle name is FLOOR MAT.

"There are a few ground rules we all accept," Lydia continues. There is no doubt in my mind who made up these rules.

I've been so intent on getting to (and into) my seat without, you know, falling over someone, I haven't really looked at the group. It's small, only six women, including Mom and Lydia.

The first thing I notice is that both Anne (the redhead) and Emo Bev from this summer's writing workshop are here. I know from the workshop they both go to the university. That must be their connection with Lydia and probably how they heard about the writing workshop, too. Anne ignores me, but Bev wiggles her fingers at me. I wave back.

Lydia continues, "Pamela, would you share those rules with Una . . . and Jessie?"

Pamela is fifty-something with frizzy gray hair and no makeup. "We discuss two or three selected topics each week," she says in a deep, resonant voice. "We are mostly interested in taking a global perspective on issues. So NO personal stories or advice given to each other during our discussions."

"Thanks, Pamela," Lydia says. "Any questions?"

Why am I here? comes to mind, but I wisely keep my mouth shut.

Mom's nodding her head to indicate she is with the program, although my guess is she has no idea what the rules are either because the truth is, she has trouble listening to rules. And then that makes it a little hard to follow them. Dad calls her his Little Anarchist. It's her favorite nickname.

Lydia consults her calendar and says, "This is a social issue discussion, and Renee gets to name the first topic. Renee?"

I hadn't noticed Renee. She's tiny like my mom, and she speaks so quietly I have to lean forward until I'm nearly falling out of my chair just to hear what she's saying. Probably why I almost miss that David is waving at me from the kitchen doorway.

He's wearing an apron, which nearly sends me into apoplexy. He looks really cute in it.

I also miss the beginning of the issue, but I get the gist. What I hear is: ". . . parents' role in supporting their children's nontraditional choices."

Or in my case, it could be, children's role in supporting her parents' nontraditional choices. I'm just saying.

Pamela starts in on how we need to move beyond the definitions of traditional and nontraditional.

David is standing in the doorway where only I can see him because of the Japanese screen Lydia has blocking the big arched opening between the living room and the library, so you can't see into the kitchen from the living room. David's stirring a big bowl of something and grinning at me.

Anne talks about the tendency children have to make choices in opposition to their parents and the different ways parents can deal with this. She cites several studies done at the University of Minnesota. Of course she does. Boring.

Now David's scooping up a finger full of some kind of batter and licking it off his finger. Gross. Well, it's kind of sexy and gross at the same time. More gross than sexy.

Bev goes next. She talks about how rebellion is a critical stage in the development of young adults and should be encouraged and honored by parents and teachers.

I crack up and then I have to hide my laughter in a huge cough. Everyone looks at me. Mom turns beet red. Sorry. But I mean really—all that black clothing, hair, fingernails, makeup. And then the things she wrote in the workshop!

She winks at me when she's finished. And that cracks me up even more.

Lydia feels it's necessary to list and define all the possible types of nontraditional choices *young people* are inclined to make. I take this opportunity to grab a glass of water from the kitchen. Evidently I was in there for a while because I missed Renee entirely.

And then it's Mom's turn. David has retreated into the bowels of the kitchen, and heavenly baking smells are issuing forth. His pastries are enough to make you fall in love with him.

Or they would be if he weren't, you know, like my brother.

I redirect my attention to my wacky mother. She starts to tell the story about Bartle, and how once he got into adolescence he could no longer conceal that he was gay.

"Even when he was sixteen, which wasn't that long ago, it was still very much frowned upon in the African-American community," she says, leading into the main point of the story, which, of course, I've heard countless times. "And his mother, my sister-in-law Mary, could not handle it. So she kicked him out of the house, and he came to live with us . . ."

Suddenly there's this embarrassed, almost stricken look on everyone's faces. Lydia holds up her hand and Mom stops right where she is, mid-sentence.

"I'm sorry, Una. The rule Pamela mentioned. No personal stories."

I can't believe Lydia's stopping her. She knows this story. She knows how relevant it is to the topic.

And I can't believe Mom stops.

Pamela gets to name the next issue. The pros and cons of legalizing gay marriage.

I have to admit my curiosity is up immediately. Is Pamela gay? Is she in a serious relationship? Does her partner want to get married?

Then I wonder why anyone would want to be married when over 50 percent of marriages end in divorce. (Sue me, I looked it up.) Or people make up strange rituals in order to stay married. For what?

Like Lydia and how she and Edward supposedly have an open marriage—modeled, Mom says, after the open marriages popular in the 1970s. I mean, as far as everyone we know is concerned it is her way of saving face for the fact that Edward has slept with every woman he's ever met if she's within a ten-year range of his age and the slightest bit attractive or, you know, if she accidentally bends over.

Lydia is an extremely intelligent, strong woman. She is at the university pursuing a PhD, for crying out loud. I mean, what is with that?

"Your turn, Una," Lydia says, sounding a little irritated.

"What?" Mom says. "Oh . . ."

Evidently she isn't paying attention, either.

"Marriage . . ." Mom's face blushes the deepest red. "What constitutes marriage? I'm still married . . . but my husband and his partner are living in the attic . . ."

"PERSONAL!" Pamela booms.

"I'm sorry," Mom mutters. I notice she makes no attempt to explain the situation or the relevance. Maybe she thinks that's obvious.

Lydia serves herbal tea after that and the cookies David just made. I sneak out to the kitchen and get more than a couple cookies. Ha!

Then of course I have a crisis of confidence and slink back into the dining room wondering what in the world I'm doing with this, you know, kissing David thing. I mean, experimentation aside, David is the boy next door who is more like a detested twin brother I'm suddenly messing around with. Oh, ick! This has got to stop!

I don't even like it all that much.

So, after the tea break, what happens?

Lydia says, "Una—you've got to leave that egotistical moron."

Is she talking about my dad?

Everyone turns to look at Mom. And no one screams, "Personal!" or shouts out, "The rules, the rules!" No, put a little tea and a few cookies in these ladies and it's a whole new ball game. They sit there nodding as Lydia says, "It can't be good for either you or Jessie to live in that mixed-up household. And how in the world can you continue to supervise Brad when he's shacking up with your husband?"

Okay, so Mom does the unforgivable.

She stands up in a fit of pique. I stand up, thinking we're leaving.

First she tells Anne she'd look a lot nicer if she wore eye makeup. (Great minds. I thought the same thing the minute I saw her.)

I sit back down.

She tells Pamela she needs to get off the stick and color her hair if she doesn't want to look like a seventy-something grandmother twenty years before her time. (Ditto my idea.)

And then she spins on Lydia, and says, "And if you don't already know, you ought to—I've slept with Edward at least a dozen times."

WTF?!!!

Mom keeps right on. "No, I'm not crazy about having Mark and Brad loving and fighting and making up on the third floor of the house I bought with my inheritance. But screwing Edward DOES take the edge off it!"

And then she runs out the door, slamming it hard, and our back door harder.

I am standing there with my mouth wide open. My mom has been sleeping with Edward? Ewwwwwww.

"Well, you know, the personal is political . . ." I blurt, quoting something on Lydia's reading list.

Lydia's mouth is now open down to her knees.

Or is it, the political is personal?

All Mom says to me when I catch up with her is, "Why in the world did I do that?"

To answer her question, my dad would say she really IS an actress at heart and can't resist the scene. I think he'd only be about a quarter right in this instance.

"You slept with Edward?" I ask. I have to. "A DOZEN TIMES?"

Mom's face turns a deeper shade of pink. "Well, no. More like half a dozen."

How in the world is she ever going to face Lydia again? How am I?

Maybe Mom can convince Lydia she was doing an improv.

And where is Bits? I cannot wait to tell her about this!

more like the eskimos

It's been almost a week since the infamous salon, and as far as I know except for some very tight-lipped civilities in the hallways between classes, Mom and Lydia are barely speaking.

I told David about Mom and Edward last night. Well, to put it more clearly, I assumed he'd heard the commotion but he must have had his head in the oven or something because he missed it. So then I figured I'd better clue him in before someone else did. But he said he already knew. I wonder who told him. He says evidently everyone at the theater knew except Lydia. I've noticed that's generally the case with these kinds of indiscretions.

Something to think about. The other thing I noticed is that once again I didn't know. Sigh. My only comfort is that neither did Bits.

Anyway, today after lunch, Lydia shows up at the back door with a sack of zucchini (Mom's been avoiding the communal garden) and they sit down for coffee. It's very late to be harvesting anything, but it's been a warm autumn so far. And dry.

Auntie Ellie and the band are scheduled to practice in the basement, but they haven't come home yet. Bits and I are hanging out watching some stupid TV show.

When we see who's here, we sneak down the back stairs and crouch on the third stair from the bottom and eavesdrop on the entire conversation.

THE SCENE:

Una hesitates at the kitchen doorway, then opens it. Lydia enters, carrying a sack of zucchini. She holds them out to Una.

UNA: Lydia. Come in. Good to see you. Zucchini? How thoughtful . . . oh, of course, they're OUR zucchini. Would you like . . . can I offer you . . . let me just put these in the fridge . . . coffee?

(*I'm picturing the passing of the phallic zucchini from Lydia's hands to Mom's waiting arms. It's a kind of archaic, archetypal, female, Goddess ritual thing when you've discovered your husband is banging one of your closest friends. Side note: the zucchini are HUGE.*)

LYDIA: Sure, thanks.

(*An uncomfortable silence ensues.*)

LYDIA: Una . . .

UNA: Lydia . . .

(*Simultaneous speech—pause—LAUGHTER*)

UNA: I'm sorry about the other night.

LYDIA: (*Holding up her hand the way she does, I'm sure, and I hear her sigh.*) Una, I'm sorry you've been having sex with

237

Edward, but I don't feel it's in any way a violation of our long friendship. Who hasn't had sex with Edward? I mean, thank goodness he hasn't started in on the teenagers . . .

NOTE: Bits and I both gasp at that one, but fortunately my mom gasped so loud that must have been all Lydia could hear.

UNA: Oh, he'd never . . . would he?

LYDIA: No, he'd never. And you can take care of yourself, can't you?

UNA: I'm not in love with him . . .

LYDIA: I didn't think you were . . . to tell the truth, I'm not sure I'm in love with him anymore. But I don't want to leave him, so I guess I'm relieved to hear you say that.

(*There's a long silence. They can be heard sipping coffee. Una sighs. Lydia sighs. More sipping.*)

NOTE: I've got a leg cramp and am frantic, wanting to move, but not until someone starts talking. Bits is poking me and poking me but I can't look at her or I'll start laughing. Good lord! How long can they sit there? Sighing. Sipping.

LYDIA: Edward says he's in love with you.

UNA: What? Oh, no . . . he's not . . . that's not . . . ohhhh, did you have to talk with him about this?

LYDIA: It's all right. It's a good thing, I think. He says that being with you cracked something open in his chest.

UNA: He said that?

LYDIA: (*nodding*) He said it's not a triangle, country-Western thing. He says . . .

UNA: Yes?

238

LYDIA: It sounds dumb. He says he loves ME more because of it.

UNA: Oh . . . (*anyone can hear the disappointment in her voice, but Lydia doesn't seem to notice*)

LYDIA: Maybe we should all be more like the Eskimos . . .

UNA: Oh, Lydia!

(*Creak of chairs. Soft laughter. Hugging sounds. Someone's crying a little. Lydia. LYDIA. PhD Woman Who Never Weeps*)

I am suddenly ashamed of myself and grabbing Bits by the arm, sneak as silently as possible up the stairs to our room.

This is different from the salon scene where I couldn't wait to talk with Bits about it. This one I have to sift through for a while. Bits can be kind of thick about things like this, but when I offer to run her lines (nonstop until she has to leave for the theater) she forgets all about it.

Mom's in her sewing room, hand stitching a ball gown hem. She does most of the hand sewing on Bartle's gowns. She says she finds it relaxing.

She doesn't look exactly thrilled to see me—an expression I'm coming to know pretty well—but I have questions that won't wait.

"Are you in love with Edward?" There. I dump it right out.

"You heard us?"

"Uh-huh." I don't tell her we were crouched in the stairwell.

"No," she says, after she's thought about it for a while. "No, I'm not."

"Then why did you . . . um . . . sleep with . . . have sex with . . . him?"

239

She lets her sewing fall to her lap and looks at me as though she's really seeing me for the first time in a long time. (A long, long, long time.)

"I've only ever been with your father," she says finally. "He was my first . . . well, everything. First love. First sex. Seventeen years is a long time. Ever since Mark told me he was gay I've been doubting myself. But it's been even worse since he and Brad have been openly together."

I nod. I can imagine. Though she doesn't show it most of the time.

"I kept wondering what it would be like to be with someone who really loves women," she says with a tiny dry laugh.

"And there was Edward," I jump in to cover the moment. "A good friend in an open marriage who may possibly hold the record for loving women . . ."

At that moment I wish I had a camera. I'd love to have a picture of my mother's open mouth.

"Mom—come on! Who doesn't know about Edward's proclivity?"

She laughs, picks her sewing back up. "You'd think by now I'd be used to your brain power . . ."

"Besides," I add. "You're the one who dragged me to that god-awful salon!"

The dryer blares in the basement. Ellie and Lee took the band over to the theater to use the proscenium stage, so I'm doing laundry. I run down and grab the clothes and bring them back to the sewing room to fold them.

Mom doesn't seem to mind talking about it. And I'm not quite done with my interrogation.

"So, what was it like?"

"What?"

"Sex with Edward . . ."

Her face turns Valentine pink and she starts to stutter.

I can't really blame her. We've hardly spoken for four months or more and suddenly I'm interrogating her about sex.

"Oh, for . . . I don't want the details . . . summary, please. An overview . . ."

She looks at me so strangely it almost makes me laugh. It would make me laugh if I weren't still so angry at her. I studiously fold clothes while she thinks about answering me.

"I loved making love with your father," she says slowly, "because of how much I love him."

Okay, I counted the word LOVE three times in that one sentence. I get it. She loves the guy.

"But . . . he doesn't . . . he's not attracted to women . . . at all."

I nod. This seems obvious given his sexual orientation, but they were married a long danged time, and here I am as evidence of at least ONE incident of copulation, soooooo . . . ?

"Well, he doesn't appreciate the female body much . . ."

Sudden illumination. I am getting from David's recent attentions that a guy who loves the female body is a good thing. I don't say this to my mom, though. I'm not self-destructive.

"And then, your dad and I stopped having sexual relations quite a while ago . . ."

"I wondered about that."

"Jessie!"

"Well, geez, Mom. I'm sixteen!"

She sighs. "Two, no three years. Long time."

"Yeah."

"The abbreviated, appropriate-for-your-sixteen-year-old-daughter version: Edward really loves the female body."

My nodding must encourage her, as she continues.

"I had no idea sex could be so much fun," she says. "Or that someone could appreciate parts of me I've pretty much always ignored. And that's ALL I'm going to say!"

Now we are both blushing. Hers I can see. Mine I can feel.

What a weird conversation!

"So"—I try to get back to normal, whatever that is. "So, you don't love Edward?"

"No," she says. "I mean, yeah, like a friend . . . We've known each other for so long. But no, not the kind of love you mean . . ."

"Like how I feel about David," I say, without stopping to think.

"You're in love with David?"

"No! The other . . ."

"You're having SEX with David?"

"Good lord, no!" I have to laugh at the look on her face. "No. He's kissed me a few times, though. Since my birthday party."

"He has?" Mom asks.

"Yeah," I say. She sounds kind of excited about this. Not what I expected.

"Well, did you like it?"

"Sure," I say, wondering if that's entirely true. "It's kind of nice . . ."

"Does Lydia know?" Now Mom's really into it.

"No . . . we're not . . . that's not what I meant. I meant that I don't want him as a boyfriend because I don't feel that way about him."

"Oh . . ."

"I love him, though. Like a friend or a brother maybe . . ."

Mom looks at me for a second like she wants to say something, you know, parentally important. "Be really careful then, Jessie."

"Yeah, I will," I say, pretty sure she didn't say what she was thinking. "I am. Careful, I mean. I don't know why he's been doing this . . . it's pretty much over, though, I'm sure. We've been doing more cooking and baking."

Mom's face is a study. That was too big a leap for her evidently.

"Mom, it's not a metaphor. We've been cooking and baking together a lot lately. Less kissing."

"Oh," she says, with a big whoosh of air. "Whew. I got nervous for a second there."

The dryer blares for the last load.

"Jess," Mom says, stopping me at the doorway. "You know, it was good for me to have sex with Edward—or with someone like him . . . Someone not married to one of my best friends would have been better. But I learned something. I need to love someone in order to be really intimate with him."

See, this is exactly what bothers me about the concept of open marriages.

"I don't know if I'll ever love someone other than your dad again. But I'm through having sex with Edward."

The dryer alarm sounds again so I go down to finish the laundry and that's the end of the BIG CONVERSATION with Mom.

It was good talking with her, though. Really good.

Talking with her about this makes me wonder if she will ever fall in love with someone like my dad fell in love with Brad. It makes me feel weird to even think about this, but I guess I hope she does. It doesn't seem fair or right for her to have gone so many years loving someone who doesn't appreciate her as a woman. And if she's right about how having sex without love isn't all that great, then I guess she'd better fall in love.

Love in all capital letters: L-O-V-E love. I wonder what that feels like.

I wonder if it will ever happen to me.

and one may in his time play many parts

Tonight I'm with my dad at his rehearsal. They've been rehearsing *Tartuffe* for about a month, and this is the first time I've gone. I figured if I'm going to see any of the process, I'd better start showing up. The show opens Friday after next. And it's a really complicated production. My dad's playing the lead, and I think he's going to be amazing. On the way over he said he hasn't done this kind of role since right out of college.

I love Moliere the way my dad loves Shakespeare. It amazes me that this French playwright wrote this kind of raucous, crazy comedy in the late 1600s. More than 350 years ago. *Tartuffe* isn't my favorite of his scripts. Not at all. But I find the religious fervor subject matter very interesting, especially given this whole end-of-the-world thing going on with all these different groups.

Which reminds me, I found a calendar Mom's keeping where every few days she jots down (in purple ink no less) how many days are left before December 21. Okay, it freaked me out. I should talk with her about it, but I don't really want to bring up the subject.

I did mention it to Grandmama last time she called.

She said the same thing she said to Loretta that day all hell broke loose.

"God is bigger than that."

It made me feel better again.

Anyway, this production is very stylized and wacky in a French farce kind of way (a lot like our house) and my dad is playing *Tartuffe* in an OVER-THE-TOP way. (Hey, also a lot like our house.) If it's ever been done before, I haven't found the reviews. And I love it!

The director, Ted, isn't on the JUMBLE artistic staff. He's someone who jobs in with us. I like his style better than Edward's. He uses a lot more improvisation in his whole rehearsal process. In fact, he starts with improv and lets the structural blocking evolve instead of imposing it. And then he does a lot of improv to develop characters and relationships. I'm sure that's how my dad got to doing this swishy interpretation of his character. He's too classically trained to go there on his own.

"Your dad is such a different kind of actor than Una, isn't he?" Bits's stage whisper in my ear makes me jump out of my seat.

Since I came to rehearsal in part to get away from her and my mom running their lines together in the kitchen (again), I'm not exactly thrilled.

"What is it?" she whispers. "I mean, Una disappears into her characters, doesn't she?"

"Yeah, she does." It's uncanny really. After a show, once Mom's out of costume and makeup, she can walk right through the theater-going crowd and if they don't know her, they don't recognize her.

"So, what is it with your dad?" she continues. "He's wonderful. But it's something else entirely . . ."

"Charisma?" David's voice comes out of nowhere.

"What are you doing here?"

He lowers his voice to a suitable whisper. "Want to go with me to the bookstore?"

"Can't, I'm waiting for my dad . . ."

David climbs over the seat and sits down next to me.

"What does that mean?" Bits asks.

"What? I'm waiting for my dad . . ."

"No . . ." She giggles. "Charisma. What does it mean?"

Bits, though my blood relation and indisputably my BFF—even with this current ongoing incessant drip-drip-dripping irritation—does not share my love of words. Example: I gave her the most amazing dictionary for Christmas once but she used it as a doorstop. To give her some credit, all the doors in the apartment where she used to live with her mother swung shut on their own. Still.

"Well, what I mean by *charismatic*," David answers, "is that he's always himself only more so."

"And there's some kind of electrical connection that happens between him and the audience," I add.

"Oh, yeah," she says. "Like how people mob him after the show."

"Yeah, like that."

Ted's called a halt to the scene they're working and they've all gone to the green room to get a cup of coffee. So we can talk out loud until they come back.

"What are you doing here? I thought you and Mom had pages and pages to rehearse."

"Edward came over, said he had to talk to Una . . ."

Oh, great!

"About the spring season . . ." she says. "I'm sure he wasn't . . ."

Before she can say anything more, David asks her if she wants to go to the bookstore with him.

They're off like a shot. He'll listen to her complain about all the voice messages she's getting every day from her mom. He'll even listen to her recite the lines from her next acting class scene. He's a sweetie like that. Almost makes me wish I were attracted to him.

Rehearsal is kind of up and down in the interesting department after their break. Lucky for me I brought along a stack of reading Lydia recommended. There's a really interesting article in there by a woman who runs that all-women theater here in the Cities—Theatre Unbound. And then there's another article about this feminist theater back in the 1970s—At the Foot of the Mountain. Comparing them is fascinating. What *feminism* was back then. How the word is still scary even now. What's that about? And then both theaters are/were strongly focused on process and collaboration.

I wonder what that looks like in production. Well, more like Ted's shows than Edward's, that's for sure.

"Well, darrrrrrling, what do you think?"

My dad sneaks up on me and grabs the article right out of my hand.

"It's going to be wonderful," I can honestly say. "And you're great!"

He beams. He is a sucker for praise. If I were less honest, I could use this to my advantage. Fortunately, he's also talented enough I don't have to lie.

"What did you think about the way I'm playing the character?"

"You mean the whole GAY thing?" I like to name things. My dad, for some reason unfathomable to me, still has a hard time saying he's gay.

Earth to Mark . . . earth to Mark . . . it's the twenty-first century. Even if you're black you can go ahead and say you're gay. I mean, your black relatives will probably ignore you and pretend they didn't hear it. But you can still say it.

He nods.

"I love it," I say, and see the relief on his face. Hmm. Subtext, subtext.

"Ted suggested I try it in an improv and everyone liked it so much, we kept it."

"I knew it!" I have to laugh. "I knew that was how it happened!"

He laughs, too. "I know it's funny," he says, hesitating a bit. "But does it work?"

"Oh, yeah, it does. It totally does. It makes the character more . . . human, I guess. More vulnerable. And funnier like you said. It changes Orgon's fascination with him—adds dimension. And it makes the whole situation with the wife have a double meaning. Sweet."

He's nodding. "I hadn't thought about it like that. I can play with that more, can't I?

"Uh-huh," I say.

His eyes go to the reader he's still holding.

"What are you reading?"

I tell him.

"Oh, yeeeessssss," he says, his voice slurring into dismissiveness. "The feminist lesbians . . ."

"Are you familiar with their work?" I ask, kind of surprised by his tone. I think he's talking about the 1970s group, but apparently not.

"Lydia brought them here a few years ago . . . I guess in their first or second year of operation." He shrugs. "You were too young to remember them?"

"Yeah, but I've been to see some of their shows," I say. "Mom and I went with Lydia and Bits to see the all-women production of *Julius Caesar.*"

"Not my cup of tea, dahhhhhling . . ."

He hands the reader back to me, a question in his whole posture.

I'd venture a guess that he's asking me, "Is it YOUR cup of tea, dahhhhling . . . ?"

"I don't know," I say, and he laughs that I've read his body language so well. "I don't know."

pleasing the masses

So, for my first directing assignment, I am in the studio theater observing a student group rehearsal of a scene from one of the stupidest plays in the history of the stupid so-called modern theater. That play is *Barefoot In The Park* by Neil Simon. Why is it stupid, you ask? Have you seen it? Then I don't need to answer that question, do I?

For some inexplicable reason my dad loves Neil Simon. My mom has better taste. My father says that Simon is the Shakespeare of the twentieth century. This makes my mother so mad her skin blotches.

My father's argument is that in his own day Shakespeare was a popular playwright who wrote to please the masses. I read up on it. He's right.

And, he says, that's what Neil Simon did and still does for that matter.

Mom says, "He's like the damned Energizer bunny . . . he goes on and on and on . . ."

Is she talking about Neil Simon or about my dad?

Since there's no directing class to do this, Lydia agreed to provide some direction to the Advanced Acting class in their scene work. This helps Mom out and takes the place of what they would have been doing with the directing students.

Mom's replaced me in the class with the first girl on the waiting list, so I know I'm off the hook for the time being with that class.

To give Lydia and Mom some credit where this particular project is concerned, neither of them picked the play. But Mom made the mistake of letting the students pick their own.

In this group, all the girls want to play the female lead and there's only one guy in the group, so Lydia is having them tag-team it. An interesting approach. There are four girls, which means I've been watching the climax recycle nonstop for an hour.

Lydia sneaks up behind me and makes me jump a mile. Why do teachers do that? She leans in and asks me to see if I can help the group that's rehearsing out in the hallway. They are having some problems with their scene.

I shoot her a LOOK but don't say anything.

All right then.

Jessie Jumble Pretends To Know Something About Acting & Directing . . .

That was a much more interesting play. The problem was a no-brainer. First I had them key their lines to movement. And then since the main character is talking nonstop through the whole scene, they had to fade in and fade out with the overlapping dialogue.

Still, I couldn't believe how they all thanked and thanked me and said I'd saved the day.

When I come back in, I sit facing Lydia so she can't sneak up on me again. Geez.

"Thanks for taking care of that," she says, sliding into the seat beside me.

I nod.

"Seriously, Jess, that was excellent."

"Thanks?"

"I don't think you realize how much you know about the theater simply from living in it all these years."

Is she serious? I don't say anything.

"The other kids think you know everything they don't. You realize that, don't you?" She places her hand on my arm. "You know, Jessie, you're going to find yourself one of these days."

"I didn't know I was lost," I quip, unable to stop myself.

Lydia ignores the attitude. "I mean it, Jess. If you're ever able to get past all the acting and singing and dancing . . . let's call it performance testosterone . . . in your family, you can easily pursue directing or even playwriting. You've got the eye and ear for it."

My mouth is all ready for another snappy, snippy comeback, but I control it. "Thanks, Lydia."

Lydia nods and then goes back to her original seat. The students have finished their tag-team scene and bombard her with questions.

I sit there, watching how patient she is with them. I don't think I could do that. But what I do wonder is if I can do what she's said I can.

One good thing is happening because Lydia had to cancel her Directing class. She's invited Professor Enomoto . . . James . . . to do an eight-week playwriting workshop. She says he'll be e-mailing all of us. And to watch the green room board.

I wonder if Emily will show up for this session.

is THIS the end of the world?

My parents sit me down and tell me that I am taking Advanced Stage Movement whether I like it or not. They do this together— and thankfully without Brad or Bartle or Bits present. My guess is everybody knew what was going down and cleared out.

Do I argue with them? Not much.

I mean, when I tell them how ridiculously clumsy I am, they both look at me like I'm nuts. And then they look at each other in a way that I don't get. And then they ignore what I said.

It's kind of hard to fight that.

"Dell is graciously letting you into her class a month into the semester," Mom says.

I don't say, "Of course she is. You run the theater. She can't very well say no." What's the point?

"She's really hard," Bits says when she gets back and I tell her that I will be joining her at her next class.

Thanks a lot. Exactly what I want to hear.

"But she's really, really good," Bits adds, realizing what she's said.

This doesn't make me feel any better. *Good* and *hard* are practically synonymous when it comes to movement teachers.

So, today is my first Advanced Stage Movement class. Please, God, if you're planning on ending the world, now would be a really good time.

Now.

Right now.

"Ms. Jasper Lewis, are you going to join the class or stand there with the door half open the entire period?"

Busted.

Ten minutes into doing improvisational rushes across the studio theater—that's where one person leads with a movement pattern and everyone else follows, and then the teacher calls out the next person to lead and they repeat this back across the studio floor, and on and on until all fifteen students have lead or everyone's lying dead of exhaustion on the floor—ten minutes in, Ms. Patterson calls a halt.

"Ms. Jasper Lewis, could I have a word with you?"

Bits shoots me a look of utter sympathy. Not empathy (the actor's greatest skill), but flat out sympathy.

Out in the hallway, Ms. Patterson gets right to the point. "Ms. Jasper Lewis, have you taken Basic Stage Movement?"

I nod. Feel the need to add, "Five . . . no, six times."

"Ohhhh!"

I am looking straight at Ms. Patterson. I can't remember the last time I had a female teacher who was as tall as I am. It's kind of unnerving to be looking her right in the eyes. I'm used to towering over.

"How about Beginning Ballet?"

"Too many times to count."

We avoid looking at each other for a beat or two.

"Beginning Jazz?"

"Ditto."

"Hmmmm . . ." Her face is turning a kind of mottled red and white. Which clashes with her hair. Interesting.

"Modern?"

"You don't want to know . . ."

"There's no need to be sarcastic . . ."

"Oh, no—I really mean that."

"Hmm . . ."

There is a long pause while neither of us say anything. I'm not used to theater people being able to stop talking this long. I start counting under my breath. I get all the way to forty-two.

"You are in Advanced Stage Movement simply because your parents are Mark and Una Jasper Lewis?"

Wow, talk about direct. Words fail me. I nod. Tears well up in my eyes, but I try the blinking and breathing trick. Go, acting!

She's waiting for me to say something.

I can't think of a thing to add to what she said.

"I've been told you graduated from high school two years early."

I nod. Though what this has to do with Advanced Stage Movement I have no idea.

"Ms. Jasper Lewis, do you have aspirations to be an actor or . . . a . . ."—she almost chokes on the word—"*dancer*?"

"No!" It comes out as a shout. Then I whisper, "No. No, my parents want me to take the class. They think it would be good for me to work with a new teacher."

"A new . . ." I didn't think her face could get any redder, but it does. She swallows whatever she was going to say. She's looking at me really funny.

"I . . . I know how bad I am. And I seem to get worse every class I take."

She nods. I'd be willing to bet she's thinking it's not humanly possible for me to get worse working with her.

Out of nowhere she asks, "How do you feel about the theater?"

"I love the theater!" I blurt out, and feel a choking sensation at the back of my throat that I don't think blinking or swallowing is going to help at all.

The look of complete surprise on Ms. Patterson's face makes me want to laugh, but thankfully I'm able to swallow that down, too.

"I'll do the best I can," she finally says. Not at all what I expected. And from the look on her face, not what she thought was going to come out, either. She must really need this job.

We return to the classroom where Ms. Patterson says, quietly and just to me, "Why don't you sit the rest of the class out? I need to think about this."

She points to the stool that's up against the mirrored wall and usually reserved for the teacher. Although I am happy to be—albeit temporarily—released from leaping and lunging and twirling across the floor, there is another feeling burbling up in my interior.

I'd like to take my locally famous parents and bang their heads together until their ears ring. Or better yet, make them sit through an entire semester of Advanced CHEMISTRY.

if you're clumsy, beat the drum

Next class period I show up filled with trepidation, but dressed for action. Leotard, tights, leg warmers, big T-shirt designed to hide the worst of my movement gaffs.

"Class, we're going to do something a little different for the rest of the semester. Since Ms. Jasper Lewis only recently joined our group, I've decided to work with her outside of class for a while. So, during class, she will be here observing, and I may ask her to assist me occasionally."

What? This is news to me. I nearly drop over in a dead faint.

I brace myself for the laughter and titters and looks of disdain from the rest of the class, but everybody stands there looking as though this is the most normal thing in the world. Even Bits.

Ms. Patterson motions for me to go sit on the stool again. So I do. My heart is beating so loud, it seems inconceivable that no one else can hear it. And I am wishing for my regular clothes.

And my new boots. Which are awesome even if Brad did buy them.

Because *Tartuffe* has been in rehearsal and is opening tonight, the class has been working on stylized period movement. All the girls run to pull on these three-quarter-length commedia skirts like the maid, Dorine, wears in the play. There are only three guys in the class, and they are fine as they are evidently. Except everyone puts on dance shoes that emulate the period.

Ms. Patterson plays some music, a tinkling, brittle, comic sound—the same music, I realize, that Ted the director selected for the show, and they all start doing warm-ups to it.

Before I realize what's happening, Ms. Patterson's at my side. Very quietly she says, "They've been rehearsing and today they are being tested on their movement patterns. Just watch, okay?"

I nod. Then she's calling pairs and they are sweeping across the floor, doing different kinds of walking styles, greeting each other without speaking, using movement to tell the story, playing the hero, the villain, the coquette, and ending with a period dance.

I can't take my eyes off Bits. She is so graceful in her blue leotard, like a luminous golden butterfly. And yet when she needs to be comic, she's so funny to watch you want to laugh out loud. God, she's good. The rest of the class pales by comparison. But they're all doing good work.

It occurs to me, watching Bits, that if she were a little older she could have played Dorine in *Tartuffe*. Her skills are already there.

What gives a person that kind of talent and certainty, I wonder, and not for the first time.

Bits would counter, "What makes you able to remember everything you speed read and do impossible math problems in your head?"

But, see, the difference is that those things come naturally to me, and I don't love doing them. Nor am I about to make a career of them.

The exam takes up about three-quarters of the class time. Most of our other teachers would let us go after that. Not Ms. Patterson.

"Good job," she says. "Get out of those skirts and shoes while I make some notations about your grades."

I offer her the stool, but she's got a clipboard and she leans against the wall while she writes.

No one says a word (which if you've ever been in a movement class with a bunch of high school students you know is *phe-nom-e-nal*). They strip off the skirts and take the period shoes off and put them away in a big crate and go stand in the corner. Unreal.

Finally, she puts her clipboard down, hands me a drum, and says, "Give me a beat in three four time."

I'm so shocked, I just start pounding on the little drum.

She listens for a minute, comes over, adjusts the speed by lightly touching my hand as I pound the drum, and then says, "Yes, like that . . ."

And the next thing I know the students are all following her lead as she takes them in three four time exercises across the floor.

I don't have to match the drum to the dancers. They are

moving to the beat I'm setting. Or Ms. Patterson is, and they are following her. It's so fluid, I can't really tell.

It feels like five minutes have passed when she stops, claps her hands, and everyone comes to a halt beside her. I stop, too.

"Good work, everyone," she says. And they all applaud. Wow. Totally unreal. "See you tonight at opening."

raised on theater stories

The entire Jumble family bedecked in magnificent costumes rallies to support my dad in his opening of *Tartuffe*, where he is playing the character of the same name. And he is MAGNIFICENT. I think it's the best thing I've ever seen him do. Mom says so, too.

How ironic is it that both my parents are doing their very best work right now when everything is changing, changing, changing? Or is it? Ironic, I mean. I'll have to think about that.

Another successful opening gets the weekend off to a great start.

On Sunday I don't have anything else to do, so I go over to help David with his baking. He's trying to learn how to make French bread and needed an assistant.

Lydia and Edward are at the theater, so we have the condo to ourselves. My mom would go crazy if she knew this, but there's a matinee performance today, so she's at the theater, too.

David kisses me a couple times while we're laying out all the ingredients and pans and things and flouring the work surface. But his heart's not in it. Or maybe it's his hormones that aren't in it.

Good grief, does he love baking that much?

That would be worse than having a gay guy as your lover. Imagine having to tell your best friend you haven't had sex in months—or years, like Mom—because he prefers baking.

"What?" He's looking at me like he looks at a recipe when he can't figure it out or he thinks something's wrong with it.

"What do you mean, 'What'?"

"What's going on?"

"With what?"

"Never mind." My heart isn't in it and neither are my hormones.

I don't know. I'm confused.

I hate being confused.

"Jessie!" Oops, I've lost count of the number of cups of flour I'm sifting.

We remeasure them, and I force myself to pay attention.

We make five loaves of French bread and play Scrabble while the dough is rising. Two of them turn out great. Good enough to satisfy even David.

He lets me take one of them home, along with two of the "failures" to have with dinner.

Since Mom forced Bartle into making dinner, this is a very good thing. We are having spaghetti so the bread is a perfect addition, especially since Bartle forgot to make a salad.

Naturally, this is the night Mom has invited a guest for dinner. Let me reword that. Mom invited my movement teacher, Ms. Patterson, to dinner. Then she forgot to tell me—or Bartle or Bits or anyone else for that matter. And then she forgot she invited her.

Awkward.

In a moment of prescience on Ms. Patterson's part (or else she has a long memory where Mom is concerned), she's brought a huge vegetable platter for an appetizer, which I immediately grab and incorporate into the dinner in lieu of a salad. Bartle has made an even more enormous batch of spaghetti than usual, so we pull dinner off with a bunch of jokes and the adults polish off two or three bottles of red wine.

It's so much fun to hear them tell stories of their early days together in the theater. I love listening to old theater stories. I was raised on theater stories.

It sounds like they were all really close back when Ms. Patterson still lived here. I wonder why I don't remember her. I guess I was too little.

The minute dinner's over, Brad has to run to the costume shop. I don't know why, since he can't possibly be working on the Christmas show yet and the other two are up and running. Bartle scoots upstairs, saying he has to work on the costumes for the show at Mixed Blood. Really, it's that he wants to avoid having to clean up. This demonstrates how seldom he cooks. He evidently hasn't figured out that when you cook someone else always cleans up.

Mixed Blood Theater actually hired Bartle! Not as the

costumer, but the costumer's assistant. I still think it's incredible given his age. He's doing most of the stitching. Along with the work he does with us, this is a great start for him.

Why is everyone in this family so talented except for me?

Loretta talked Bits into going to church with her. I can't believe she said yes. I thought she'd be back by now, and I really wish she was—she'd corner Ms. Patterson and keep her talking about New York City all night long!

My mom starts the dishes while my dad and Ms. Patterson go out to the living room to put on some music. She mentions that she saw *Memphis* when she was on Broadway and my dad wants to hear all about it. It's his favorite musical ever. (This is a title that changes with some frequency. But he has held on to this one for at least two years now.)

He and Ms. Patterson sing along.

When Bartle hears the start of "Everybody Wants to Be Black on a Saturday Night," he comes tearing down the stairs and he and I join in. He and my dad demonstrate a dance routine they picked up at the Cabaret Club (gay bar over in Minneapolis), and it's so campy it has us all in stitches. Ms. Patterson joins them, and Mom comes out of the kitchen to see what I am hooting about and cracks up, too.

Mom's about to drag me out there to help finish the dishes when Ms. Patterson says, "Mark, I wonder if you'd help Una. I wanted to have a word with Jessie about class . . ."

My stomach clenches up. For a while there I'd almost forgotten about class.

Defenses—along with my shoulders—rise up to my ear lobes. "Ms. Patterson, I'm sorry you have to put up with me in that advanced class, but . . ."

"You can call me Dell," she says, smiling. "And there's no need to apologize."

Maybe my shoulders drop an inch. Maybe.

"It's nothing," she says. "I . . . I wanted to talk with you away from the theater and the other students."

"Okay."

"I've known your parents since we were almost as young as you are now."

"I'm sixteen."

"Okay, yeah, I was eighteen when we first met at the U. Your parents were a few years older. And they were such a big deal on campus."

That's no surprise.

"You don't remember me from back then, do you?"

"No," I say, and I could swear she looks disappointed, which is weird.

I'm about to ask her what I'm supposed to remember when she asks me another question.

"Do you remember when you . . . started feeling so . . . awkward . . . in your dance and acting classes?"

"Always!" I say. A no-brainer.

"Really?" She sounds genuinely surprised. "From when you first started taking classes?"

"Yeah," I say. "They had me in dance classes from age four, I think. Before I started school."

"So, what do you remember about those early classes?"

I open my mouth to answer, but then close it again. These are the pictures I was looking at this summer. I remember hearing my parents tell stories about the classes, about me being taller than all the other kids. I remember them saying I was the only biracial kid there.

But those are their memories, right?

I shake my head.

She waits.

In the silence we can hear my mom and dad out in the kitchen. He's telling her (his voice has suddenly gotten really loud like it does when he's excited about something) about a revival of the musical, *Purlie Victorious*. And then his voice drops and I hear my mom laugh. A loud, hooting kind of laugh. I can picture them out there. Such a familiar scene from my entire childhood. But that now almost always has Brad in it.

I can't even remember what Ms. Patterson asked me. Oh, about the classes when I was really little.

I shake my head again. "I don't remember, I really don't."

"Okay." She pauses to think. "Do you remember the first time you heard someone—other than yourself—say something about you being awkward or clumsy?"

Why is she asking this? I don't have a clue. But, here's the thing. It seems like I should be able to remember this. I mean, if it's something I feel so strongly, then why do I have this blur of memories that aren't really memories? Like this awkwardness is a truth about me that goes back to birth or something. That's stupid. Doesn't make any sense.

I shake my head again.

Grandmama would say, "You keep shakin' your head like that, your brains are gonna scramble." I smile.

"It's okay," Dell says. "I thought it might be helpful if we could pinpoint when this started. But it doesn't matter. Don't worry about it."

"What are you going to do?" I ask.

"Go slowly," she says, with a really sweet smile. "We've got all the time in the world, don't we?"

My parents come back into the living room and my dad puts his new CD on, the one he's been shouting about out in the kitchen—a revival of one of the first all-black musicals, *Purlie Victorious*. Evidently it's taking Broadway by storm.

Bits comes back when we're in the middle of listening to that one. "Why are you listening to church music?" she asks, a look of alarm on her face. I can't say I blame her after a day with Loretta.

"It's a new musical on Broadway," I answer.

"Thank god," she says, and wonders why we all laugh.

Then my dad puts on "Mysterious Ways" from *The Color Purple*. He turns the volume up till the gospel music is shaking the house to the rafters. Bartle comes back downstairs. And we end Sunday singing like we're in Grandmama's Baptist church.

"This is the real deal," I say to Bits, and she nods.

She can't believe Ms. Patterson is singing in the middle of our living room and once they've turned the music down, she monopolizes Dell until she leaves, thankfully without talking with my parents about how terribly I'm doing in her movement class.

For once, I'm grateful to Bits for her New York obsession.

you win some, you lose some

Tuesdays are the most boring days of the week with no classes and nothing particular to do. Mondays aren't so bad because I'm usually doing lots of house chores. Laundry. Cleaning. Grocery shopping. Pathetic. What am I, Cinderella? Wednesdays and Fridays are taken up with the movement class. And helping Lydia with the scene work for Mom's class.

I can't wait for the professor's workshop to start.

Today I spend most of the morning over at Grandmama's trying to worm her cinnamon roll recipe out of her. David wants it, and I thought for sure that would convince her to give it to me.

"I don't have a recipe," she says, making a pan of fresh corn bread for me to take home with me. "It's a pinch of this and a handful of that."

Try telling that to Chef David. He'll have to come over here and watch her do it himself.

Afterward, I head over to the green room to talk with Bits

between her classes. We've been listening to all the stored voice-mail messages from her mom. Loretta uses voice mail with Bits the same way she sends postcards and text messages to Mom. They're worded pretty much the same, too. Evidently her cult instructions don't include audience analysis.

When Bits goes to the restroom, Lydia grabs me and says she wants to talk with me in the library. What's up now?

"Jess, you probably heard, we decided to go with my adaptation of *A Christmas Carol* instead of *Little Women*," Lydia begins.

She means for the holiday show.

"You did? Why? I thought for sure you'd want to do *Little Women* since you've already completed the adaptation." She did that last semester for a project for her playwriting class at the U. It's a feminist version. I read it. It's really, really good.

"Timing," she says. "You know that the Guthrie does *A Christmas Carol* every year and the Children's Theatre Company does it pretty often, too. This year, they aren't doing it, so it's a great time for us."

"Makes sense." I love the CTC's version, am only moderately in like with the Guthrie's more traditional version. We've never done it, as far as I know.

"Have we ever done it?" I ask.

"No," Lydia says. "I'm working around the clock to get the adaptation done. I'm writing it for a very small cast where people will play multiple roles."

"I like that. What made you decide to do that?"

"Well, for one thing, so we don't have to hire outside actors. So the set's not as complicated. More profit margin." She shakes her head. "But it will make it more interesting for the performers, too."

"And the students?" I am holding my breath. Please, please, please don't ask me to be in it.

"Only in the olios between scenes."

Olios are like intermission acts, usually with music and funny stuff. It's a JUMBLE tradition to have them as part of the Christmas show no matter what the show is, but that doesn't mean I want to be in them.

"Bits is going to have a bigger role," Lydia continues, "one where she crosses in and out from the scenes to the olios."

"Nice."

"Yeah, really nice."

"Will Loretta let her do it?" I have to ask. Bits's mom is RABID about her not being involved in anything that has to do with Christmas.

"Lee's given Bits permission, and we're going with that. She doesn't know about the full extent of the part yet, so don't say anything, okay?"

"Okay." Why is she talking with me about this?

"I don't know if you've heard, but I'm directing it," Lydia says.

"Wow! That's great!" No wonder she was so amped to be teaching directing again. What a shame that class didn't make it.

"I'd like you to be my assistant director, if you're interested."

Sweet.

She hands me the rehearsal schedule. "Your parents are psyched," she says with a smile.

Mom, too? I want to ask but bite my lip.

"So, do you want to do it?"

"Are you kidding? Of course!"

She hands me a piece of paper with a description of the duties of an assistant director. I pretty much already know what they are. I've been sitting in on rehearsals since before I could walk or talk. But it's good to have it spelled out in such a practical way.

No surprise, the first thing I notice is that I'm the one responsible for running lines with the actors. Well, there you go. That's one thing I know for sure how to do.

I go back to the green room to see if Bits is still there. She is. And I'm about to tell her about *A Christmas Carol* when in walks David and . . . Emily.

"Oh, there you are, Jess . . . we stopped at your house but . . . Hi, Bits."

"Hi," Bits says, with a strange look on her face.

Emily has a strange look on her face, too.

"I wanted to introduce you to . . . my friend . . . girlfriend," David says, "Emily."

"Emily," I say at exactly the same time he says Emily.

And Emily says, "Hi, Jessie!" at the same time we are both saying "Emily." No wonder Bits looks confused.

"You know each other?" David asks.

"Yeah," I say. "From the writing workshop this summer . . . you didn't tell him?"

"I didn't put it together," Emily says. "YOU'RE the Jess he was talking about . . ."

Bits appears to be choking. I reach over to pat her on the back but realize she's not drinking or eating anything.

"Are you all right?" I ask.

She nods but apparently still can't speak.

Neither can David. And he's turned very VERY red. Tomato-ketchup red. I'm kind of stunned. I mean, I wonder what he's told Emily about me. And how long they've been seeing each other. I guess I'd better ask.

"Have you two been . . . seeing each other . . . very long?" I manage to spit out with only one or two little stutters in the middle.

"No," she says, smiling and shaking her head.

"Couple weeks," David adds.

Okay, a couple weeks. Yeah, that's about how long David's been acting kind of strange. No serious kissing sessions during that time. Only a teensy weensie bit around the edges of cooking and baking. Now I know why.

I'm suddenly glad Grandmama held back her cinnamon roll recipe.

Does that mean I'm jealous?

No, not exactly.

I mean, it's not like I ever wanted to be David's girlfriend. I didn't. I don't.

And I'm the one who never returned Emily's e-mail. I could have. I'm not even sure why I didn't.

I mean, it's not like I can't be friends with her if she's with David.

It's just sort of weird.

I glance at Bits and notice that now her eyes are bugging out of her head. I know that look. She is FURIOUS. Okay, how weird is that? I'm not furious and I'm the one who's been . . . ya know . . . messing around with David and being his nonstop sous chef.

Now David's mouth is working again and he blathers on and on about how they met at the bread place down on Snelling, and then he went to see a showing of Emily's photographs at the coffee house right there by Jamba Juice.

I mean, when did this happen? The same time I was trolling down Grand Avenue looking into cafés and coffee places hoping to run into her? How embarrassing!

I can't think of a word to say.

And how is it they've been going out for two weeks and she never put it together that he's from the JUMBLE Players? Of course, given how he feels about the theater, he probably never even mentioned it. Other than cooking for us, he's never wanted to be involved.

Bits, who is usually more socially adept than I am and very personable (in that save-any-uncomfortable-social-situation kind of way), has not said one single word.

"This is my cousin, Bits," I finally give in and tell Emily. "David's probably told you about her."

Emily nods. "Hi," she says. Then to me, "Tony and Maria?"

"Uh-huh." I nod and smile.

Bits has grabbed her bag and jacket and she pulls me toward the stage door. "We've got to go," she says through gritted teeth.

"Okay," I say, trying to get her to look at me. She won't.

"Catch you later," I say to David and Emily and let Bits pull me out the door. Then it hits me—the writing workshop!

I pull away from Bits and stick my head back in the door. "Are you taking the next writing workshop?"

Emily nods.

Okay, then.

Bits waits until we're safely away from the theater, which also means we're past the costume/set shop and nearly at our steps, then explodes, "Can you believe that? Are you okay? What a tool!"

"I'm a little surprised, but I'm fine, why wouldn't I be?" We head for the kitchen. "I don't really see how David's a tool."

I pull two cans of pop out of the fridge and toss one to her. We pop the tops and take long sips. She's looking a little more normal. I could ask her what's going on. But I don't. See, I didn't even know she knew about David and me and the kissing. 'Cause I've been modeling myself after my mother and haven't told her.

I take another sip.

"You're not upset?" she asks finally.

Not the way you think I am, I'm thinking.

"No," I say, checking in with myself. "No, I'm not."

And the thing is, I'm really not. I mean, it's kind of like the universe has handed me the answer on how to stop making out with David and go back to being . . . friends. And if I'm friends with David, there's no reason why I can't also be friends with Emily. Right?

"I'm good," I say, smiling because it's true.

But because I'm not upset, now Bits has nowhere to go with her anger. And I can see she's still madder than hell.

Very interesting. Indeed.

just breathe . . .

Ms. Patterson's asked me to come in an hour early on Friday so we can work together before class. And she may want to work with me after class for an hour or so. She'll decide on a day-by-day basis, she says.

I have to get out of the house, I'm so nervous. That makes me at least fifteen minutes early. The Advanced Acting class has just let out, so the studio theater is empty and the green room is full of students eating their lunches before their 1:00 p.m. classes.

I wave at Bits and head for the studio theater.

I'm standing in the middle of the room still holding my tote bag when Ms. Patterson comes in and closes the door behind her.

"Jessie, I thought about our conversation and for now, I think we'll do what I said. We're going to move slowly. Today we'll start out with some floor work. So why don't you lie down on the floor facing away from the mirrors."

Not the kind of floor work I'm expecting.

I lie down but can feel myself stiffening up.

She laughs, and says, "You can relax. All you have to do today is breathe, and fortunately you're already doing that."

Breathe? What does she mean, breathe?

"I'm going to adjust your head," she says as she does it, putting a stack of paperback books underneath the back of my head, which oddly enough is a lot more comfortable. "And now I'm going to make an adjustment to your shoulders . . . and now to your back."

"You might tuck your legs up if that's better for you. You've got long legs like me."

She adjusts my legs, then my feet.

"All right," she says. "Now I'm going to lie down also, in the same position. I'll be doing the exercises along with you, okay?"

"Okay," I say. But what does this have to do with stage movement? Or any kind of movement for that matter.

"How we breathe is the basis for everything we do. It's the life force, isn't it? So that makes sense on a metaphysical level as well as a physical one."

Okay, I get that.

She has us focus on the way our bodies feel lying on the floor. Noticing all the places that the floor is supporting us. And then to notice how the breath moves in and out of its own volition. I probably am forcing it a little, she tells me, because I don't know exactly what's happening or what's coming next. But continue to be aware of that and keep breathing and noticing.

After a while she has me let out a big sloppy whooshing sound on an out breath. And then just allow my breath to return. Notice where it goes in my body. Does it stop in my chest? Does it go down into my abdomen? Do I feel it in my back?

Then she has me make an *F* sound on my exhale. As if singing note *fa*, only not singing, whispering. She does it along with me so there's no reason to be self-conscious.

I notice that the floor doesn't feel hard anymore.

I'm so focused on my breath, going in and out, in and out, in and out.

And suddenly she stands up, and says, "Great. That's it for today. I want you to observe in class again today. And if you can meet me an hour before the next class, we'll continue our work together."

I get up, thinking, oh good, I've got at least half an hour to go hang out in the green room, maybe grab something to eat, but the door opens and students start coming in and there's Bits. An entire hour has gone by as we were "just breathing."

How strange. Yes, the clock says 1:05. How did the time go by so fast?

Ms. Patterson hands me the small drum and motions me over to the stool.

"All right, class," she says. "Warm-ups."

where we live

Nearly everyone from the summer writing workshop is back.

"I teach playwriting and dramaturgy at the University of Minnesota," Professor Enomoto says by way of reintroduction. "Lydia Benedict asked me to come back this fall and do a writing workshop focused on playwriting."

"Isn't that what we were doing last summer?" Bartle asks.

"Yes, but only in three sessions, so we couldn't get very deeply into how the writing exercises work in direct relationship to playwriting."

Emily raises her hand and the professor nods at her. "Does it matter if we're not really focused on becoming a playwright?"

"Not at all," he says. "What kind of writing are you most interested in?"

"I'm a photographer," she answers. "I want to get better at keeping an art journal that includes words."

"This is perfect for that," he answers. "Anyone else have questions or concerns about their fit with the workshop?"

We all shake our heads. I have no idea if I'm really interested in becoming a playwright. But I love plays. And words. And I really liked the three sessions last summer. So, why not? And I also like this odd group of students. For some reason, seeing Sister Mary Margaret sitting there wearing her old-fashioned wimple makes me smile.

"Most drama for the stage focuses on ordinary people in extraordinary circumstances. Shakespeare's famous quote, 'All the world's a stage . . .' still applies to the live theater."

I'd been doodling in my notebook, but hearing the professor reciting my dad's favorite quote makes me pay closer attention.

"On the stage," he continues, "we generally don't go in for all the special effects of explosions and car chases the way films do. We have to engage and entertain an audience that is sitting so close to us we can hear them breathe and cough and gasp and laugh."

Or we can hear the dead silence that happens when they aren't at all interested. I've sat in audiences where that happened. I can't even imagine what it must feel like to be one of the actors onstage when some husband dragged along to see Shakespeare for the first time falls asleep and snores!

"Setting is very important," the professor is saying, "because it provides the container for all the conflict and humor and resolution. What I like to call the world of the play. So that's where we're going to begin."

"Where?" Troy asks.

The professor smiles. "We're going to start with place. Go for the details. We'll write for twenty minutes on this first prompt . . ." He pauses and looks around the room. "Does everyone remember the guidelines for our writing?"

Bartle blurts out, "We write in response to a prompt . . ."

Emo Bev adds, "Once we start writing, we keep writing . . ."

Tim Chang pipes up, "We don't put our pens down, we keep writing until the time is up."

The professor's beaming. "Don't think too much, don't edit . . . just write. Okay, good. The first prompt is 'Where we live.'"

Piece of cake, I'm thinking. I describe our house, how much my mom loves it, how the cats found us, who all lives in the house. How they all got there.

"Time," the professor says, looking up from his own writing. I love it that he writes with us. I've never had a teacher do that before. "Okay, you can wrap up that last thought . . ."

Everyone else but Sister Mary Margaret is still madly writing. She's looking out the window.

"All right, we're not going to read your free-writes this time, but since we will be building on this idea of place and setting today and in the weeks ahead, it would be useful to go around the circle and say the place you wrote about."

He nods at Sister M&M to begin, and she says, "Los Angeles," and then blushes bright pink. I wonder why.

I'm next. "Our Victorian house," I say.

Emily says, "A fractal of light." What? What does she mean by that?

Bev says, "The reservation." Then she adds, "Leech Lake."

Troy says, "The JUMBLE green room." Suddenly I'm wishing I'd written about the theater not our house.

Tim Chang says, "San Francisco . . ."

I'm fully expecting Bartle to say, "Our Victorian house." I mean, that's where he lives, so why would he say anything else, right? But instead he says, "My mom's house . . ." Bartle hasn't lived in his mom's house since he was sixteen. When she kicked him out. What is with that?

And then it's the professor's turn. "Denver," he says, with a tiny shrug. "Where my family relocated after the Second World War."

"No QUALIFYING!" Bartle shouts.

And we all bust out laughing, including the professor. He had to say "No qualifying!" so many times during that first summer session.

"Okay," the professor says, standing up and tripping over the edge of the area rug. "You got me on that one."

"Professor Bumble," Bartle whispers to me.

"What?"

"He's so clumsy we should call him Professor Bumble . . ."

"Did you have something you wanted to share with the group?" the professor asks, in typical teacher fashion.

Bartle grins. "Nope."

I'm grinning, too. I love that name. Professor Bumble.

"All right then, let's do another free-write. We're going to add ten minutes to it—so it's a thirty-minute write. It's the same prompt, only you can't write about the same place."

Oh. That's interesting.

"The prompt again is 'Where I live' . . . Go."

My head is still caught up in other people's responses. Bartle hasn't lived in Northeast Minneapolis for so long. Why would he write about his mom's house? And what did Emily mean by a fractal of light? You have to start writing the second the professor says go, so since my head's not in it yet, I'm doing what he always says to do when you're stuck.

I don't know, I don't know, I don't know . . . (He also says to use your favorite swear word over and over. He says it's stimulating. Ha!)

And suddenly I'm in that closet under the stairs with the bolts of brown corduroy. My hide-and-seek fall-back hiding place. What is that about? But I'm describing it. I'm smothering in there. I'm too big for the space and there's not enough color. The dusty fabric makes me sneeze. I have to pee. I'm writing crazy shit that I'm never going to read out loud. And we have to write for a half an hour. Which is a really long time to write without lifting your pen from the page. Especially if you are writing about a space the size of a tiny half bath that's stuffed with bolts of fabric.

My pen is moving and moving and moving. Now I'm in the attic of our house. Now I'm in that crazy hoarder house where Bruce and Albert live. Now I'm in the room I share with Bits. This is one of those times I won't know what I wrote until I'm able to read it.

But I'm sure not going to read it out loud in the workshop before I've had a chance to read it to myself.

And the real question is will I ever have the courage to read in here?

all hallow's eve
and a hurricane

It's a JUMBLE Players tradition to stop everything and celebrate Halloween. It's my mother who refers to it as All Hallow's Eve. It's also my mother who is responsible for this tradition—for some reason Halloween is her favorite holiday. Maybe this is a way of making up for her own lost years, since the CLP folks don't celebrate any holiday, especially Halloween.

This year, Halloween falls on a Wednesday. Classes are canceled and, because of the terrible hurricane on the East Coast, our huge party is now also a fund-raiser for hurricane relief. This is mostly Ms. Patterson's idea, I'm pretty sure. She's frantic because she can't get in touch with close friends in New Jersey and all flights are canceled so she can't hop a plane. Her anxiety is contagious.

So this year the students' parents are also invited to the party and Lydia has set up a computer with an online donation site and we're taking other donations, too. Very civic minded. I like it. It's refreshing. Sometimes I wish my parents were more into that kind of thing.

Okay, the party. Students can check out costumes from the costume shop. There's food and music and games. This year Auntie Ellie and Lee are playing and singing while we're eating. Just the two of them, not the whole band. Which reminds me, the last two times the band has been between gigs, Lee stayed at our house. I don't know if it's because Bits is there. Or if it's also because of Auntie Ellie. I'm pretty sure he's crashing on the futon in the basement laundry room. Which is not all that horrible after the going-over I gave it this summer. He's been with Auntie Ellie's band the longest of any of them. But lately it seems like he and Auntie Ellie are morphing into a couple.

Bits makes a twirling entrance on point.

"You are too cute for words." I mean it. Bits is going as Tinker Bell in Peter Pan.

"It's this sparkly leotard Una loaned me . . ."

"No, I'd say it's the fifteen layers of tutus that make the costume!"

"One for every year I took ballet," Bits says, twirling again and executing a series of ballet moves meant, I'm sure, to suggest flying. If she could she'd have us rig her up with a rope and pulley.

"Where did you take ballet before you came here?"

"CTC. Sylvia was a really good teacher. I was sorry when my mom pulled me from there."

"You remember your teacher from when you were . . . how old?"

"Five and six, I think. Yeah, she was great."

Well, that's weird. How come I can't remember my dance classes from back then? I'd ask Bits, but she didn't start with us until she was ten and I was eight. That was when Lee joined Auntie Ellie's band. I remember that. Before that I only saw her at family gatherings. And not many of those because Loretta was kind of boycotting my mom's marriage to a black man.

"What about your first dance teacher here?"

"Yeah, I liked her, too."

"I meant—who was she? What was her name?"

"Ms. Svenson," Bits says. "Here, will you stick this on my head?" Bits is waving this sparkly net thing that Bartle glued to a kid's plastic headband for her. It's sort of a wacky tiara. The kind of thing you look at and think—oh no, that will never work—and then once it's on Bits's head nestled in all that curly golden hair— voila! Magic!

"Don't you remember her?" she asks. "You were in the class, too."

I was? Huh.

"This is your best year yet!" I snap a couple pics of her with my iPhone.

Bits pulls out her phone to take a picture of me, but I duck behind the refreshment table. I am dressed—for at least the fifth year in a row—in my gypsy costume. I really don't like wearing costumes, which is yet another reason why it would be stupid for me to want to be an actor. But if I take my hair out of the braids and let it go wild and if I put on some layers of funky clothes and wear a lot of costume jewelry, I don't even need makeup. Instant gypsy. This is a good thing, too, since I also don't like wearing makeup. (Ditto on the anti-actor thing.)

Bartle's been over at the shop helping Brad with some last-minute party prop or something, so I have no idea what he's wearing but I heard rumors at dinner last night that he was considering going as Lady Gaga. A six-foot-three, black Lady Gaga—this I've got to see!

Grandmama isn't coming. She's not a big fan of Halloween. She'd rather stay at home and pass out candy to the kids who show up at her door.

I've got three bags of food to unload. This party isn't catered. And David's not cooking, either. It's more of a semi-organized potluck extravaganza. With ribs and chicken and fish from our favorite BBQ place (Dad and Brad contributed this).

So the costume parade comes first (kind of like we do at the first tech rehearsal). Edward, Lydia, Ms. Patterson, Bartle, and Ted are judging. My parents will lead us in some games (yup, Mom organized this). Then we eat.

We're in the middle of the costume parade when David and Emily arrive. David hasn't come to this party for two or three years, so that's a bit of a surprise. They're not in costume, which makes me wish I hadn't given in to Mom at the last minute with the gypsy thing.

Bits waltzes by in the costume parade. She's smiling at me but glaring at David and Emily. What is with her?

So far no one is forcing me to participate in the costume parade. Hallelujah!

"You look beautiful," Emily says, pulling out her favorite digital camera and snapping some shots of me before I realize what she's doing. "I love your hair like that."

David's grinning at me. He knows how I feel about this wild mass of hair.

"You do," he says. "You look beautiful."

Bits wins first place. A no-brainer. Susie, Troy, and Susie's other nemesis Anita win honorable mention. We're halfway through a wild and crazy game of dueling charades (another tradition) when suddenly the door bursts open and in comes Loretta, looking like it's the charging of the bulls.

This is totally weird. I mean, it's been months since I've even seen her. And she never comes to the theater if she can help it. What is she doing here?

She heads straight for Bits, grabs her by the arm and starts yanking her toward the door.

She's so focused on Bits, I don't think she's even noticed that Lee is here, too. He and I run for Bits at the same time.

Loretta is admonishing, halfway under her breath, "What are you doing celebrating like a pagan when Armageddon is so near . . ."

"Mom, stop it!" Bits squirms, trying to pull away.

Loretta acts like she doesn't even hear her. If anything she pulls harder.

"Stop it," Bits hisses, squirming and tugging to get away. "Mom, stop!"

Loretta grips Bits's wrist so hard, Bits winces.

"Signs of the end," she says, her voice getting louder. "Hurricanes and devastation . . ."

"Daddy!" Bits calls out, and Loretta's head snaps around and she sees Lee.

She tightens her grasp on Bits and pulls harder. The whole theater crowd has stopped what they're doing and everyone's standing there watching. In silence. Loretta doesn't even seem to notice. She's too busy muttering all the signs that the world is about to end.

Auntie Ellie and Mom are frozen in place, which is a good thing because they're blocking the front door. My dad and Edward are poised in the open doorway that leads back to the studio theater area and the stage door. The last thing anyone wants is for Loretta to succeed in dragging Bits out of here.

Now Loretta is spewing Bible verses from Revelation. Nightmare imagery . . . words, words, words.

The escalating imagery must shake Mom out of her trance, because all of a sudden she goes at Loretta like they're kids and fighting over their favorite toy.

Loretta still has Bits in a vise-like grip, and she doesn't let go, even with Mom batting at her. Mom's at a disadvantage because she's a lot smaller than her sister, so I grab Bits's other hand. I see Lee start to move around behind Loretta. I'm pulling on Bits's hand, but Loretta won't let go. I hang on. I guess I figure if she takes Bits she's also got to take me, which is harder to do since I'm a lot taller. I don't know. I haven't thought it through. Loretta is outnumbered here, but she's still got hold of Bits and she's got that super strength of someone unhinged.

Over against the wall, Emily is crouched behind David and

she's taking pictures. I mean, she's a photographer, but still, it seems kind of weird.

I see Lydia slip up the stairs to the office. I hope she's not calling the police. She can't do that! If the police come, they could take Bits away and that would be terrible. On the other hand, I'd like to see someone lock Loretta in jail and throw away the key. She's a lunatic.

Now Lee's right behind her, and he grabs Loretta fast and yanks her so that she lets go of Bits and Mom and I pull Bits over to Auntie Ellie. Bits is rubbing her wrist and looking like she's going to cry (something she hardly ever does except in a scene onstage).

My dad and Brad join us, everyone in a protective circle around Bits. So I slip away to the office to see if I can keep Lydia from calling the police. I know it would be the thing to do in most circumstances but not this one. What's really important now is that Bits stay with us.

It turns out Lydia's calling her friend from the U who is a child advocate lawyer. I don't know exactly what that is, but it sounds like a good thing.

Lee escorts Loretta out to her car. Lots more yelling. Nothing like a terminal relationship to bring out the LOUD in some people. I'm suddenly grateful for the untraditional way my parents are breaking up. Finally Loretta drives off, and Lee comes back inside. Bits is pretty shaken up so he and Auntie Ellie take her back to the house. Mom decides she'd better go, too.

I want to go with Bits, but Lydia asks if I'll stay and help with the food.

So my dad and Brad and Bartle and I stay to wrap up the party.

Ms. Patterson takes this opportunity—while the parents are all standing around with their mouths open in shock and horror and disbelief—to gather them up for Hurricane Sandy donations. Somehow, Loretta has provided the perfect segue into disaster relief.

Bartle, by the way, has managed to pull off a fairly stunning version of Lady Gaga. Who now is reduced to sweeping around the room serving teenagers and their parents punch.

"Love your shoes." Try to imagine Bartle wearing eight-inch wedge heels. Even I have to stand on tiptoe to grab a glass of punch, the tray is up so high.

And where in the world did he get that wig?

"I wish I could see through these glasses!" He's copying those glasses Lady Gaga wears that have a big pattern on them, in this case a black-and-white retro check. I'm guessing when Lady Gaga wears the glasses, the pattern isn't made with a marker!

"You're lucky you haven't stepped on someone . . ."

"I wish I'd stomped all over that whack job Loretta!"

I agree.

"Anyway, my peripheral vision is SICK!" he smirks, sweeping away. Oh, so that's why he's holding his head at that weird slant.

David's helping serve the food. I'm in the kitchen getting ribs and chicken and fish out of the oven when Emily appears behind me.

"Here," she says, quickly pulling the memory card from her very cool digital camera and slipping it into a little case. "Bits might need this as evidence if she ever has to testify against her mother."

Suddenly her picture taking makes complete sense. "Thanks," I say, taking it. "A lot."

Emily nods and smiles. "Sure. I felt like a ghoul out there shooting those pics. But, hey, it is Halloween!"

She pops a new card into her camera. "Always come prepared . . ."

"Quick thinking for a ghoul," I say.

"Here," she says, grabbing the smaller platter of wings and leading the way out to the lobby. "I'm starved. Abusive, crazy mothers always do that to me."

You see. This is why I like this girl.

The rest of the party's a dud after all that drama, so once everyone's eaten they split. I'm kind of surprised the parents let them stay that long, but hey, who doesn't like a good spread?

As I'm about to head home, Lydia hands me a copy of her adaptation of *A Christmas Carol*. "I finished it last night," she says. "Sorry it's so late."

"I'll read it tonight," I say.

"Why don't I give you the rest . . ." She counts out copies for Bits and my parents, two more for Auntie Ellie and Lee (they're providing the music for the show). "Bartle and Brad can share a copy, can't they?"

I nod. I doubt Bartle will read it, though he should.

"I'm so glad Una had the sense to get Bits out of that house this summer and keep her," Lydia says, lowering her voice so only I can hear. "She knew better than the rest of us how crazy Loretta might get . . ."

So that's what happened.

I'm glad, too. And proud of my mom for thinking ahead and taking action to stand up for her niece.

So why does my stomach hurt? And why am I blinking back tears every step of the way to our house?

finding water

At the next writing workshop Professor Bumble talks for about fifteen minutes about what's new in playwriting. And then he talks about what's always going to remain at the center (the old writing-about-what-you-know thing).

"This is my favorite writing exercise," he says. "I use it over and over in classes and also for myself when I'm stuck with my own writing. Using the prompt, I remember . . . make a list of things you remember from different years in your life."

"Write down the year, too?" Emily asks.

"Yes," he says. "Write as many different I remembers as you can in twenty minutes. Starting now. Keep your pen moving."

At first I'm having fun. The memory kind of pops up, usually with an image, and I almost always know the year—or how old I was. But then all of a sudden, I realize I'm not really having my own memories. It's like all my points are tied in with family pictures or stories I've heard my family and our friends tell.

I almost put my pen down I'm so shocked. I want my own memories.

Professor Bumble opens the workshop up for discussion and it turns out everyone is having a similar experience.

"Yes," he says, "that's completely natural. It's how it starts. The stories that other people tell and that are told, especially about photographs . . ." He looks at Emily and she's sitting up straighter.

He continues, ". . . They sort of imprint themselves on us. So we remember them first. A lot of people never get beyond those stories. But when you play with it and keep going, you eventually do get beyond that. Like digging down through a lot of sand to get to water."

That's fascinating.

So, he has us do it again for another twenty minutes. He says don't worry if you repeat memories. Write whatever comes.

We all check in after that and most everyone is still writing from photographs and family stories. Only now they're aware that's what they're doing. Me, too.

"Okay," he says. "We've got an hour left of today's workshop. Let's move to a variation of this prompt. This one is even better. We'll write for forty-five minutes. The prompt is 'I don't remember' . . ."

Lots of funny reactions to that, of course.

Bartle says, "Like after a night of drinking and running around and what you don't want to remember?"

Everyone laughs, even Sister M&M.

It's a long time to write, the longest we've ever written. My mind jumps all over the place. From the ongoing drama at our house to my conversations with Dell about movement and dance to my irritations over the deepening relationship between Bits and my mom to the differences in my relationships with the two sides of my family. I write and write and write about what I don't remember.

Everyone is writing furiously, including the professor. He lets us go on writing and then when we wrap it up, it's time to go home.

I'm glad because I want to read it through by myself before I make any decisions about sharing it with anyone else. But I'm also tired of saying, "I pass."

We're walking out, and Emily says, "That was crazy. How can a prompt about what you don't remember make you remember like that?"

I nod. "It's powerful, this kind of writing, isn't it?"

"Yeah, it surprises me every time where the writing takes me."

I know what she means. The prompts make the writing go deep and deeper. It's like reading something someone else wrote about me and knowing it to be true.

dancing in the dark

It's another Friday and another crazy movement session with Ms. Patterson. Ten minutes of breathing exercises on the floor, in the dark.

Now she's put on this wild music with a lot of drumming in it. Native American flutes, too.

"Just stay on the floor like you are."

Okay. What does she think I'm going to do? Jump up and start dancing?

"Pay attention to what parts of your body want to move to the music," she says. "And let that happen."

I have no idea if she's doing it, too, because she keeps the lights off and even though my eyes have adjusted some, it's so dark in here I can't really see her.

Her voice comes out of the darkness, blending in with the drums and the flute, "I'm doing this with you." What is she? A mind reader?

"I find this a great way to relax and warm up between classes."

Okay. I guess.

"It's also a great stress reliever," she adds. "I've been doing this a lot this week, what with the hurricane and everything . . ."

"Did you ever get through to your friends?" I ask her.

"Yes," she says, "thanks for asking. I got through to one of them and he says everyone's okay, though some are still without power."

I love this music. The beat is irresistible.

I let myself move a little and after a while it's easier.

Even if I do look like a stranded ostrich . . . or . . . yes . . . a giraffe . . . lying on its side on a sand bar, gyrating occasionally. Who cares? It feels good. Almost fun.

And it is relaxing like she said.

Now she's changed the music. More drumming. African this time, I think.

"Let's continue the same thing. Let your body move to the music while staying on the floor. Remember to breathe."

I'm moving my torso a lot more to this music. I mean, who could NOT move with this beat?

Or not breathe for that matter!

The time flies by again. Ms. Patterson flicks on the light as I'm getting up from the floor, and says, "Good."

I'm surprised at how easy it is to work alone with Dell like this. She's not at all scary, the way she often is in class.

Today in class, I beat the little circular drum again. Ms. Patterson works with the students on cleaning up and improving some technical movement skills. The last fifteen or so minutes of class she's working with the students to pull all the movements together, and then moving them across the floor.

"Ms. Jasper Lewis," she says, and for some reason I giggle, "Every so often change the beat and let them respond to your drumming."

"Okay," I gasp, trying to stifle this unholy urge to laugh. What is with me?

"Oh, and that vocalization thing you've been doing under your breath?"

What vocalization thing?

"Do that loud enough so we can hear it."

I nod, although I'm not even sure what I was doing. What was I doing? I'm about to panic, but then I see Bits smiling at me. She knows evidently. Tell me!

"Start with three four time and then do your thing," Ms. Patterson says, moving to her corner of the room. Thank goodness she's not standing right next to me.

So I start drumming. And then, of course, I know instantly what I was doing before. Although I sure hadn't intended to do it out loud. I was doing this thing my dad and I do sometimes when we're listening to musicals where we don't know the words. Kind of like scat singing in jazz. It's second nature, I guess.

I kick it up a couple notches on the volume scale. Bits grins.

Oh, this is a first! Me scat singing in class!

When Ms. Patterson calls a halt, she says, "Okay, next Wednesday we will begin our new unit."

She doesn't say whether or not she wants me to join the class. I guess she'll tell me on Wednesday.

"That was wicked, Jessie Jumble," one of the boys says on his way to the dressing room.

"It was," Bits says as she joins me. "It was most definitely WICKED!"

Even more history in the making! Jessie Jumble laughing as she leaves a movement class.

jessie jumble,
assistant director

Once again—history in the making. It is Saturday, November 3, and I am sitting here in the first rehearsal for the Christmas show and I am happy to say that I am NOT in the cast.

Happy, happy, happy.

I'm sitting where directors always sit—in the center of the first section of raked seats—two seats over from Lydia.

I can't wait to see how Lydia works.

She's telling them about the production and then we're going to do a read-through. So far, that's pretty typical.

Bits and I read through the play last night.

Before we started she had me listen to her mom's recent voice mails. Ever since the Halloween debacle, Loretta's been threatening to let her apartment go and move with some of the other CLP "messengers" to a little town up in Northern Minnesota. It's not that far from where she and my mom grew up. There's a commune or something like that up there.

She tells Bits this in short bursts of crazy-sounding voice-mail messages.

One's about her stockpiling food.

Several are about how she intends to take Bits with her.

Bits is afraid Loretta will do it without warning. You know, grab her and force her to go, too.

"If I had to live in a little town with only religious fanatics for friends and no theater anywhere in sight I'll shrivel up and die."

Well, yeah.

I drag her down to the kitchen so Lee and Auntie Ellie and Mom can hear the messages, too. I'm not sure why Bits was keeping them a secret. Sometimes I worry that Loretta has her under some kind of mind spell, just because she's her mom.

They all freak out.

Mom says she will call that child advocate lawyer person Lydia found for Bits. Something has to be done to protect Bits. I mean, we can't watch her every second.

Anyway, after dinner, Bits and I went upstairs and read through the script. When we went back down to talk with Mom about it, turns out she and my dad were reading it in the kitchen. So the four of us read through it a second time together.

We all agree it's the most incredible adaptation of *A Christmas Carol* we've ever seen. We've been to all of them in the Cities and seen all the movies ever made of it so it is definitely an informed opinion.

Rehearsal is about to start. The stage manager has just called the cast in and they are all up onstage. It's a cast of six adults and five kids. Edward's playing Scrooge. I don't know why but that cracks me up. Everyone else has multiple roles. Bits and the other students will be doing the olios and they aren't written yet.

The cast is: Edward, my dad, my mom, Ms. Patterson, Ted, and two other actors who work with us a lot—Barry and Jean. Then Bits plus four of the theater school students: Susie, Jeff, Anita, and Mike. (They're all dancers, too.)

Ms. Patterson is choreographing it. There will be a lot of group movement in addition to the Fezziwig dance scene.

Brad and Bartle are doing the costumes, and Auntie Ellie and Lee are doing the music.

The full read-through is about to start.

I am so excited I could SHOUT! But I am the assistant director and that means I am quietly and surreptitiously taking notes.

my own private poll

It's election day, and I'm so nervous I can't sit in the house reading or (for sure) I can't start watching election coverage this early in the afternoon. Even though it's raining, I have to get out of the house for a while. It's no better in the green room. I sit there for a while playing games on my laptop, then give in and spend an hour helping Susie learn her lines for Advanced Acting. She is way harder to work with than Bits—she whines—but much more appreciative.

I bug my parents and Brad and Bartle until they all go and vote in order to get me off their backs. Bartle and Brad were planning on going anyway. My parents forgot it was Election Day. Sometimes I can't believe them.

There's a break in the rain mid-afternoon so I decide to take a walk around the area and count the VOTE NO signs and do my own private tally of who's ahead in the race for president. Yes, I know our neighborhood isn't exactly typical. And I know a tally based on yard signs isn't even vaguely accurate. Even so, I walk up Summit all the way to Dale and then come back on Grand Avenue. Turns out there are a lot of VOTE NO signs and it's looking pretty good for presidential reelection, too. Raises my spirits a tad.

On a whim, I decide to zigzag the last several blocks back and forth on the side streets between Grand and Summit. I'm not ready to go back home or to the theater, and even though it's raining again, I've got on my slicker and it's not that cold.

I haven't talked to Bruce and Arthur since right after they got back from the Mayo Clinic and I'm only a half block from their house, so I decide to pop over there.

Bruce answers the door. He's got a red, white, and blue party hat on.

"What do you think?" he asks.

"Nice hat," I say.

"Oh, the hat," he says with a little smile. "I put it on today for Arthur. I meant the amendment." He points at the sign, which is standing a little crooked.

I walk over and adjust it.

"Are we going to defeat this measure?" he asks me.

"It's about even right now," I say. This is a surprise to nearly everyone I know because the assumption earlier in the year was that the marriage amendment would pass with flying colors like it has in every state that's had one.

Brad wouldn't even let himself get into it until the reports started coming in that it was neck and neck. What if Minnesota could be the first state to defeat one of these amendments? That would be sweet.

"It's the only thing that's keeping Arthur going right now," Bruce says, his voice choking up on the words.

"What do you mean?" I choke on the words, too. "I thought he was doing better after the treatments."

"Oh, Jessie, he's really failing. I don't think he'll be with us much longer."

This makes me sad. Arthur is such a funny old man. So full of life and so interesting.

"I'd ask you in to see him," Bruce says. "I know he'd love to see you, but he's not doing very well today."

I give Bruce a hug and look away as he wipes tears off his cheeks. "Tell him we're thinking about him and hope he feels better." What good are words when someone's dying? I don't know if they're any good at all.

Bruce points at the sign and says, "If this amendment goes down in flames, it'll give him a new lease on life, I'm sure."

jessie jumble, movement consultant (not!)

It's my before-class session with Dell again. She's got relaxation music on. We're on the floor doing stretching and breathing exercises. I definitely need these relaxation exercises today. I am so hyper-jazzed about the election results I can hardly sit still.

The marriage amendment went down, as Bruce would say, in flames! It was close, but not nearly as close as people expected. And President Obama is in for another term. Even my apolitical parents were excited about that.

I remember four years ago, how important it was to my dad to have the first African-American president. And Grandmama . . . I heard stories from Grandmama then about things that happened down South that even my dad didn't know about. Grandmama cried when President Obama won. She hardly ever cries. And I know she voted—four years ago and yesterday. She'll be wearing that I VOTED sticker for a week!

It's interesting to me that what they see is a black man and what I see is someone who's biracial like me.

"Jessie," Dell says, interrupting my political reverie, "I wanted to ask your advice about something."

"You do?" I ask.

"I do," she says, with a laugh.

"Okay."

"I've had a unit planned for the class that's a logical follow-up to the period movement unit we completed last week. We'd focus on the student chorus Lydia's using in *A Christmas Carol*, work on period movement for the show."

"Yeah." (As in: of course, and why would she need my advice about that?)

"But, I'm thinking this is an area these students have had a lot of experience with. Am I right? I mean, the theater does something like this at least once a year, right?"

"Yeah," I say. "You're right."

Not that it's something I've ever managed to perfect or, let's get real here, even get vaguely proficient at—hence the previously mentioned nightmare the last time I was forced to do the Christmas show. But we're not talking about me.

"So," she says, hesitating a second. "So. Before I moved back here I was taking an African dance class. At Alvin Ailey's company. For about a year."

"Sweet."

"Yes," she says. "Very sweet. I'm not that great at it—the movement's really different from anything I've ever done. But it is so much fun. And the thing is, it's terrific for extending and expanding students' skills. That's why I took the class."

"Makes sense."

"Well, that and there was this guy that was really . . ."

"Hot?"

She smiles. "Umm-hmm. Anyway—learning it moves you through diametrically opposed movement patterns from all the areas where our traditional ballet training has us secure or set in our ways."

Us? "You mean them, not me, right?"

She laughs again, nods. "And me."

I wait. I don't know what to say. Actually, I don't know what she's asking.

"Are you asking me if I think it's okay to teach African dance to a bunch of white kids?" I ask. I mean, I'm the only student in the advanced movement class that isn't white. "Or are you asking me if I think my parents and the Benedicts would be okay with it?"

"I thought it was the first," she says, sitting up. "But I guess both. Should I just ask them?"

I sit up, too.

"Nah," I say. "If they think enough of you to hire you to teach us, then they trust what you know and your instincts about crafting the classes."

She smiles and looks kind of relieved.

"So," I say. "Should you teach African dance to a bunch of white kids? Why not?"

I think she knows I'm testing her with this white kids comment. She's not rising to the bait.

She nods, "Go on . . ."

"I mean, you'd have more credibility if you were black. And even more credibility if you were African! But if you've taken lessons and can pull it off, it would be something completely different for them to learn. We haven't ever studied African dance. And I, for one, would love to see some of our star pupils—yes, even including my cousin Bits—come up against something they don't know how to do."

We both chuckle a little at the thought.

"You're not expecting me to be good at it because I'm half black are you?"

"No," she says, laughing again. "I have no idea if you'll be any good at it. But my guess is they won't be. At least, not at first. So, full disclosure here . . . it did occur to me that it might level the playing field long enough for you to make a safe reentry into the class."

I don't know how I feel about that.

But I like it that she's this honest.

"Or maybe not," she says, standing up. "I haven't figured out how truly hopeless you are. Yet."

"Wow!" I say. "It is refreshing in the extreme to have a theater school teacher say right out that I'm hopeless. Good thing my parents aren't here . . ."

"Yes," she says, laughing. "Indeed."

"You know, someone should have said that when I was six and maybe I'd have a clue by now what I'm supposed to be."

"Jessie . . ." she starts, and then stops as if she's deciding if she's going to say something. The way she pauses, I'm pretty sure she changes her mind, which gets my curiosity up immediately.

What she says is, "You're actually pretty remarkable."

I'm about to do that withdrawal thing. You know, the clam-up, pull-back, shut-her-down thing. But there's something about the way Ms. Patterson doesn't pay attention to my nonverbals that stops me. I wait, glad the room is still dimly lit.

"Your outsides haven't caught up with your insides yet."

This gets my full attention. What is it my mother always says? Oh, yeah. It *resonates.*

"No," she says, "I don't mean I think I can turn you into a dancer or even an actor . . ."

"Ahhhh, shoot!"

"But I do think you are heading, maybe even on the verge, of a complete collision of outsides and insides. When that happens, maybe you'll be able to see yourself the way the rest of us see you."

My (teenage) mouth opens to say something snotty, you know, on basic principle. But then I close it. Something about what she said feels, I don't know, right.

For just a flashing second.

And then the flash has fled and I am, once again, clueless.

oh my god, oh my god, oh my god

It's Friday, before movement class again. I'm calling Ms. Patterson Dell pretty much all the time now. I have to remember NOT to do that in our actual class. When I do it at home, Bits gets all pissy about it. It's all I can do not to point out that she omits the *Aunt* in front of Una.

We do the alignment and breathing work with me sitting on a stool this time. And it's easy to do. No big deal.

"I've adapted these exercises from some work I did with the Alexander Technique," she says. "Ever heard of that?"

I actually have. Some of my mom's actor friends take lessons. I tell her that.

"If you're interested, I'll give you a book to read."

"I'm always up for reading a new book." Goes without saying.

Then she says, "Jessie, I want to thank you for our talk the other day. I've decided to go ahead with the African dance unit."

"Good," I say.

"So," she says, smiling. "I've got the music here. It would help me a lot if we could do our warm-ups to it. Okay?"

"Sure."

She puts the music on, and says, "Let's move to this. Don't try to do anything you've seen before. Don't even try to imagine what you're doing before you do it. Just inhabit the music like we did last time when we were lying on the floor."

I start to get down on the floor, but she says, "Let's stay up this time and just move."

She slides the light dimmer down a bit. We can see a little, but the lights are real low. I get that she doesn't want me to keep checking myself in the mirrors. That's fine with me!

And we start moving.

At first I'm doing what I always do. I'm thinking too much.

How am I supposed to move? What's it supposed to look like? Exactly what she said not to do.

Then, something happens. My feet feel the beats. They move.

My arms swing to the beats that are . . . well, yeah . . . arm beats.

My head moves to the head beats on my . . . how did this happen? . . . incredibly resilient neck.

And then all the beats come together and I have no idea what I look like, but it feels so right. So I keep doing it.

A few minutes into it, I see Dell stop dancing. I figure it's to watch me but, you know, I keep right on. I don't want to stop.

Finally, she takes the CD out and turns up the lights. She doesn't say anything to me about how I did.

She says, "Do you want to observe again or do you want to join the class today?"

I open my mouth to say—surprise—that I'll join the class, but I chicken out at the last second and say, "Observe, I think."

I admit it. A little part of me—well, maybe not so little—was hoping she'd say something nice and encourage me to go ahead and join in. Or even require me to. You know, like a typical teacher.

She doesn't do that, but she says. "All right. But I'd like you to join us next session, okay?"

"Okay," I say. I mean, come on, she's the teacher. She could be telling me to join the class right now. Or she could be telling me to stay on the stool for the rest of the semester.

She opens the door then and all the kids are waiting in the hall and come trooping in.

I almost change my mind again. I mean, I'm remembering the writing workshop and how much I really wanted to read but kept saying, I pass . . . But then I decide that in this case, it's okay because I really do want to watch.

Dell takes the class through what look like very basic African dance movements, first without the music, which is pretty much all drums, and then with the music.

They all have a terrible time learning the movement. Even Bits. Even Susie.

"Here in the U.S. in most classic dance and movement study," Dell says when they stop to take a break, "we treat the dancer's body as a whole unit. But African dance treats the body as something called polycentric."

Suddenly she turns to me. "Jessie, do you know what polycentric means?"

"A system with several centers," I say without even stopping to think. "The term often used is unity in diversity."

She asked me, but she looks really surprised that I answer.

"Exactly," she says, smiling slightly. "So when applied to the body in dance, it means that the body is divided into several different areas of movement. And each area is able to move to different rhythms within the music."

Lots of groaning to that description.

"Couldn't you show us a video of people doing it?" Susie asks.

"I could," Dell says, "but I'd rather not. I want you to learn the movements from the inside out."

When I get home I've got the house to myself for about half an hour before Bits gets home and I try the movements. Without the music of course.

I actually think I've got most of them.

Oh, not in a performing kind of way.

But in a physical way. Accurate, I guess. Not the best word. *Organic* maybe. *Integrated*. I'm thinking maybe that's what Dell meant when she said "from the inside out."

There's a part of me that wants to say it's because it's African movement and I'm tapping into my black roots, which go all the way back to Africa. But maybe even more than that, it's because it's so different. It's counterintuitive to all the so-called training I've received. Which clearly had no impact on me and I learned to become even clumsier out of sheer self-consciousness.

This movement is so different, there are no expectations—in

my body, in my mind. And while that's screwing all the good movement students up, it's working for me. For the first time.

Okay, don't overthink it.

Think instead about what Dell said the other day.

Maybe this is that collision she was talking about.

Oh, my god.

Is this really happening?

when in doubt, distress it . . .

That's what Brad always says about costume design, especially when he's designing for a proscenium stage. He says nothing makes costumes look more fake and amateurish than to have them all bright and shiny like every single character walked out of the same department store.

This is a discussion we have at the kitchen table with some frequency, especially now that Bartle's all into costuming, too.

"A benefit of being black," he says, straight-faced, "is that you can't see the dye all over me the way you can on a white boy like Brad."

Brad throws a slice of bread at him.

Food fight!

Mom stops it before it gets seriously under way.

I've never been particularly interested in set or costume design, but I see what Brad's talking about. It's like creating a moving painting with people and clothes and lights and props. And, of course, try to do that without the director.

You can't.

Lydia is focusing almost exclusively at the moment on the main story of *A Christmas Carol*. She does a lot of improv, which she then cleans up so that the scenes work and what she calls the *stage pictures* are pleasing to the eye. Our actors are incredible, so she doesn't do much coaching. She throws them into scenes together and they come up with wonderful stuff.

But the kids are sitting around waiting to work on the olios and getting really bored. Dell is in a lot of the scenes Lydia's working on, plus she's busy with choreography or she could be working with the kids. But the main problem is that Lydia hasn't decided how she wants the olios to work this year. My guess is she would abandon tradition and dump them if they weren't the students' only opportunity to be in this show. The parents expect to see theater students in it.

So we are in that stage in rehearsals where everyone is kind of irritable and scratchy. Lydia sends the adults off to work on smaller scenes together. Mom and Edward go off to work on Scrooge and Ghost of Christmas Past while Dad goes with Dell and a small group to work on Christmas with Tiny Tim.

Lydia and I stay in the theater to finally focus on the olios. All she's done so far is to dress the kids in period costumes and have them wander around singing Christmas carols. Boring. Like every other olio we've ever done in a period Christmas show. Plus, they don't make any kind of sense in the context of the story.

All of a sudden it hits me.

"Lydia," I whisper. "I've got an idea."

"Well, I'm glad someone does," she says, right out loud, not even bothering to whisper. "Wait a sec . . . Bits . . ."

"Yes?"

"Would you take the group to the music room and run through your carols a couple times while Jessie and I talk?"

"Sure . . ."

"Give us fifteen minutes, okay?"

I jump right in. "Bits could be the ringleader of a street gang. Of the period, of course. Urchins—you know, like in *Oliver*. Kids with no parents and no money and no place to get out of the cold—so they're out on the streets begging for food."

Lydia's nodding.

"It's Christmas, so they're singing carols, hoping to get money . . . you know, to buy food. Or maybe they're even singing for food."

"I like it," she says.

"They could look into the windows of the houses before they knock on the doors . . ."

"And run into Scrooge on the street," Lydia adds.

"Yeah, exactly. But that means you'd have to use some of the adult actors in the olios and you weren't planning on that."

"But that's okay," she says, pausing to think about it. "There's no need for formal dialogue. They can all improvise once it's set up."

"And you wouldn't have to use everyone—not if they need to make costume changes or if they've just been in a scene playing one of the ghosts or something . . ."

"Jessie, I can see it! This is brilliant . . ."

It is? Sweet.

"Listen, why don't you go get the kids and take them to the studio theater and work on the olios using this new idea. If you're ready at the end of rehearsal, we can try running one to see if it works. If not, no problem. We'll do it tomorrow or the next day."

My mind, meanwhile, has gone completely blank. It's a big sheet of white paper. Blank. And now there are HUGE typed words in capitals on it that say, I HAVE NO IDEA HOW TO MAKE THIS HAPPEN. But see, there I am, thinking like Edward not Lydia.

Lydia would be collaborative.

She'd get them to do it. So I don't have to know how. Yet. Right?

Okay, so Bits is their ringleader. What I have to be able to do is communicate to them who they are and what they want and what they're trying to achieve.

And they will know how to do it because they are the actors and dancers.

What a concept!

So, off we go.

I tell them the idea and there is a wild babble of excitement. None of them were all that happy strolling around the stage singing Christmas carols.

Susie, of course, has to complain. "But I LOVED my costume with the fake ermine trim and the muff . . . awwww . . ."

"Another year, Diva," Bits says, cutting her off before she's had a chance to dissolve into complete whinedom.

Cracks me up. It's not like Susie's even WORN the costume.

She's only seen drawings of it. I quickly jot down so I don't forget—TALK WITH BRAD! I hope he's not completely freaked out over the changes this will require.

We run some improvs, and they get it immediately.

So we stage the first olio like a street scene where they encounter Scrooge first and he says no (I play Scrooge and am very Scrooge-ish), and then they beg for food from other people who are on the street. Singing for their supper, basically. I make a note of which adult actors we'll need for the scene.

The next olio I have them go down the aisles of the theater and beg from the audience. I won't know exactly how it works until we're back in the main stage theater, but I think it will work really well. One or two can sit or stand on the edge of the stage.

I quickly jot down—LIGHTING CHANGE. TALK WITH LYDIA ABOUT LIGHTING THE AISLE.

We work on that one some more, and they really get into it. The olios have already broken the fourth wall because they are talking to the audience and singing directly to them, too. But when they leap off the stage and go into the audience, that's a whole new level of interaction.

What's really fresh is that when they sing the well-known Christmas carols immediately after begging, suddenly the songs mean something different. More. The third olio will be the one where they are looking through the windows at the lit houses and then they beg at the door. We work a little on that scene so that they're using the song for the actual begging and that works even better.

We get three of the five olios fairly well set. And just before the regular rehearsal is over, we go back to the main stage and Lydia asks if we're ready to show the cast what we've been working on. I say yes, and then she asks if I'll describe what we've been doing. So I do.

Then we run all three olios, including the one where they come down and beg from the audience. Everyone goes crazy for it.

Brad's there watching. Maybe Lydia called him, I don't know. Of course he sees immediately what this means in terms of costumes, but instead of being annoyed he's relieved. Now the kids don't need a bunch of new costumes. We can pull most of them from stock. They need to be . . . guess what . . . dyed and distressed.

We all offer to help, but Bartle declares himself Queen of the Dye Pot.

On the way home, Mom and Dad and Brad and Bartle are all saying what a great idea it is. Bits tells them what a good job I did directing.

And you know what?

She's right.

Imagine that.

jessie jumble joins in

Rehearsals are crazy all week. My head is buzzing all the time, what with directing the olios (we're working on them separately from the main show and then coming together for the last hour to pull in the rest of the cast as needed). Bits sometimes has to run back and forth, since she's in other parts of the show. But it's working pretty well.

The writing workshop is great. Professor Bumble is having us do a lot of writing without reading out loud. He says we're using the process to gather material that we will come back to later to write actual scenes. I'm so busy right now most of the time I end up not even reading what I wrote.

And then there's movement class.

Dell and I are still meeting for an hour before each session. We do the breathing exercises and the relaxation techniques.

Today she puts on the African music again and we move in the semidark room. She's upped the dimmer a little, so we can see ourselves a bit in the mirror (and we can see each other, of course). She doesn't try to teach me any of the moves she did in class on Wednesday, and I'm glad.

It would feel . . . I don't know . . . like cheating, I guess.

She also doesn't say anything about what we're doing.

Right before class is going to start she says, "Jessie, you're going to participate today, aren't you?"

"I am," I say, gulping down the last vestige of fear.

So the kids come in, and Dell says she's going to go back over the basic African dance moves they worked on last session.

They all start moaning. Even Bits!

"We're not getting it," Bits groans.

You have no idea how strange it is to hear our perennially Ms. Positive moaning and groaning.

"I don't think my body can move like that," Susie adds. "It needs everything to be in unison."

"Oh, come on Suze," Anita says. "You're the best dancer in here. If you can't do it, no one can."

Two things happen then. Bits perks up. She likes to think of herself as the best everything where the theater is concerned. (One of the reasons I think she may actually make it on Broadway.) So, no more moaning out of that girl. And Susie, of course, perks up even more.

"Listen," Dell says. "It was exactly like this in the classes I took in New York. If you've been classically trained—which means starting with ballet, then these movements and rhythms are very different."

She doesn't say, especially if you're white, but I know she

means that. She's told me already what it felt like to be one of a handful of white students at the Alvin Ailey Dance Theater. It's smart of her not to say anything about that now, though. It would take their complaints in a whole new (and not productive) direction.

"The best antidote," she says, "is the movement itself." And then, as if we haven't talked at all about this, "Jessie, you'll join us today, won't you?"

Nice. She makes it super easy to go stand in the group with the rest.

After about five minutes of doing it and seeing all of us in the mirror (of course she's got the lights full up for class), I see that I am getting it and they still aren't.

Oh, don't get me wrong, it's not like I'm great at it or even that good. It's that my body is moving in the same ways that Dell's is. And it fits with the music. And their bodies are moving against the music most of the time. Like if you isolate the movement they can do it. They're all advanced students and good dancers so they can copy anything. But when you put the moves with the music, they are out of sync.

Seeing that helps me loosen up a little. Because I can feel in my body that I'm doing it right. This makes me tear up, and I feel like I could sit down in the middle of all this movement and bawl my eyes out. I can't remember when I felt like my body was doing the right thing.

Well, except maybe a little when I was kissing David. Sigh.

Fortunately, Dell doesn't say anything about how I'm doing. She's a really good teacher.

But when we take a break, Bits says, "Jessie, you've got it!" And she's so surprised—can you say flabbergasted—by it that if she weren't my cousin I'd be tempted to smack her.

"Yeah, you do!" Susie says. "That was sick!"

Sick is her word of the week.

I smile. Now I don't feel like smacking anyone.

When we start back up again, suddenly I notice that they've all gotten behind me, which basically pushes me to the front row and they are scrambling to stand where they can follow me. (All five foot eight, giraffe of me.) Another first.

It's still nothing but technique, but Dell seems satisfied.

On the way out of class she asks me, "Have you had any luck remembering your early dance class experiences?"

"No," I say. "It's all still a big blank."

"Oh well," she says, with a smile. "No big deal. I'm sure you'll remember."

a jumbled up thanksgiving

A Jumble Thanksgiving is a wonder to behold, so when my dad and Brad announce that they're going to visit Brad's family in Kansas, I am not very gracious in my response. Even my dad looks a little hurt over my inability to support him as he goes off to meet his new in-laws.

I don't speak to him for several days and then on the day before Thanksgiving when they're about to get in the rental car for the long drive to Kansas, I give in and nearly knock him over with the strength of my hug.

As they drive off, Mom takes a deep breath and says, "I don't know if Bartle told you, but he and Tim Chang are going out to San Francisco for the long weekend."

"What?" I yowl. "Did they leave already?" What is with everyone? Sneaking off instead of telling me what they're doing?

"No, they're leaving tonight on a red-eye."

Well. Here it is Wednesday of Thanksgiving week. When

were they planning to clue me in? Seriously, you'd think I was the high maintenance one in the family.

I'm not.

I'M NOT!

"Auntie Ellie?" I hear the whine, try to dial it back.

"You remember—she and the guys won't be back from their gig in St. Louis till Sunday. They'll be back for first tech."

I do know. I forgot. Even with Bits wailing over not being able to spend Thanksgiving with her dad. Tears come flooding into my eyes, and I bend down to pet Maggie, who is winding and winding around my ankles. I don't care if Auntie Ellie stays in St. Louis for a month. What am I crying for?

Mom doesn't even notice the tears. I swoop up Maggie and bury my face in her luscious fur, forgetting it's Maggie and not Brick or Lettuce or Judge. Maggie twists in my arms, bites my finger and leaps to the floor.

I wipe away the tears and turn my attention back to my mother who is still staring out the door as if by doing so she can get my dad back.

"What are we going to do?" I don't say, the three of us. That would be me, Mom, and Bits.

I love Thanksgiving at our house. I love the food. I love the house full of people and noise and music. I love the stupid games we play in front of the fire after pie and ice cream. I love the annual Thanksgiving Fashion Show where everyone dresses up and parades around the house and I get out of dressing up by being the one to take pictures galore. This is the one time of year everyone joins Bartle and Tim Chang in drag—I've documented every outrageous costume! One year Auntie Ellie, Mom, and I decided to dress like men to counterbalance all the frills. Bits was there, too, that year and she was the emcee. I love the late-night turkey sandwiches and being stuffed to the point of groaning.

It's like Mom's inside my head going through the Thanksgiving litany of greatness.

We both shake our heads.

We don't say out loud what I'm sure we're both thinking: What are we going to do, just the three of us?

"What about Grandmama?" I ask.

Mom reaches over and smoothes down my bangs. She hasn't done that in a long, long time.

"This is her year to go to Mary's." (As long as Aunt Mary is busy disowning Bartle, we aren't speaking to her, so Grandmama alternates holidays.)

"I'll go see if Bits has any ideas," I say, though what I feel like doing is running upstairs and slamming my door. Not an option. Bits is still asleep up there. But not for long.

I'm so depressed I can barely drag myself up the stairs. Of course that might be because all six cats have materialized out of nowhere and are winding around my ankles all the way up and into my room. Meowing. At the tops of their lungs.

"What are David and his parents doing?" Bits asks, rubbing her eyes to help her wake up. I should have brought her a cup of coffee.

We race downstairs to see if Mom's thought of doing something with the Benedicts. I think she's trying to avoid Edward in informal settings, but that's more like a when they're alone kind of thing.

David comes in the back door just as we hit the kitchen.

"I want to grill a turkey," he says to Mom.

"Well, hello to you, too," Mom says, grinning up at him.

Bits is standing there in her pajamas, turning beet red.

"Go get dressed," I say, since she's obviously embarrassed about something. Must be the pajamas, right?

"You're fine," David says. "You're way more covered than you were in that bathing suit on Sprinkler Day at Summer Street . . ."

Now she's sputtering. But she sits down at the table with a cup of coffee and a doughnut.

"The turkey?" I ask, curious in spite of myself.

"I want to grill the Thanksgiving turkey," David says. "Do you guys have plans?"

Turns out Emily is staying in town for the holiday weekend. It's too short a time for her to go back East. But the dorms close, so she's planning to stay with them. Only they don't have an extra bedroom.

"She can stay here," I say, and Mom nods her head immediately. We have tons of room, especially with everyone gone.

Bits gets up and leaves the room. I'm assuming to put her clothes on.

The weekend is starting to look brighter to me.

"The theater, or here?" I ask.

"Oh, let's do it here," Mom says. "I need a break from the theater. Even if it's only a day or two."

Wow. I don't think I've ever heard my mom say that before.

"That's if our grill works for it or do you need the big one?" she asks.

"Your grill's perfect," David says.

And the two of them sit down to figure out the rest of the menu. And then he runs off to tell Lydia and Emily the new plan. I suggest we put Emily in Auntie Ellie's room, and since we were washing her sheets along with ours anyway, this is easy to do. Auntie Ellie never minds if her room is used as a guest room. She's here so seldom she's not even attached to it.

My mom throws herself into helping David with the dinner preparations. Bits helps them while Emily and I clean the house and get things ready. Emily's never cleaned house before—her parents must be loaded—and is fascinated by all the cleaning products I've accumulated. It's like teaching someone from a tropical climate how to walk in the snow. Hilarious!

"You clean your dorm room, don't you?" I have to ask.

"Well, yeah . . ." she says. Obviously she doesn't. Scary.

We have a great time. Lydia and Edward tell the funniest stories about when they were first married and Lydia was an even more "rabid feminist" as Edward affectionately dubs her.

David's grilled turkey is the best we've ever had.

Mom has a glass of wine with dinner and doesn't even bother with the scotch later on. After the Benedicts go home, the four of us make popcorn and watch old movies for hours and hours.

Bits is kind of crabby all weekend. I think maybe she's missing her mom, although honestly I can't imagine why. And when I ask her about it she denies it and nearly bites my head off.

Other than that, it's a surprisingly good weekend.

A Jumble Thanksgiving with a twist.

tedious, tedious tech

My dad and Brad get in so late Saturday night we don't even hear them. In the morning we all sleep really late, and then Bartle and Tim get home less than an hour before first tech for *A Christmas Carol*.

They are so hyped up, they throw down their bags in the entry hall and yell up the stairs for Dad and Brad to come down. Then they simply explode with their news.

"We're moving to San Francisco!" Bartle shouts the minute we're all together in the kitchen.

All kinds of wild excitement with everyone shouting and laughing and asking questions.

Turns out they had a fabulous time and some of Tim's friends knew about jobs they could get. Bartle says there are tons of costuming opportunities.

"They even have a gay ball I could do dresses for . . ."

"My family out there has a place we can stay until we can get our own apartment," Tim has to interrupt Bartle, who sounds like he could talk nonstop for three hours, he's got so much to say.

"I didn't know you had family out there," Mom says.

Me, neither.

"My favorite aunt and her teenage kids," he says. "She has a little pool house that she uses as a guest room. We can stay there for as long as we need to."

"I love San Francisco," Brad says.

"I can't believe I've never been there," my dad adds.

Suddenly my heart sinks even lower. Oh, my god, what if my dad and Brad go, too?

"When?" I finally manage to choke out.

Why does everyone seem so happy about this?

"Not till after the first of the year," Bartle says, running over to give me a hug. "You can come visit us."

I nod. Honestly, I have no desire to go to San Francisco. Even for a visit. What is wrong with me? I'm the only person I know who doesn't want to go running off somewhere else.

Well, no, that's not exactly true. I don't think Mom wants to go anywhere, either. For some reason I don't find this comforting.

It's a relief to head over to the theater for first tech. Emily tags along since she can't go back to her dorm until 6:00 p.m. I warn her it's going to be tedious.

"Tedious?" she asks.

"Tedious, tedious, tedious . . ." I answer. I've heard this said about first tech so many times it's engraved in my head like stone.

And of course I've hung out at tech rehearsals since I was a little kid.

But this is the first time I've been in a tech rehearsal as an assistant director, so all of a sudden I'm realizing firsthand what's really going on and why it takes three times as long and makes the actors feel like they are back at square one.

And then that makes them cranky and impatient.

And then that makes it even more tedious.

Emily shrugs when I tell her she could go find David or something if she's bored. She's got her digital camera out and she's snapping shots left and right. The cool thing about Emily is that as long as she's got a camera in her hands she's never bored.

So we plod along . . . STOP! and START! and STOP! and START! as we work with the tech people to fold in all the technical aspects of the production. You have to work it until the lights and sets and sound and costumes and props are essentially invisible and seamless.

I'm madly taking notes for Lydia through the costume parade. That goes really well. Brad's done a great job blending stock costumes with brand-new designs.

After the costume parade Lydia looks at the lights and then looks at the lights while the actors stand onstage in their costumes getting crabbier and crabbier and finally she has BJ mark it. And then I write down the setting. So does he. And then they walk through the scene. And then we mark it. And then we do it with sound. And she listens. And she listens. And she sets it. And we write it down.

Then there are costume notes here and there, and I write those down while she's telling them to Brad.

The only piece of it that's pretty much set are the props because the actors have been using them in rehearsals. But now the people who are doing the set and prop changes have to get that down.

Yeah, it's tedious all right. But here's the thing.

I LOVE IT.

I wish I were Lydia, listening and watching and making the decisions. With someone else being me and writing it all down.

Honestly, since it's the first time I've done it, I'm even loving writing it down.

David comes to get Emily around five, I'm assuming to take her to campus. But at seven, the two of them serve us sandwiches and soup they fixed. I don't remember David ever doing this before, but it's way better than ordering pizzas, which is what we usually do. We don't get out of there until nearly nine.

Lydia comes to look over my shoulder as I'm jotting down the last item.

"Wow," she says, "I was going to ask you to type those up, but your handwriting is so clean I can read it just fine."

"If I'd been thinking I'd have brought my laptop," I say. "Then I could print them out for you."

"Next time," she says, taking the notes and glancing over them some more. "Jessie, you did a great job. Thank you."

"You're welcome." We walk out of the theater together, and the lights go out behind us. All except the blue tech light right in the middle of the stage.

"I really . . ." It's hard to put this into words. "I really enjoyed today."

Lydia busts out laughing.

"What are you laughing about?" I ask, hoping it's not AT me.

"I did, too," she says. "I don't think I've ever admitted that to anyone before. I love first tech rehearsal."

We're both grinning like idiots.

"You're going to be a great director, Jess," she says, giving me a quick hug before heading home.

I'm at our door when it hits me. Lydia said, "Next time." She must plan to use me as her AD in another show.

"What are you grinning about?" Bits asks, still sounding like a cranky actor at first tech.

I don't tell her. This is one of those things that's more satisfying kept to myself.

"Where's Emily?" I ask, and then Bits really bites my head off.

"With David, where do you think?"

"Hot chocolate," I say back.

"Huh?"

"Follow me to the kitchen and I will make you a cup of your favorite hot chocolate. It sounds like you need it."

"With whipped cream?" she whines. See, there she goes again. What is with her?

"How else?"

dig deeper

Bartle and Tim Chang have done nothing since they got home Sunday but talk, talk, talk San Francisco. It's actually a relief to have them switch back to wondering if Professor Bumble is gay and laughing over his clumsiness. I'm that desperate to have them change the subject. Sigh.

Sister M&M turns from the window when I throw myself with some gusto into my usual chair between her and Emily.

"Are you going to read today?" she asks without even saying hello. Her voice sounds strained.

Gee, she always seems so calm.

"Depends on what we write," I say. She answers with a nod and a smile.

"I am," Emily says. "I'm tired of always saying I pass. I can't write for beans, but I think I need to start reading anyway."

"Yeah, me, too," I say. "I make up my mind yes and at home in my room it seems doable in the extreme. Then we get here and do the writing and I still think I'm going to read and then I open my mouth and out comes 'I pass' . . . What is with that?"

"Me, too," Sister M&M says. "Exactly like that."

Then she laughs.

"What?" Emily asks, smiling back at her.

"Well, except that I'm in a convent when I'm thinking it."

I don't know why, but that cracks us up. She cracks up, too. You can't howl with laughter and still look and feel frantic. Even when you're wearing a wimple.

Professor Bumble shoots the three of us a stern glance that dissolves immediately into a grin. Probably because of the Sister.

"Today," the professor says, "we're going to dig deeper."

Uh-oh.

"Bring it on!" Bartle says. Someone really needs to sit on that guy. He's getting on my nerves big time.

"What I want you to do is take about five minutes to look through all the list writing we've been doing for several weeks now. Glance over it quickly and look for a phrase or a sentence that has a kind of zing when you read it. Circle it. And keep looking."

Troy has his hand up.

"I'll let you know the next step when we're done with this," the professor says. He's good.

This sounds interesting. I can't really imagine any of my phrases or sentences having a zing—whatever that is—but who knows?

We all dive into our notebooks and silence reigns.

When Professor Bumble calls time, I've circled at least five. Huh. I glance at Sister M&M's notebook and she's got several pages creased at the corners. Emily's got some stuff marked, too. And across from me, I can see Bev wielding a neon green pen.

"All right," the professor says. "Now glance over what you've marked and pick one to use as your prompt—as a jumping off place for your writing."

We comply. Even Bartle manages to do it without commenting.

"Now, let's write for half an hour. I know these longer writes are hard to sustain, but the rule still applies. Once you start writing, don't lift your pen. Keep it moving even if you have to write a phrase over and over. Don't stop."

He makes it sound like a marathon. Which it kind of is. I shake out my hand to make sure I'm ready.

The sentence I picked was actually a question prompted by my work with Dell. Walking backward in time, what's on the other side of the CLUMSY door?

We write and write and write and write. And Professor Bumble hit the nail on the head—it's hard not to stop. You naturally want to stop and think. To put your pen down or stick it in your mouth and chew on it. To gaze off into space for a while. But as usual, he doesn't let us. Even though he's writing, too, he's like a mom with eyes in the back of his (her?) head. Every so often he'll glance up and say, 'Keep those pens moving. Repeat something if you have to.' Or swear. I for one always write 'oh shit, oh shit, oh shit' until something else comes . . .'"

We all laugh, even Sister M&M, and we keep on writing.

What happens to me in these long free-writes is that at some point I don't really know anymore what I've written. So when we stop to read it, it's almost like reading something someone else wrote.

I think that's how you do what he said—dig deeper. I think it takes you beyond (or maybe below) the critical voice in your head that's saying how stupid you are, how inane what you're writing probably is. All that self-critical crap.

So, the second he stops us, we all page back to read what we wrote. But he interrupts us this time, right away.

"Okay, now go back to the pages where you marked your prompts and pick a second prompt. Don't read what you wrote yet."

How funny—it's hard not to go back and read it. I look around and everyone is struggling with this.

This time I take a phrase, *Got-to-be-Good Girl.* I like the hyphens and the alliteration. I don't even remember what context I used it in.

"All right," he says, "This time we're writing for twenty minutes. Same deal. Go."

Crazy, crazy, crazy. Those are the first three words I write and then I'm off and writing.

I'm pretty sure I know what he'll do next. Yup, I'm right.

"All right," he says, as he stops us. "Don't stop to read. Go back and pick a third prompt. This time we're writing for fifteen minutes. Go."

Mine is "I don't remember my first dance teacher."

Only, here's the deal. About five minutes into the free write, I DO remember my first dance teacher.

Her name is Ms. Della.

She was my teacher when I was four and five and six.

Ms. Ardella Patterson.

And she thought I hung the moon.

the ghost of christmas present

Lydia and I are pacing across the back of the theater. Every so often we catch each other's eyes, shake our heads, and go back to our chosen spots (she's behind the center section and I'm next to the exit that's stage left).

"I've always thought it was pretentious of Edward to do this," she whispers to me one of the times we almost collide. "And here I am doing it, too."

We have a little fit of laughter, hanging on to each other for a couple seconds. Then we somehow manage to stand still, smile, and greet people as they are coming into the theater.

All the reviewers came last night for final dress and two of our favorites are back again tonight. I wonder if they do that at all the other theaters in town. Of course, they have perfect seats in the middle of the center section (right where Lydia and I sat while we were rehearsing).

Oh, my gosh, Professor Bumble is here! He stops to talk with

Lydia and waves at me. Then I'm busy talking to David and Emily and it isn't until the show's about ready to start that I notice where the professor's sitting. He's in a row with Bartle, Tim Chang (who, bless his heart, is once again in drag), and ... SISTER MARY MARGARET! Now, that is a funny sight. That is so funny it could be a skit on *Saturday Night Live*. I point them out to Emily, and she races around to get some good shots without them noticing.

How sweet of Sister M&M to come.

I'm surprised at how wonderful the music has turned out to be. Auntie Ellie and Lee are both classically trained musicians. They've done a wild job of taking well-known classical pieces and updating them. Auntie Ellie is on the piano, and Lee is on electric guitar. During the part where the other band members are there, Lee is playing the drums like he usually does. Sweet.

Finally, the lights dim, the curtains sweep to each side, the lights come up, and the show begins. Lydia and I pace through the entire thing.

At intermission I slip backstage to avoid talking with any of the audience members. I'll save that for after the show. Besides, I want to tell Bits and the other kids how well the olios are going! They are doing a wonderful job. And Mom and Bits were amazing as the dual-personality Christmas Past. It was such a weird concept, but given how much they look alike and how easy it is for them to match each other's voices, it turned out to be Lydia's best idea ever.

Edward is great as Scrooge. I didn't expect him to be. He's different from the rest of the company. They all have out-there personalities and his is more interior. And using that for his characterization makes Scrooge so real and makes you care about him even when he's being a real jerk at the beginning.

The second half of the show is even better than the first. I can see all these tiny adjustments Lydia made that I maybe questioned when she was doing it and they all work. The audience leaps to its feet and gives the cast a standing ovation for so long that they do an encore of one of the olio Christmas songs, with everyone joining in.

And then we throw the best party ever.

This is the start of the holiday season. We have a huge Christmas tree this year, covered with a crazy combination of traditional ornaments and hand-made ornaments. Lights hanging everywhere. Pine boughs sending out that heady scent.

The theater hasn't been lit up like this since my graduation party six months ago! It's gorgeous. Everything's gorgeous.

The board of directors are here again, so the food is catered like at the first fall show. But this time David and Emily have done the baking and all of the French pastries David's been teaching himself how to make are incredible.

Emily's everywhere at once, taking photographs. If she keeps this up, we may have to hire her. She gets off three or four shots of me as I'm thinking this, and I foil the fifth by sticking a huge shrimp dipped in cocktail sauce into my mouth. Leaving the tail hanging out. Of course, she shoots it anyway.

Bits is surrounded by people telling her how wonderful she was. All my recent jealousy evaporates into thin air. I'm so happy for her I could bust. This is her first real role at the theater. She's done a ton of student productions and had her share of small chorus roles. But she's never had this kind of main stage role. She was fantastic as the ringleader of the street gang in the olios. But the biggest breakthrough for her was matching my mother moment for moment as the Ghost of Christmas Past.

My mom is a consummate actor. For Bits to be able to match her . . . well . . . there's just no stopping her now.

The crowd around her thins when the caterers bring out our signature BBQ'd ribs, chicken, and fried fish. Not exactly health food, but everyone swarms the buffet tables.

Bits keeps looking around, and I wonder who she's looking for. It hits me all of a sudden that she looks sad.

I slip up behind her and give her a hug. "Are you okay?"

It seems like a silly question. She's got to be over the moon.

"Uh-huh," she says, smiling, but still with those sad eyes.

"What?"

"Oh, nothing," she sighs, but smiles again. "I invited my mom. I . . . I guess I thought maybe she'd change her mind and come . . ."

At that moment David comes sliding across the floor (yeah, the guys who polished the wood floors got a little over enthusiastic). He's carrying a tray of mini chocolate tortes with whipped cream on them and in them.

"For you, mademoiselle?" he asks, extending the tray out to Bits. "Crafted especially with you in mind . . ."

For once Bits doesn't say something cutting to him. She grabs one of the tortes and takes a huge bite, looking at him over all that chocolate and whipped cream, her hazel eyes gleaming.

We both reach out to wipe the whipped cream off her nose, but David has pulled a handkerchief out of his pocket (yeah, a real cloth one) and he does the honors.

"I made the fruit tarts for Jessie," he says with another sweet smile.

"For *moi*?" I say, suddenly remembering Bartle's crazy French accent the day Loretta blew her top last summer. He hasn't done that again. "They are delicious."

"What did you make for Emily?" Bits asks, her mouth again full of chocolate and whipped cream.

There's one of those funny moments of silence and in that moment you can see all three of us knowing he didn't make a dessert for Emily and all three of us wondering what that means. But then we see Emily snapping photographs of us and we turn to her and pose, all of us making silly faces and the moment passes.

That's when I notice that Professor Bumble appears to be following my mom from one spot to another.

What's he doing anyway? He must be trying to get her attention but she keeps moving away from him right before he succeeds.

"I've got a feeling about that man," Grandmama says at my elbow.

"Good or bad?" I ask.

Before she has a chance to answer, someone taps on my arm. It's Sister M&M.

I introduce her to Grandmama.

"I've got to get back to the convent," she says. "This was a wonderful evening. You should be very proud of the work you did on this production."

"Thank you." I am so surprised I don't even stumble over accepting the compliment.

"I noticed in the program that you conceived and directed the olios," she says.

"That was in the program?" I've been so busy with the Christmas decorations and last-minute stuff on Lydia's list, I hadn't even stopped to look at a program.

"I think you'll make a wonderful director if that's something you're interested in doing," she adds.

"Thanks! I am interested in directing." I really am. Wow. "Thanks."

"I'll see you Thursday," she says. "If I don't leave right this minute Mother Superior will lock me out."

Now there's a mental image I wouldn't mind using in a scene.

We take the party back to our house the way we always do.

Everyone's making a huge fuss over Bits. She is loving it!

"I was assistant directing when I met your mom," my dad says. He's putting some music on so we can all dance. We didn't do much dancing at the theater this time. Everyone was too busy schmoozing the board members.

"You were?" I say, taking the plastic off the new CD my dad just handed me. "What's this?"

"*Billy Elliot*," he says. "From the stage version. I meant to get it when it came out and kept forgetting."

"We're going to dance to this?"

"Oh, no . . . all right . . . you pick something . . ." He stands aside to let me at the shelves. "It's a harder job than people think . . ."

"Picking dance music?"

"Noooooo—being an assistant director."

"Hmm."

"You did a very good job," he says, reaching out and selecting first one CD then another from the ones I've been sorting through.

"Thank you," I say, not for the first time this night. I'm starting to like the way that phrase is rolling off my tongue.

"I love this house," Emily says, grabbing me and pulling me onto the dance floor where she's already been dancing with David and Bits and Bartle and Tim Chang. Their wildly gyrating throng parts to allow us in.

"Yeah," I say, "it's a nice house." I guess. I mean, it's okay. My mom loves it. I like how close it is to the theater more than anything.

"No, I mean all of it. Your family. All these people. The theater . . ."

Bartle has pushed us all into a line to do this dance from the 1960s called The Locomotion. My dad taught it to us for one of our end-of-the-year musical reviews. It's fun to do if you're not tripping over your own feet and tonight for some reason (maybe because I'm trying to teach it to Emily) I'm not.

"I wish I didn't have to go home for the holidays," Emily says with a little sigh.

"Oh, do you?" I grab her shoulders and turn her around for the next side step. "I suppose you do . . . Connecticut?"

"Yeah, just outside of New York City."

"Right. When are you leaving?"

"I haven't gotten my ticket yet, but I'm aiming for Friday, December 21."

"The day the world is supposed to end," I say, doing a pretty mean spin to end the dance.

"The world is ending?" she sounds confused.

"Yeah, you know—what Bits's mom was yowling about at Halloween."

"Oh, the Mayan prediction thing . . ."

"Yeah, Armageddon on the twenty-first. Are you sure you want to fly that day?"

"Why, do you think it's dangerous?"

I whack her on the arm. "Joke."

She hits me back. "I'll be back on New Year's Eve. Or the day before if I can swing it."

Oh, my goodness, who put Bette Midler on? Well, let me see, that would be one of the gay guys, I would imagine.

David and Bits are doing a dance my mom and dad did in another one of those reviews a while back. I can't believe they know the choreography. Especially David.

"Why don't you want to go home?"

"Did I actually admit that to you?"

"You did."

"My parents are from old money and they want me to be a society girl . . . can you imagine? Gag . . ."

"My only frames of reference for that are old movies and the rich theater kids . . ."

"You're lucky," she says with a smile. "And yes, it's that tacky."

"I can't imagine you in that scene," I say. I really can't. I mean,

Emily's looking gorgeous tonight for opening. But she's doing it in her usual army fatigues. And combat boots. Vintage, lace-up combat boots.

"That's the best compliment you could give me," she says.

When my dad sees what David and Bits are doing, he grabs Mom and that's when I notice who she's talking with over there in the corner. Professor Bumble! Did my mother drag the professor home with her?

Evidently I say this out loud, because Emily answers, "No, he came with Lydia."

Oh, right. They know each other from the university. Whew. That was a little too weird for words for a second there.

We all stop dancing and talking to watch the performing foursome. Bits and David are giving my parents a run for their money. I glance at Emily to see . . . well . . . if she minds. But she's looking at me so I guess not.

You know, it really is strange that David knows that routine.

"Do you think that boy is gay?" Bartle asks, right in front of Emily.

"Nope," we say in unison and then laugh.

Then it gets even better. Dell, who has been lurking in a corner talking with Edward suddenly grabs Professor Bumble and pulls him out onto the dance floor.

She is at least four inches taller than he is.

And then there's his whole clumsy thing.

But, big surprise, the man can dance. Maybe it's because Dell's leading. He sees me and waves. He's got this huge smile on his face.

I haven't said anything to Dell about her being my first dance teacher. Things were so crazy getting ready for the show to open and class was cancelled today because of that. Besides, I'm not absolutely certain my memory is real. I mean, if it's true, why hasn't she said anything to me? Or why didn't my parents mention it?

"You have any popcorn?" Emily asks, interrupting my reverie.

"Let's go see."

David and Bits join us in the kitchen once the Bette Midler marathon is over.

It's not until I'm falling asleep with Bits snoring on the other side of the bed that I realize it's been a truly wonderful night.

And the first time in longer than I can remember that I haven't spent the entire party worrying about my parents.

just in case we didn't get the message

Saturday morning. I'm the first one up. As usual. It doesn't matter how late I've been up the night before, I'm an early riser. It was a really good after party. After a really good party at the theater. After a really REALLY good show.

The first thing I notice after I've got the coffee on is that Lee is asleep on the couch. At least he's made it up out of the basement. Although I thought for sure he was in with Auntie Ellie the other night. I don't know why I don't just ask someone. I keep forgetting, I guess.

I've started to clean up some of the mess from the night before but stop at the living room so I don't wake him up.

I'm on my second cup of coffee when Bits wanders in, her hair a tousled mess around her still partly made-up face.

"There's some makeup remover in the bathroom," I say. It's

not good for your skin (even beautiful, yes, flawless skin like hers) to sleep in stage makeup.

"Good morning to you, too," she mutters.

She's standing in front of the coffeepot staring at it like it will pour her a cup and add cream and sugar.

I get up and do the honors.

"You weren't drinking last night were you?" I ask.

"Are you out of your mind? I don't drink."

"You were wonderful."

"Thanks."

"You're welcome." See how good I'm getting at responding like a normal person. Perhaps you've noticed that I don't have a lot of role models for that.

For example, Bartle has stumbled down the back stairs and poured himself a huge cup of coffee. Geez, where did he get that mug? He totally wipes out the pot I just made.

I get up to make a second pot of coffee. We've still got a crowd waiting to rise.

That's when the doorbell rings.

"I'll get it," Bits says.

She's opened the door before it hits me who it's going to be. It's Saturday. The pesky CLPs, of course.

But not just any CLP this Saturday morning, the day after the opening of *A Christmas Carol*. Oh, no. It's Loretta. Standing there, all gauzy and spacey-looking with another woman, clutching their star-covered, yet still churchy, totes.

Let's say ALL HELL BREAKS LOOSE.

Because that's what happens.

"Mom!" Bits shouts.

This wakes Lee. Who is, thankfully, still wearing last night's clothes. But he's a bleary-eyed, hungover, wild-haired mess. Still, he joins Bits at the door.

Loretta is doing her End of the World spiel. There's a strong emphasis this morning, as you'd expect, on this wicked old system of things.

I turn to go back to the kitchen and guess what . . . here comes Auntie Ellie. She is wearing next to nothing (it's not Christmas yet, so she hasn't gotten the bathrobe that Mom actually did take the time to make her like she said she would the last time Auntie Ellie ran through the house naked). Wow.

Next, Mom comes down the stairs. She, fortunately, is fully clothed. Bless her little heart. She's even combed her hair.

Behind her, though, is Tim Chang. I'm not going to describe what he's wearing. Nope. Not going to.

So far, no professor. Or Dell. I'm praying that means they went home.

But right then Bartle comes barreling out from the kitchen.

Try to picture all of this happening—one, two, three!!! Like perfect staging in the proverbial French farce that is our household.

"Who drank the last of the coffee?" Of course that's my dad. He wanders out to the front door wearing only pajama bottoms, unconsciously flexing his upper chest muscles while holding the empty pot.

"Good lord!" he fairly shouts. And that brings Brad the rest of the way out of the kitchen behind him.

And there's Grandmama behind Brad. Wearing a pair of my

dad's pajamas. What did she do? Stay upstairs with them last night? She's never done that before.

I have two choices.

One is to stand here and watch so I can record all of this for posterity. I'm thinking it will make a grand scene for my playwriting workshop.

The other is to grab the coffeepot out of my dad's hand and go make another pot of coffee.

Evidently I'm in competition with Brad over this, but I'm a bully, so I win.

I know I should stay and record. I mean, when will I get another chance at a scene like this? But I can't. I just can't.

I hear Loretta shout that it's thirteen days until Armageddon. I glance back in time to see her wave a pamphlet so close to Bits's nose, Bits has to jump back.

You bitch, I'm thinking. Your daughter just did the most beautiful acting job you can imagine, and you weren't there to see it. And now you're here screeching at her about the world ending? I can't watch. I can't.

Unfortunately, that leaves my sense of hearing, which is acute. Not that it needs to be in this case.

I make the coffee while Lee shouts at Loretta.

I stand and watch it brew while Loretta shouts at both Lee and Bits.

I hear my mom enter the fray, shouting even louder than both of them at her sister.

It sounds like Loretta's trying to grab Bits because I hear everyone screaming, "Let her go! She's staying here!"

That draws me over to the doorway in time to see Auntie Ellie shove Loretta and shout in her deep, husky, BOOMING voice, "If you don't get off those steps, you insane bitch, I am calling the cops!" Since I know how Auntie Ellie feels about cops, I'm impressed.

The door slams. And the living room erupts into a babble of noise. I can't see Bits. She's so small and everyone is surrounding her.

I can't help myself. I think of Babylon. The Tower of Babel. Sodom and Gomorrah, pillars of salt. The horsemen of the apocalypse in Revelation.

I go back out there.

Lee and Auntie Ellie have Bits on the sofa and they're consoling her. Mom is standing in the hallway staring at the closed closet door. Everyone else is milling around trying to look useful and succeeding only in looking like they just got out of bed and haven't had their coffee yet.

Except for Bartle, who's at the window with the curtains pulled back.

"That other woman's got Loretta by the arm and is pulling her back to the car," he says. "Oh, shit! Loretta's yanked herself free."

We all gasp.

"She's coming back!"

Auntie Ellie gets up, searching her skimpy nightclothes for her cell phone. Nope, not there.

Mom, who has finally quit staring at the closet door and returned to the living room, sits down.

"No," Bartle reports. "No, she's not."

Auntie Ellie sits down. Mom stands up.

"The woman's got her again," Bartle says. "They're standing still and she's talking to her."

"That other woman didn't say one word at the door, did she?"

Tim Chang and I push in behind Bartle. We watch as Loretta hangs her head, sobbing uncontrollably.

"Oh, shit," Bartle says, "She really is coming back this time."

Auntie Ellie stands up. Mom sits back down. It's like they're attached or on strings or something.

"No," I say, "No, the woman's leading her to the car . . ."

Auntie Ellie sits back down. This time Mom stays there with her. I seriously wish I'd gotten that on video. Where is Emily when we need her?

The woman and Loretta get in the battered minivan and sit there.

And sit there.

And sit there.

Finally the car starts up, coughing and sputtering, and then, while we all hold our collective breaths, it drives off.

"Hallelujah!" Grandmama says, her hand raised in the air as though she's at church.

In the silence that follows I can hear the coffee maker doing it's final grinding noises.

"Anyone want a cup?" I head back out to the kitchen.

As everyone gathers around the table to drink their coffee, with Bits in the very center of us all, Grandmama says, "God is bigger than that."

"Amen," I say, and I say it right out loud.

I suddenly remember what Emily said last night.

"I love this house," she said.

She was talking about this family.

This cracked, crazy, frazzled, and reconfiguring family.

Yes. Me, too.

making it a family thang . . .

Hoping to catch Dell before class, I go over half an hour early. Sometimes she warms up for a while before class even when she's not working with me. This time I get lucky. She's there and doesn't seem to mind that I'm interrupting her breathing exercises.

I've spent every spare minute of the last three days digging through the crates of photos looking for what I know has to be there. I remember when I was transferring the photos from the cardboard boxes to plastic crates seeing photos of me from dance classes when I was little and wondering about them. But do I have any idea which crate? Nope. I mean, the only constant here is that there are a lot of photos of me.

Isn't that proof that my mom loves me? I mean, she was always the photographer. Yeah, pathetic, I know. Back to the photos.

Photos of me in shows, of me and Bits, of me and our other distant cousins, of David and me at our birthday parties, me in the costume shop with Mom back when she worked there.

Me in the orchestra pit while my dad's performing. Me in the office with everyone sticking labels and stamps on big mailings. Me each summer of Summer Street. Me at Grandmama's house. And on and on and on.

When I finally find the dance class photos the first thing I notice is that I'm really cute. Really, really cute. Taller than all the other little girls, yes. Quite a bit darker. Most of them are blond—I mean, we do live in Minnesota after all. But I'm actually kind of pretty.

And I'm also not clumsy looking. Not at all.

Wow.

It's Tuesday night when I finally hit pay dirt.

Ms. Della.

She looks a lot younger than she does now. Not that she's all that old now. Her early thirties I guess. But ten or twelve years ago she would have been nineteen or twenty maybe. Only a year or two older than Bits and David and Emily are now. Only a couple years older than me.

The photos say 2000, 2001, 2002 on the backs.

In one photo she's got long, straight hair. Red like it is now. I guess it's natural. Ha!

She was really thin. She's still thin, but now she's more muscular.

There's a series of pictures where she's working with me on ballet moves. My extension is better than good. It's . . . it's . . . incredible. And I'm smiling. The picture, though, that starts to stir some actual memories—instead of me feeling like I'm looking at photos of someone else's life—is one where we're having a big party.

There are several group shots. It's in an old warehouse over by the university, probably where the theater was before they got the grant and were able to buy the old mansion. Balloons and banners and a big cake and tons of people.

And then there's a shot of the two of us. I'm holding the bunch of balloons and she's holding me on her lap.

Two of the balloons say, "Good luck!" and "Break a leg!" And there's one that has a big heart on it and NYC. New York City. So, they're her balloons.

I think I've got it figured out, but I want to see what she has to say about it.

I hand her the picture.

And she starts to cry.

And, to my complete surprise, so do I.

Then she closes the studio door. And she gives me a big hug, which I give her right back big time.

"You remember, huh?" she asks, wiping at tears that keep rolling down her cheeks.

"I'm so sorry I forgot you."

I have a million questions and there's no time right now to ask them. We've only got a few minutes before class is going to start.

"I lost touch with your parents for several years. New York was not an easy adjustment after living here all my life."

"It's weird they didn't say anything to me when they hired you . . ."

"I was surprised, too . . ." She hesitates. "Actually, I was more surprised that they hired me."

"Why?"

"When I left . . . see, I got this great opportunity . . . but not only was I leaving the teaching, but I was doing a show here. Choreographing it. I pulled out in the middle to go to New York. With hardly any notice . . ."

"Oooohhh . . ." My parents hate it when people do that. Especially my mom.

"Your mom was really angry about that. We both said some things . . . I know I regretted . . . that's the main reason we lost touch."

It surprises me that she's telling me this. But I want to hear everything she has to say.

"I was feeling so bad about having left like that, and then not staying in contact with you."

She stops, swallows hard, to keep herself from crying again, I think. "Especially not staying in contact with you."

This is so strange. But the more I remember about Dell, the less strange it seems.

"So," she says, letting her breath out in a whoosh, and continuing, "I was looking for you that first day . . . I . . . I couldn't wait to see you . . . but then it was clear that you didn't know me at all. Not just that you didn't recognize me but like you'd never even heard of me before. I should have said something right then. Normally, I would . . ."

"Why didn't you?"

"I was on my way over to talk with you . . ."

"I know! Bits ran up to ask you about New York, didn't she?"

"Uh-huh. That girl is obsessed with NYC!"

"She is!"

"To tell you the truth," Dell says, getting back on track. "I caught on to your whole 'I'm so clumsy, I'm so awkward, I don't fit in' persona thing right away that first day at orientation and it stopped me dead in my tracks. It was so NOT what I was expecting. And then, since neither Una nor Mark said anything or made any attempt to reintroduce us, I decided to wait and see if you'd remember on your own."

It makes sense. Especially given her kind of rocky relationship with my parents.

"Of course, I didn't expect to see you in my movement class, either."

We both laugh over that first class and how she handled it. It was really perfect, if you think about it.

I'm running over in my mind everything my parents have said about Dell since school started, but I'm coming up with next to nothing. Knowing how they are, though, that's not all that unusual. They've probably forgotten how important she was to me back then. They both tend to think of themselves first in most situations.

"Did you know Bits back then? I mean, you know she's my cousin, right?"

Dell is nodding, but she says, "I do know that, but she hadn't started taking classes here when I was still here."

For some reason, I'm really glad about that. "She must have started right after you left." I'm thinking about what Bits said about her teachers at the Children's Theatre and her first teacher here.

"Even when you came to dinner and you were telling theater stories . . ."

"I know," she says. "I really thought that night we'd clear this up. But we were talking about the university and those first JUMBLE Player productions . . ."

"And my parents . . ."

"Yeah, your parents . . . even when they're not together . . ."

We both shake our heads and start to laugh.

There's a din out in the hallway where the students are waiting for Dell to open the door and let them in.

"We've got some catching up to do," she says with another quick hug.

For the first half of class, Dell works with the kids setting up their dances for the recital that marks the end of the semester. It's only a week and a half away. They're all going to be demonstrating the different period movement patterns they worked on before I joined the class. And then, she says, we'll end with a big group number doing the African dance moves.

So, once they are all set with their assignments, we start to practice the choreography she gave us last session. She's going to be dancing with us. Everyone's pretty much gotten over the hump of learning these moves. They have trouble every time she teaches a new move, but then once they get it, they get it.

I'm not having any trouble learning the moves. And now I'm wondering if, on some physical level, I remember working with Dell when I still believed I could dance. Maybe that's what's making the difference.

We're in the middle of the second run of the group number when my dad pokes his head around the doorway.

"Hi, Mark," Dell says. "Do you want to join us?"

He's in the room in a flash.

"I've never done this kind of dance before," he says. "It looks like too much fun! Soooo, show me."

The kids are all giggling and acting goofy. Mr. Big Shot deigning to come dance with the Advanced Movement class. Bits shakes her head at me.

Dell runs through a quick review of all of the moves. And the funniest thing happens. My dad cannot get it. He is as bad as Bits was at the beginning.

Dell corrects him. He watches himself in the mirror (because clearly he thinks he's got it) and then he sees he doesn't. And then, of course, he's determined to get it.

Dell says, "We're going to perform this at the recital. Do you want to be part of the group?"

By this time, he's backing away, shaking his head.

"No," he says, "I'd only slow you down."

"Well," she says, "why don't you watch us perform it now. We could use an audience—and then you can decide for sure."

She puts the music on again and we do the whole thing. And my dad is sitting there on the stool, watching, with this priceless look on his face. I wish we were videotaping him.

When we stop, he applauds and applauds.

And then Dell says, "If you change your mind, Jessie can show you the moves."

Makes my day.

doing the right thing

When we get to the writing workshop there's a note saying that the professor is out sick today. Bartle's thrilled, as he's got some last-minute work to do for another small costuming gig he snagged a few weeks ago. He drags Tim with him to help.

I don't want to go home yet and I don't want to hang out in the green room so I ask Emily if she wants to go to Caribou instead.

"Sure," she says, "but can we go on down to Penzey's first? I want to get David some spices for Christmas."

Now that is a seriously perfect idea. I wish I'd thought of it.

We wander from one side of the street to the other, stopping in Pier 1 to look at this year's ornaments and going back across the street to check out a little import store. We've been to the spice place and are just about to cross the street to head back to Caribou when I happen to glance down the side street and see Bruce out on his front lawn. It looks like he's struggling to get the VOTE NO sign out of the ground.

I motion to Emily to follow me and take off down the street at a run. I've been wanting to check in on him and Arthur, but have been too busy.

He smiles when he sees me. "We won," he says, nodding down at the sign that he still hasn't managed to pull up. It's probably frozen into the ground by now.

"I know," I say, introducing Emily. "Can you believe it? No one thought Minnesota would come through like that."

He's still nodding, but there are tears in his eyes. "Arthur was over the moon about it!"

"I thought he would be"—I turn to Emily—"Arthur's his partner."

"That's why I left the sign out so long . . . so he could see it . . . and . . ."

"How is he doing?"

"Oh, honey," Bruce says, tears sliding down his cheeks. "Arthur passed away . . ."

He sags against me as I give him a big hug, and he feels so fragile and frail in my arms.

"When?"

"A week after the election," he says, wiping at his cheeks. Emily hands him a tissue and he blows his nose. "Oh, Jessie, he was so happy. I'm glad he lived to see that. Those last weeks, I'd come back to the house after going grocery shopping and he'd ask me for a count of the signs . . ."

"I was doing that, too!"

"Do you mind if I take a picture of you and Jessie?" Emily asks, pulling her trusty camera out of her pocket.

"Why?" I ask, just as Bruce says, "Why not?"

We all laugh.

"I don't know," she says. "Something about this feels historical."

"Emily's a great photographer," I say, and then Bruce and I smile at the camera.

"I'm sorry we didn't know about Arthur," I say.

"I meant to call you," Bruce said, "but I couldn't find your number. And, you know, I'm not on that e-mail thing . . ."

"Is there anything we can do for you now?" I ask.

"Well, no," he says. "Not unless you've got someone who wants to buy this house."

I look up at the rundown but adorable little Victorian jammed between two huge turn-of-the-century farmhouses. And my heart plummets to the bottom of my feet and stays there. It's exactly the kind of house that Brad has been wanting and searching for. Five years? Six?

"You're planning to move?"

"I've been wanting to join my daughter in Miami for about ten years, but Arthur wouldn't budge. She's got a little place waiting for me, and I'm heading out of here the minute I sell this house."

"You have a daughter?" I guess I shouldn't be surprised. "Were you married?"

"Didn't I tell you that?" Bruce asks.

"Huh-uh," I say, shaking my head.

"Well," he says, "it was a long time ago."

"Have you listed the house yet?" I ask, trying to keep the tremble out of my voice.

Emily doesn't know anything about Brad's search for a small

Victorian in this neighborhood. All I have to do is keep my mouth shut and no one will ever know the difference.

"I had some Realtors come look at it. You know what a mess it is inside. They want me to clear it out and do some basic upgrading before I put it on the market."

The house really is pretty bad. But see, that's what Brad needs to get into this neighborhood. He needs to be able to make a low offer on a house with lots of potential. And then put in the elbow grease to make it beautiful. I'll bet Bruce would sell it without even going through Arthur's stuff, anything to get on that plane to Miami.

Emily's looking at me kind of funny. I wonder if I said something out loud. I do that sometimes.

But she's looking at Bruce. Oh, he must have said something.

"What?" I ask, pulling my attention back to the present moment. "I'm sorry, I was thinking about something."

"Oh, it's nothing, dear. I just said that I can't even begin to think about trying to clear this place out . . ."

I take a deep breath to steady myself, hoping it will blow out some of the fog in my head.

I don't want to say this. I don't want to even think about this. But it has to be said.

"Bruce," I say, slowly, so . . . you know . . . I'll keep breathing. "I am pretty sure I have a buyer for your house."

On the walk to Caribou I tell Emily all about Brad's passionate—and lengthy—search for a small Victorian. At first she's really excited, but then she picks up on my mood.

"Why did you ask him to give you twenty-four hours?" she asks, cutting right to the heart of it.

"So I can decide whether or not to tell Brad and my dad."

"Why wouldn't you? Oh, I get it—you don't want them to move?"

I shake my head. Blink back tears that have been pushing against my eyelids ever since I hugged Bruce for the last time and we watched him hobble back into the house. He looked so . . . old. I didn't even know he had a daughter. Honestly, I had no idea he'd ever been married.

"Did you think they would stay in the attic?" she asks. "I mean, indefinitely?"

"No . . . no, of course not . . . I don't know. I guess I was buying time. Everything's changing. My mom's been, whewwww . . . so strange . . . ever since my dad came out. I'm pretty positive she wants him there, but you know, it's not really all that healthy for her to have him there."

"What do you mean?"

"Well, it's like she spends half her time pretending nothing's changed . . ."

Emily's silent look is a kind of question.

"Like . . . you know, he comes down and showers in her bathroom and they hang out together in the kitchen and talk and plan things for the theater. They laugh and listen to music and tease Bartle. When we all go out, she and my dad dance together and on the surface everything is just like it always was."

Emily's nodding.

"Then we come home, and he and Brad go upstairs. You know, you can feel it. They can't wait to get upstairs."

I've never said any of this out loud before. It's almost like the words are coming before the thoughts.

"I don't mean just to have sex." Then I can feel myself blushing. Up until recently I never even thought about my parents having sex—not even with each other—and suddenly the topic keeps coming up.

Emily's still nodding. She looks interested. Nothing seems to embarrass her.

"It's not like it used to be . . . when he was sitting on the couch watching TV until four in the morning and then falling asleep there. Hardly ever going up to bed with my mom."

It's so easy to talk to Emily. She doesn't interrupt or think she knows better. She doesn't defend my dad like Bartle does. Or defend my mom, like Bits always does. She just listens.

"And then . . . after they go upstairs . . . Mom crashes. And she heads for the liquor cabinet. I'm starting to worry about her drinking . . ."

"Do you think she's an alcoholic?"

"I don't know. I never did before." We walk in silence while I think about it. "It seems really situational. I think if she could accept this change, she wouldn't do that so much . . ."

"So, what do you think will happen if you tell your dad and Brad about the house?"

"You mean, why am I so afraid?"

"Yeah . . . okay . . . What are you so afraid will happen?"

"Brad will be over the moon and he will make an offer imme-diately. My dad will be mostly happy for him—and for them."

"And your mom?"

"I'm almost positive she will be furious at me. I already feel like I've lost her, but this . . . this may do it for real . . ."

"So, there's a lot at stake . . ."

I nod. "Yeah, I have to think about it some more . . ."

We're at Caribou. We go in and order large extra-hot lattes. Shortbread cookies. Sit down at a table near the window where we can watch people walk by. Neither of us pulls out our laptops.

We sit there without talking. I hand Emily my cookie. No point in trying to eat it when I'm having a hard time swallowing the coffee.

After about twenty minutes, Emily says, "How come I know that you're going to tell them about the house?"

How does she know that's what I've decided?

"I have to, don't I?" I say, making it irrevocable. "I mean, it's the right thing to do . . . isn't it?"

All the way home I think about how to do this. Should I tell Brad when he's by himself? Or maybe I should tell Mom first and let her tell them.

In the end, I wait until we've all eaten and are about to have some ice cream, and I say, "I saw Bruce today. Arthur died about a month ago and Bruce needs to unload his Victorian as soon as possible."

My mother makes this strangling noise. But I don't even look her way. I don't dare.

I look straight at Brad and say, "He's selling it as is. I thought you'd want to know."

There is a general hubbub. I don't think I've ever used that word before. *Hubbub.* Bartle and Tim shout with joy! They know what this means to Brad. My dad is torn between beaming and trying to figure out how my mother is reacting. Join the club.

Auntie Ellie and Lee both look pleased, but a little concerned. That would be on account of Mom, I imagine.

Mom's sitting there, staring down at the tabletop.

Bits is looking at Mom and looking at my dad and Brad. She's avoiding looking at me.

Mom looks stunned. Kind of like she's forgotten we're all still there.

Auntie Ellie catches my eye and shrugs. Even she can't figure out what's going on with Mom.

At least she's not screaming at me. Or at my dad and Brad.

And she's not stomping up the stairs and slamming herself into her room (you know, like a teenager).

Brad wants to know the details, of course, so I recite them, glancing every few seconds over at Mom.

Bits is at the counter making a pot of coffee. That is, like, the second time ever she's done that. The first was when she was trying to get me out of my room last summer. A sign of great agitation.

"Have you ever been in the house?" I ask Brad, when I'm done telling him everything.

"No," he says. "Is it nice?"

"It can be," I say. "But Arthur was . . . well, Bruce calls it a packrat, but I'd say more like a hoarder. It's pretty bad. " Brad needs to know what he's getting into.

"Do you have any idea what condition the house is in structurally?"

"All I know is that Bruce said the Realtors he's talked to wanted him to do some basic repairs and upgrades . . . that doesn't sound like there's anything really awful going on other than the mess, does it?"

Now Brad's beaming. "No, it doesn't."

He looks at my dad, and my dad's nodding at him with a big smile on his face.

"We've got to put an offer in first thing tomorrow morning!" Brad says, and my dad gives him a big hug.

My guess is Bruce will snap it up.

"Coffee's ready," Bits says, her voice cracking.

Mom looks up.

"You're going to love that house," she says with only the slightest quaver in her voice.

She has everyone's attention. Trust me.

"It's perfect for the two of you."

My dad and Brad are looking at her with huge eyes.

"Did you say Bruce wants to leave as soon as possible?" she asks me.

"Uh-huh . . ."

"Then the timing couldn't be much better," Mom says. "We can all help with the clean-out in January when the theater's dark. I'll bet we can even get Chris and his crew to help."

We're all nodding. We look like a bunch of bobblehead dolls.

"That is, if David's doing the cooking . . ." she finishes, looking at Bits for some reason.

Bits smiles and nods at Mom.

Finally, Mom turns and looks at me. "It's a good thing you went for that walk today, huh, Jess?"

Well, it's not exactly heartwarming or anything, but at least she's on board and isn't tearing up the place or heading for the scotch.

Just as I think that, she gets up and goes to the cupboard.

Or is she?

Nope, she's pouring herself a cup of coffee.

"Why don't you call Bruce tonight?" she asks Brad. "It's only seven-thirty. You've got his number, don't you Jessie?"

Auntie Ellie follows me out of the room. Bits has already gone upstairs to work on her lines for her advanced acting final, which is tomorrow morning. Auntie Ellie gives me a big hug and says, "You are so incredible."

I'm assuming, given the hug, she means that in a good way.

the writing workshop that DOESN'T end

The professor is late today. He arrives in a flurry of coat and scarf and gloves and papers, which he spills all over the front of the room. Bartle leaps to assist him and there's a mad scramble with papers going every which way.

PROFESSOR: My car keeps stalling out.

TIM CHANG: What kind of car do you drive?

PROFESSOR: Do I have to say?

TIM CHANG: Now you do.

ALL: *(Laugh)*

PROFESSOR: A KIA.

ALL: *(Shriek with laughter)*

I don't even know why we're laughing. I know exactly nothing about cars, yet somehow I know this is a car worthy of ridicule.

"When I become an Associate Professor I'll buy a new car," he says.

"I hope that's happening soon," Bev says.

"Tell you what," Professor Bumble says. "Come spring I'll rip the doors off my KIA and maybe that will give it more character . . ."

He says this while opening up a huge container of teriyaki chicken. "Tim and I decided to surprise you with some good Asian appetizers."

Tim's beaming. I hope he brought his mother's fabulous egg rolls! He did!

"We'll write in a little while," the professor says, his mouth full of chicken. "I wanted to tell you how much I've enjoyed working with you."

"Are we going to continue the workshop in the spring?" Emily asks.

"I'd like to," the professor says right away. "I was talking with Lydia about that. We've done some wonderful writing this session, but we haven't really gotten very far into the crafting of scenes and playwriting in general."

"Yeah, what is with that?" Bartle asks, his mouth full as usual. Then he cracks up laughing.

Fortunately, so does the professor.

"We're going to miss you, Mark Bartle," he says. "Are you sure you and Tim won't change your mind about San Francisco and hang in here with us?"

They laugh. They are so already gone.

"How many of you are interested in continuing in the spring?"

We all raise our hands, even Sister M&M.

"I know it's hard to stop talking," the professor finally says, "but let's grab our notebooks and do one last writing exercise, okay?"

We all stop eating and grab our notebooks.

"How about the prompt, 'I'll rip the doors off'?"

We all look at him with blank faces.

"Oh, come on," he says. "It's a metaphor. Shorter write today . . . ten minutes . . . go . . ."

When we stop to read, it turns out the professor, Tim Chang, and I are all ripping the doors off our inhibitions. Scary.

Bev is ripping the doors off the racist, sexist facade of academia. (Good luck with that, Bev!)

Bartle is ripping the doors off the black community's view of homosexuality. (Way to go, Bartle! This is the first nonpersonal, intelligent thing I've heard him say in the workshop. Maybe ever.)

Sister Mary Margaret is ripping the doors off her vocation.

"Your vacation?" Tim Chang asks her.

"Her *vo*-cation," the professor gently corrects him.

"I'm going to stop being a nun," she says, her voice still quiet and calm, but you can hear the determination in every syllable.

She gets the biggest response of everyone. And we all make her promise that she will come back to the workshop in the spring. Not only do we all like her a lot, I know I want to see her without the wimple.

The professor hands back all the pages we've been typing up and turning in to him. He says to wait until after the workshop to look at the comments, but I sneak a peek anyway.

He's written so much on my pages there's no way I can read it without him noticing. So I flip to the very last page where he's written:

You have such a strong voice, Jessie. And a true feel for dialogue. I look forward to working with you next semester!

When I glance up, he's looking at me. He smiles and nods.

He talks the rest of the workshop about what he calls having a writing practice. He says it is critical whether you're trying to write plays (like we are) or with any other form of writing. He says it's like doing daily meditation. For some people it's like saying prayers. Or exercising.

I've been thinking lately about keeping a journal. Something like the writing exercises we do in his workshop, only on my own and every day. Maybe I'll buy myself a notebook for Christmas and give it a try.

Professor Bumble says I have a strong voice. I guess I'd better use that voice and read some of my exercises out loud next time, huh?

"I've started a photo journal," Emily says, as we're gathering up our things to leave.

"What's that?"

"Oh, everyone," Professor Bumble calls after us so that we all stop and come back into the room for a minute. "I'll post the start date of the workshop. Be sure and hang on to the new writing that you've done. Type it up so you know what you've got and bring it with you to our first session along with what I just handed back. We're going to start right in at the beginning with scene construction."

"What's a photo journal?" I ask Emily again as we're walking out of the building.

"Well, I'm not really sure yet," she says, laughing. "Kind of like a blog, I guess, only I'm not posting it online. Photos. Lots of photos. And a little bit of writing."

"Sweet."

"Sweet, Jessie Jumble," she says, smiling that dazzling smile. "Sweet like you."

a sideways celebration

December 18 is Bits's eighteenth birthday. Numerically that seems significant. Not to mention it's the birthday she's been yowling about for . . . well . . . YEARS.

It's a Tuesday, everyone's home. The only thing left of the theater school semester is our movement recital on Thursday. The last weekend of the Christmas show is coming up, and then the theater will be dark until the end of January.

We've always meant—all of us—to have a big celebration for this birthday. For one thing, it's the birthday that liberates Bits from Loretta's parental control. No need anymore to fret about outcomes if Lee had to take Loretta to court over custody. This has always been a big issue because on the surface Loretta looks like the more reliable parent. She's got a nine-to-five job. She's active in her church. Lee, on the other hand, is a drummer in a folk rock band and moves around all the time. He's never had a regular job and he doesn't make a lot of money. Not only that but he hangs around with all us crazy theater folk. I'm just saying.

What doesn't show up is that Loretta is way crazier than your run-of-the-mill CLP (I mean, they all seem like pretty nice people, though they are a little overexcited about Armageddon, while she is—you know—NUTS). And Lee—for all his instability—is the one who understands Bits and wants her to pursue her dreams.

The other reason we all wanted this birthday to be a huge celebration is because Bits has never really had any birthday parties because Loretta's religion doesn't let her celebrate birthdays, either.

But for some reason the party just can't seem to come together.

First of all, there's the whole buying the house deal. Brad made his offer the morning after I told him about it. We looked it up online and checked the houses near it, both the huge ones and the other comparable Victorians, so we knew roughly what everything is appraising at. Brad went in really low with his offer. I know from watching real estate shows on HGTV that it's what you'd call an insulting offer.

Only not to Bruce. The house has been paid off for years. Any amount is gravy for him, especially since he's going to live with his daughter. And lucky for us, the cats are going with him.

Brad's already approved for financing and he's got a good down payment.

So Bruce snapped it up, exactly like we hoped he would.

This morning, Dad and Brad drag me with them when they

go to sign the last of the paperwork and do a final walk-through of the house.

It sounds like Brad and my dad can take possession right after New Year's. It may be the shortest escrow in the history of the world.

Bruce is selecting a few things to ship to Florida, but for the most part, he's selling it as is, with everything in it.

I leave when they start going over the house room by room. I'll see the part I've never seen when we're in HAZMAT SUITS doing the clean-out.

No one's home when I get there so I have time to wrap the presents I got for Bits. I've learned my lesson where books are concerned, although I did get her one on New York City. I also got her a gift card for the store that sells dance clothes. And I got her a CD of this new Broadway show that's getting rave reviews. I think they are things she'll like, but nothing feels very personal. I'm feeling really disconnected from her right now.

I try calling David, but he's not answering.

Bartle's off with Tim Chang somewhere. I hope they're back for dinner anyway.

Auntie Ellie and Lee are gone, too. My guess is they are probably out buying last-minute birthday gifts.

And where is Bits?

I leave Emily a voice-mail message suggesting she come for dinner in case we manage to pull off a cake and presents.

Finally, I give up and watch old movies all afternoon.

I doze off on the couch watching TV and when I wake up, everyone's home and the doorbell is ringing with a pizza delivery.

David's in the kitchen showing off this enormous chocolate torte he's made for Bits's birthday. Bits is in there, basking in the attention, looking adorable in this retro dress from the 1950s that Brad found for her. It's his birthday present to her, but he wanted her to wear it for her celebration.

Mom is making a big salad.

We're just about to sit down and eat when Auntie Ellie and Lee get home. They're loaded down with presents, too.

It's sort of a sideways celebration, but Bits couldn't be happier. That is, until she listens to a voice mail from Loretta.

"You think you're so talented and special," Loretta's voice sounds hard and mean. "You're eighteen years old today. Enjoy it while you can. In three days you're going to be . . . you're not going to be . . . anymore." Then, right when it sounds like she's threatening to kill her only daughter, her voice turns sweet in a sugary sappy kind of way, and she ends it with: "But there's still time to repent and be saved. You don't have to end when the world does. I love you."

The woman is schizophrenic. Seriously.

We end the evening—after everyone has had fits over Loretta's voice mail—listening to Broadway shows, making fudge (Bits can never get enough chocolate), and eating popcorn.

Emily never does show up, and I don't think Bits is one bit disappointed about that.

the heartbeat of the dance

Today is the stage movement recital. It's not a big deal. Parents come, of course. The other classes are required to come. All the teachers and actors and staff show up. It's always held in the late afternoon and on the last Thursday of the semester, so there are no conflicts if people want to go to dinner afterward or something.

I'm a little nervous about the recital, but not that much. I'm only in the African dance and it's so wild and so much fun to do. We're not wearing costumes—Dell got us some wonderful pieces of hand-dyed cloth to tie on over our leotards and tights. It's from Ghana, I think she said. We're dancing barefoot, of course.

We're expecting the usual small crowd, but when it's time for the recital, we're stunned to see that the theater is almost full. Our shows last weekend were like that, too. Dell says she thinks it's because of the school shooting in Connecticut last week. Even though that was way out on the East Coast, the effects rippled everywhere. It's like all the parents gather up siblings and aunts and uncles and cousins and grandparents and neighbors and drive to the theater when their kids are doing something here because they don't know what else to do.

I throw my jacket on over my dance clothes and go out to watch the first three-quarters of the recital. Of course, my parents are here. All three of them are sitting together. Bartle and Tim came. They're sitting with Grandmama. Some of the writing workshop people are here, too—Professor Bumble is with Sister M&M. Even Auntie Ellie and Lee are here, sitting way in the back.

The first part of the recital is like watching figure skaters do their technical skills skating. Interesting but not exciting. Bits does it so well, my guess is everyone is watching her most of the time. I know I am. It's great for the parents to see because it so clearly demonstrates the level of training the kids get in technique. As Lydia would say: the recitals are a great marketing tool for the theater school.

I look around to see if Loretta came, but as usual, she's not here. She's missing so much and she doesn't even know it. I'm glad she's not here today, though. I already know from her text messages and voice mail that she took the school shooting and ran with it. For her, it's another sign of the end of the world.

I slip away when the last segment is being done—the one that's keyed to *A Christmas Carol*. Time to get ready for the African dance.

Backstage there's a wild but muffled scramble as everyone gets out of rehearsal skirts and shoes and finds their fabric pieces. The pieces are all different sizes and shapes and patterns. Different colors, too. Some people have them around their heads. Others cinched like a halter top. Two of the guys just have a thin strip tied around their necks like a bandana.

Mine is around my waist. I was going to wear it around my head, but Dell insisted that I undo my braids and let my hair go crazy.

While we're changing clothes, Dell puts on some of the African drum music to help us and the audience make the transition. It's a completely different feel and beat to what we're going to dance to, lower energy for one thing, but it gets the audience in a mood. Well, that's what she says. It's getting me in a mood, so she's probably right.

Anyway, before we come on, she goes out and thanks everyone for coming and like every event since the shooting, she says a few words about the tragedy in Connecticut. We've got a fund-raising effort going on out in the lobby. And the kids have all been cutting out snowflakes between classes and during rehearsals every day.

Then she gives a brief description of what we're going to do—describing the African dance and how it's being taught here in the States. She talks about the polycentric rhythms. She even manages to get in some points about Alvin Ailey's company. She's good.

And then she comes backstage and the wild, crazy, raucous drumming music erupts from the speakers and we all ERUPT from the sidelines and through the backstage curtains and the dance begins.

The funny thing is, I don't remember a thing about it.

One minute I'm busting through the center back curtains with

Dell and it seems like a moment later the dance is over and the audience is shouting and applauding and pounding their feet on the floor. They're all standing up and whistling and waving their arms. No wonder actors get so hooked on applause. This is insane. As in: insanely . . . WONDERFUL!

It's a student recital, not a formal performance, so after taking a bow, we all plunk down on the edge of the stage and we're mobbed.

I'm mobbed.

Lydia, Edward, Brad, my dad, Bartle, Tim Chang, Grandmama, David, Emily, the professor, Lee, Auntie Ellie, other workshop people, half a dozen theater students . . .

I've slid off the stage and been enveloped in a hugging, shouting, back-slapping, congratulatory throng made up of all the people in my life.

I can hear my dad saying to Brad, "I tried learning it . . . I couldn't get a step of it . . . can you believe her?"

"She's blacker than you are . . ." Grandmama says to my dad. He laughs and whacks her on the arm.

David plants a huge big-brother kiss on my cheek. And Emily gives me an even bigger hug. "I'm speechless," she says. "Jess, that was incredible! How did you learn to do that? My God, woman, is there anything you can't do?"

Bartle picks me up and swings me around effectively dispersing the crowd, which is kind of a relief because I'm not used to this kind of attention. In the past when a huge group of people have converged on me, it's generally to make sure I haven't broken something.

Then I turn around and there's Mom. Tears are rolling down her cheeks and she's grinning this ENORMOUS grin and she throws her arms around me and hugs me tight, like she's never going to let me go. She hangs on and so do I.

"Oh, Jessie," she says. "Oh, Jessie, baby . . ."

Later when we're backstage retrieving rehearsal skirts and taking off fabric pieces and finding our shoes, Dell tells us all what a great job we did.

"Now, that's my girl," she whispers to me.

bringing it home

It's a Thursday night and everyone's tired, so we gather up our stuff and head home. It's hard to believe the entire fall season is nearly over. All we have left are three performances of the Christmas show and then the theater goes dark until the end of January.

"Can you believe Christmas is only four days away . . ." Auntie Ellie says, with an uncharacteristic sigh, as she plumps down on the couch, Lee right next to her.

"Every year I say I'm going to figure out Christmas gifts at Thanksgiving," Mom says with a little laugh. "And every year I'm scrambling the last couple days of the Christmas show to get it all done."

"You were fabulous, Jessie," Auntie Ellie says, then catches herself. "You and Bits were both great!"

Mom's nodding. "You were!" she says, looking right at me.

"Thanks."

The smile on Bits's face is a little stiff. She's used to being first when it comes to performance praise. Well, after my mom and dad, I mean. I love hearing that I did well. All the attention at the theater was nice, too. Yeah, I loved it.

What I really loved, though, was doing it. I just wish I could remember the whole thing.

"Grandmama, why don't you stay over so you can help us with the tree tomorrow morning." My dad has just come back down from the attic and of course Brad's right behind him. These are the things I'll miss when he and Brad move out. I mean, my parents aren't even together but they've been planning Christmas as if they were.

I hear the kitchen door opening and the stomping of boots in the mudroom. Then David and Emily pop through the kitchen door.

"I hope you're ordering pizzas," David says. "Mom and Dad are going out to eat and said we had to come over here."

Bartle is organizing the pizza order so chaos ensues.

I'm too tired to care what they order. I'll eat whatever it is when it gets here.

There's a sudden jangle in the room. Three iPhones signaling a text message simultaneously. Mom, Bits, and I pull out our phones in unison to check. We've been spending too much time together.

It's a message from Loretta, sent to all three of us at once.

Armageddon will be here in less than ten hours. I am heading north. It's probably too late for you. But I'm not God. L

Mom reads the text out loud while making small shrieking noises. I would rather be an only child than have a sister like Loretta.

I don't know how Bits can be as . . . you know . . . normal and together as she is after being raised by that nut job.

Now her face just gets hard and set.

Lee motions her over, and she plunks down between him and Auntie Ellie.

"I'm relieved, honey," Lee says. "At least now we can stop worrying about her trying to grab you and take you with her . . ."

"Yeah," she says, her face relaxing a little as she snuggles in with them.

Auntie Ellie gives her a hug, too.

"We have an announcement," Auntie Ellie says, looking quickly at Lee. I'm assuming to see if he minds what she's about to say.

Mom smiles in a way that tells me she knows what's about to be said and likes it.

"Lee and I are moving into the attic when Mark and Brad move into their house."

"Hey, that's great." My dad and Brad look pleased.

I'm thinking, What's the big deal? You already live here and Lee's here all the time, too.

"Lee's just gotten a great teaching opportunity at the Open School for Music. And I'm going to take some classes at the College of Art and Design . . . we're not going on the road anymore."

Sweet. This is major. Too bad for Bits it couldn't have happened about ten years ago.

We've just finished devouring a sausage and pepperoni New

York–style and a Hawaiian when "Boogie Woogie Bugle Boy" goes off. Could our UPS guy, Al, be delivering this late? I've ordered all my gifts online this year and am squirreling them away in my closet as they arrive. Harder to do this year since Bits is sharing my room.

It's Dell . . . and behind her, looking like he's hiding there . . . Professor Bumble.

Dell's waving a DVD. "We went back to the theater to get this after we ate," she says, visibly excited. "I can't wait to look at it."

My parents both want to see it right now, too.

Auntie Ellie and Lee move closer together on the couch so Dell can sit down. Mom waves the professor to the armchair and sits on the floor next to it. Everyone else grabs dining room chairs or plunks down on the floor, leaving me standing there feeling once again like that very tall and very awkward giraffe.

Do I even want to see this? At the moment, I don't think so.

It felt really good to be doing it. And from how everyone's reacting, I must have done a good job. But do I want to see myself doing it? No. I'm pretty sure how it feels in my body is way better than what I'm going to see.

I start for the kitchen, thinking I'll go make coffee or something, but Dell motions me over and says, "Let's watch it together."

I sit down on the floor by Dell's feet. Bartle's working the DVD and he's fast forwarded through all the technical stage movement stuff to the African dance.

My stomach is way more jittery than it was backstage before we went on. I have to cover my eyes. But the music. Oh, that music. And I uncover them again.

Is that me?

That can't be me.

That tall, slim dancer with the African cloth around her waist. With her long, dark, curly hair swinging around her face as she moves. Dancing next to red-headed Dell and . . . you know . . . keeping up with her.

That can't be me. I mean, how crazy is that?

That's me.

Dancing.

Everybody gets all into it again like at the theater. Now I'm just plain embarrassed.

I leap up, tripping over Dell's feet. I have to get away from everyone for a minute. And breathe. I run upstairs to my bathroom and think about putting my hair back into braids. But I can't do it.

I'm kind of liking it wild.

This is the collision Dell was talking about. I know it is.

I almost want to stop it.

Almost.

When I come back down the stairs, they're playing the DVD again, this time for Lydia and Edward, who've popped in after eating dinner down the street at Brasa. Lydia is going wild over the African dance, as if she were seeing it for the first time.

"Show me how to do it," she says, waving her arms in a way that makes Dell duck back. I wonder if Lydia had wine with dinner. Do you think?

"Come on, Dell," she says, "just some of the basic moves."

Mom wants to learn, too. My mom's a really good dancer, so I'm curious to see if she's any better at it than my dad was.

I've stopped halfway down the stairs, so I stay there on the platform. At the moment, I don't want to get pulled into this action, I just want to observe it.

When Dell's got Lydia and Mom going with a couple basic moves, Bits gets into it, too, helping to keep them going. Mom drops out after a few minutes, laughing at her own clumsiness.

"I've been wondering," Dell says to Mom, "about that dance teacher that took over for me when I left here ten years ago."

"What about her?"

"Her name was Anya wasn't it? I can't remember her last name . . ."

Mom nods. "That sounds right. Anya. Lydia, do you remember that dance teacher, Anya—what was her last name?"

"Svenson," Lydia says, without even stopping. She's almost got the arm movements down and she's cleared out a pretty big circle of space around herself. Get down, Lydia!

I see Edward over in the corner, his drink halfway to his mouth, watching her. There's a little smile at the corner of his lips. He is loving this!

"Did she teach for you very long?" Dell asks, watching Lydia with what looks like alarm.

"Only one season, I think . . . I can't remember exactly." Mom can't take her eyes off Lydia either. I hope she doesn't pull something. "Not very long. Why?"

"Well, I was mostly wondering if Jessie took classes from her."

"Yes," Mom says. "Of course."

"More than one?"

"Uh-huh," Mom looks kind of puzzled. "Ballet. Two semesters. And I think she took Modern or Jazz from her, too. Why?"

Yeah, why? I'm wondering. I lean farther over the stair rails so I don't miss any of this.

Bits has been showing Lydia a new move and suddenly Bits turns and says to Dell and my mom, "I remember that teacher. She was my first teacher at the theater."

That's right. Bits told me that a while ago. When I was doing those writing exercises and trying to remember my dance teachers.

"She's the one who told Jessie she couldn't do ballet moves because she was black."

Bits says it in a really offhand kind of way. Like it's no big deal. And she turns back to show Lydia another move.

But Lydia's stopped dead in her tracks. And Mom and Dell are standing there with their mouths open.

"Mark!" Mom says.

He's talking with Brad about something and hasn't heard the conversation, I don't think, but hearing the tone in Mom's voice now he turns and walks over. "What's going on?"

"Bits," Mom says, "tell Mark what you just told us."

"About what?" she asks, stopping mid-move and looking genuinely confused.

I'm frozen on the stair platform, leaning on the rail. I couldn't move if the house was on fire.

"About Anya Svenson and what she told Jessie . . ." Mom says, her voice now crisp in a way that would certainly make me pay attention.

"Oh, that," Bits says—you can almost hear the BIG DUH! Then she really looks at everyone. You can see her taking it all in. "Oh," she says, visibly regrouping.

"She told Jessie she couldn't ever be any good at ballet because she's half black."

"Jess," Dell says, turning to me like she's known all along I'm frozen right behind her on the stairs. Her voice is very gentle. "Do you remember Anya Svenson?"

"No," I say. "No, I don't remember anything about my dance classes after you left, not for two or three years at least."

"You don't?" Mom sounds so surprised at this. Have I really never told her that?

"What happened to her?" Dell asks Lydia.

"We let her go after a year," Lydia says slowly. I can't read her face. "We had a lot of complaints about her from parents."

"Not racially motivated, I don't imagine?" my mom asks. She knows Lydia would have told her and my dad right away if that were the case. This is one thing they are all on the same page about.

"No," Lydia says. "No, of course not."

"Well, Jessie was the only student of color in the class at that point," my dad says. The muscles around his jaw line are twitching the way they do when he's absolutely furious.

"Why didn't you tell us about that, Bits?" Mom asks, her voice also very controlled.

I move down a step.

"I don't know," Bits says. "I guess I figured Jessie would if it was important to her."

"Did you tell your mom?" My mother's not letting up on her.

"No!" Bits says. "No, I never told my mom anything about my theater classes. They just make her mad."

Now she's backing away, and when they turn to me, she slips off into the kitchen. She can't wait to get out of here.

"You never said anything, Jess," Mom says. And I have to admit, I feel this enormous relief. It would be so horrible if I'd told my mom and she hadn't done anything. If she didn't think it any more important than Bits apparently does. "Why didn't you tell us?"

"You don't remember, do you, Jess?" Dell asks, pulling me the rest of the way down the stairway and giving me a big hug.

"I . . . I don't . . ."

There's a tiny glimmering of memory now around the edges. A minuscule flash of something that then gets swallowed up immediately. And then another tiny flash.

"I don't . . . know."

But then I do.

"I . . . I guess I believed her . . ."

When I can get away, I head for the kitchen, too. I've got to talk to Bits about this. But she's not there.

David and Emily are playing dominoes at the kitchen table.

"Upstairs, I think," he says when I ask where she went.

She's in our room changing her clothes.

"What are you doing?"

"Spilled juice on my sweater," she says, not looking at me.

"How could you not tell me about what that teacher said?" I have to know this.

"Why would I tell you?" she asks. "You were there."

"Not when it happened . . . a little while ago, when I asked about your first teachers here at the theater and you told me about her . . . when you told me how much you liked her . . ."

"I don't know," she says, but she won't look at me. "I wasn't thinking about YOU in the class. You asked about me."

"I was trying to remember my early dance teachers," I say, very slowly. As if to a child. "I told you that . . ."

She shrugs, looks down at the front of the sweater. She won't look at me.

I have to ask it. I have to. "How could you like someone who told me I couldn't dance because I was black?"

"I was nine . . ." she says, her voice sounding defensive.

"You're eighteen now," I say.

"You're making a big deal out of it," she says, taking the sweater off and digging through the closet looking for a different one. Or maybe she's looking for a way to get me off her back.

"Bits," My voice is shaking, and I don't want it to be shaking. "Bits. Until that teacher, I loved to dance. After that teacher I thought I was clumsy and awkward and I hated everything about going to dance class. You of all people know that. You don't think that's a big deal?"

She shrugs.

Maybe I'm being unfair. She was pretty little then. But she was two whole years older than me. She spent every waking minute that she could at our house. You know, that house where half the people are black and half the people are white and I'm—you know—I'm that ZEBRA her mother was always going on and on about.

I wait, blinking back tears. Bits processes things more slowly than I do. She just needs a little time, I'm thinking. To realize what this means to me.

She shrugs again. "What's the big deal?" Now she looks straight at me. "That's ancient history."

I'm speechless.

"Anyway," she says, her voice matching that look I saw earlier. "Tonight you're the star."

"You really don't get it." I'm so angry it feels like my head is going to blow off. "You are so selfish . . . you know if you don't start caring about other people you're going to end up a sociopath like your mother."

"My mother's not a socio . . . what's a sociopath?"

"A dangerous lunatic NUTCASE!" I scream back at her.

"You're the selfish one," Bits yells back. "You're a spoiled brat who has it all and you don't even realize it. You make me sick!"

And then she runs out of the room.

What just happened here?

Bits and I have never had this kind of fight before. Oh, petty squabbles, sure. Like sisters, I've always assumed.

But this?

This is . . . I don't have any words for what this is.

I sink down on the bed, too upset to even cry. I'm still angry, too. I meant what I said.

This is a big deal to me. If she knows me at all or cares about me one little bit, she has to know this matters to me.

when the world begins again

"You okay?" Emily's head pops around the door frame.

I start to say yes, but then I can't. I shake my head.

"Can I come in?"

I nod. "Where's Bits?"

"Last I saw, in the kitchen with David," Emily says, walking over to the window and looking out into the dark night.

I don't know what to say. I don't know Emily well enough to gauge where she stands on the racial stuff. Oh, she's shown that she's totally okay with the interracial marriage thing. That's not what I mean.

Oddly enough, what I don't know is how much she gets about what it means to be white. She's white. She's really cool, but she's white. And not just any white, either. She's from a really wealthy white family.

I like her so much. I'm suddenly really afraid to find out where she stands on this stuff.

"I want to talk with you," Emily says, "about the racist dance teacher and all that. I'm not avoiding the subject . . ."

"Okay," I say.

". . . but before we do that, I wanted to tell you something I don't think you know."

"What?"

"Bits is in love with David," Emily says.

"No, she's not . . . she's . . ." I stop. Oh, my god, Emily is totally right. "You're right. Oh, my god, you're right."

She's nodding. "I am."

"I mean, that completely makes sense out of why she's been so weird about you," I smack myself on the head. "Oh. I'm an idiot. I've been thinking she's jealous of my friendship with you and also protecting me because David and I were . . . you know . . . kind of messing around a little. You knew that, right?"

"Yeah, David told me," she laughs.

"Well, but what about Bits?"

"Jess, David's in love with her, too. I think he always has been."

"Well, why wouldn't he just go after her then?"

"He didn't think he had a chance with her."

"Why not?"

"I don't know . . . she's so focused on acting and going to New York," Emily pauses. "Maybe her mom, too. David sounds scared of Loretta."

Who isn't?

"Are they together?" I'm really confused now. I mean, weren't David and Emily together at the recital this afternoon? Didn't they come over here together?

"I think they are in the process of figuring it out . . . now . . ." she says. "That's why I wanted to tell you."

It's important, but I'm not sure I see what it has to do with the fight we just had.

"You know, I think it's affected your relationship with Bits for a while now," Emily says. "Probably since you and David were first . . . you know . . . doing the experimental kissing thing." She grins.

"I'd be embarrassed right now," I say, trying to smile, but not managing it, "if I weren't so miserable. I said horrible things to Bits."

"Yeah, but not about this," Emily says.

"No, not about this . . . about the dance teacher . . . her reaction."

"Did you mean what you said?" Emily asks, cutting right to the chase.

I take my time answering. I want to make sure I'm telling the absolute truth.

"I did," I say. "I do. But I wish I hadn't been so angry . . ."

"Well, the anger shows how important the issue is to you. You hardly ever yell or pick fights," Emily says.

That's true. When I get angry I close up. And when I get really angry, I do that weird spurting tears thing. This is a kind of angry I've never been.

"Maybe she needed that wake-up call," Emily says.

"Yeah?"

"Yeah," she nods. "Tell me what she said. Tell me exactly what she said and you said."

I tell her.

"I don't see how she can be a live-in part of your family and be that screwed up where the racial stuff is concerned."

She gets it, I'm thinking. She gets it.

We talk for a long time. I tell her about the years and years of feeling clumsy and awkward and like I don't fit in at the theater. I tell her about being two or three years younger than all my high school classmates and still smarter, so I never fit in there, either, though it was a good place to hide. And I tell her all about what Dell's done for me this semester and how important it is to me to have her back in my life.

Emily's amazing. She listens. I think she's like one of her cameras. She aims herself at me and puts all her energy into getting all the details. You know. Just right.

"Has it been hard for you?" Emily asks, when I finally wind down. "You know . . . finding out your dad's gay . . . having him living here with his partner?"

This is literally the first time in over six months that anyone (and yes, I mean anyone) has asked me that question. Which, by itself is kind of mind-blowing if you think about it.

Even Bits. Even David. Didn't ask me that.

Mom didn't.

My dad let me ask him questions, but he's never really asked me how I'm doing with it.

The good thing, I guess, is I've had lots of time to think about it.

"The hard part . . . I mean, it's never been about him being gay . . ."

"It hasn't?" She sounds incredulous.

"Oh, sure, it shocked me because I didn't know. Everybody else knew . . . except for Bits . . . she was clueless, too. So, yeah, it shocked me for about two or three hours."

"HOURS?" Emily laughs, then claps her hand over her mouth when she sees I'm serious.

"I know. Crazy, huh?" Now I laugh, too. Wow. My face actually moves.

"You're incredible," she says.

"Nah, I'm not . . . it just did. It started making sense right away. I must have already absorbed it, you know, by osmosis or something. But the hard part was knowing he would leave. I couldn't bear the thought that he would leave."

She waits.

"I've never told anyone this," I hesitate for a second. I've had this thought so many times, for years and years. And I've never told anyone.

She doesn't say anything. She waits.

"Until very recently . . . no, until today . . . I have only felt like myself when I am standing between my black father and my white mother. You know? Like there is no Jessie Jasper Lewis on her own. I'm not a stand-alone. Like I need people to see that when you add up my talented, handsome black father and my itsy-bitsy, adorable, white actress mother, you get . . . ME . . . and no matter how smart I am or how I can remember everything I read or my A+ grade record or the crazy high test scores . . . none of that added up to . . ."

"Jessie Jumble," Emily says.

"I engineered it so my dad and Brad would move back in here. I thought I was doing it for my mom, because she seemed so lost. But really it was for me. You know? So I could walk downstairs in the morning and there they'd be at the kitchen table and there I'd be, too. Oh, I know, it doesn't make any sense. At all . . ."

"No wonder it was so hard for you to decide whether or not to tell your parents about the house coming on the market . . ."

I nod. She gets it.

"You did it, and it turned out to be what your mom wanted, too."

"Yeah, that was a . . . well . . . surprise." It really was. I thought Mom was going to disown me for it. Instead, she's been way more like herself. And she's hardly even drinking anymore. I don't really understand. But I'm hoping one of these days she and I can talk about it.

"You said that this feeling of . . ." She's struggling for the words. ". . . of not being a person in your own right . . . you said you felt like that until . . . today . . . ?"

"It's Dell." I surprise myself saying this. I haven't thought it through. So what? I'll think it through telling it to Emily. "The dance class turned out to be the best thing that could happen to me this year. Other good stuff, too. The directing. I love the directing. Not just doing it but all the reading I'm doing. I love it. But the work with Dell—that's so personal."

"What do you mean, personal?"

"Not relationship personal . . . not like that . . . personal like it's my body. And how I move. And breathe. And it's just me. It's not my dad. It's not my mom. It's not even Bits. It's me and listening to myself and knowing I can do something I didn't think I could do."

"It's knowing who you are," Emily says, pulling her camera out of her pocket.

Good lord, she's not going to take a picture of me NOW is she? No.

"Oh, wait a minute. My iPad's in my bag." She goes to get it and then, sitting down next to me on the bed, she shows me a long string of photos she's taken since the first summer writing workshop. Of me. At first I don't even want to look at them. I don't like photos of myself as a general rule.

But then I see why she's showing me. I see what she's seeing. What she was seeing all along.

We've only known each other since July. But even without knowing what was going on with me, she's recorded it somehow. There are shots from the first summer session of the writing workshop. My face is stiff and kind of hard. I look sort of like my mom. I see how in the second session of the writing workshop, the one this fall, my face is so much more open. And laughing.

And she took pictures of me working with the kids in the olios. Yeah, that's me.

But the best ones are from today. From the African dance. From afterward when everyone was coming to congratulate me.

She takes the iPad back. "Here," she says. "Just a couple more."

"Wait a minute." I grab the tablet back from her. "What did you name that album?"

"All the world's a Jumble," she says and she sounds kind of embarrassed.

"All the world's a jumble?" It sounds familiar, but I don't know why.

"That quote from Shakespeare your dad is always saying . . . All the world's . . ."

"A stage," we say in unison.

"I saw the way you responded when Professor Bumble said it," she adds.

"My dad always . . ." I start to explain but she interrupts me.

"Yeah, I know. I've heard him say it, and you answer him with the second line . . ."

"And all the men and women merely players . . ."

"And then you both finish the last three lines . . ."

"Dumb, huh?"

"No," she says, looking at me so funny. "No, it's not dumb. It's . . . it's not."

"It's not?"

"No, it is incredibly smart and funny," she pauses. "It's just . . . I'm so in love with . . . your family."

We click to the next photo and laugh. It's one from when everyone surrounded me after the dance.

"I just thought all the world's a Jumble made more sense," she leans in to look closer at the shot.

"I like it," I say. "All the world's a Jumble."

"Look at you," she says, leaning in even closer. "Jessie Jumble."

Yeah, that's me.

the end of the world

"What are you doing up here?" David sticks his head around the door frame.

We both jump.

"Where's Bits?" he asks.

"I thought she was with you," Emily says, putting her iPad back in her duffel bag.

"She's not with you?" I was assuming they were still down there, you know, figuring out their relationship stuff.

"Maybe she's in the living room with everyone," David says. "But I thought she was coming up here."

I'm wondering what Bits told David. And if there's a side in this fight, I'm wondering which side he's on.

"Did you two have a fight or something?" he asks.

"Didn't she tell you?"

"No," he says. "I asked her, but she wouldn't say."

"Let's go find her . . ." I don't really want to see her. But I have to sleep in the same room with her tonight. So there's no point in putting it off for very long.

Out of habit we go down the back stairs and through the kitchen. Brad's there making a pot of coffee.

"Seen Bits?" David asks, and Brad shakes his head.

But that doesn't mean she's not out front with everyone else.

My dad's playing the piano and singing a Leonard Cohen song. The professor and my mom are deep in discussion in the reading corner. Lydia and Edward are . . . of all things . . . slow dancing to my dad's song.

David grins at them as we go by, and they don't even notice. Well, well, well. It must be the end of the world all right.

Bartle and Tim Chang are sitting on the floor playing Scrabble with Grandmama who is queening it up on the love seat. I'd be willing to bet a large sum of money that she's winning. Auntie Ellie and Lee are talking with Dell. Is Bits with them?

No.

When we go back to the kitchen, Brad is finishing up the coffee. Without saying much, we fan out. Emily checks the downstairs bathroom. David runs up to the second floor main bath. I run down to the basement, though I know that Bits would pee in the yard before she went down there by herself.

We meet back in the kitchen.

No luck.

I run up the back stairs to the attic. There's even less reason why she'd be up there, but this is getting weirder by the minute, so I figure I'd better check. And I stop on the way back down to look in Mom's room and in her bathroom. Nada.

"She's not up there," I say, the second I'm in the kitchen again. "Is her coat here?"

The three of us jam through the doorway into the mudroom. Why we didn't check there first I have no idea. I guess we assumed she was in the house. It's nearly midnight. It's freezing cold outside. Where could she go?

"Let's go check out the theater," I whisper.

"Why are you whispering?" David whispers back.

"We had a big fight," I answer. "Where else would she go?"

"Does she have a key to the theater?" Emily whispers, too.

Evidently it's catching.

"No, but there are always some hanging on that hook over there . . ." I check it and there are two sets. I don't know if that's all we have right now. It's always changing. "You got any better ideas?"

They don't.

I go into the living room and tell my mom that we're walking over to the theater to get some popcorn since we're out. This is something we do all the time. Go back and forth between our house and the theater pantry.

We layer on our jackets and hats and gloves and, at the last second, I grab a flashlight off the shelf in the mudroom.

It's a short walk to the theater. Except for the night lights, it's

414

dark in there. I can't imagine that Bits would be hanging out in there by herself.

Not unless she's shut herself in the studio theater and is rehearsing something. She does that sometimes when she's upset about something her mom did or said.

We go in just in case.

It seems crazy, but we go all over the building, calling out her name before we're satisfied she's not there.

A thought has been nibbling at me ever since we left the house, but I don't want to think it. And I sure don't want to say it out loud.

Of course, I do anyway.

"Her mom's . . ."

"You don't think she would?"

"You heard that text message," I say, and by the feeling in my gut, I know this is it. "It's Armageddon night."

"Yeah, but Loretta said she'd left already. For up north."

"I know." What he says makes sense. But Loretta doesn't. And Bits . . . well, she's all tied up in her mother, even though she's been with us so much. "But the world is supposed to end tonight."

"You don't think Bits believes that . . ." Emily says.

"No, not at all. But I think it's like Mom says about her own childhood. She believed her mother. It took her a long time to get over it. Bits is still . . . connected to Loretta no matter how crazy Loretta gets about this end-of-the-world stuff."

"When does it end?"

"Huh?"

"The world . . . when is Armageddon supposed to arrive?"

"Technically tomorrow, December 21, at 5:12 a.m."

"But she's afraid of her mother. Why would she go over there?"

"Maybe to see if her mom's still there so she can say good-bye . . ."

David's looking at me like he knows there's more.

"It was a bad fight, David," I say. "I said things that were really . . . hurtful. About her and about her mother."

"Okay . . ."

"We have to go over there," I say. It's the last thing in the world I want to do. But we have to.

"Should we get your parents?" Emily asks.

"No, let's not get them involved. Yet."

"Yet?" David's voice comes out a squeak.

"Let's go over there and if Bits is there, let's bring her home . . ." I say, suddenly determined. "And we can always call them if we need them . . ."

"Yeah," Emily says, "we're out already. They won't miss us for a while. How far is it?"

"I wish I had a car," David says. This is becoming one of his litanies that's almost as pervasive as Bits saying, "When I'm eighteen I'm going to New York."

"It's only a few blocks," I tell Emily. "Down on Marshall. Not a great neighborhood but we should be fine."

We take off walking so fast we can't talk much.

There really isn't anything to say.

Please, God, let her be at her mom's apartment and not on her way with Loretta to that commune in Northern Minnesota.

Now we're finally on Marshall. It's more industrial here than anything else, but there are still a few old houses on the street. Loretta rents the top floor of one of them. You enter their apartment from an outside staircase. It's wood and really icy. From where we're standing the apartment looks dark.

I go first. David second. Even though Loretta has known him since birth, he has the disadvantage of being a boy. A worldly boy. And Loretta doesn't know Emily at all.

I knock on the screen door.

There's no answer.

I knock again, louder this time. Nothing except that an icicle falls off the edge of the roof and just misses Emily's head.

I yank the screen door open, knock a third time, calling out, "Bits! Loretta? Anyone home?"

The whole place is very quiet. It's late, so people could be asleep. But it's so quiet, I don't think anyone's home upstairs or down.

"What are we going to do?" I have that sinking feeling in my stomach again. "Okay, so Loretta is gone like she said in the text."

"What if she took Bits with her?" Emily's voice is shaky.

David pushes me aside and pounds on the door. "Bits!" he shouts. "Bits, it's us—open up!"

I reach around him and try the door. It opens.

"The door's not locked." I step into the dark kitchen. "Loretta?"

I try the light switch by the door, but the power's out.

David reaches into my pocket.

"What are you doing?"

"The flashlight . . ." he says.

I grab it and hand it to him. He shines the flashlight and steps ahead of me. It's very dark in the apartment, but we can see from the flashlight beam that the room is empty. Not just empty of people. It's been cleared out. All that's left are two kitchen chairs and an old table. Some stuff lying around on the floor.

I know this place, and he doesn't. I grab the flashlight from him, shine it down the hallway.

The bathroom is at the end of the hall. The door's shut, which seems kind of odd. And then, in the dim light of the flashlight, I see that a ladder is lying flat on the floor. It stretches from one open bedroom doorway, across the hall in front of the closed bathroom door and into the second bedroom.

There's something really weird about that.

"Bits!" I yell again. "Are you in there?"

And that's when I hear it. A scrabble of sound. And then I hear her coughing. She's pounding weakly on the inside of the door.

"Jess? Is that you? Jess?"

"It's me . . . us . . . Are you okay?"

"I'm locked in. Get me out of here!"

"There's a ladder blocking the door," I yell back at her. "We've got to pull it out of the way . . . hang on . . ."

The ladder is one of those big old heavy wooden ladders. I don't even think they make them anymore. I'm pretty strong, but when I grab one end of it, I can't lift it.

David grabs the other end and Emily comes to help me. With the old, slanted wood floors, it's hard, even with three of us, to get hold of it in order to shove it or pull it one direction or the other.

We can hear Bits sobbing in the bathroom.

"Talk to us," I yell at her. "Tell us if you're all right."

"I'm . . . I'm . . . okay . . ." she says, but I don't believe her.

"Did she hurt you?" David asks, panic building in his voice, too.

Bits starts to cry again. I have no idea what that means.

"Okay," Emily says, taking charge. "We have to do this together. Count to three and then you pull, David, and we'll push. We need to get this into the larger of the two bedrooms."

"It's the other way around, then," I say. And we scramble to change places.

"One, two, THREE." We go at the ladder like crazy people. And we manage to shove it and drag it into the larger empty bedroom. I can't believe how heavy this thing is. Why is it even up here?

I pull on the bathroom door, but it still doesn't budge.

Then I push. No movement.

"How did she lock it?" I yell.

"I don't know," Bits says, coughing again. "The regular lock inside here is broken."

David grabs the flashlight from me and sends the beam all up around the outside of the door. And we see it immediately. Up high, on the right. There's one of those wood blocks nailed to the door frame. So simple. Like you'd use to keep a cabinet door shut if it had a tendency to fall open or something.

It's nailed tight, but it's easy to open if you're on the outside. All you do is turn it.

That's what David does. The door swings open into the hallway.

And Bits stumbles out and into David's arms. She's coughing like crazy and crying.

We all hug her at once and then lead her out to the living room.

"When I got here," she sobs. "Everything was gone already. Mom was still here."

She starts to cry again so hard she can't talk. And then that makes her cough even more.

"Don't talk," David says, but she has to. And we need to know what happened.

"She . . . at first she wanted me to come with her . . . I said no . . ."

She coughs and coughs and coughs.

"Why did you come?" I ask, then am overcome with guilt. "It's my fault, isn't it? You came because of what I said about your mom . . ."

"I . . . no, it's not your fault . . . I just wanted to see her before . . ." She starts to sob again. "I got scared. I thought, what if the world really is going to end and I never see her again? I mean, she's my mom . . ."

"I'm so sorry," I am. I meant what I said, but I wish I could take it back anyway.

"No, I'm sorry," Bits says. "I knew what I was saying. I didn't mean it. I wanted to hurt you. I'm so sorry . . ."

"It's okay," I say. It's not, but it will be.

"And you were right," Bits sobs. "About Mom. When I said I wouldn't come with her, she yelled at me and said I was filled with the devil and that she didn't want me to come with her. She said I was evil. She hit me and hit me . . . and then she dragged me down here and pushed me into the bathroom."

"Oh, God," David moans. I know. I can't believe it, either.

"I couldn't get out . . . I couldn't get out . . . and it was so cold . . ."

"Sshhhh," I say, reaching out to hug her again. "Where's your coat?"

Standing here talking, the cold has crept up on us. This apartment is freezing. I mean, it's cold like the heat has been turned off for a while now. No wonder Bits is so cold and coughing again.

"Your coat? Where's your coat?"

"I'm looking for it," Emily says. She's taken the flashlight from David.

"I don't know," Bits says. "I took it off when I first got here."

We look everywhere for her jacket, but it's gone. Fortunately she's still wearing her boots.

"Come on," I say, "we've got to get out of here in case Loretta's coming back."

That gets everyone moving.

I take off my jacket and give Bits the thick sweater I'm wearing underneath. My jacket's too heavy for her, so I put it back on over my long sleeved T-shirt. I give her my scarf to go around her head and her shoulders.

"Put these gloves on," Emily says. "I've got pockets."

"Let's go to the bus stop and call Lee," I say. "It's heated. And that way we'll be gone if Loretta comes back, but they can come get us. I think they should see the apartment."

"No," Bits says, "no, I want to walk. It's not far. We can tell them then and they can do whatever they want . . . I want to get out of here."

"Are you sure you're okay?" David's voice about breaks my heart.

"I'm okay," Bits says. "She mostly hit me in the face. I can walk fine."

We surround her and start walking. She's not as strong as she thinks she is, though. My guess is Loretta got in some punches Bits doesn't even remember.

So after she's stumbled a couple times and then slipped on the ice, David picks her up and with Emily on one side and me on the other, he carries her the rest of the way home.

We make quite a sensation when we come in the front door.

They were starting to wonder why we were staying at the theater so long. Bartle and Tim were suiting up to come get us. Imagine the surprise when we stumble in, David carrying Bits. In the full light of the living room, her bruised face tells the whole story.

"Loretta did this to you?" Lee asks, his voice incredulous. "She hit you?"

Auntie Ellie and Lee both throw their arms around Bits.

Mom's grabbed me and is hugging me so hard I think she's going to crack a rib. "You're all right!" she says with a little sob. "Thank God you're all right!"

I hold on and hug her back. Then my dad's there, too. And we're all hugging and talking over each other.

Mom and Auntie Ellie take Bits upstairs to rub her down and get her into warm, dry clothes.

"I was wrong," it hits me all of a sudden.

"About what?" My dad asks.

"Loretta . . . she wasn't planning on coming back . . ."

"What do you mean?" Lee asks.

"If she'd been planning to come back, she'd have locked the outside door."

"Lee," Auntie Ellie calls down the stairs, "Can you come up? Bits wants you."

"I'll be right there," Lee shouts back, and then to me, "I don't follow you . . ."

"She'd have locked it so no one else could get to Bits. It was open. She left it open so Bits could be found . . ."

"Oh, of course, you're right . . ."

"I'm so glad you kids went after her," Brad says.

"But you should have told us so we could go with you," my dad says, looking and sounding surprisingly fatherlike. I find that comforting.

Mom comes downstairs then. She follows me into the kitchen where Grandmama's making coffee.

"Grandmama, can you put some hot chocolate on for Bits?" I ask.

"Already have," Grandmama says. Then she turns to Mom. "This girl of ours has quite a head on her shoulders, doesn't she?"

And Mom says, you know, right in front of me and looking me straight in the eye, "She does. I am so proud of her."

And then when Grandmama leaves the room, she tucks her arm in mine and says it again. "Jessie, I am so very proud of you."

I'm not even sure why. But here's the thing. That haze that's been over my mom's eyes since June. It's gone.

And I know after this we'll talk again. Like we used to.

I don't know when but right now it doesn't even matter.

Auntie Ellie and Mom try to get Bits to crash in Auntie Ellie's room, but Bits insists on staying with the rest of us. All of us. It seems like that's the only place she feels safe.

"What time is it?" she asks. She smells like the Ben-Gay they put on her chest. And her voice is ragged. But at least she's stopped coughing.

"A little after three . . ." David says, checking his phone. I notice he can't stop looking at Bits. Funny how so many things can change in one night.

"What time did my mom say the world was going to end?" Bits asks.

I answer, "5:12 a.m." You can always count on me for the details. Shit.

"Could we . . . do you suppose we could all . . . I don't know . . . stay here together until . . ."

"Honey, you don't believe that do you? You don't think the world's really going to end?" Lee says.

"No, Daddy," she says. "No . . . I don't." Then she laughs, a kind of pitiful little laugh. "But I won't know that for sure until five-thirteen."

Everybody howls. No one's really making fun of her. It's just so BITS.

Bartle says, "I propose that we have an End of the World Countdown Party."

"Are you hungry?" David asks Bits.

And we all answer, "We're starved."

Everyone goes into action. You'd think we'd rehearsed it. Like having an End of the World Countdown Party was an every Thursday night event.

My dad builds up the fire.

Edward and Brad go to make the adults some new drinks.

"I should go," the professor says, looking around for his coat.

I'm kind of surprised he's still here. But I'm even more surprised when my mom says, "No, James, stay . . . I want you to stay."

And Professor Bumble blushes about ten shades of red and smiles so huge his dimples almost leap off his face.

All right, Mom. Do you realize what you're doing here?

Then I look more closely at my mom. Oh, wow. I haven't seen that look . . . I haven't seen THAT look for a really long time. Years.

My dad's by the fireplace and he gives me a thumbs-up. Well, all right then.

Grandmama and David are in the kitchen making us a snack. Which, given who's doing it translates into: A FEAST. I go out to check.

Yup, she's frying chicken. He's making corn bread. And she's telling him the secret of her cinnamon rolls. Grandmama, you slut.

Bits is curled up with Lee and Auntie Ellie on the love seat. All three of them, tucked in under a comforter, looking like a family.

After we eat, my dad and Brad build up the fire again.

Bartle proclaims in his most theatrical voice, "It's 5:00 a.m."

And we all settle in to count down the last twelve minutes.

David and Bits and Emily and I are all lying on the rug in front of the fire. All six of the cats have joined us. They came down for the chicken liver Grandmama fried up for them. And then they stayed.

It's the Jumble Family, with a new face or two, a few new twists and turns.

No one's talking much.

We're all just hanging out, waiting.

You know. For the world to end.

And for it to begin again.